TREASURE
of the
WORLD

ALSO BY TARA SULLIVAN

The Bitter Side of Sweet
Golden Boy

TREASURE
of the
WORLD

TARA SULLIVAN

G. P. Putnam's Sons

G. P. Putnam's Sons

An imprint of Penguin Random House LLC, New York

Copyright © 2021 by Tara Sullivan

Visit us online at penguinrandomhouse.com

Library of Congress Cataloging-in-Publication Data
Names: Sullivan, Tara, author.
Title: Treasure of the world / Tara Sullivan.
Description: New York, NY: G. P. Putnam's Sons, 2021. | Summary: After a mining accident kills her father and leaves her brother missing, twelve-year-old Ana puts her dreams on hold and goes into the mine to help her family survive in their impoverished Bolivian silver mining community.
Identifiers: LCCN 2020040827 (print) | LCCN 2020040828 (ebook) |
ISBN 9780525516965 (hardcover) | ISBN 9780525516972 (ebook)
Subjects: CYAC: Silver mines and mining—Fiction. | Bolivia—Fiction. |
Family life—Bolivia—Fiction. | Child labor—Fiction.
Classification: LCC PZ7.S95373 Tr 2021 (print) | LCC PZ7.S95373 (ebook) | DDC [Fic]—dc23
LC record available at https://lccn.loc.gov/2020040827
LC ebook record available at https://lccn.loc.gov/2020040828

Printed in the United States of America
ISBN 9780525516965

1   3   5   7   9   10   8   6   4   2

Design by Eileen Savage | Text set in More Pro

For Dad, who loves Bolivia

TREASURE
of the
WORLD

1

Even though I hate getting up before dawn to make coca tea for my family, I have to admit that there is nothing so stunning as watching the sun rise at the top of the world.

Holding a match to the pile of dried dung, I blow on it softly until the flame catches. Once it's going strong, I put the beaten tin pot on top of it and breathe on my chilled fingers, looking forward to the tea. It will be warm and filling, and because it's only water, I'll be allowed to have as much of it as I want. I toss a handful of coca leaves into the pot and stand, hugging my arms around myself as the orange sun shoulders its way out from behind the rough red slope of the Cerro Rico.

Behind me, I hear the soft shuffle of feet as Abuelita joins me from the house.

"Look at that, Ana," she says, tipping her wrinkled face to the sunlight. "Only God has a better view."

I smile. "I bet God is warmer."

"Probably." She laughs. "How's the tea coming?"

"Almost ready."

"Good. Your brother woke up with that cough again. A cup of coca tea would do him good."

I frown, worried. It seems like Daniel is always fighting off one chill or another. Although we're not even a full year apart, it usually feels like I'm much older because I'm always taking care of him. He just gets sick so easily. If the rest of us get a sniffle, his turns into bronchitis; if we get a fever, his turns into pneumonia and he'll still be fighting to breathe weeks after the rest of us are better. This high in the Andes, there are only two choices for temperature—cold, and colder. Today is the first day of February, right at the end of summer. I chew on my bottom lip. If Daniel is struggling this much now, I hate to think how sick he could get when we get to June and July, the depths of winter.

I hand a cup to Abuelita and follow her inside, carrying the pot. Papi doesn't like weak tea, but I don't want Daniel to have to wait longer than he has to. I put the pot on a folded *manta* that Mami has placed in the center of the room. We all dip our cups in, sipping until our bellies slosh. The tea will take the chill off the morning and trick us into thinking we're full for about an hour. Then we'll start chewing coca leaves to dull the real hunger that comes from working on an empty stomach. Mami helps Papi buckle an acetylene tank to the belt on his miner's coveralls and hands him his lunch sack as he walks out the door. Abuelita sits off to the side with Daniel, rubbing his back as he coughs between sips of tea. I get dressed for school, sure I'll be going by myself again, but Daniel surprises me.

"Mami, can I go to school today?" he asks. "Please?"

She walks over and smooths his thick black hair away from his forehead. She hides it in a caress, but I notice she lets her hand rest there an extra moment, checking for fever. This time, bronchitis has kept him home from school for over a week.

"I don't know, *mi hijo*," she says, concern lining her round face, "your cough is still pretty bad."

"I feel fine, really," he protests. "Ana will make sure I'm okay, won't you, Ana?"

I shoot him a glare for making me a part of this.

"If we left now, we could walk slowly," I say, leaving the decision up to Mami.

For a moment I'm not sure what it's going to be, but then Abuelita chimes in and settles the matter.

"Let the boy go. He'll never learn anything sitting around the house."

And so I find myself starting the long, slow walk to school with Daniel beside me, his thin frame bundled in two sweaters to combat the early-morning cold.

The Cerro Rico, the mountain we live on, is huge. If you crane your neck upward, you can see past the brick-colored summit to the dry, pale sky beyond. Sometimes the road runs right along a cliff face and you can see down to the city of Potosí at the base of the mountain. If, instead of looking up or down, you stare at your feet, it feels like the red road stretches on forever. What you don't see, no matter how you tip your head, is any green at all. This region of Bolivia is so high up there's not a tree or a bush or a blade of grass anywhere. Just red and yellow and gray stripes of rock and the never-ending dust that slowly sifts into your clothes and cakes the inside of your mouth, claiming you, camouflaging you so that, if you stay here long enough, even you can't tell where the mountain ends and you begin.

We go slowly, like I promised Mami, and we stop to rest a bunch of times, sitting on boulders along the side of the path whenever a coughing fit takes Daniel, until he catches his breath and can walk again. The way to school is mostly downhill. Even so, on a normal day, with Daniel walking full speed, it takes more than an hour to get there over the rough, rocky paths scraped across the mountain's face and chipped out of its sides. Today, it takes longer.

Turning the last corner, I see our school below us, a tiny dust-colored building surrounded by a cinder-block wall, wedged into a crack between a cliff face and an ever-growing pile of slag from a nearby mine entrance. It crouches there, between the cliff and the cliff's guts, looking like it might be crushed at any moment.

I hear the static hiss and scratch of Don Marcelino's ancient speakers echo off the cliff. We're going to be late! I dart a glance at Daniel. I know I promised Mami we'd go slowly, but we might make it in time if we run. We're practically the same age. It's not like he needs to be babied *all* the time.

"Think you can run?" I ask.

He nods.

When we get to the front, Daniel bends double trying to catch his breath. I feel a little bad for pushing him. Grabbing a rock from the ground, I tap it against the peeling blue paint of the tall metal gates.

Doña Inés, one of the helpers, opens the gate. It creaks and groans on its dust-caked hinges. She smiles when she sees Daniel.

"Welcome back," she whispers, one hand on her huge belly. Soon it will be another helper who opens the door because Doña Inés will be having her baby. We duck around the door and scamper into the courtyard. Doña Inés shuts the door softly behind us.

The rest of the school is already lined up by age in the tiny packed-earth courtyard. Don Marcelino stoops at the base of the flagpole, twisting the wires at the back of his battered stereo and muttering. For once, I'm glad the technology is misbehaving. It gives us the chance to sneak in late without anyone noticing.

Daniel and I both hurry to join the end of the line for twelve-year-olds. Even though I'm older by almost eleven months, they put us in the same class. I try not to let it bother me too much. Daniel steps into place behind me, and I shoot him a grin over my shoulder that we made it. Daniel smiles back, his teeth a flash of white in his skinny face.

Just then, Don Marcelino wins his battle with the ancient speaker and the opening strains of the national anthem blare at us.

As we all straighten to attention and sing along, saluting the flag, my eyes wander to the rows on my left. The messy gaggle of four-, five-, and six-year-olds is a huge, unmanageable pack. There are at least thirty or forty of them, still not all facing forward even now that the music is playing. But then, year by year, the rows get shorter. By the row of twelve-year-olds, where we're standing, there are only six of us. Victor, Juanillo,

Emily, Wilma, and Álvaro are standing to my right: they're the only five students in the whole school who are older than me.

The music cuts off and Don Marcelino addresses us, like he does every morning, standing tall in his dark slacks and patterned wool sweater. His voice booms and his square-framed glasses make his face look very impressive, but still I ignore him. I don't need to listen to Don Marcelino because all he ever does is talk about big things: pride, patriotism, work ethic. I don't come to school to learn about the big things. I know those from home.

Pride is what makes you not tell people when your papi hits your mami.

Patriotism is what makes you not curse Bolivia when you get so tired of living on this one mountain that you could scream.

And work ethic is something a child of six from the Cerro Rico knows more about than Don Marcelino ever will. He comes up here every day in a pickup from the city of Potosí. He's not a miner.

I tune him out, letting my eyes lift over the solid walls of the school to the high cliffs stretching beyond them, wondering whether today will be the day when I finally learn something that will lead me off this mountain and toward a future I actually want.

———

"Thank God that's over," mutters Daniel as we get our mugs of thinned-down oatmeal and go sit in a corner together after Don Marcelino's speech. The younger kids wait in line, impatient for the food. One of the few benefits of being older is eating first.

I sip at my steaming cup. "Yeah," I agree.

Susana, Alejandra, Robertito, and Óscar—the other twelve-year-olds—sit with us, along with a few of the eleven-year-old boys Daniel is friends with. Even though he's thirteen, Victor joins us too. Victor's smart and kind, with an easy smile. He's in the year ahead of us when we line up because of when his birthday falls, but we've been friends for as long as I can remember. He never makes Daniel feel bad about being sick, and he has never made me feel like I'm somehow less for being a girl, like Papi and some of the other boys do. Even though I giggle and joke with Susana and Alejandra, Victor is my best friend.

For a few minutes all of us focus on the food, scooting sideways on the bench until everyone fits. No one gets breakfast at home. Once we're done, though, everyone starts chattering. Óscar and Daniel are discussing La Verde's chances in this year's Copa América since they made it to the quarterfinals last year. Robertito interrupts.

"Hey, guys, did you hear? They found Mariángela's body."

"Wait—what?" Susana squeaks. "Her *body*?"

Mariángela used to go to our school. She was a few years older than us, so we weren't all that close, but she had been kind and we looked up to her when we were little. She stopped coming to school about two years ago and, just before Christmas last year, took a job as a *guarda* for one of the big mines on the other side of the Cerro. Then, in mid-January, she vanished.

When the miners reported for work in the morning, she wasn't standing by the mine mouth guarding the tools. She wasn't with the equipment. There was no one watching the pile of high-quality ore. Worse, she hadn't gone home. For the past two weeks people have been looking for her.

"Yeah," says Robertito grimly, "they found her in an abandoned mine mouth on the other side of the Cerro. She's dead."

Being a *guarda* is lonely, dangerous work. I swallow against a lump in my throat. It's not hard to imagine a gang of robbers—or even a pack of miners, drunk after leaving work—coming up on Mariángela and her not being able to fight them off.

Susana and Daniel pepper Robertito with a hundred questions about what he knows, but I try not to listen as they gossip about what must have happened to her.

With a shudder, I tune them out and turn to Victor, who, I notice, is unusually quiet. Normally Victor would be right in the middle of everything, but today he's not his typical sunshine self.

I elbow him gently. It's not like him to stare into his cereal with a frown tucked between his eyebrows and ignore everyone.

"Hey, what's up with you?" I whisper under the buzz of the other kids' conversation.

"Nothing." He pastes on a smile, but it doesn't crinkle the sides of his eyes. Now I'm actually worried.

"No, seriously," I say, putting down my own mug and facing him. "What's wrong? Are you upset about Mariángela? Did something happen at home?"

Victor lives alone with his papi ever since his mami died three years ago. Even before his papi paid for all the expensive medicine for Victor's mami, they weren't rich, and ever since she died, they never seem to have enough money. Sometimes his papi gets too sad to work and they go awhile without food.

Victor shrugs.

"Is your papi okay?"

"Everything's fine, Ana." I can tell from his tone that he doesn't want to talk about it. I give him what Abuelita calls my "signature glare." *You could save the miners a lot of drilling and blasting,* she teases me. *Glare at the mountain like that and you'd bore a hole right through to the other side in no time.*

Sure enough, Victor cracks. He glances away and starts to pick at a loose thread on the rumpled La Verde shirt he always wears.

"This is my last day of school." His voice is barely above a whisper, but I hear it anyway.

"What?"

Victor winces. I guess my voice was louder than I meant it to be. The rest of the kids break off their conversation and stare at us. Victor flushes. Then he straightens his shoulders.

"I'm not coming to school anymore. Starting tomorrow, I'll be joining my papi in the mine."

I stare at him. Victor's face, usually so happy, looks sadder, older. When he sighs, it's not hard to imagine the ghost rattle of silicosis in his lungs.

If he becomes a miner, you might not get to see what he's like when he's older, a horrible voice hisses in my head. A lot of miners don't live more than ten years after starting work. I slam down firmly on the thought, not letting it breathe. I refuse to think about that number and my best friend.

9

"It'll be fine, Victor," I say. "Maybe the price of mineral will go up and your papi will have enough without the extra you'll bring in."

Victor nods, but his face is tight.

Susana, Alejandra, Daniel, and Robertito all make sympathetic noises. The prices of zinc, tin, and most of the other metals and minerals that come out of the Cerro Rico were good until 2014, but recently they've been so low that most mining families are struggling more than usual.

Óscar grimly finishes his oatmeal. "I'll be there soon too, probably," he says, punching Victor lightly on the shoulder. "Don't clean out the mountain before I join you."

Victor forces another smile, but it's all teeth and no joy.

None of us asks him when he'll be back.

Somehow that makes it worse.

Knowing that Mariángela is dead and that Victor will be leaving school puts me in a sad mood the rest of the day. I struggle to pay attention in class and my cheeks fill with heat when our teacher has to call on me twice before I hear him. Even then I don't have the answer prepared. Usually, I'm completely focused at school, working hard to be at the top of the class. But today . . . today is awful. Things that feel a lot more important than a math lesson have gone wrong and my brain whirs to try to find a way to fix them.

I like fixing things: I'm always trying to find a way to do things just a little bit better. But I have no control over Victor leaving and you can't change death, so today my brain spins and spins but doesn't get anywhere.

Victor stays quiet for the rest of the day too. When we sit together again for our lunch of watery soup at noon, I try to bring him into the conversation, but he just shakes his head and stays quiet. School lets out for the day right after that, so once we finish eating, it's time to gather up my satchel and notebook and head home. I'm thinking hard about what I'm going to say to Victor, but when I meet Daniel at the big blue metal door, I don't see him anywhere.

"Hey, where's Victor?" I ask.

Daniel pokes his head out. "There he is." He points. "He must have got a head start."

I push past him, out the door. "Victor!"

Victor turns. He's already twenty meters up the road that leads toward El Rosario. He and his papi live in a little house perched right on the edge of the gully overlooking the entry lot. I wonder what it's like to wake up every morning and see your future below you.

We live in the other direction, farther down the mountain, but I jog to catch up to Victor.

"Victor, I . . ." I trail off when I get to him. What am I going to say? That I'm sorry he has to leave school? That this isn't fair? He already knows those things.

"What, Ana?" Victor's eyes look tired already. I notice he didn't bring his notebook home with him. He must have left it at school so some other kid could use the empty pages.

"I'm going to miss you," I finally manage. "Take care, okay?"

"Okay," he says, but even I can tell he doesn't believe it.

I watch until Victor turns the bend, then I retrace my steps to where Daniel is waiting for me and join him for the long walk home.

The younger kids stay behind because Don Marcelino will give them a ride down the mountain in his truck. They look funny, twenty of them packed into the flat bed of the truck, but it's a nice thing to do for their little legs. The bigger kids, like Daniel and me, walk.

For a couple hundred meters, there are other kids our age on the road with us, and Daniel chats and jokes with them. Daniel is cheerful, like he always is when he gets to go to school. Being sick and stuck at home with nothing to do bores him. I bring him work so he doesn't fall too far behind, but that only fills an hour or so of the day. It's not the same as being at school all morning, every day, surrounded by friends. It lights him up from the inside.

It also exhausts him.

In twos and threes the other kids branch off the road to find their own paths home. We wave at them. Eventually, it's just us hiking our way up and around the Cerro.

Walking home is even slower than our trip to school in the morning, when Daniel was fresh. On the steeper slopes we have to stop every ten steps or so for him to lean heavily against my shoulder and take deep, shuddering breaths. In my mind, I try to figure out how much farther we have yet to go and how long it will take us. We don't have time to dawdle: Mami needs us home to work. Still, I'm afraid to push Daniel.

I study his face. He's pale and his cheeks are shiny with sweat even though we're going so slowly.

I walk to a boulder slightly off to the side of the road.

"Take a rest," I tell him. "We'll keep going in a minute."

It's proof of how tired he is that he doesn't fight me on this. Instead, he collapses against the boulder and closes his eyes, focusing on evening out his breathing.

The air is thin up here. The Cerro Rico is 4,800 meters above sea level. Whenever tourists visit, or even people from lower down in Bolivia, they gasp like fish and get horrible headaches and nausea. We call it *sorroche*—altitude sickness. The extreme altitude is why water boils at a temperature so low you can cook a potato for days and it will still be hard in your soup. Even cars and trucks struggle to work up here. I heard Papi grumble once that a car will last three to five times as long at lower altitudes just because there's more oxygen in the air which lets it burn fuel efficiently without straining the crankshaft. Not that we have a car, but still, he was offended by the thought. Those of us who live here don't notice it so much, but when I hear Daniel wheeze, it's all I can think about: whether, if he had air with more oxygen in it and we could get him away from breathing in dust full of arsenic, lead, and other things that weaken your body—if we were somewhere else, anywhere else—he'd be okay, even with his asthma and his constant lung infections.

I scowl and aim a sharp kick at a rock near where we're standing.

Unfortunately, the rock is not loose scree, like I thought it was. Instead, it's a small spike of the mountain, still very firmly attached.

I swear loudly, grabbing the toe of my sneaker in both hands.

Daniel's eyes pop open at my cussing, and seeing me hopping around on one foot, he starts to laugh.

"Shut up!" I snap. "It's not funny."

"Sure, sure," he says, still chuckling, "you're not funny."

It's only when he winks at me that I realize he's changed the words around to mean something different, like he always does.

"Gah!" I take three steps off the path and aim a kick at another, much smaller rock. Satisfyingly, this one goes flying.

"Take that!" I shout after it.

"Good work, Ana." Daniel is gasping for breath again, but this time it's from laughing so hard. "That rock definitely had it coming."

And I want to stay angry, I really do, but no matter how annoying he can be, Daniel has always known how to find the words that poke my mad feelings in the sides until they giggle. I stare at the offending rock, now a good two meters off the path, and can't help but smile.

"It did, didn't it?"

"Mmm-hmm," he says, face completely straight even though his eyes are sparkling. "Definitely. That was one bad rock. Good thing it's gone now. Would have been a disaster if it stayed there."

I shuffle my feet in the scree, my bad mood settling onto my shoulders again like a condor perching on a carcass.

"Yeah," I grumble.

Daniel tries to catch my eye. "What's wrong, Ana?"

I can't admit that I wish I could get him better air to breathe, so I say the other thing that's been weighing on me all day.

"You heard Victor. He's not coming back to school."

Daniel grimaces. Kids work. Unless you're rich or something, families can't get by on what the parents make. In the city you see kids doing lots of jobs. They sit beside kiosks or *mantas* laid out on the ground with things to sell: coca leaves, hats, used shoes. Some get jobs washing the sidewalks or collecting trash. Kids shine tombstones and shape bricks and carry loads. They wash windshields and collect scrap metal for smelters. They sell their size, their energy, and their time. Crippled or disabled kids beg. Boys and young men dig trenches, work the ore refineries, or shine shoes. Girls work as maids for fancy families or help out in shops and restaurants. Up here, though, there aren't that many jobs. Boys mine. Girls break rocks.

"That stinks," he says.

"Yeah. I don't think he wants to work in the mines."

"No one wants to work in the mines," Daniel says flatly.

There's no arguing with that, so I don't. For a few minutes we sit in silence, each leaning against the big red boulder, lost in our own thoughts.

"Luís and Araceli are gone too," I muse.

Daniel quirks a brow at me, but I know he can see where I'm going.

"And remember? Óscar said that he might need to start working soon too. Alejandra told me later that her parents were starting to talk the same way."

"So?" Daniel asks, but he's not meeting my eyes anymore and his face has smoothed out like a bedsheet, the way it does when he wants to hide the lumps in his feelings from me.

"So"—my voice roughens without my permission—"that means, in the whole school, there are only going to be four kids still older than us. And now even *our* friends are starting to leave." I scuff my poor abused sneakers into the path, digging through the centimeters of brick-colored dust that cover everything on the Cerro Rico, exposing the hard, cold mountain beneath. I find the courage to say my fear aloud, but even so, it comes out as a whisper. "I think I'm running out of time, Daniel. I'm getting too old. Any day now, I'll be next."

We both know there's no way that Daniel could ever be a miner, not with how often he's sick and how weak his lungs are. Since we were little, Mami has always talked about how Daniel will need to finish secondary school down in the city and get a job there. We've all known he was too special, too fragile, to stay up here. But me . . . I almost never get sick. They've never had those conversations about me. Never mind that I'd like to leave the mountain too—go to the city, maybe even attend university—I've always known that my job is to help out my family in whatever way they need. That means that every day I get to go to school feels stolen from an ugly future. One day, though, we all know that I'll be asked to stop going to school and work full-time as a *palliri* with Mami and Abuelita. Girls like me don't get choices like the ones I dream about. All our choices are bad ones: like whether we want to waste a day walking down the mountain and back up carrying heavy cans of clean water, or whether we want to drink the runoff from the mines, which we know will make us sick.

For a long moment Daniel just sits beside me, face outlined in the harsh afternoon light, staring at the empty sky. Then, like flipping the switch on an air compressor, Daniel turns on a smile.

"So we'll run away together," he says. "Far away from here. Far away from the mountain and the mines. Far away from the rocks and the cold. We'll run until we find a green valley like Abuelita talks about in her stories, and we'll sink our toes into the soft black soil and grow so much food that we both die fat."

The words are musical and familiar. It's something we've repeated back and forth to each other so many times since we were little that I could recite it in my sleep. I finish it. "Or we'll find a city that sparkles with electric lights and good jobs and we'll both make lots of money and be happy forever?"

Daniel nods. "It's what we've always dreamed, right?"

"It's what we've always dreamed," I agree. But with my friends dropping out of school one after the other, the words feel hollow today.

I pick up his backpack from the ground and loosen the straps so I can wear it over mine.

"Come on," I say. "If you've caught your breath, let's get going again. Mami needs us home sometime before next week."

Daniel heaves himself off the boulder and starts walking beside me, and I bend double, gripping the four backpack straps, fighting against the steepness of the slope and the darkness of my thoughts.

2

Just over two hours later we crest the last rise home. Even before we see them, we can hear the irregular pounding and cracking of Mami and Abuelita checking the refuse pile of rocks in the gully near our house for bits of metal missed by the miners. I dump our schoolbags near the door and pick my way over the uneven pile until I reach them.

"*Puangichi.*" I kiss each of them on the cheek and switch into Quechua because Abuelita never went to school and doesn't speak Spanish.

"*Allyisiami,* Ana," she replies. "How was school today?"

I don't like questions like this. I like *Three-fifths added to four-thirds is how many fifteenths?* And *Describe the way the Bolivian government is divided between our two capital cities.* Those types of questions have one right answer and you can learn them or figure them out. *How was school?* is one of those questions that you have to answer differently depending on who's asking you. If a teacher is asking, I have to say *Good*, no matter what I'm really feeling, so as not to be rude to a community leader. If a friend is asking, I'm supposed to complain so they have the chance to complain too if they want to. If Mami or Papi is asking, I have to tell them something impressive I've learned, to give them a reason to let me go again tomorrow. Papi likes to see numbers. He'll check my math notebook and, if I've gotten a problem wrong, will make me copy it over ten or twenty times until I have it memorized. Mami likes to see my writing. Sometimes, when no one else is around, we'll take out my notebook and read through what I've written together. She'll trace the curves of the letters with her fingers and I'll help her sound out the words. Mami had to start working when she was nine, so she only got two and a half years of school. I've already been in school more than twice as long as my mother.

With Abuelita, it's a little different. Abuelita loves stories. She doesn't want to see a row of neat, correct numbers, or a well-lettered sentence that someone else dictated. She wants something to think about while she works as a *palliri* with Mami. It's hard, boring work sifting through rock chunks all day long, and she's been doing it every day for longer than I've been alive, so I try to give her a good story. It doesn't matter if it's happy or sad, gossip or fact; she'll treasure any story like a new shirt and spend the day folding and refolding it into her memory. Sometimes, months later, she'll pull out a story I told her, but it will have all kinds of additions and changes from the original. That's how I know she spends her days embroidering them.

Today, though, the only stories I focused on all day long are the ones about Victor leaving school, Daniel needing better air, and the tragedy of Mariángela. None of those is something I want to bring up now. I'm also not about to admit my worries about my own future. I like to believe that, if I never talk in front of my family about the fact that I'll one day have to start working full-time, then it will never occur to them and I'll get to stay in school forever.

I shoot Daniel a panicked glance. He rolls his eyes. Daniel thinks I'm stupid for believing this. *Just because you don't talk about the wind doesn't mean it won't blow you over the cliff,* he says. But even so, he comes to my rescue.

"Did you hear? They found that girl's body."

"What girl?" asks Mami, her hands stilling. "The missing *guarda*? Mariángela?"

"Yeah. A group of miners found her body yesterday in a ditch on the far side of the Cerro."

"*¡Ay, Dios!*" What few phrases Abuelita has in Spanish are all religious.

This tidbit is interesting enough to keep Abuelita and Mami asking Daniel questions for a while. And though I'm grateful he saved me from having to answer Abuelita, I hate that this is what he distracted them with. It was bad enough when she disappeared . . . at least then I could pretend that maybe she just decided to run away to a better life. I could imagine her, with her shy smile and ready laugh, in a green field or a sparkling city. But now, knowing she's dead, knowing the Cerro Rico has taken another person I knew . . . it makes me feel sick to my stomach.

". . . and she was only fifteen! Such a pity."

I can't stand it anymore. "Can we talk about something else, please?"

Mami and Abuelita stare at me. Daniel raises an eyebrow in my direction. It clearly says, *You asked for a distraction and now you're complaining?*

"It's . . ." I mumble. "I knew her. I . . . I don't want to talk about her anymore like this."

"Of course, *mi hija*," Mami says gently.

Abuelita sucks on her teeth. I can tell she's disappointed but also doesn't want to upset me. "Girls shouldn't be working so close to the mine anyway," she says loftily. "*La Pachamama* gets jealous."

"I thought you said Mother Earth gets jealous if women or girls go *into* the mountain?" I ask, scrunching up my face, trying to remember, sure that's what she said last time. Trying to figure out if this is a real thing or another story she's embroidered.

Abuelita snorts. "In, on, near. It makes no difference. You shouldn't take chances with *la Pachamama* like that. If Mother Earth gets jealous, she will collapse the mining shafts to keep her men to herself. You remember when that whole section of the top of the mountain collapsed five years ago?" She nods emphatically. "*La Pachamama* was angry. No one should challenge a power that strong."

A cold, slightly slurred voice speaks over my shoulder before any of us has the chance to respond.

"The 2011 cone collapse happened because the tunnels underneath were empty and unstable, and no one had shored them up before moving on. There was nothing mystical about it, Mamá. It's physics."

Abuelita closes her mouth and the rest of us stiffen slightly. None of us contradicts Papi. Mami gets to her feet and walks over to him.

"How was your day?" she asks, taking his helmet and satchel from him. The satchel is oddly stuffed. It should be empty. He would have chewed the coca leaves and drunk the alcohol that was in it this morning while he was working. From how unsteady he is on his feet right now, I know he drank more than what was in the bag. I'm curious what might be in there and why he's home so much earlier than usual, but I know better than to ask questions when I don't know how drunk he is.

"It was a good day," he slurs. Papi's face, usually all angles and hard lines, is softened around the edges by the drink. "A very good day! They came . . . the news came . . . from the city. The prices of zinc and tin are up. There's money to be made in mining again!"

We all make appreciative noises, but they're not enough for Papi.

"You all"—he sways slightly on his feet before recovering himself—"you all don't know how hard I work to feed you. The price of mineral went up! We should celebrate! Mónica! We should . . . celebrate . . ."

It seems to me that maybe Papi has done enough celebrating with his miner friends already. Mami steers him into the house, making soothing noises. Now that Papi is home, she will focus on making dinner. Daniel, Abuelita, and I bend our heads to our task without talking. Talking annoys Papi.

The price of mineral went up! I think, remembering my words to Victor this morning and feeling weirdly like I made it happen. Maybe this will be a good thing. Maybe he really can make some quick money and come back to school.

I pick up a rock from the pile and smash it against another until one of them cracks. I peer carefully at the cross section, rubbing my finger along the rough ridges, squinting for the stripes of color or texture changes that would mean there's enough of something in it—zinc, aluminum, tin, maybe even a spiderweb thread of silver—to make it worth selling. Nothing: the middle is a uniform, pockmarked reddish rock. I toss the useless halves down the slope and pick up another one. And then another and another and another. Only when we run out of daylight, nearly five hours later, do we stop and head inside.

Abuelita holds her outmost skirt to make a pouch. I pick up the pile of rocks the three of us found that we think are worth trying to sell and set them inside it for her to carry. They fit easily. Even at a higher price, we won't make much off that. Sighing, I loop Abuelita's free hand through my elbow and guide her over the uneven ground to our house. She puts the pile of rocks beside the door and we go inside. Daniel, carrying the schoolbags, is a step behind us.

Three of the walls of our one-room house are built from chunks of reject stones loosely mortared together. Once, when Daniel had pneumonia and needed to stay home sick for a month, he complained it was like living in a cave of failure, but I try not to listen to him when he's crabby. The fourth wall of the room is chipped into the side of the Cerro Rico itself. I'm sure it saved the builders some time and energy to borrow part of the house from the mountain, but the cold radiates off it and there are days when I feel like I can never get warm, even indoors. Winter, summer, it doesn't matter. Nights are always cold this high up the Andes.

Mami carries in the pot of soup she has made and serves it into bowls, handing Papi his before anyone else. We sit in a circle on the floor since our house is too small to fit a table, chewing on the softened strips of llama jerky and freeze-dried potatoes in the soup. I'm hungry, but I know better than to rush.

We usually eat in silence, so I'm surprised when Papi finishes his bowl of soup and starts talking.

"Mónica, pass me my bag."

Mami puts down her bowl immediately and fetches it for him. I bite down on the inside of my cheek, annoyed. He could have reached out and picked up his bag, but instead he made her get it for him. Not that she had far to go: our house is tiny. But still. He was finished and she was still eating. I duck my head so that he won't accidentally read something in my face he doesn't like. It's better to let Papi have his little victories. Then he doesn't feel the need for bigger ones.

Mami hands him the bag without a word.

Papi opens the flap and digs inside. We all stare at him. Though none of us said anything, I guess we were all curious about what was in it.

When Papi pulls out a miner's zip-front coveralls and helmet, for one second I think that he wasted our money buying himself a spare set of work clothes. There's no point in spare clothes. They get filthy by the end of any day of mining, so there's barely a point in even washing them. Mami only cleans the clothes he wears inside the coveralls, his sweaters and slacks and shirts, never the coveralls themselves.

It's only when he throws the outfit into Daniel's lap that I realize they're not full-size coveralls and that he didn't buy them for himself. My heart stops.

I hear a soft gasp from Mami. Abuelita starts to mutter quietly under her breath. She's probably praying, but I don't look over at them. My eyes are glued to Daniel.

He's frozen, his spoon halfway to his mouth. Then he puts down his spoon and bowl on the ground beside him.

"What's this?" he manages, his voice slightly choked. His hands hover over the clothes, like he's afraid to touch them.

"Pedro Sánchez is bringing his boy to work," Papi says gruffly, scraping the last of the pot of soup into his bowl and chewing. "I got César to approve a second slot on the shift. Since he was adding one boy, I figured I could get him to add two. You start tomorrow."

There is a beat where it feels like no one breathes; the only sound, Papi's slurp and chew as he works his way through his second helping.

Daniel's hands settle on the coveralls. He doesn't say anything.

"Mauricio..." Mami starts softly, hesitantly.

Papi's eyes snap to her, the hardness of the mountain in his stare.

"He's so young," Mami goes on. I'm biting the inside of my mouth again. She is brave, so brave! With Papi's attention on

25

me like that, I would never keep talking. "The Sánchez boy, Victor, he's older. Let Daniel go to school a little bit longer. We have enough to get by, especially if the price of mineral is going up; we'll be fine. And you know he's not strong..."

Papi slaps his open palm onto the floor beside him. We all flinch. Mami stops talking. Daniel doesn't say anything, but I can see his fingers tightening in the material in his lap. His knuckles are turning white.

"No one says a son of mine is weak." Papi slaps the floor again. "No one says he's only slightly better than an invalid or a girl."

None of us have said anything like this, so it must be something he overheard at work. My wide eyes dart to Daniel. Papi is a proud man. There's no way we'll talk him out of it if he thinks Daniel staying home somehow makes him look bad.

"I say it's time for him to go," Papi shouts. "He's going."

Mami might be about to say something more, but Daniel gets to his feet. He bunches the material of the suit in his fists.

"It's fine, Mami," he says. "I'll do it."

Then he turns and goes to our bed and curls up in the blankets like a pill bug that has been poked, his back to us.

"That's my boy!" says Papi loudly, but none of us answer and the rest of the evening passes in a tense silence.

Even after Papi falls asleep, we don't say anything, afraid to wake him, but Mami cries quietly as she cleans the dishes. When I'm done with my chores, I go outside, even though it's cold, and stare up the starlit path. This morning I said the price of mineral would go up and it did. Then, this afternoon, I had worried that we were running out of time. And now Papi is

26

making Daniel leave school and join him at work. I feel like I jinxed us. That, by saying my fears out loud, I brought the attention of the devil of the mines or the Pachamama or whoever upon us and they made Papi make this decision. I bury my head in my arms and try to think of a way out of this. Nothing good has come out of anything I've said, but just in case the magic pattern holds, I speak out loud to the stars.

"Papi and Don Sánchez will change their minds, and Victor and Daniel will be allowed to come back to school." I squeeze my eyes shut and will it to be true, but nothing immediately changes. Eventually, the wind forces me inside. I lie on the pile of blankets I share with Daniel and Abuelita and curl around my brother, hugging him close to give him what heat I can. I drift off to sleep to the rattle of his breathing.

The next morning, when Mami shakes me awake to make the tea, Papi is already up, brash and happy even through his hangover. Daniel knocks his tea back in three quick gulps the way the miners drink liquor at a funeral. Papi sips his tea and laughs, all smiles again now that he's gotten his way.

"You'll do fine," he's saying to Daniel, patting his hunched shoulders. "I spoke to César and he's going to start you on his team. César will take good care of you."

Daniel doesn't answer and I can see the tight lines along his face from where he's holding in his words by sheer force. Usually, when Papi's sober, Daniel sasses all of us freely. It's who he is. With him quiet, I'm not sure whether to talk or not.

"We shouldn't even be on this mountain," Abuelita breaks

in, her voice sounding extra thin this morning. I pour her some more tea to soothe her throat. "Our people."

"What's that?" Papi asks her, the smile on his face looking like an afterthought.

"When the Inca ruled this land, the emperor had miners working all over his empire."

I settle back and sip my tea. When she uses that rolling tone, Abuelita is launching into a story. I'm glad. It's got to be better than anything else we'd talk about this morning.

"But when Huayna Capac, the Incan emperor, came to this mountain, planning to dig for silver," Abuelita goes on, "the land heaved and rolled beneath his feet, and an echoing voice came from the earth. It said, *You shall not mine here! This silver is meant for others*." She throws her arms wide, indicating how big the voice was, and even though her own voice doesn't get any louder, it's almost like I can hear the mountain booming its command at the emperor. "And the emperor listened," she says, settling her hands around her cup of tea again, "and decreed that this hill was never to be mined. And that's where this whole region got its name—the emperor named the mountain *Potoc'xi*, a thunderous noise."

I can't help myself. "I thought you said the Inca called it *Sumaj Orcko*, beautiful hill?"

"Beautiful is for emperors who don't need to work in order to eat," Papi says flatly. His smile is a dish left out too long that has started to spoil. "The Spaniards called it the *Cerro Rico*: the rich hill."

"The miners call it the Mountain That Eats Men." Daniel's voice is barely a whisper.

"All names are true," Abuelita says before Papi can answer Daniel. "The prophecy given to Huayna Capac was fulfilled, because then the Spaniards came and conquered the Inca, and took the silver for themselves. So much silver that, had they wanted to, they could have built a solid silver bridge from Bolivia, across the Atlantic Ocean, all the way to Spain, and still had enough left to carry across it to give to their greedy king."

"And what exactly does this have to do with anything?" Papi's definitely not smiling anymore.

"We are descendants of the Inca." She points a finger at Papi, the way she must have when he was still a small boy and had to mind her. "We were never supposed to mine this mountain. The earth itself decreed it and only sorrow has met those who go against the decrees of *la Pachamama*." She meets his eyes. "Leave the boy. Let him go to school."

Papi's eyebrows scrunch in a scowl and I want to shrink into myself. None of us ever speaks out against him. Papi glares at his mother. Abuelita holds her chin high and meets his gaze. Daniel, Mami, and I sit like statues, eyes darting between them.

Papi stands up and grabs his helmet. "Legends and non-sense," he growls, and walks out the door, barking for Daniel to follow him.

Mechanically, Daniel gets to his feet. He picks up his new helmet and buckles the attached acetylene tank to his belt. Mami hands him a satchel with water and coca leaves in it and kisses his forehead. Without a word to any of us, eyes still on the ground, Daniel walks out the door.

With them gone, it feels like a bubble of tension has popped.

Abuelita sags where she sits, clutching her teacup. Blinking away tears, Mami grabs a comb and steers me onto the stool in front of her.

"Mami, I can comb my own hair."

"Hush," she says, and I leave it at that because, though we both know that I'm able to do this for myself, it feels nice to let her baby me. Plus, I realize I can give her a gift by letting her do my hair. At least then she can feel like she's been allowed to take care of one of her children this morning.

Pulling out the messy braid I slept in, she starts to drag the comb through my thick black hair, starting at the bottom and working her way up so as not to yank on the snarls.

"He'll never make it," says Abuelita softly.

Mami's hands pause for a second, then keep up their smooth movement. "He'll be okay for just a few days," she says. "With any luck, by then Mauricio will see that he's not made for mining."

"You really think Papi will change his mind?" I ask her.

"Well, it's happened before," she says. "Your father . . . he can be very stubborn, but he can change his mind too. You might not remember—you were only five—but he didn't want to let you go to school."

"Really?" This is news to me.

"*Mmm-hmm.*" Mami dips the comb in water and slicks it through my hair. "Do you remember, Elvira?"

"Oh, do I ever," says Abuelita. "He went on and on. He said that his mother hadn't gone to school, and his wife had barely gone to school. He wasn't about to send his daughter there." She deepens her voice, imitating Papi: "*She could be more useful around the house. Besides, a girl is just going to get married and have babies. What's the point in wasting time sending them to school when they could be working?"*

I feel a twist of anxiety when I hear her say that. It's not something we talk about, but I know, along with leaving school to work, that it's expected I will get married and leave the house. It makes me sick to my stomach to think about it. Marriage is a cave-in you can't dig out from under.

"So what happened?" I ask, to move the conversation away from my future marriage. "How did you change his mind?"

Mami's fingers gather the hair at my crown and start weaving it into a tight braid. "Little by little, over time. Your grandmother would lament the things she wasn't able to do because she never got an education, and I'd tell him how much I wanted you to be smarter than I was, how important it was for me. We'd talk about the possibilities it would open up for you. I think we even started to complain about how you were always underfoot and how much more work we'd get done if we could just get you out of the house for a few hours each day." I can hear the smile in her voice even though I can't see it.

"Eventually," says Abuelita, "he came around. And, once you were going, it was easier to just let you go and keep everyone happy."

"So, you see"—Mami ties off the end of the braid and lays her hands on my shoulders, dropping a quick kiss on my cheek—"there is hope, *mi hija*. We'll work on changing your father's mind. Until then, we just need to keep Daniel encouraged and try not to anger your Papi too much, okay?"

"I'll try," I say.

Half an hour later, hair scraped into a braid so tight and perfect that the skin on my face feels stretched and my eyes pull at the corners, I leave for school, retracing the steps I took yesterday with Daniel.

Even though Mami and Abuelita assured me that this won't be forever, I still worry. Is Papi walking slowly enough that Daniel won't start coughing? With any luck, they won't be walking at all if he and Papi managed to catch a ride to the mine on one of the ore trucks. If they did catch a ride, is Daniel even now reporting to Don César and being told the schedule for the day? Is he walking into the main entry tunnel at El Rosario, the big mine, or will he be assigned to a smaller branch? Can he still see daylight or is he lighting the open flame of his acetylene headlamp to fight away the darkness? How is he feeling? Is he scared of what might happen to him? Angry at Papi for making him go? Jealous of me for staying behind even though I'm older and not sick?

As I walk, I pass the used-up mouth of a mine from long ago. I wish I had something with me to sacrifice to beg for Daniel's safety. And Papi's too, I guess. But I don't have anything in my bag other than my notebook and a pencil. I'm not a miner and I will get food at school, so Mami doesn't let me pack anything from home.

I pause for a moment, staring into the half circle of blackness in front of me. I pull off my bag and rip out a piece of paper, folding it. On one half, I write out the twelve times table, as neatly as I can manage, for Papi. On the other side I write:

We will run away together. Far away from here. Far away from the mountain and the mines. Far away from the rocks and the cold. We'll run until we find a green valley like Abuelita talks about in her stories, and we'll sink our toes into the soft black soil and grow so much food that we'll both die fat. Or we'll find a city that sparkles with electric lights and good jobs and we'll both make lots of money and be happy forever.

And then, because it feels like it fits, I add the word *Amen.*

With Abuelita's warnings about the jealous Pachamama ringing in my mind, I don't go near the mouth of the tunnel. Instead, I fold the paper around a rock and throw it as far as I can into the mountain. It lands in the darkness beyond what I can see. Closing my eyes, I say a quick prayer to whoever might be listening that my father and brother will be safe.

With one final whispered, *"Please,"* I turn away from the darkness and hurry to school.

3

At school, I can't focus. All day long I'm haunted by thoughts of Daniel and Victor, both on their first day in the mines.

"Where's Daniel?" Susana asks when we sit down for our morning oatmeal. "Is he sick again?"

That's usually the answer for why Daniel isn't with us, and oddly, today I wish it were the reason. I shake my head. "Papi took him to work," I whisper.

"Oh no," says Alejandra.

I nod.

Susana pulls me into a one-armed hug and leaves it at that. There really isn't anything to say. But while we sit there and sip our breakfasts, the twin losses of Victor and Daniel make it impossible to smile. It's only as I'm getting up to return my cup that I see a notebook tucked under the bench. I pick it up and flip through it. Victor's messy handwriting covers every centimeter of every page of the first two-thirds, even the margins. When I get to the last page with writing on it, I see the note:

Whoever finds this: it's yours. I don't need it anymore.

Fighting back tears, I shove the notebook into my satchel and wait for the school day to start.

During geography, when we work on maps, I wonder how Daniel and Victor are finding their way through the maze of underground tunnels. In science, I remember Papi's comment about physics, and only barely stop myself from trying to calculate the probability that the mountain will fall in on itself today, crushing my brother and my best friend beneath unknown tons of rock. In language class, a square of sunshine slants across my desk, and no matter how I try to focus on the teacher's words, they float by me like balloons with cut strings. All I can think about is that Victor and Daniel aren't seeing the sunshine right now—haven't seen it for hours, won't see it for hours more. In handwriting, my letters are all jumbled on top of each other like a pile of rubble; in dance, I'm a landslide. By the time math rolls around, I'm desperate to lose myself in the clean, well-behaved lines of numbers, but not even they occupy my mind enough.

You have to do something, I tell myself. But just as strong as that impulse is the voice that says, *You don't have any good choices. There's nothing you can do.*

And though I spend the rest of the class turning options over in my head while my pencil scribbles its own way through my math, by the time school is over at noon, neither my plans nor my numbers have added up to anything.

At home, I head over to the slag heap to work as a *palliri* with Mami and Abuelita, like always. Today, though, it feels different than it did yesterday. I don't comment on the tear tracks through the dust on Mami's face. Abuelita doesn't ask me how my day was.

"Mami," I say, gathering my courage. I've spent the day thinking, but the best I've been able to come up with is not something better, it's just a different shade of bad. "Do you think if I left school and worked with you and Abuelita as a *palliri*, we could make enough extra money that Papi would let Daniel stop working in the mine sooner?"

"Ana!" Abuelita gasps. "You can't leave school! You've only got a few years left and then you can make it to secondary school. Hasn't that always been your dream? To go off to university and get a fancy degree?"

I look down at the scuffed toes of my sneakers. "Yeah," I admit, my voice barely above a whisper. "But it seems selfish to chase a dream that may not even happen when Daniel is in the mines. Maybe it would just be for a little bit . . . ?"

Mami runs a hand over my hair. "It's always a risk to pause your dreams," she says. "You might not get the chance to restart them."

I look into her eyes and wonder what her dreams were before she married Papi, but the sadness I see in them keeps me from asking.

"It's a generous offer," Mami says, "and it speaks to your kind heart. But if we pull you both out of school, I think it will make it easier for Mauricio to stop thinking about school at all for either of you. We're trying to get Daniel back into school, not you out of it."

I nod, grateful that's her answer and I can let go of a little of the guilt I've been carrying. If I'm going to school to protect it for Daniel, instead of stealing it from him, I don't feel quite as bad.

The afternoon stretches on and we break the rocks in silence, each of us lost in our own thoughts. It feels like the clink of our rocks against each other is the ticking of a giant clock, counting down the seconds until we see that Daniel is okay. Finally, at dusk, I see two figures in miners' coveralls walking toward us.

"It's them," I say, pointing.

Mami and Abuelita stop immediately. When Papi and Daniel reach us, both equally filthy, twin wads of coca leaves shoved into their cheeks, Mami takes their bags and helmets, fussing over them. Their faces are blackened with rock dust, the whites of their eyes stark against the layer of filth. You can see a straight line across their temples where the helmets rested, keeping the grime off their foreheads. Daniel unzips his coveralls and hangs them on the hook inside the door alongside Papi's. Then he collapses to the floor, rubbing his chest and wheezing. I'm used to seeing Papi dressed as a miner, coming home from work, but it's a shock to see Daniel that way. I poke him in the shoulder.

"You're gross," I say, even though that's not what I meant to say at all. "Go wash."

For a moment, Daniel stares at me, and I want to take my

words back and tell him I don't care how dirty he is, I'm just glad he's safe. But he stands up and walks outside to the blue plastic barrel where we store our water. A moment later I hear him splashing. I pick up a rag and join him.

"Here," I say, handing him the rag.

Daniel rubs his face and hands, but we can both see that there is still grime in the lines of his knuckles and caked deeply under his nails. *The mark of a working man,* Papi always says whenever he shakes hands with someone who has calluses on his palms and black half-moons under his fingernails.

"Are you okay?" I ask when I can't take it anymore. "How was your day?"

"How do you think?" snaps Daniel. His eyebrows knit and he scrubs harder at his hands, digging the now-filthy cloth into the ridges and running it along the tips of his fingers. When it's clear that's worked as much as it ever will, he throws the cloth to one side and tries to scrape out his fingernails using the nails of the other hand. The grime is caked deep. He's not making much progress.

Daniel struggles with his nails a moment longer, then he stops and leans against the side of the barrel, staring at his hands. His knuckles tighten on the rim and he closes his eyes. When he opens them, he doesn't look at his hands anymore, but picks up the rag and gives it to me.

"Thanks," he says, and turns to go inside, his voice flat, his narrow shoulders slumped.

"Daniel!"

He pauses in the doorway.

"Everyone missed you at school today."

It's only as the words leave my mouth that I know they're absolutely the wrong thing to say.

Daniel tenses as if I'd hit him, and he turns away and walks inside without another word.

———

Dinner is beyond awful.

Mami keeps finding excuses to touch Daniel, her fingers flitting out like butterflies to land on his arm or brush across his hair. Papi thumps Daniel on the back so many times you'd think he were choking, telling him he's a man of the mines now. Abuelita sits in her corner, wrapped in blankets and silence, glaring daggers at Papi. Daniel doesn't respond to any of them. Guilt burrows through me like a mine tunnel, leaving me feeling hollow and unstable. I don't even taste the soup.

After dinner, things don't improve. Usually, while I cleaned up with Mami and Abuelita, Daniel would do homework. But he doesn't have any homework today. I was so wrapped up in thinking about our problems I forgot to ask his teachers for his work. I feel like a double failure: once for going to school when he couldn't, and twice for not remembering to bring school home for him.

The gap in our routine feels like a missing tooth: you know it's only a small loss, but it's so close to you it feels huge and you can't stop probing it. Finally, after an awkward quarter of an hour, Daniel goes outside. I see him as I wash the dishes, perched on a rock up the slope so he's higher than our roof, wrapped in a blanket to keep off the chill.

When Papi reaches into Mami's apron pocket, takes a

handful of the grocery money, and walks out the door, we all know we're unlikely to see him again before tomorrow. As soon as he's out of sight, Mami follows Daniel. She settles by him and takes his hand. Dusk blurs their edges until they are no more than two shadows on the rock, one staring down at the unreachable city below, the other staring up at the equally unreachable stars.

When I move to join them, Abuelita puts a hand on my arm, stopping me.

"Let them be," she says softly. "There's nothing you can do."

I want to believe that I could find the magical words to make Daniel feel better. But I remember math class and the fact that I don't have another choice to offer him, and I let Abuelita turn me away and distract me.

"Where's your homework?" she asks. "Come, do it here next to me."

With another pang of guilt at living the life Daniel has left behind, I take out my notebook. Abuelita sits beside me, stitching up the rips in old clothes we'll be wearing again.

I stare at the line of numbers marching down the left side of my page; the row of unanswered questions that each have a single right answer if only I can find it. But I can't make my brain chase them. I stare at the blank page, my fingers frozen.

"The Inca fortress of Saqsayhuamán was built with some of the largest blocks of stone used in all of the Americas."

I glance up from my math. Abuelita's whole body is curled around the mending in her lap, but even so, I know her focus is on me. I smile and also pretend to be focusing on what's in front of me.

"There is no mortar holding the stones together," she goes on, her thick-knuckled fingers working the needle methodically, "and these blocks, though they have rounded corners and are all a jumble of interlocking shapes and different sizes, are so perfectly aligned that even now, hundreds of years and many earthquakes later, you couldn't slide a sheet of paper between them if you tried."

Abuelita finally looks at me. Though her body is frail—her bones birdlike and her knuckles twisted knobs that move slowly and painfully through her daily tasks—her eyes are clear and sharp.

"How did the Inca manage this, Ana, when the nearest place that these stones could be quarried is across a deep river valley?"

I blink at her, but she waits for my answer.

"Um . . ." I chew my eraser. "They . . . put them on carts? Had animals pull them?"

"The Inca never invented the wheel. They had no horses, no oxen. Their only beasts of burden were llamas." Her eyes pierce me. "Llamas can't carry more than thirty-five kilos. The biggest of these blocks weighs over a hundred and seventy tons. The walls are four hundred meters long and sixty meters high."

I stare at her, thinking hard. But I don't come up with any answer to the puzzle.

"I don't know," I finally admit.

"No one knows," she says, sniffing like she didn't expect anyone to know any better. She lets the mystery stand another minute while I chew on my pencil some more, then she goes on.

"Modern people like to focus on all the things the Inca didn't have. No wheel. No oxen or horses. No money system. No written language. But do you know what they did have? What allowed them to build mysterious marvels that baffled the imagination of their conquerors?"

"What did they have?" I ask, breathless.

Abuelita raises an eyebrow pointedly at my blank homework page.

"Our ancestors"—she leans over and pokes me to punctuate every word—"had. Very. Good. Math."

I laugh, and Abuelita returns to her sewing without another word.

Still smiling, I start my sums.

I wake up in the middle of the night, the cool white moonlight icing everything around me like a cake. Daniel is sitting against the wall, wrapped in a blanket. I sit up and rub the sleep crusts from my eyes.

"Sorry I woke you," Daniel whispers.

"That's okay," I whisper back. The moon-bright room shows Mami alone in the bed and Abuelita asleep on the floor mat next to me. Papi's nowhere to be seen, so I scoot over and sit next to Daniel, my shoulder nestled against his, blanket wrapped tight to keep out the cold. "You look like a woolly *salteña*."

He barks a short laugh at the image of himself as a meat-filled pastry, then lapses into silence.

"Couldn't sleep?" I finally ask.

Daniel shakes his head.

"Is it that bad?" When Daniel was a baby, he learned to walk in order to keep up with me. When we were kids, he trailed my footsteps to school. But now he's entered a place I've never been, and I struggle to imagine his new reality.

After a long pause, Daniel nods.

"The work's hard. It's obvious I'm no good at it. But the work's not the really awful part." He shakes his head slightly. "It's super hot and humid in the mine and the air smells funny, and you know there's less oxygen left with each breath. It's so hard to breathe in there, I have to keep stopping. And then Papi gets upset because I'm not as strong as the other boys . . ." He trails off and his head sinks onto his knees, so his next words are muffled. "I shouldn't even be there. I hate it."

I snake an arm out of my blanket and give his shoulders a squeeze.

"We'll find you a way out," I promise.

Daniel rocks his head back and forth on his knees, disagreeing with me.

"We will," I whisper even more stubbornly. "I spent all day today thinking about it."

"Oh?" Daniel lifts his face and raises an eyebrow at me. "And? What did you come up with?" His voice turns sour. "Will we run far away from here? To a green farm with black soil or a city that sparkles with electric lights and good jobs?"

"Far away from the mountain and the mines," I agree. "Far away from the rocks and the cold. We'll both make lots of money and eat until we're fat and be happy forever."

Daniel's laugh is hollow. "That's all just a stupid kid's dream, Ana. Neither one of us is ever going to make it off this mountain."

I let the fake smile slip off and really look at him. At his thin shoulders he's hunching so tightly and his delicate face he's scrunched into a scowl.

"You've never said that before."

"Well, it's true," he says softly. "Dreams are for little kids. I'm not a little kid anymore. Didn't you hear Papi at dinner? I'm a man of the mines now."

I don't like thinking of my brother as a man. Men are big and scary. They drink beer and liquor and hit their wives when they're angry. I don't want Daniel to have to be anything other than Daniel: a bit annoying, a bit of a mischief-maker, but still my brother.

"Daniel," I ask, trying to move away from whatever has put that emptiness in his voice, "what makes those kid dreams?"

"Huh?"

I bump him with my shoulder. He turns to face me.

"What makes those kid dreams?" I ask again.

He considers my question.

"I guess . . . I mean, I'm nearly twelve now, like you. When we were like seven or five or whatever, we used to think that things would get better—*poof!* But now . . . now we know that's not going to happen, right? They're kid dreams because we just imagined ourselves into a city or onto a farm. But we have no way of actually getting there. That's what makes them fake."

"You're right," I nod. "What we need isn't a dream, it's a plan."

"A plan," he repeats. Tasting the idea; trying it on.

"Yes," I say firmly. "A plan with actual steps that will get us off this stupid mountain for good."

A yawn cracks Daniel's face. "Okay, Ana," he says. "You let me know when you come up with one."

"You should lie down again and try to sleep," I tell him.

"Whatever, Mami," Daniel teases. But he does what I suggest anyway.

As I roll into my blankets beside him, I even out my breathing to encourage him to do the same. I know he'll need his sleep if he's to face another day in the mines tomorrow. But long after Daniel finds an uneasy sleep, I lie awake, trying to come up with a plan to buy my brother back the life he should never have had to give up.

The next day starts the same as the one before it: Papi and Daniel head off to the mines, I head off to school, Mami and Abuelita hunker down to break rocks. Again, I struggle to focus on my work at school, though at least I do remember to get an assignment for Daniel from the teacher this time. Given how tired he was last night, I don't know that he'll have the energy to learn after a day spent in the mines, but I get it for him anyway.

The afternoon breaking rocks with Mami and Abuelita stretches for what feels like forever, especially when the end of shift comes and goes and there is no sign of Papi or Daniel. The three of us work quietly, side by side, waiting. But as dusk draws closer and closer and they're still not home, Mami gives up pretending to work and starts down the road to find out what happened to them, leaving us without a word.

Abuelita and I glance at each other.

"I guess I'll go start dinner," I say.

Grabbing the beaten metal pot on my way out of the house, I fill it from the blue plastic barrel of water beside the door and walk over to our little clay stove. As I struggle to light it, I wrinkle my nose at the metallic tang of the water and the smell of the animal dung. We get the water from a little stream a short walk away, but it mixes with the runoff from the mines and always smells strange. If we go down to the city of Potosí, we can get clean water from taps, but then we have to carry the heavy cans back up the mountain. That water doesn't last very long.

Mami told me that when she was a little girl, before her father moved their family up to the Cerro, chasing a mineral boom, she lived in the valley. There, fires were made from wood and twigs and had the most wonderful-smelling smoke. Her family's farm was small but full of color. She would get all dreamy-eyed remembering it and wave her hands around as if she could paint a picture of it in the air for us. In some ways, Mami loves stories as much as Abuelita does; she just likes to talk about the way things are, not the way they were hundreds of years ago. *Green waves would turn into silvery sheets of barley at harvest time,* she would tell us as she tucked us in at night. *The dark earth tumbled out piles of brown and yellow potatoes, and the tall quinoa stalks wore tufts of purple, and red, and gold, each crowned like a king.* I always wished I could see it. Our mountain is only painted in bands of black and brown and rusty red, and I've never smelled woodsmoke. The Cerro Rico is high, high above the tree line, so there are no trees or bushes to burn. I feel the old anger against this mountain well up in me and it makes my fingers clumsy. I push too hard on my match and not only does it break, but the rest of the packet falls into the pot of water at my feet.

"Dammit!"

I fish the soggy box out of the water and shove the heels of my hands into my eyes to keep myself from crying. *They're only matches,* I tell myself severely. *They don't matter.* But they're also our *only* box of matches, and though I know I haven't damaged them permanently, having to wait until they're dry before I use them means that I won't be able to have dinner ready by the time Papi and Daniel get home. For some reason, that feels like the biggest tragedy in the world.

A warm hand settles on my shoulder and I startle.

"A bit over-the-top to pull God from his busy day to damn a broken match, don't you think?" Abuelita shushes me, her wrinkled hands smoothing the angry tears off my cheeks. "Now, what's the matter?"

"It wasn't just a match," I say, holding up the soggy offender. "It was the whole box."

"Ah," says Abuelita, her lined face serious. "Yes, of course. Much more worthy of divine attention."

I can't help it. I smile.

"Well, it kind of *is* a big deal if I can't get dinner cooked because I was too clumsy," I say. "Papi will be mad if he comes home and there's no food ready."

For a moment Abuelita just looks at me, and I can't read her expression. We don't usually talk about Papi and what he does when he's angry, but she lives in our one-room house with us. She knows what I'm not saying.

"Well then," she says, getting up and dusting her hands on her layered skirts, "it's a good thing there's more than one way to light a fire." She disappears into the house and reappears a moment later carrying Papi's spare acetylene helmet. Running her fingers around the band, she pulls out an almost-empty cigarette lighter.

"We shouldn't waste that," I say automatically.

"I don't plan to."

Abuelita turns on the acetylene to get the gas flowing, flicks on the lighter in a surprisingly smooth movement, and lights the spigot in the middle of the reflector plate. Then she tucks the lighter back into the band and holds the lit helmet out to me.

"You want me to light a cook fire with *acetylene?*" I manage.

"Why not? You need a fire, don't you?"

I shrug miserably, not wanting to take the helmet from her. Papi never lets me touch his mining stuff. When I hesitate for a moment longer, Abuelita sets the helmet gently into my hands.

"What your father doesn't know can't hurt us," she says.

Fingers shaking, I hold the flame against the pile of dung. After a minute, the pile catches, the persistent breeze no match for a continuous acetylene-fueled fire. As soon as the fire is well caught, I snap the valve shut to cut off the flow of gas and hand her the helmet.

"Thank you," I mumble, placing the pot of water on top of

48

the flames. Abuelita returns the helmet to the house, and I add a handful of diced llama jerky, fresh carrots, and diced *chuño* to the pot.

The water has just boiled when a shout from the house snaps me out of my daze.

"Ana!"

I jump to my feet at the panic in Abuelita's voice.

"Come quickly! They're back! Daniel is sick!"

4

Daniel's cough is raw and hacking and so intense it bends him around himself and he can't stand up. It's why it took the two of them so long to get home: Papi had to carry him.

Daniel's fever is back too, raging through him, burning him alive. Being in the mine has triggered his bronchitis, worse than it was before.

I sit beside him on our pallet of blankets holding a cool, damp cloth to his forehead, trying to bring his temperature down and wiping the blood-flecked spittle off his cheeks. In between his coughing fits, I try to spoon broth into his mouth, but so far he's vomited up anything he's managed to get down.

In the background, Mami yells at Papi that this is why Daniel should never have gone to the mines, that he's too fragile for that kind of work, that her baby is dying. Papi yells at Mami that she should shut the hell up, that she doesn't know what she's talking about, that she's turning Daniel into a weakling. I'm not surprised when I hear him hit her, which is when Abuelita starts shouting at both of them to stop it.

I don't turn around. Instead, my shoulders curve forward protectively, keeping Daniel and myself out of it.

The fight ends when Papi storms out of the house, shouting that he'll be damned if he's going to work alone tomorrow, the price of mineral is too high, and he'll not have it said that his son's a cripple.

When he's gone, Mami comes over to me.

"I can sit with Daniel, *mi hija*," she says. "Go to sleep: get some rest."

But I shake my head.

"You need it too," I say. I didn't take a beating, after all. "Besides, I don't think I could sleep even if I went to bed. Please let me stay up with him."

Mami drops a kiss on each of our foreheads and leaves it at that.

While my mother and grandmother sleep, I sit, hour after hour, late into the night, and think about all the things I heard over my shoulder. Papi, saying he's not going to work alone tomorrow. Mami, saying Daniel's in no shape to walk out the front door, let alone go into the mine.

The problem is, I believe both of them.

Even after Daniel falls into a fitful fever sleep, I sit awake, staring around our tiny house, thinking. There has to be a better way, even if it's not a good choice.

The price of mineral is high. It should make life easier. It should be a dream come true. Instead, it's destroying my family.

Daniel's right. Dreams are for little kids. What I need now is a plan.

I don't go to bed until I have one.

———

Usually I sleep deeply and silently, but tonight when I fall asleep, a dream is waiting for me.

In it, I'm standing barefoot on the rutted rock path that leads into the mountain, and the arched entrance to the mines looms dark in front of me. The cold from the mountain stabs up through my heels and the wind whips over the ridge and raises goose bumps on my arms and calves. I'm amazed at how real it feels because I know it's a dream. Standing there, cold seeping up through me, wind whistling over me, I stare into the maw of the mountain and, in the way of dreams, I feel the Mountain That Eats Men inhaling and exhaling. When it sighs, the smell of dust and death washes over me and I cannot imagine that anything could be worse, until the next moment when the wind pulls around me and whistles into the black cavern and I realize the mountain is breathing me in.

I stand there, unable to move, as the mountain heaves beneath me, learning my smell.

———

I wake bathed in sweat and feeling more exhausted than when I fell asleep. Shaking my head to clear it, I roll out of bed. The small amount of warmth I managed to put into the alpaca-wool blankets overnight is instantly gone and my sweat chills me even more as I struggle into my shoes. As cold as it is to be awake, I'm glad to leave sleep behind.

Everyone else is still asleep—even Papi, who must have come home at some point—as I pull my thick black hair into two braids and wind them in a tight, bobby-pinned crown on top of my head. I layer on a shirt and my least-favorite sweater and pull on jeans and my heaviest pair of socks. Before anyone else wakes up, I take what I need from the house and hide it outside.

"That's a different style for you," comments Abuelita when she joins me while I make the morning tea. She tries to pull me into quiet conversation, but I'm having trouble shaking off my dream from last night and stay quiet. It's almost like I can feel the slow rise and fall of the mountain under my feet even though I'm awake. Besides, of everyone, I think I'm about to upset Abuelita the most and that hurts my heart.

Through the open door I hear the unmistakable sounds of Papi waking up, and I know that I have to move now.

"Here." I hand her a cup of tea. "Could you take this in to Daniel, please? I'll follow in a sec with the rest of it."

Abuelita takes the cup and heads into the house. As soon as she's gone, I unwrap the bundle I hid around the corner of the wall. In it are Daniel's coveralls, belt, boots, and acetylene headlamp.

Battling a hollow, gnawing feeling in my chest, I pull them on.

Beneath me, the mountain sighs.

The fight I cause with my appearance is, in some ways, more epic than the fight last night. Even Daniel props himself up on his elbows and shakes his head at me. Mami is shouting things that are so scattered and unconnected to each other that they don't make any sense and Abuelita has gone pale and is trying to pull the uniform off me by force. Papi, for once, is sitting quietly on his stool, watching all of us fight. When he finally speaks, everyone in the room freezes.

"And what," he says to me coldly, "do you think you're doing in your brother's clothes?"

Abuelita and Mami step away, leaving me alone to face the coming storm.

I swallow and force out the words I practiced.

"You said you needed to bring a kid with you to work today. Mami said that Daniel is too sick to go. You're both right, so I'm going instead of him."

Papi's face darkens like a building thundercloud.

"Do you think being a miner is a joke, girl?"

I shake my head and the helmet I've wedged over my coiled braids jostles.

"No, sir. But I'm older than Daniel and right now I'm stronger than he is. Whatever he was able to do, I know I'll be able to do." I play my best card. "He can't work with a fever and there's no point wasting days when the price of mineral is so high."

Papi rubs a thick hand over the lower half of his face, considering.

This is enough uncertainty that Abuelita loses it. She turns on me. "Have you not listened to a word I've said?" she shrieks. "*La Pachamama* does not allow girls into the mountain. It's ill luck!"

"But, Abuelita," I try to soothe her, "the tourists do it all the time. The Americans and Europeans, when they come to visit the mountain, they ask for tours of the mine and everyone lets them in, no problem. Nothing happens when *those* women go into the mountain. Why should something happen if I help out, just until Daniel is better?"

Abuelita is furious, but instead of answering me, she turns and yells at Papi. "No, Mauricio, absolutely not! This is ridiculous! You can't let your daughter go into that hell hole."

I can see at once that she has made a big mistake. Papi's face, which had lightened in amusement to see me being yelled at by my grandmother, twists into rage at being scolded.

"Quiet!" he roars at her. "I'll not be told what I can and can't do under my own roof!"

Abuelita stretches her thin neck and squawks at him, angry as a wet chicken. "I'm your mother!"

"And I'm no longer a boy and you'd do well to remember it." He's on his feet now. "I am the man of this house! What I say goes."

"But *la Pachamama*—"

"Damn the Pachamama and the devil and all the saints too while you're at it!" he bellows. "No one quotes hocus-pocus to control me!" He looks me up and down, and I try not to flinch under his glare. "The mines are no place for a girl," he starts, and I wilt, thinking I've lost. But then Papi goes on. "However, her brother is too sick to work right now, and she makes a good point that this is not a time when there is a day to waste. The price for zinc is higher than it's been in ten years. Tin is on a rebound too. I'm not going to waste this opportunity because Daniel has a sniffle. Until the boy's back on his feet, Ana will take his place." When Mami starts to talk again, he holds up a hand to stop her and points at Daniel. "If you don't like it, focus on making *him* better."

He slams his helmet on his head and stomps out the door.

"Ana! Come!"

I glance an apology at Mami and Abuelita. Mami is shaking and Abuelita won't meet my eyes. Daniel looks shocked, but he's still wrapped in blankets and propped on pillows. He'll get a chance to heal. I know I've done the right thing.

Without a word to any of them, I follow Papi.

———

Papi doesn't talk to me as we walk the long road to the big mine entrance on the other side of the mountain where he works. The Cerro Rico has hundreds of mine entrances, some huge, some no bigger than the little manhole near my house. I sometimes think about all the tunnels snaking their way through the rock and wonder how the whole thing, hollowed out from the inside, doesn't fall down around us.

The big mine is a long way from home, nearly two hours of walking, and we're not lucky enough to meet up with any trucks going our direction, only trucks coming down the mountain. We stand aside and let them pass. It's downhill for the first hour until we get to the intersection with my school. I give it a wistful glance, then follow Papi up the road leading away from it for the last forty-five minutes of steep uphill walking.

Finally, we round a last blind curve and the El Rosario mine stands before us. The cleared area in front of the main tunnel is a hive of activity—the tromp of heavy boots competing with the *whump-whirr* of the air compressor machine and the rattle of an electric jackhammer.

I feel deeply that I don't belong here. Sure, I've come to the mine before, once or twice, when Papi forgot his lunch sack. But every other time I've come here as Ana, Mauricio Águilar Agudo's daughter, who was doing a nice, daughterly deed. People smiled at me and patted my head.

But now I'm not running an errand, not wearing a skirt. Instead, I'm in a dusty miner's suit, cinched tight at the waist. There are mud-caked boots on my feet, and my braids are wound around my head so that the helmet doesn't wobble. The acetylene tank is strapped uncomfortably to my right hip and a spike jabs into my left. Over my shoulder, in Daniel's bag, are a simple lunch, a few handfuls of coca leaves, and the small plastic water bottle I carried with me when I left home. No one is smiling at me now.

"Well," says Papi, cracking his knuckles one by one and looking around him, "now you just need to convince César to let you stay. Don't make me regret bringing you." He sets off at a brisk walk across the lot.

I swallow. I didn't realize I would have to have this fight with more than just Mami and Abuelita.

Heart hammering in my throat, I force my feet to follow Papi as we walk toward the chaos of the mine entrance. Men strain, their feet slipping in the gray sludge as they struggle to keep huge wheeled metal bins of rock fragments on their narrow tracks. I scrabble sideways to get out of their way and bump into a column of workers lighting each other's acetylene lamps. The glow from the open flame on their helmets shadows their faces even in daylight.

"Sorry," I mumble, and hurry away.

I hug the rock face, scuttling to catch up to Papi, who is standing in front of a tin-roofed hut off to the left of the gaping archway. Just as I get there, a man comes out. I pull up short to avoid smashing into him and recognize César Jansasoy Herrera.

"Don César," I squeak. I hate how high and girlish my voice sounds, but I can't help it, so I don't try again. César is a huge slab of a man: his shoulders are wide, his face is wide, his knuckles are wide. He's the kind of strong you can see coming ten meters away, not the ropy, sneaky strong that Papi is, that surprises you when you're not expecting it.

About to walk past, César does a double take when he hears me and peeks under the brim of the helmet at my face.

"Ana?" he asks, shocked.

I nod and glance at Papi, but he just waves a hand for me to go on. "Daniel is sick today. We were hoping you'd let me take my brother's place, just until he gets better . . ."

"Ana . . ." he starts, holding up his hands in front of him in apology, but Papi claps César on the shoulder. Even though he's shorter and slimmer than César, Papi moves with an intensity that tends to make people do things his way. Steering César away from me and other listening ears, Papi leans in and starts talking to César in a low, focused voice. I can't hear their words, but it doesn't take hearing to see César shaking his head back and forth. This is not good. I can't imagine how angry Papi will be with me if this doesn't work out. Not only will he have to go home this evening and have his mother's way be the way things are, but his work buddies will have watched him fail to convince his boss. None of that will go well for us. I break into a cold sweat under my awkward gear. This idea is all my fault. I have to make it work.

Without any more thought than that, I run over and grab César's hand in mine.

César startles and tries to pull away, but I hold on tight.

"Please, Don César," I beg. "It's not for long—a couple of days only, maybe a week! Let me try to work here for just today. If you think I can't do the job, then you can tell me to go and I'll leave. Let me try. Please."

"Ana . . ." he starts again. His filthy face wears a soft expression under his metal hat, like he's unsure what to do with me.

I race on before he can make up his mind, trying not to stare at his hands, so big that I can barely fit both of mine around one of his, rough and ridged from years of wrestling metal out of rocks. I force myself to keep going before I can let myself think too long about what kind of work I'm signing myself up for. There is no gentleness in a world that forms hands like those on César Jansasoy Herrera.

"I won't be any trouble—I learn things really fast, just as fast as Daniel, maybe even faster, and I work as hard as my brother too. Even harder because I have good, strong lungs. I won't be any trouble at all. Please . . ." I stare up at him imploringly. I have no idea the right way to go about asking for work. I know that César has a young daughter, only six or seven I think. I don't know if it will help or hurt me that he has a girl too, but I need him to say yes.

César scrubs one giant, filthy hand over his face. Papi says nothing.

"One day," César finally says. "Then we'll see."

"*Agradiseyki!*" I gasp, finally dropping his hand. "I promise you won't regret it."

"We'll see," César repeats. Then, to Papi, he says, "I had Daniel scheduled with me again today, and you, Francisco, and Guillermo in zone five. Does that work for you? I'll stay with her and make sure no harm comes to her."

Papi waves a hand as if he has absolutely no concerns about the idea of harm coming to me. "Be good." He points a finger at my face. "If you disgrace me, you'll regret it."

I nod shakily. As if I didn't know that.

Papi trudges into the mine without a backward glance, and I'm left alone with César.

For a moment César stands there, eyes scrunched closed. Then, with a sigh, he says, "Come on, then, follow me," and starts walking, muttering under his breath. I hear a word that sounds a lot like *babysitting* and vow to work as hard as I can to not make this kind man's life any more difficult than I already have.

I scurry to keep up with him, tucking my head down to avoid the curious stares of the other miners.

"César! Who's that?" shouts one of them, a long string of a man. He's so skinny his cheeks cave in except for where he has a huge wad of coca leaves shoved in one. It makes his face look bumpy and off-balance.

"Mauricio's kid," César answers.

"And you're taking her in?" Bumpy asks, the shock plain in his voice.

"It's not permanent," César grumbles.

I wish I were invisible. It's clear that Bumpy and his crew aren't happy to have me here. But César doesn't waver: his voice is level, his pace is steady. Bumpy doesn't say anything else, but I hear the sound of spitting. I tell myself that the men are only clearing their mouths of coca to have a new mouthful, but I have the horrible suspicion that they're cursing me.

Seconds later, my concerns about Bumpy and his crew are replaced by a new fear. Without breaking stride, César enters the mine, the cave darkness swallowing him whole.

I can't do this! I think. For a heartbeat, I flinch away from the shadow's edge. I can't see more than an arm's length into the tunnel and it doesn't help that air tubes snake in around the edges, hissing and whistling. It sounds like the mountain is whispering, and it reminds me of my dream.

Daniel, I remind myself. *Think of Daniel. He did this sick and with bad lungs. Papi has done it for years. Surely you can do it for one day.*

And with that, I take a deep breath to steady myself and plunge into the inky depths of the mine after César.

5

As soon as we enter the mine, César takes me to meet the devil.

"This way," he grumbles, no more than a dusty hump in the darkness ahead of me. It's difficult to keep up with him: the tunnel slants and turns, disorienting me, and my feet slither around in the mud and scree underfoot. I'm clumsy in Daniel's boots. When I put a hand out to catch myself, the rough rock gouges my palm. I curl my fingers into the pain and feel wetness pooling in my nail beds. I ignore the sensation as best I can and scramble after César.

When he stops, I nearly run into him. I throw my hand out to the side to stop myself from falling on my butt and making even more of a fool of myself than I have already. My injured hand smacks into the rock face and I gasp.

César turns around at my noise. I follow the glow from the acetylene lamp on his helmet and see that I've left a bloody handprint on the wall of the tunnel.

"Sorry," I mumble, and curl my hand into my sleeve to wipe it off.

"Leave it," he says, stopping me. "Maybe if you give the Tío this taste of your blood, he won't take any more. Come." He gestures me forward and I shuffle up until I'm level with him. "Meet the Tío of this mine."

In a grotto carved out of the side of the tunnel in front of us hunches a life-size statue of the devil. The flickering light from the candles stacked around him glints off the broken glass teeth in his mouth and rims his light-bulb eyes. His clay horns almost reach to the ceiling. His nakedness is nearly hidden by a pile of coca leaves and he's surrounded by a sloppy ring of open bottles of alcohol and lit cigarettes. I chew the inside of my lip nervously.

César takes a cigarette out of his pocket, lights it in the flame of the acetylene headlamp, and puts it in the devil's mouth. "Tío, this is Ana Águilar Montaño, sister to Daniel Águilar Montaño, the boy who started two days ago. We want you to know her and not harm her." He turns to me. "Do you have anything to give the Tío?"

At first, I shake my head. I barely have enough for myself, let alone anything extra to give to some statue in the middle of a mountain. But the Tío's head is wreathed in smoke from the cigarette and he's staring down at me out of his light-bulb eyes, and I realize I'm afraid. I reach into my pouch and pull out a handful of coca leaves and hold them out to César. He sprinkles the leaves on top of the pile already there.

"You should bring gifts to the Tío. Outside"—César points up the echoing tunnel toward the exit—"we pray to God. But down here, the devil is in charge and you must follow his rules, or he will kill you. Do you understand?"

I have never been further from understanding anything in my life, but I nod, wanting to get away from here.

"So"—César dusts off his hands and turns from the statue—"let's go find you something to do for the rest of the day that's worth your brother's pay and won't get you killed, *hmm?*" With that, he leads me deeper into the mine, farther and farther from the light of day.

By the time César stops again, I feel a creeping panic. Being down here is like being in a nightmare, one of those where I'm trapped in a tight space and can't get out—but this is worse than any dream because I know there's no waking.

César turns to say something else to me and his eyes go to my forehead.

"You never lit your helmet," he says.

When he reaches for my head, my instinct is to pull away, but I stay put. His giant hands close over the edges of my helmet and I feel the sweaty tug against my hair as he lifts it off my head. He reaches over and taps the tank strapped to my hip.

"This is your acetylene," he says. "The gas travels through here"—his giant finger traces the clear tube that runs from the tank, over the top of the plastic hat, to the beaten-tin disc centered at the front—"and comes out this spigot." He turns a switch at the base of the beaten-tin reflector plate and touches the spigot to the flame on his forehead. A twin fire springs up on the front of my helmet. "You adjust the flame by turning this valve"—he demonstrates—"but you never turn it off, even if you're with the main crews and their electric lights."

"Why?" I ask, settling the helmet on my head, super aware of the live flame only centimeters from my face and hair. César studies me seriously.

"Because fire only burns when there's oxygen," he says. "If your flame ever goes out, it means you've come to a place in the mine that is full of other gases . . . arsine or carbon monoxide, for example, and you need to get out as quickly as you can." He raps on my helmet with a callused knuckle. "If your flame can live, you can. Remember that, Ana. If it dies, it's only a matter of time before you will too."

I swallow against a throat gone suddenly dry. A few seconds ago I was only worried about the mountain around the tunnels. Now I'm afraid of the tunnels too. I nod to show I understand, gripping my hands behind me so he won't see them trembling. César takes off again through the narrow tunnel, his broad shoulders blocking my view of where we're going. As we pass a gaping black hole in the floor, he pauses and turns to me again.

"This is where Daniel and I were working yesterday," he says softly. His eyes are sad. My gaze is pulled to the yawning hole in front of us.

"Down there?" My voice is a squeak. When I tip my head toward the hole, the weak light from my lamp glances off the rough sides of the narrow shaft but doesn't come anywhere close to showing me the bottom.

"Yes, but we're not going to work there today. I think maybe the air was bad and that set off his lungs. I'll check it later."

I stare at the gaping hole in the floor before me. Was that what happened to Daniel? Has the bad air of the mine already started killing him?

César puts his hand on my shoulder. I feel like I might buckle under the weight of it. "Come," he says, "we're working somewhere else today."

The main entry is a long, smooth tunnel, wide enough that people can get out of the way of the ore carts that run along the narrow-gauge track in its center. But once you leave zone one, "tunnel" is no longer really accurate. Instead, the various paths that have been chipped or blasted or eroded from the mountain dip and weave and crisscross each other like the middle of an anthill. There are chimneys you have to climb up and down on spindly ladders; chasms you have to balance across on wobbly planks; passageways you have to slide through on your belly like a snake. You have to look down so you don't trip on the spikes and ridges of harder rock jabbing up from the floor and so you can make sure not to splash when the standing pools of toxic orange water reach over your ankles. Looking up is a bad idea. There are places where the acid condensation on the ceiling is so strong it stings if it drips on your skin. Plus, if you do look up, you can see how bowed and rotten the support beams are.

We've descended steadily for almost forty-five minutes and the idea of hundreds of thousands of pounds of rock over my head, just waiting to collapse and crush me, is making me twitchy. I'm starting to long for daylight and the wide-open spaces of the Cerro Rico like I never have before. The air gets hotter and hotter the deeper we clamber into the guts of the mountain, and as I scramble to keep up with César, I'm sweating freely.

Finally, we arrive at an open chamber César introduces as

"zone eight." The zones are named in the order they were discovered, not in any meaningful, organized way. I wish I had a map since the numbering doesn't do much to help. I feel completely lost in here. There are three miners chiseling against the far wall of zone eight. César leads me to the end of the line and takes out his spike. I copy him. He shows me how to hold the spike against the wall and pound it with a rock. My split palm screams at me when I do this, but I don't complain. Instead, I try to match my pace to that of the row of miners. The miner closest to me is a boy about my age, but he's working with the same deadened determination as the others. It's only when he turns to glare at me when I can't match his rhythm that I see who it is.

"Victor!"

His jaw drops in astonishment. "Ana?"

I can't help my grin. In the middle of the darkness of this terrible place, in the middle of this terrible day, seeing my best friend's face is as welcome as sunlight.

"Victor, it's so good to see you!"

"What are you doing down here?" he asks, stunned.

The man beside Victor barks at us to get to work and stop yapping, so we set our spikes and beat them with the rocks in time with the rest of the miners. It takes me a few minutes to learn the weight of the spike and the impact on the rock, but soon I've figured out the pattern of the movement and I know what to expect. Once I catch the rhythm, even though my muscles are aching from the repeated motion, I can use my brain for other things. Like answering Victor's question.

"Daniel got sick. Papi and César are letting me work in his

place until he gets better." At Victor's horrified face I add, "It's only temporary."

"There's no way they should have let you down here. It's too dangerous!"

That stings.

"Too dangerous for me but not for you? A falling rock will smush you as easily as it would smush me. We're basically the same age, Victor! The same size. And Daniel is sick. If it's too dangerous for me, then he *definitely* shouldn't be here."

"None of us should be here," mutters Victor. "Kids aren't even supposed to work in the mines. But it *is* more dangerous for you. You're a girl."

"So?"

"There are no girls . . . I mean, the men down here . . . they won't like that you're here, and some of them . . ." Victor trails off, uncomfortable. "Just promise me you'll never go anywhere without César or someone he has specifically assigned you to."

I hear the truth behind Victor's words. I update my worry list to include not just the rock, the air, the toxins, the devil, and the Pachamama, but also the non-mystical inhabitants of the mountain.

I glance nervously at the man working beside Victor and, with a start, realize that he's Victor's papi and that César sent the last man in the spike-driving line away. Victor and his papi are the only ones on my left. César is working to my right. None of these men are a danger to me. César has sandwiched me in safety. I feel a warming in my heart for the quiet supervisor.

"I'll be careful," I promise Victor.

We work, repetitively chiseling holes in the rock, long

beyond when my arms and shoulders are burning and my eyes are blurry from fatigue and rock dust. Finally, César checks the line and says the holes are deep enough. *Deep enough for what?* I wonder, but I'm too tired to say anything out loud. I slouch against the far wall, sweat rubbing the suit against me uncomfortably. Black spots are dancing in front of my eyes, whether from the bad light or from working for hours with nothing to eat or drink, I'm not sure. Then César opens a bag at his feet and I'm suddenly at attention again.

"Is that ... dynamite?" I gasp.

"How did you think we make the tunnels?" Victor laughs. "Or get the rock rubble to sort for ore?"

I swallow and shrug, not sure what to say. I mean, of course I knew that miners used dynamite. How many times have I seen my father walk out the door with sticks strapped to his belt? Too many to count. But standing inside the mine, surrounded on all sides by the rough, dark rock, the idea of blasting away at it is beyond terrifying. How careful is César when he sets the charges? How is he sure he won't blast a hole that brings the whole mountain down on us? I dig my fingers into the palms of my throbbing hands. The pain takes my mind off the dynamite.

Sort of.

When the last charge is placed, César lights the long fuse and says, "Let's go!" and we hustle in a dusty line, uphill through the tunnels toward the entrance. I always wondered why ants moved so quickly; now I feel like one, scuttling through the earth, no thought in my mind beyond survival.

César yells, *"¡Dinamita!"* as we climb back to the surface. Out of crevices and chimneys, other miners appear and join us. *What about those who traveled deeper than César's voice can reach?* I wonder. *How will they know to get out in time?*

By the time we make it to the main tunnel and zone one, our ant line has swollen to almost twenty shuffling men, with one miserable girl in the middle. The noise of our breathing and the clinking of our gear is the only sound.

When we finally break out into the harsh clear light of midday, I want to sob with relief. The sky! The sky stretches above me, no rock pressing down. The air I breathe is thin but pure, and the light comes from the sun, not some miserable gas flame on my forehead. A muffled boom makes me glance over my shoulder, and I feel a rumble under my feet. The miners count the number of explosions aloud, to make sure they all detonate. When they get to ten, the men break into smiles, saying how good a sign it is that the Tío didn't withhold any this time. About half a minute later, a puff of dust comes out the mouth of the mine, driven through the tunnels by the force of the blast.

I look up at Victor's house, perched on the edge of the cliff above El Rosario. I wonder if they can feel the blasts through their floor when they're at home.

The miners share coca, tea, and a cigarette if they have one. I see Papi among them, seeming relaxed, but he doesn't come over to me and I don't feel brave enough to go bother him. I sit away from the group and drink some water. Victor crosses the wet silt to join me.

"Enjoy the break while you can," he says. "We'll be back at it soon enough."

I nod, exhausted.

"Chew some coca," suggests Victor. "It'll help you feel better."

"I gave it to the Tío."

Victor seems uncomfortable when I say that, though whether it's because he believes in the devil or doesn't, I'm not sure. Either way, he reaches into his sack and hands me a fistful of dried green leaves. I thank him, shove a few in my cheek, and put the rest in my pouch for later.

"The miners took me to the Tío on my first day too," Victor says.

"Yeah?" The bitter taste of coca floods my mouth, and though I do get a mild boost of energy, it isn't nearly enough to combat the fatigue of the work I've already done.

"Yeah. Old Francisco told me the story—how we think we're just calling him 'uncle,' but really, the Spaniards put the statues in the mine tunnels when they forced the Inca to work in them. They told them the statue was a god—a *dios*—that would kill them if they left early. Over time that word—*dios*—came to be *tíos*."

"That's messed up," I tell him. I bet Abuelita knows that story. I wonder if she believes it. I wonder if that's part of the reason she's so mad at me right now.

"I know, right?" says Victor. "At least we can come up here and take a break without thinking some god is going to kill us for it. The Spaniards made them work in the mine for months at a time, and they never saw the sun."

That makes me shiver.

"I know it's just a statue," he says softly, as if he's afraid of being overheard, "but it still gives me the creeps."

"Me too," I admit.

Though, to be honest, the devil statue was only one of many

things today that has creeped me out. I feel the other miners' eyes on me as they talk in voices too low for me to hear. Determined to make the most of my short time aboveground, I ignore them and stare at the sky.

Too soon, César is walking among the miners, getting everyone on their feet for another six-hour shift. When he gets to us, he pauses. He jerks his head, indicating that he wants Victor to get a head start.

Victor gives my hand a reassuring squeeze and hustles to join the line of miners reentering El Rosario, pulling his helmet on as he does so. I stare after him. I hadn't noticed he was holding my hand.

When the rest of the crew has cleared out and it's just the two of us in the entry lot, César crouches down in front of me and meets my eyes.

"You could go home," he says quietly. It's a statement of fact. Not a criticism; not a command.

I lift my chin.

"I could," I say, "but I'm not going to."

César considers me for another minute, then nods.

"Okay," he says, and gets to his feet.

Standing to follow him, my muscles ache from the unusual work. But the pain in my back and arms is nothing to the pain in my soul as I walk toward the dark mouth of the mine and push myself into the shadows once again.

———

We're working away when, with a rattling groan, the air compressor dies. So far, the space we're in has been filled with the constant noise of the humming motor and the *shush* of the pressurized air through the hoses.

Victor waves a hand over the opening.

"No air," he confirms.

César grunts in annoyance. "Come on," he says, and turns up the tunnel.

We fall in behind him again, retracing our steps to the outside. No one wants to stay behind in a section that's not being ventilated. I wonder if it's my imagination, but it already feels like there's less air to breathe; that it's hotter; that our flames are duller than they used to be. I tell myself it's my imagination. But all the same, I hurry behind César and Victor.

When we get to the main entryway to El Rosario, I immediately scuttle out of the way, back to where I was sitting earlier. I'm glad to have any excuse for a bonus break and I sink down gratefully in the sunlight. I expect Victor to join me, but instead I see him head directly to the compressor with the men. I wonder whether I should have gone over there too, but decide to stay where I am.

César hefts the dented yellow chassis off the outside of the compressor and the men lean in to examine the guts of the machine. It's like each of them is a dusty *yachac*, trying to read the cause of illness in its entrails.

But after about ten minutes of standing around, muttering, and pointing, Victor's papi wanders away to smoke a cigarette on the far side of the lot. Only Victor stays with César. I drift closer, curious despite myself.

"... and lift that hose there," César is saying when I get close enough to see what's going on. "Keep your fingers well away from those fan blades!"

Victor is forearm-deep in the machine, following César's instructions. His face is intent, but unlike when we have to concentrate in the mines, or even when we had to concentrate in school, he seems relaxed. Almost as if he's enjoying himself.

"Like this?" he asks.

César nods. "Now, while you hold that out of the way, I'll clean the dust out of this filter. Once that's done, let's see if I can get the engine to turn over . . ." César's head disappears behind the bulk of the air compressor. I hear clanking. Victor keeps his hands exactly where he was told, but he cranes his neck to see what César is doing on the other side of the machine.

I don't understand what's so fascinating: it's a machine. Just another hulking, clunking piece of scrap that is struggling to work in the altitude. Don't get me wrong: I appreciate the air that the compressor delivers into those hellish tunnels. But I just don't see anything interesting about the thing itself. Its rusted guts twist between colored wires and black rubber hoses. None of it makes any sense to me.

"Hey, Victor," I say.

"Not now, Ana," he says, never taking his eyes from what César is doing.

I shrug and return to my sunbeam, leaving him to his machine.

About half an hour later I hear a cranky *chunk-chunk-chunk* that changes to a steady drone, accompanied by a whoop from Victor. I look over to see him and César grinning at each other over the top of the whirring machine. They struggle to replace the chassis now that it's shaking from side to side, but eventually they manage. I can again hear the snaking hiss of air through the tubes.

César claps Victor on the shoulder and hands him a rag from his pocket to wipe the thick black stripes of engine oil off his arms and hands.

"Let's go!" calls César, buckling his helmet on.

The rest of us fall into line behind them and head to where we were working before. The air tube hisses comfortingly when we get there, and the four of us settle once more into the routine of the work.

"What was that all about?" I ask Victor.

"Hmm?" His face still wears a happy, distracted look. "Oh, see, it turns out, not only had the dust gummed up the filter, but some debris had made its way into the fan. The grit made it so the blades couldn't turn, which overheated the motor and made the whole thing fail." He grins. "Once we cleaned it all out, César was able to reset the thingy—I forget what he called it, I'll have to ask him later—and get the whole compressor working."

"Uh-huh," I say.

"What?"

"And you would rather have been doing that than getting an extra half-hour break? I'm sure César could have figured that out without you."

"Maybe," Victor admits, looking off into the distance. "But I liked helping."

"Whatever," I say, teasing.

But Victor is serious.

"No, really, Ana. Look at what we do all day—smash this, lift that—it's all just movement, but none of it is going anywhere. But this . . . it was different. I worked hard at something for a little while and then, because of what I did, it was better than it was before. It was kind of nice. That doesn't happen much."

I don't tease him again because he's right. There's not much up here that any of us does that moves forward. So much of our work is just what has to be done in order to do more work or survive another day. I imagine how it would feel if I could make something better, truly better with my efforts.

"Okay," I say, giving him a soft punch on the arm. "I guess that does sound like fun."

Victor grins at me and we both get back to work.

———

I thought the worst part of my day was behind me when I finally exited the mine at six o'clock. For some reason I'd forgotten about the hour-and-a-half walk home. And if that slow, agonizing trudge around the mountain wasn't already adding insult to injury, at the end of it I had to go inside and face my family.

When we finally come around the last bend of the mountain, I see the far-off shapes of Mami and Abuelita standing in the door together, their hands unusually idle. When she sees us, Mami slumps in relief. I hurry my steps, desperate to be home and have this day behind me.

When I walk in, Mami seems torn between fussing over me and venting her frustration at me.

"Get out of that suit," she snaps. But when I do, she hangs it up for me and holds my face in her hands, resting her forehead against my sweaty one. "Are you okay?" she whispers.

"I'm fine, Mami," I say, because Papi's standing right there and I'm not about to admit weakness now. I go outside and wash my face and hands. The cut from this morning has scabbed and reopened so many times that the cuff of my sweater is stained with blood. I scrub at the cut the best I can, wincing at the fresh pain. The lines on my blackened fingers look like they've been traced with ink. Remembering Daniel's first day, I don't even bother trying to get it out.

I walk inside and slump onto the floor. Mami hands me a bowl of stew and a spoon. Abuelita hasn't spoken to me since I walked in. Disapproval radiates off her like steam rising off boiling water.

Daniel's still not well enough to join us, and soon after we finish our tense dinner, Papi heads out. Now that I'm working for the money he's drinking through, I feel mad all over again, but I force myself to let that go.

We're washing the dishes together when Mami notices my cut palm.

"What's that?" she asks, grabbing my hand and examining the wound.

"I cut my hand today," I say, stating the obvious.

"You can't let that get infected!"

Not satisfied with my cleaning job, she scrubs at my palm with the hard block of soap until tears sting my eyes and then she pats it dry and wraps it in a clean cloth. I think she's done, and I move to pull my hand away, but she holds on for a second. We stand there as she stares at my hand, clasped between us.

"Promise me you'll stop," she finally says, squeezing my fingers gently. "We'll find another way. You can't keep doing this."

I glance at where Daniel is tossing fitfully on our shared bed and then at the door where Papi has vanished.

"I have to," I answer softly.

Mami follows my gaze. She lets me go without another word.

———

That night, my dream changes.

In the washed-out light of dreams, I stand outside the mine. But this time when the mine inhales, it sucks me into it. I'm pulled, screaming, into the darkness, only to be met by a grinning devil. Two cigarettes are smashed in his broken-glass teeth; one is burning, the other gone out. The strings of drool slathering his jaws stink of alcohol. I press myself against the wall opposite him, but the sides of the mine are hard and offer no escape. My movement calls his attention and the devil's glowing eyes meet mine.

So, you think you're a miner now? he asks, his voice a death of snakes and a rending of metal.

I shake my head, but as I do, I feel the heavy bob of the lantern on my forehead, the uncomfortable press of the belt at my waist.

The devil laughs.

I wake up.

For a moment I lie there, gasping, bathed in sweat and a

terror so complete I don't know if it has a bottom or edges. Then I force myself to get out of my blankets and go outside to the latrine.

The freezing night air cuts like a knife through my clothes, but the misery returns me to my body. When I climb into my covers, I push a fold of the blanket between my teeth so that their chattering won't wake Abuelita or Daniel. I force the air in and out of my lungs around the blanket. Slowly my body relaxes. If only I could do the same for my mind. Because the truth is more frightening than the dream.

The truth is that tomorrow I'm going to have to go back and do it all again.

I stare at the ribbed sheet of tin over my head and let the tears creep out of my eyes. It takes me a long time to fall asleep, and when I do, the devil's laughter echoes through my dreams.

6

Next morning, Mami can't meet my eyes and Abuelita still isn't talking to me. I try once to start a conversation, but she holds up a bony hand and walks out of the house. I pull my hair into double braids again and let my eyes wander around the room. At the end of my bed, one of them has laid out my nicest skirt and favorite top, clean and folded, a gentle option to Daniel's filth-encrusted miner's suit hanging across the room on the hook. But Papi is waiting for me, and Daniel's thin breaths wheeze through his half-parted lips. As usual, there isn't a good choice.

When I step out of the house with Papi, Mami's eyes snap up from her washing, but when she sees what I'm wearing, her lips thin and she bends her head again. Abuelita is nowhere in sight. Everything aching, I head up the road toward the mine, the weight of their disapproval heavier than the mountain itself.

I didn't think there could be anything harder than going into the mine when I had no idea what to expect.

I was wrong.

Standing in front of the entrance to El Rosario in the milky predawn light, I know exactly what lies ahead of me. And that makes it so much worse.

Papi leaves me at the edge of the lot to find his work crew without a backward glance. I hesitate there until a shoulder bumps mine. I flinch, but then I see Victor's infectious grin and I relax.

"Hey, Ana," he says.

"Hi, Victor."

"Where are you working today?"

"I don't know."

"César's right over there." He points. "Let's go find out."

With Victor beside me I find I can brave the walk across the open space. Even the stares and the whispers of the other miners, though they still unsettle me, don't frighten me as much as they did before.

We catch up to César at the edge of the mine, talking with a crew of men who are working the slag heaps.

"*Puangi*," I call, and his eyes meet mine. I can tell he's not exactly happy to see me, but I don't offer an apology. I worked hard yesterday. "Where do you want us today?" I ask. "Same place?"

César scowls slightly. "We're not blasting today. Victor,

you're in zone two with your papi. I already gave him instructions."

"Got it," says Victor. "Catch you later, Ana." He lights his helmet and waves to me, then jogs off to find his father.

César turns to me.

"You'll be hauling ore out of the mine for the breakers to work on." I can tell, from the way he says it, that I'm not going to like this job. Then again, I didn't like yesterday's job either. In all honesty, it's probably a mercy to use a different set of muscles than yesterday.

"Okay."

He sighs in response and points me toward a three-man crew pushing a large metal bin on wheels along the narrow-gauge track that runs into the mine.

"Don César said I'm to work with you today," I say, trying to come across as someone who belongs here; someone you'd be okay having assigned to your team for the day.

The two men on my side of the bin stare at me stonily for a moment, taking me in. Then the man on the other side straightens and I see his face. I feel something in my chest loosen.

"Oh, hi, Papi."

Papi *humphs* and glares at the other two men.

"Guillermo, Francisco, behave yourselves today. This is my daughter. She's helping out until my son gets better."

Francisco has a long, gaunt face. His skin is weathered and the lines bracketing his mouth hint at frowns rather than smiles. He looks old, but sometimes it's hard to tell with a miner. They often look a lot older than they really are. Guillermo is much younger than Francisco, but his smooth, narrow face holds suspicious eyes. Neither of them looks very friendly.

"Hi." I give them both a small smile and a wave.

The men give me sullen nods in return, but I can see that Papi is the leader of this little crew and I know I'll be safe enough. Again, César is taking care of me.

"Let's get going, then," says Papi. And with no more introduction than that, we're off.

Gathering ore turns out to be a backbreaking job, even more so than hand-drilling holes in solid rock. With two of us in front, and two behind, we push the heavy rail bin into the mine. We have to strain against it on the downhill slopes and push hard the few times the track slants upward. Then, when we get to the part of the tunnel nearest yesterday's blast zone, we load chunks of rock into the bin. Some of the rocks are small enough for one person to do, but sometimes it takes two of us to lift them.

The pile we're working from is on the floor of zone one. Another crew has the job of loading the rock fragments from zone eight into baskets and slings and carrying them up to us. As awful as it is to be on the ore-cart crew, I am very glad I didn't get assigned to carry rocks over the wobbly-bridged ravine and up those spindly ladders.

Once the trolley is full, we have to push it back out. The cart is so heavy at this point that we all have to strain behind it to get it to roll uphill, and whenever there is a small downhill, we break into a run to get some momentum behind us for the next time the tunnel slopes up. Other miners in the tunnel leap out of our way when they hear the rumble of our wheels because the mine carts have no brakes. Next to me, Guillermo whispers about a miner who didn't get out of the way in time and was crushed by the rolling tons of rock. His eyes glitter when he sees his story makes me uncomfortable. I like him even less.

Shivering against the image his words put in my head, I push harder, praying for everyone to get safely out of our way. There are so many ways to die in here, I'm losing count.

We make it out of the mine to the slag heap and dump the cart over. I consider it a minor miracle that we've all survived so far, but no one else seems to notice. Instead, we head in and do it again.

And again.

The day drags. The few times the men have enough breath to talk, they leave me out of their conversation entirely. Papi seems content to pretend I'm not there at all except when Francisco or Guillermo decide to make a dirty joke. Then he reminds them I'm here and they all lapse into sullen silence.

The first six hours of our shift pass mostly in this uncomfortable quiet; the clang of rocks hitting the inside of the ore bin the only sound marking the passing of time. At the midday break, I collapse on the ground and close my eyes, my body a misery and my mood bleak.

I lie against the pitted red rock and stare at the sky. I've never felt so starved for the sky before. I survey the entryway to the mine, examine the tired, dirty faces of the men and boys. I see Francisco and Guillermo sitting at the far end with Papi and another group of miners. Francisco is scowling at whatever the other men are saying, and it looks like Guillermo is tuning everyone else out instead of participating. Maybe it's not me; maybe they're just grumpy people. I decide that, after lunch, I will make more of an effort to talk to them. Nothing can be as bad as the boredom of doing awful work while everyone ignores you.

Victor's arrival breaks up my bitter musing.

"Hi," he says, lowering himself beside me and pulling off his helmet. He carefully extinguishes the flame and sets it next to him before he pulls out his lunch pack. I glance over and do a double take.

"Are those *potatoes*? In a *sock*?"

Victor's grime-streaked face splits into a grin, his even teeth startling against the dark rock dust coating his skin and lips.

"What's so weird about having potatoes for lunch?" he asks innocently.

"That," I say sternly, pointing in case he missed it, "is a *sock*."

He shrugs and runs his hands through his hair. It's straight and black, like all of our hair, and his sweat makes it stick up at crazy angles. He doesn't smooth it down.

"Yeah," he admits. "But it's a *clean* sock."

Glancing across the entry lot, I see Victor's papi unpacking his lunch. The look on his face when he gets to his sock-wrapped potatoes is priceless. I snort a laugh and roll my eyes at Victor, pulling out the plastic bag Mami wrapped around my lunch.

"Want a piece?" I hold out the llama jerky.

Victor grins and reaches for it, but I don't let go of the other end.

"You can only have it," I say, very solemnly, "if you don't put it in any of your socks."

"I promise," says Victor. His straight face is only ruined when he winks.

We eat quietly for a little while, and then Victor drifts off to chat with some of the other boys who work the mine. I wonder, if he stays out of school and if I go back to school, which one of them will replace me as his best friend.

Shaking off the thought, I lean on my elbows and tip my face up so the sun shines on it. Reaching into my pack, I grab my coca pouch and savor a few swallows of water. Then I spit out the old, pulpy leaf wad I chewed all morning and fold fresh coca into my cheek. The brittle leaves crack when I bend them and their dryness sucks the moisture out of my mouth. I wait for my saliva to soften them and think about the mess at home. I can't stand the thought of having another night like last night. I need to find a way to make this up to Mami and Abuelita.

Then I smile. Thanks to Victor, I think I may have an idea.

———

When the whistle blows to signal the end of the midday break, it's far too soon. Every muscle complains when I stand; every bit of my mind rebels at the thought of burying myself alive again.

I hobble over to where Papi, Francisco, and Guillermo are removing the chunks of rock they'd placed on either side of the wagon's wheels to keep it still while we rested. Francisco completes his task in mechanical silence, pointedly ignoring me. I join Guillermo's side and brace myself to push the cart again. Then we're off, rolling into the mine.

The first time I trip, I'm not sure what did it. It's only the third time that I see Guillermo's foot. My patience already frayed by the long day and the men's sour mood, I whirl on him.

"Knock it off! What's wrong with you?"

Papi's eyes flick to us when I speak, but then he ignores us again.

Guillermo doesn't even try to deny it; he just chuckles in my face.

"Clumsy little girl."

I glare at him, and as I do, I realize that under all the grime masking his face, he's not much older than me. He has just the faintest fuzzy outline of a mustache starting.

"What's your problem?"

"Everyone was talking about you at lunch." He gives me a snarky smile. "Do you want to know what they said?"

I hesitate. Although, yes, I do want to know what the miners are saying about me, I don't want to tell this unpleasant boy that. Besides, given his tone, I don't think it was anything I'd enjoy hearing.

"They said," Guillermo goes on without waiting for my answer, "that you were an abomination. That your presence is going to bring the wrath of the Tío down on us. That the best thing would be if you left and never came back, but stayed where you're supposed to be."

"It's not permanent," I mumble, reflexively echoing what César said to the unhappy miners the first day I arrived.

"Nope," Guillermo says, "it's not. And the less permanent it is, the better. So why don't you do us a favor, little girl, and find your feet aboveground?"

I stumble when his leg swipes forward again, catching

myself against the side of the ore bin to keep from falling. I burn inside at his words, but Papi is on the other side of the bin, and I don't want to do something that he would consider embarrassing. I know I have to be careful, especially if all his buddies spent lunch telling him off for bringing me. That will have made him angry. He'll either push back against all of them if he decides this was his idea, or he'll take it out on me if he decides I'm to blame. The fact that Guillermo and Francisco and all the others think I *want* to be down here is laughable. This wasn't something I picked because I thought it was a good choice. I picked it because I had no good choices. Guillermo swipes at my feet again and I dodge out of his way.

"Grow up or shut up," I snap at him, and move to load the cart from a slightly different angle so as to avoid his feet.

I spend the next two runs trying to keep as much space as possible between myself and Guillermo. Naturally, this means I end up closer to Francisco. I decide, if Guillermo's going to be a jerk, I can use all the allies I can find. Even if he does look ancient and dour, at least he won't be immature enough to trip me like some bully on a playground. So the next time Francisco bends with me to lift a particularly bulky piece of rock into the bin, I speak up.

"Do you have children, Don Francisco?" I ask, figuring that's a safe topic.

Francisco points his chin at Guillermo, whose turn it is to break up the larger rocks. "That's one," he says. "I have four boys."

Great. They're related. Now that I look, I can see the resemblance. Both men are tall and wrapped in wiry muscles from the hard labor of the mines. Both have similar narrow faces, though Guillermo is merely slim, while Francisco tips toward gaunt. When Francisco reaches into his coca pouch and adds a handful of leaves to his cheek, one side bumps out, and in a flash I realize why his face has been niggling at me. He's the same man who spat on the ground when I first arrived at the mine, the one I called Bumpy. I struggle to keep my smile in place, a whole lot less sure than I was a moment ago about him being an improvement over his son.

"That must be busy. I have only one brother at home."

Francisco pins me with a glare that is not at all friendly, and my next words shrivel and die.

"You should be at home and your brother should be here," he says seriously.

"I . . ." I lick my lips to gather my courage and try not to choke as the tastes of rock and sweat fill my mouth. "I'm just here until he gets better."

Francisco shakes his head solemnly. "Your father"—he drops his voice and gestures at Papi loading the ore cart—"should never have let you come down here. We will all be made to pay for your stupidity."

I feel like I've been punched.

"I won't be here long," I mumble.

Francisco shrugs and sets his shoulder to the side of the ore cart. "The damage is probably already done," he says.

I'm glad we're pushing the cart again and I need my breath for other things, because it keeps me from answering.

Francisco doesn't talk to me again as we heave and strain the bin out of the mine. He doesn't talk to me when we stand off to the side and swing the bin on its hinges so it dumps our load of debris on the pile. When we head back in and he still hasn't spoken to me, I start to think that maybe we're done, but as we scrabble with our feet against the angled floor, using our bodies as brakes to keep the bin from freewheeling out of control, he starts talking again.

"You say you're only here until your brother gets better," Francisco mumbles around the coca wad in his cheek. "Either you're an idiot or a liar. I worked with that brother of yours for a day, and let me tell you, that's all I needed to be able to tell: that boy will never make a miner. Always wheezing, barely able to keep up, let alone work in any meaningful way. If you're waiting for him to get better and stay better, you'll be working here the rest of your life."

Guillermo, the tripping jerk, clearly eavesdropping, chimes in.

"Even if that scrawny runt does come back and César decides to keep wasting good pay on him, the mines will kill him quickly enough."

I glance at Papi, knowing he must be able to hear this, but he won't meet my eyes.

I clamp my lips shut to avoid saying something that could make him angry at me and focus on my feet. Luckily, we've arrived at the slag site again and I can vent my frustration. Even though my muscles cringe, I throw myself at the pile of rock, heaving pieces that are too big for me into the wheeled bin with a fury that makes the men shake their heads at me.

How dare they—how dare *they talk about Daniel and me like that! How dare they insult me and then turn around in the same breath and say my brother is going to die?*

I spend my energy before my anger has burned off, and it leaves me feeling shaky. I slump against the cold side of the hinged bin and rest my cheek against its grime-crusted surface. The others leave me alone. Every time one of them throws a rock into the bin, I feel the reverberation through my cheek, into the bones of my face.

The thing that really kills me, though I hate to admit it, is not that these strangers said those horrible things, but that Papi heard them say it and did nothing. Not a word of defense for either of his children. Almost as if he agreed with them.

I do not cry.

Finally, unable to bear the others working while I don't, I heave myself off the side and bend over to pick up another rock.

In and out, in and out. Again and again and again for another six hours. I don't lag behind once. When we finally stop at dinnertime, I think I might have caught a glint of new respect in Papi's eyes for my hard work. But by then I'm too tired to care.

When I walk in the door, I'm thrilled to see that, even though he's still pale and covered in fever-sweat, Daniel is sitting up in bed. I squat just off the edge of the pallet we share, not wanting to get grime all over where we sleep.

"Hey," I say, taking off the helmet and tucking it under my arm. "How are you feeling?"

Despite the fact that he hasn't done anything but sleep for most of two days, he stares at me through red-rimmed eyes that have deep purple bags under them.

"Better," he says. "Ana . . . I'm sorry."

"For what?"

"You know . . . if I weren't so sick, you would never have had to go into the mine."

"Not your fault you got sick," I say, because we both know he's right.

"Still. I'm sorry. I know how awful it is."

I consider telling him it's not awful or that he'll be better in no time or that I don't mind. But none of those things are true, and unlike Daniel, who treats it as a competitive sport, I don't like lying. Instead I ruffle his sweat-dank hair.

"You're worth it," I tell him. I stand and strip off what I'm starting to think of as *my* miner's coveralls and go outside to try to wash off some of the filth before dinner.

When I get outside, Abuelita is hunched by the dung stove, stirring the soup. She glances up when she hears me, but when she sees who it is, she turns away again.

I stand by the blue plastic water barrel and slowly rub the rag along the lines of my impossibly dirty hands and face. Then, putting down the cloth, I head over to the stove and hunker beside my grandmother. For a moment we stare into the flames together, quietly.

"Once, there was a boy who was a miner," I start, trying to mimic the rolling storyteller sound of Abuelita's voice. "This boy's mother had died a few years ago, and now there were only him and his father, and they lived in a little house. His father was no good at cooking and keeping the house up, so the boy figured out how to boil water and wash clothes and did his best to keep the place clean. Then one day, the boy and his father were packing to head off to work in the mine, and the boy realized that he didn't have any bags to put their lunch in."

Abuelita is looking at me now, I can see out of the corner of my eye, but I don't turn, not yet.

"The boy was frantic. It was almost time to leave, and he had to pack his lunch and his father's or they'd be late for work! He checked all around, but he couldn't find any plastic bags. No jars with lids. No box or container of any kind. He thought about tossing the potatoes straight into the work sacks, but they were full of dirt and rock bits. That seemed like giving up, and this boy isn't one who gives up easily. Then," I say, and I turn to Abuelita, "he had an idea. The boy raced over to where he had hung the laundry to dry after washing it and pulled a pair of socks off the line. Then he stuffed three potatoes into each of the socks and put them in the two lunch packs." I smile at her. "Imagine his father's face when he opened his lunch sack in front of all of his friends at the midday break!"

Abuelita cackles, delighted.

I smile at her. "Victor did that today."

She purses her lips for a moment more, but she can't resist a good story.

"Did he really?" she finally says, standing to lift the pot of soup.

"Yup," I say, reaching out to help her. "And when I teased him about it, he argued that the socks were clean! He didn't see any problem with that at all."

"Those Sánchez boys!" She laughs. "Too much creativity by half. You'd never know it now, but Victor's father was exactly the same. Now, when *he* was a boy . . ." As Abuelita launches into a story of her own, I know that she's taken the first step toward forgiving me.

Each holding a handle, we walk the pot inside and sit down to eat dinner as a family.

7

My days slip into a routine and February sneaks away like a thief. Every morning before dawn, I haul my aching body out of bed into the chilly air and pull on my filth-encrusted mining outfit. I barely remember what it feels like to be clean. Half asleep, I follow Papi on the long walk to the edge of El Rosario. I wait outside, staring into the jaws of the mine, until I get assigned to a crew. Then, work. Hand drilling. Blasting. Breaking rock. Hauling ore. Each task feels harder than the last. I spend my first six hours down in the belly of the Cerro Rico sweating in the hellish heat and straining every muscle I've never used past its endurance.

When we break for lunch, I sit off to the side with Victor, drinking in the only half hour of sunlight I'll get to experience for the whole day and eating whatever Mami was able to spare from home. *Work like a miner, eat like a miner,* Mami jokes when I tell her not to give me too much. I worry that she and Abuelita are skipping meals to feed me more. But with the extra bolivianos I'm bringing home—the ones that Papi doesn't get to first—we have been able to buy more food, so maybe it's all okay.

After lunch, it's back into the mine for another six hours. By this point the heat and my exhaustion have made me clumsy. I rarely have the energy to talk to anyone during the afternoon. By the end, I shuffle around mechanically, doing the best I can to complete the tasks set for me. These are my most dangerous hours, because my mind is muddy and my reflexes are slow. When the full carts whisk by me, I press myself into the wall and turn my face to the side, but don't leap to safety. I don't pay as much attention to my flame. Sometimes when they blast, I don't even count to make sure all the charges detonate. These are the hours when the devil visits me. Working beyond the edge of exhaustion, I hear the echo of his laughter in the vibration of the pneumatic drills, and flickers of his eyes and teeth haunt the edges of my vision. I shake my head to clear it like a llama tries to clear its face of flies, but it never works. In those long hours, the devil tracks my every move.

At the end of a day of work I come aboveground with the feeling of someone who's been buried alive clawing their way to the surface. It's dark by then, and I stumble home with Papi down the narrow mountain path, praying that I won't trip over the edge and die. When I get home, I strip off my stinking suit, mechanically eat whatever Abuelita has prepared, let Mami massage some of the aches from my shoulders, and fall into bed.

I fall asleep every night hungry for more food.

I wake every morning hungry for more sleep.

I get neither.

And still I get up, and do it again.

———

It's now the second week of March and I've worked at El Rosario for just over a month when Papi decides that Daniel is well enough to go back to work. Daniel's bronchitis had deepened to pneumonia, which had taken nearly three weeks to heal. I had figured once Daniel's fever was gone, his cough had settled, and he was eating regular food, Papi would have had him straight back into the mines. But for whatever reason, Papi left Daniel home another week beyond that. None of us brought it up, and so Daniel's days home multiplied quietly.

I was torn about it, really. It was good to see Daniel get a bit of color in his cheeks, but I was still working in a living hell every day and it was hard to come home and see him sitting on the slag heap with Mami and Abuelita, breaking rocks and chatting when I had to spend the day in the land of the devil, hauling ore and dodging insults and kicks when César's handpicked guardians were too far away. I didn't *want* Daniel to have to go into the mines . . . but I didn't want to keep going there myself either. After only two and a half weeks working in the mines I had started to walk like an old person, hunched over, bones aching. And after my one week in zone six, where the air smelled slightly garlicky, I developed headaches and a cough I still haven't been able to get rid of. *Nothing like Daniel's coughs, of course,* I keep reminding myself, but they hurt all the same.

So when Papi tells me to take off my mining gear this

morning, I don't complain. I do as he says, feeling relieved and upset all at the same time. Daniel takes it from me and pulls it on, and it's hard to figure out the emotions on his face. I give him a quick hug on his way out the door.

"Say hi to Victor for me," I tell him.

"Okay," he says, and then he's gone.

I glance around our one-room house for a moment, not sure what to do with myself. Mami and Abuelita are still staring out the door at Papi and Daniel, shrinking in the distance.

"I guess . . ." I start, then clear my throat and start again. "I guess I should go to school?"

"No," says Mami firmly, turning from the door. "You've earned a rest. Take the day and sleep. We'll get back to normal tomorrow."

I'm just as pleased, really. Not only am I beyond exhausted, but I was actually kind of nervous about going back to school. The way the older miners have talked about me behind my back for the past month hasn't been fun, and it kind of shook me that someone as young as Guillermo would hate me for doing what I did. I worry that maybe the kids at school will judge me the same way. I don't want to see those same glares on the faces of people who used to be my friends.

I roll into the covers and fall into a deep and dreamless sleep.

When I wake, I go outside and scrub until my hands are raw. I'm not going back to school until I have clean hands.

The icy water stings and the lye soap is rough, but even so, my hands are still faintly gross and my fingernails have definitely seen the inside of a mine. Giving up, I dump out the wash water. Then, because Mami has declared it's a vacation for me and I have no work to do, I start playing with the puddle of mud it makes, scooping it up and making little figurines. It's something Daniel and I used to do when we were younger and we were both home playing while Mami broke rocks and Papi worked in the mines. It makes me feel all squishy inside thinking about how different those days were, and I feel bad all over again that Daniel is working in the mines right now.

It's not your fault he's there, I remind myself sternly. *In fact, you're the only reason he wasn't there this whole past month. The only reason he got a break was because of you.*

It's all true, of course, but it doesn't make me feel much better. I make a special little mud figure for him. I'll give it to him tonight after work.

———

"What's that supposed to be?" Daniel's voice is tired but curious as he turns my figurine over in his hands. "A butterfly?"

We're sitting side by side in the moonlight again, our family asleep around us. Dinner was weird. I thought they'd all be in a good mood with having the girl out of the mines and the boy back in them, especially since Daniel didn't come home sick this time, but instead Papi snapped at everyone about everything. Mami and Abuelita looked unhappy too. I decided to wait until they were all asleep to give Daniel his present.

"It's an angel," I say, slightly embarrassed he can't tell what it is.

He raises an eyebrow.

"Why did you make me an angel?"

"Remember when we used to make toys out of mud when we were little? Well . . . now I know what the mines are like. I feel kind of bad that you have to go at all."

He raises an eyebrow at me, clearly not seeing how these things connect to a mud doll. I feel a little stupid, but I charge ahead.

"You said that you hate going into the mines because the air is so bad. When I was down there, it always killed me that there was no sky." We've been speaking in Quechua, but for the pun to work, I switch into Spanish. "I thought maybe it would be nice if you could take a piece of *el cielo* down with you." In Spanish, the word for *sky* and the word for *heaven* are the same.

Usually, Daniel loves puns. But tonight, instead of laughing, he smiles sadly.

I hold out my hand.

"It's dumb. I'll take it back."

He closes his fingers around it and tucks it away.

"Nah. I like it."

We sit side by side for a few more minutes, not saying anything. I try to think of something about being in the mines that was good to ask him about.

"Did you meet up with Victor? Or have you made other friends?"

Daniel shrugs. "Victor works with his papi. And most of the other boys who work there are older than me. I don't really have any friends."

"Are the men nice to you?" I ask, remembering Guillermo and Francisco.

Another shrug. "César's okay. A couple of the others too."

"Seems like you didn't get sick today." I'm scrambling for positives. "Do you feel okay?"

"Do you hear any coughing?" Daniel snaps. "I'm fine."

And with that, I've run out of good things to ask about.

"Um . . . so, what zone did you work in today?"

Daniel closes his eyes. "You can stop," he says. "I know you're trying to make me feel better or something, but it's not working."

I stare down at my hands.

"It's just . . . today was really bad," Daniel finally admits.

"Hard work?"

"Yeah, and not even just that. Half the miners are mad that you were there at all. And the other half—Papi included—think you were a better worker than I am. It's like, they're mad at me if I'm sick and they're mad at me if I'm not."

I blink at him.

"Papi thinks I was a good worker?" He never said that to me.

Daniel snorts. "Yup. Apparently, I'm a weakling that can't keep up with a girl."

"I'm sorry."

"Not your fault," he mumbles. But I can't tell if he means it.

"Give it some time," I say finally.

"I don't know if I *have* time, Ana," he says bitterly. "I don't know how much longer I can take it."

"You planning to run away to a green valley or a sparkling city?" I say, trying to make a joke of it. Trying to get that defeated, frightened look off my brother's face.

But Daniel doesn't laugh.

I've almost made it to school the next morning when it all hits me—my conversation last night with Daniel, feeling bad that he's not going to be able to come to school anymore, how angry and mean Papi was this morning, my own mixed feelings about coming to school. I can see the big blue metal gates, but my feet freeze on the path, not able to move forward. I duck off the path and hide behind a large boulder, trying to find the courage to go in.

"Are you okay?" chirps a voice at my elbow.

I startle.

A pretty little girl is staring at me, her face scrunched up in concern. She has round, bright eyes, cheeks chapped red by the mountain wind, and crooked braids down to her shoulders tied off with pink plastic clips. She's vaguely familiar: she's one of the little kids from this side of the mountain that go to my school. I think she's with the seven-year-olds. Or maybe the eight-year-olds. Try as I might, I can't come up with her name.

"Are you hurt?" she asks.

Nowhere anyone can see. I shake my head, trying to even out my breathing before I try talking.

"Because if you *are* hurt," she goes on seriously, "I can try to help. I'm going to be a doctor when I grow up."

That pulls a small smile from me. We all had big dreams when we were little. Daniel had wanted to be an army man when he was her age. My friend Susana wanted to be a movie star. I've never really been sure what I wanted to be, so I said

I'd do Susana's hair and makeup. But a *doctor*? This little girl's imagination has carried her away for sure. I've heard of some men and women from the mountain getting jobs down in the city—mechanics, construction workers, hairdressers, beauticians, preschool teachers. But no one I know of from the mountain has ever become a doctor. Might as well plan to grow up to be a unicorn.

She considers. "Should I go get a teacher?"

"No . . ." I manage. "Thanks. I'm okay."

Over the rocks, the first scratchy boom echoes: Don Marcelino's speakers beginning the national anthem. The little girl holds out a hand.

"Come on," she says. "We'll be late."

And folding my hand into her much smaller one, I let myself be led into school by the tiny dreamer.

"Where have you been?" asks Susana as I slip into my place in line.

I'm not sure whether she means being late or having missed the last month of school, but the answer is the same either way.

"I'll tell you later," I say. Don Marcelino is just starting his daily talk. Today it's about *Community*. You can hear the capital *C* every time he says the word. I glance to my left. The little girl waves at me with an encouraging smile. I lift my hand a tiny fraction in response. The unicorn beams.

"What's that girl's name?" I ask Susana.

Susana follows my gaze, her face creasing with thought.

"César's daughter? Hmm. Belén, I think?"

"She's César's daughter? César the shift supervisor at El Rosario?" I look at the little girl with more interest.

"Pretty sure," says Susana. "What about her?"

I could tell her I can see reflections of César's kindness in Belén, but that would raise questions about my time in the mine. I could tell her the girl comforted me on the path when I couldn't handle my feelings over Daniel. But I don't want to answer those questions either.

"She wants to be a doctor," I say softly.

Susana snorts. "Little kids and their crazy ideas. She'll end up a miner's wife, like all of us."

I don't say anything to that because, really, what is there to say? Little Belén won't think she can grow up to be a doctor for very much longer. She probably only has a year or so left before she permanently pauses her dreams and accepts that what she sees around her is all she'll ever get a chance to be. *Girls like her don't get good choices,* I remind myself.

Suddenly, Don Marcelino is interrupted by the blaring of a horn outside the gate. We all turn in our rows and watch as Doña Inés waddles over and cracks the gate open. For a moment we watch her listen to whoever's on the other side, mildly curious. But when she turns around and I see her wide eyes and ashen face, I know this is no ordinary visit.

"Don Marcelino," she calls. "Get your truck and come quickly! There's been a cave-in at El Rosario!"

8

A cave-in.

For fifteen heartbeats, no one moves.

Then people are running, shouting.

I realize that I am one of those people.

"Don Marcelino!" I scream.

Don Marcelino had set off at a sprint as soon as Doña Inés shouted out the news, not even pausing to turn off his precious speaker, which is still playing patriotic music in the background. Keys in hand, he's now at his truck. That's why they came to get him, of course. I bet they've called everyone with a flatbed pickup in good working order to help cart the wounded to the medical centers at the base of the mountain. The teachers are helping to pull open the heavy gate as quickly as they can. He'll be gone in a moment.

I grab the edge of his open truck window.

"Don Marcelino!"

"Ana," he barks, his glasses slightly crooked on his face,

"this is not the time. Get out of my way!" His face is pale and his hands are shaking so badly that he's having trouble getting the keys into the ignition.

"Let me come with you, please!"

He stares at me.

"My father and brother work in El Rosario," I go on, my words tripping over themselves. "Please!"

He manages to get his key in the slot, finally, and the engine roars to life. His eyes flick to the open doorway, then to my face.

"Get in," he says.

"Thank you!" I gasp. Racing around, I pull myself up. Some of the other older students and even a few teachers vault in with me. There isn't anyone at my school who isn't connected to the mine somehow. Everyone wants to help, if they can.

We crouch in the truck bed and hang on to its rusted edges for dear life as Don Marcelino rattles the ancient vehicle up the winding, rutted path to El Rosario. I know he's probably pushing the engine to its limit with a grade this steep, but all I can think is, *Faster! Faster!*

The pockmarked red-and-black-striped rock face whizzes by a few centimeters beyond the side-view mirror, but even so, I lean off the side of the truck, trying to see farther—around that bend, into the future. Into the past.

How bad is it?

I can't wait, don't know how to make my heart slow its furious pounding.

And then, all of a sudden, I don't have to. Don Marcelino swings the truck around the last bend and shudders into the open entryway to El Rosario.

The truck stops, and my heart stops with it.

With the screech of the brakes still echoing in my ears, I jump out and try to get my bearings.

It's chaos.

People rush and jostle.

Bodies and rubble litter the ground.

The air is filled with dust and noise—high wailing cries, drawn-out moans.

I look around frantically, whipping my head back and forth.

My lungs burn.

My brain chokes on the sounds.

I force my feet to take me to the first person on the ground in front of me. It's Bumpy—Francisco. He's sitting, clutching his head, his eyes out of focus. Blood oozes through his fingers. He's hurt.

My fingers shake as I touch his shoulder. Even if I hate him, I can't leave Francisco without help, but I have no comfort to give. No medicine. No bandages. No water.

I feel useless.

I shake off the helplessness and run to Don Marcelino.

"There's a man here, he's hurt!" I leave them together and move on to the next hunched form.

I kneel in front of him, and the silt-laden mud of the mine entrance coats my leggings, chilling me. I push my hand against his shoulder to tip his face off the ground.

It's Papi.

But Papi's face is like seeing a familiar house after the family has been evicted for not being able to pay the rent. He's not there anymore.

I pull my hand away as if I've been burned and clutch it to my chest.

He's dead.

My father is dead.

It feels like I can't get enough air.

The wind whips rock dust into my face.

It sticks.

I must be crying.

A keening noise.

It's me.

I brace myself on the ground and the rock is cold and hard under my fingers, ragged-edged like my heart.

"Help!" I manage, but it's only a whisper.

I feel a warm hand on my shoulder and see César standing over me. His face is haggard and filthy. His eyes are gentle.

"Don César . . ." I manage, "my papi . . ."

César gathers me off the ground and holds me in the protective cage of his arms as I sob. Over my head I hear him barking orders at the other men to find something to cover Papi with and move him over to where he can wait for a truck that isn't carrying the wounded.

I have to tell Mami, I think numbly. *She doesn't even know he's dead yet. I have to tell her, and Abuelita, and Daniel.* My head snaps up. *Daniel!*

César lets me go.

"Daniel!" I burst out. "Where's Daniel?"

César looks around with me. Figures dart in and out through the smoke boiling from the mine entrance, trucks arrive and leave, people who aren't miners stream through everything, trying to help but adding to the confusion.

I wrench away from César.

"Daniel?" I lurch through the debris. *"Daniel!"*

I reach out, again and again, touch a dust-covered shoulder, turn a wounded face to mine, grab a hand. I stare into the glassy eyes of the living and the dead.

My brother is nowhere to be found.

I see César and Don Marcelino helping other people. I see Victor, rocking with his head in his hands. I see women and children trying to help carry their men out of this place.

I don't see Daniel.

The dust and the acrid smoke that linger over the mountain taste like death. Grit lodges in my molars, and every time I try to swallow, a small avalanche scrapes its way down my throat, raw from screaming.

Where's Daniel?

I hear nothing but pain, see nothing but confusion, taste nothing but the mountain. I don't know how long I stay, but I stay after the wounded have been carried away in trucks. I stay after Don Marcelino drives home with my father's corpse. I stay until the last of the miners leaves for home and a special shift reports for duty, heading into the still-smoking tunnel to start to clean up the mess so that business can go on as usual, exactly like it has every day for nearly five hundred years.

I stay until César forces me to go home, promising me he'll go in with the next crew and search for my brother.

I walk home without Daniel.

———

I stagger into the house after a walk home I don't remember, sobbing.

"Hush." Mami places a cool hand to my face. She looks a hundred years old.

For a moment she holds me, and I collapse against her comforting warmth, wishing we could stay like that forever. But eventually she lets me go.

"Go fetch hot water. We need to prepare your father," she says.

A feeling of unreality settles over me when I realize that Papi is lying in their bed, like usual. But now he's a corpse and she and Abuelita need to get it ready for burial. I hurry to obey. I don't want to watch them strip the body.

When I come in again, the pot steaming in my hands, we begin. Mami and Abuelita do most of the work. I wash his hair and try to scrub the rock dust out of the creases of his face with a rag. Pushing on his face is like pushing against cold clay, slowly setting. It doesn't feel like touching a person. I shiver.

Mami and Abuelita pray aloud as they wash and dress him in his best clothes. He's heavy and it's a struggle to get his arms and legs to move. We end up having to cut the back of his shirt and jacket and then re-secure them with a few loose stitches. I take a sharp knife and trim his nails. Lying there on the bed, arms by his sides, he's cleaner than he ever was in life.

"It's almost like he's sleeping," Mami says around a sob.

I stare at the thing that used to be my father and don't say anything. Yes, his eyes are closed, but I can't bring myself to agree with Mami. It doesn't at all look like he's sleeping. His face is gray. Rigid. It's as if the mountain, not content to simply take my father from us, is slowly turning him into stone.

"A woman who loses her husband is called a widow," Abuelita murmurs. "A child who loses her parent is called an orphan. But there is no word for a parent who has to bury their child. It shouldn't happen. How can God be so cruel?"

Mami snaps at that. "At least you have a body! I've lost a husband and a son in one day! Where is my son's body for me to mourn?"

"No!"

I realize the shout was mine.

"No," I repeat, forcing a more reasonable tone of voice. "You haven't lost a son. Papi is dead, but Daniel's only missing. He'll be home soon."

For a moment they just stare at me.

"Oh, Ana," Abuelita says finally. "Once the mountain takes someone, you never get them back. Once, there was a man—"

"Daniel's not dead," I grind out, cutting off her story. For once I don't want to hear what Abuelita has to say. My brother's not dead. He *can't* be. Beyond the impossible heartache, it would just be too cruel. If Daniel and Papi were both dead, it would mean that all our lives were truly over. It would leave us with no men in the house, forever. Without a man's salary we couldn't make rent. It would mean I definitely would have to quit school to make money. It would mean sooner, rather than later, I would have to get married.

Unable to watch them cry any longer, I turn and walk out the door into the deepening night.

When I finally lie down, I barely sleep, and when I manage to, I have no clear dreams, only a crushing feeling of fear. Every time I wake, my eyes fall on my father, laid out on the bed, and my mother asleep on the floor beside him, and it feels like the waking world has become its own nightmare.

Around four thirty, even though it barely counts as morning, I force myself to get up, light a fire, and make tea. The ritual of the motions soothes me and gives me a chance to think.

I carry a mug of tea in to Mami. I don't let myself glance at the bed when I hand it to her.

"I'm going to ask Don Marcelino if we can borrow his truck to take Papi to the cemetery," I say. I don't add that I'm also going by the mine to see if they've found Daniel.

She nods, but her face has an absent expression on it, and as I close the door behind me, I wonder whether she really heard me.

The path down the mountain to school is a dark wash of a road over the streaked brick and tan rock of the mountain face. As I walk, I pass little entrances to the mine—small mouths that choke quickly on their own darkness. On the edges you can sometimes still see the dried blood from last year's llama. The miners sacrifice one every year and bathe the lintels of the mine they're working in with its blood to convince the devil inside not to drink their blood instead. I glare at the rusty brown stains. They didn't do their job.

An odd feeling wraps around me when I arrive at school. Even though school won't start until eight, there are already people there at a quarter to seven. Through the blue metal gate I can hear the shrieks of the little kids who arrived early, playing, and the subdued burble of older voices, waiting for their work day to start. It all seems surreal.

How can it be just another day?

I stand there, my hands splayed on the door, my forehead resting against the peeling blue paint, waiting for my racing heart to slow. Finally, I'm able to pick up a little rock and knock on the gate. The clanging brings Doña Inés, clutching her belly. I stare at it for a second, wondering how she feels about bringing a child into this world after what happened yesterday.

"Ana!" she says, opening the door for me to come in. "I heard about your father and brother. I'm so sorry. How are you?"

"I'm fine," I lie. "Where's Don Marcelino?"

She points to the teachers' block.

I walk there without thanking her. It hurts to talk.

The doors of the teachers' block are open to the courtyard: the school psychologist's room, Don Marcelino's office, the toilets. I push through the middle door. Don Marcelino is sitting behind his desk. There are papers piled everywhere on it, and a battered ancient laptop is open to one side, but he's not looking at the papers or the laptop. He's not preparing his morning speech. Instead, he's resting his head in his hands, his glasses pushed up into his hair, as if he can't bear to see the world. I know how he feels. I clear my throat. He startles.

"Ana," he says. I see him slip a mask of *I'm okay* over his face. He pulls his glasses onto his nose and runs his fingers through his hair, official once again. "How is your mother?"

"My mother's fine," I say, and I wonder, having used the word *fine* twice in as many minutes, whether it is ever true.

"What can I do for you?" His eyes are kind. I take a deep breath.

"I was wondering if you would help us bring my papi down the mountain to the graveyard?" I pause for a moment. When he doesn't answer immediately, I rush to clarify. "In your truck. Like yesterday?"

"Ana, I . . ." He trails off. Then he, too, takes a deep breath. "Yes. Tomorrow, before school, I will come by your house. It will be early . . . Will that give your mami enough time to arrange things?"

"Yes," I say, relieved. "Thank you, Don Marcelino."

When I turn to leave, he stops me.

"Ana."

"Yes?"

"Will you stay?"

I think about a standard school day: saluting the flag, drinking my oatmeal, lessons on the cracked chalkboard, reciting answers, singing, practicing my dance for the upcoming festival. I think of Mami right now, sitting alone beside the lump of clay slowly turning to stone that used to be my father. I think of resting my head against the gate, working up the courage to even be able to knock on the door of normal.

"No," I say finally. "I don't think I can."

Don Marcelino doesn't say anything. His face is very sad.

I walk out of his office.

It is only when I'm at the fork in the road that I realize he might not have been asking about today, but about me continuing at school at all now that my father is dead. I'm just as glad this hadn't occurred to me in Don Marcelino's office.

I don't know the answer.

———

I should go straight home, but instead I turn my feet in the direction of El Rosario. One night with no word was too much: I have to go back to the mine and see if they've found Daniel.

They'll have cleared the debris from the mouth by now and they'll have dug through to wherever he was trapped, and they'll have given him water and coca and wrapped him in blankets, and he'll be waiting for me.

I hurry my steps. When I get to El Rosario, work seems to be going on as usual. I run up to the first miner I see and ask him where César Jansasoy Herrera is. The man points at the shed to the left of the mine.

When I open the door, I see that it's a toolshed, but with most of the tools having been pulled out to clean up yesterday's mess, there's space for a single rickety folding chair. César is slumped in the chair, head resting against the wall, helmet in his lap, sleeping the deep sleep of the exhausted. I hate to wake him, but I need to know. I shake his shoulder gently. César jolts awake.

"Oh! Ana." He sits up and scrubs his hands over his face.

"Don César. Did you find my brother?"

César's eyes are sad.

"Not yet," he says simply. "I've had every man searching, but no one's found him yet."

"But what if he—" My voice hitches. "What if he's trapped?

What if he lost his way in the mine and couldn't get out and is stuck down there somewhere, hungry and thirsty and running out of air, and can't find his way to the surface?"

Spots dance in front of my eyes and I have to sit on the ground, light-headed at the thought. I press my hands against the floor as if I could feel Daniel's heartbeat through the thousands of tons of rock between us. There's a creak as César gets out of the chair, and I feel him lift me into it as if I weighed no more than a baby.

"Put your head between your knees." César's hands guide my shoulders. "Breathe."

I follow his murmured instructions, and slowly my vision widens out to normal and I can sit up without feeling like I'm going to fall over.

César is kneeling in front of me, so we're eye to eye.

"I promise you," he says softly, "that we will comb through every pile of rock moved by that blast and search every tunnel leading away from the site. We miners take care of our own, Ana. And your brother, even though he had just started, was one of us. Okay? Will you tell your mother that?"

"Okay," I say shakily. "Thank you, Don César."

César gets to his feet.

"My condolences to your family," he says, and heads out of the toolshed and back into the mine with tired steps. Even though he spent the night helping clean up the disaster instead of sleeping, he's not taking any time off.

For a minute I sit there, not wanting to leave the place where I still have to believe they'll bring Daniel out at any minute, but eventually thoughts of Mami and Don Marcelino's message get me to my feet.

I try not to listen to the voices of the miners as I walk across the entry lot, but my ears hear them anyway.

Well, it can't have been a dynamite problem, can it? Everyone here knows you have to announce a fuse setting and then count off the detonations once you're outside.

It must have been a gas explosion. Someone must have burst through the rock to a pocket of gas. When that gas hit his flame, the whole thing would have exploded.

I bet it was that missing kid. If it was his flame that touched off the gas, he would have been vaporized. There wouldn't be much of him left to find, would there?

I want to cover my ears with my hands and run, but I settle for taking longer steps. I've almost made it when the man I spoke to earlier calls out to me.

"Hey, aren't you that girl who came into the mine? The one that caused all of this?"

That stops me in my tracks.

"Excuse me?"

"Yeah," says another miner with him. With a sinking heart I recognize Guillermo, my main tormentor during my time working at El Rosario. "That's her all right." He spits on the ground between us. "I said you should never have come here, girl. See what you've done?"

And with that my courage breaks, and I press my palms to my ears and run as fast as I can away from the mine toward home.

9

When I get home, neither Mami nor Abuelita have moved from where I left them this morning. They're both still sitting near my father's bed, hunched over, staring at him. The mugs of tea I left are cold and untouched beside them.

Abuelita glances up when I come in.

"Our people have been mining this mountain for over four hundred and seventy years," she says dully. "And in all that time, the price of metal has always been blood."

"Abuelita—" I start, but she cuts me off.

"Overwork killed the men in the mines. Mercury poisoning killed those working in the refineries. And in the Casa de la Moneda, where they turned the silver into coins? They died there too." For a moment I think she's done, but then Abuelita goes on. "They had mules, at first, four of them, that would walk in a circle their whole lives, chained to the giant turnstile, creating the power that pressed the metal into coins and bars. But the mules died too quickly—they didn't last more than four months each. It was too expensive to keep getting new mules. So they replaced the four mules with twenty African slaves. The Spanish crown sent thirty thousand of them here, to Potosí, to work in the mint. But they died too, every one of them. And so the work came back to rest on our people, the Inca, because we could survive hell the longest." She meets my eyes. "Do you remember I told you they could have built a bridge from here to Spain with the silver they took from this mountain?"

"Yes, Abuelita," I mumble.

"They could have built a bridge twice as long with the bones of those they killed to get it. Do you know how many have died here, on this mountain, Ana? More than eight million people. Eight. Million." She reaches out and smooths Papi's suit across his chest. "So many people. One more shouldn't feel like such a big difference. But he was my son."

I give Abuelita a small hug, but I have nothing to say that will make it better, so after a second of holding her, I let go and walk over to Mami.

"Mami, come on, we have to go into town and get things arranged for tomorrow." I pull on her arm until she stands.

"Tomorrow?" she murmurs.

"Yes, tomorrow. Don Marcelino is coming with his truck to take Papi to the cemetery, but we have to get things set up today."

Mami blinks as if she can't quite place where she is. Then her eyes clear and she nods.

"Yes, the cemetery," she says.

I breathe a sigh of relief. Though Mami never challenged

Papi directly, she was always working around him, making things happen: she protected the majority of his pay from waste, she planned carefully for what we needed, and she managed our lives with quiet ability, always looking out for us. It's been scary having her be so blank, to have to be the one to plan and look out for her.

Mami grabs her shawl and kneels beside the bed. I think she's going to pray some more, but instead she pushes her hand under the mattress. The corpse on the bed lurches a little as she fishes around for something, as if it's about to sit up, then it settles again when she pulls her hand out. I fight the bile climbing up my throat and focus on my mother.

"What's that?" I ask.

"Money," she says simply, and tucks it into the deep pockets of her many-layered skirts. My mother, like most of the women on the mountain, dresses like a traditional *cholita*: blouse, cardigan, eight or ten colorful woolen knee-length skirts, one layered over the other, braids, and, when she wants to dress up, a bowler hat on her head. Today is one of those days. Brown bowler firmly in place, hands knotted in the shawl around her shoulders, she gives me a once-over. I glance at my long-sleeve T-shirt and dirty pink leggings, my too-small sneakers. "Go wash your face," Mami says firmly, "and change into some clean clothes. Nice ones." She turns to Abuelita. "Will you come, Elvira?"

Abuelita puts her hand on top of Papi's.

"No, I'll stay here with my son."

Mami nods, and I hustle off to get dressed.

Fifteen minutes later, we're on our way down the mountain.

I didn't know how nice Mami expected me to dress, so I rounded up. I'm wearing clean black leggings, a sweater that I know Mami likes, and my church shoes, even though they're not the best suited for the two hours of walking we've got ahead of us. I even combed and rebraided my hair. I'm not giving Mami one more thing to worry about.

When we get to the church in Potosí, we join the other mining families there. I see Victor, his eyes red-rimmed, talking quietly to Padre Julio. I realize his father must have died yesterday too. With his mother dead, there's no one to do this but him. I catch his eye and give him a weak smile of what I hope is encouragement, but he looks away from me.

Does he blame me for this too? My stomach twists painfully at the thought and I don't go over and talk to him. I don't want to know if my best friend hates me.

My eyes hunt through the rest of the families there, bunching them into groups, doing a roll call of the dead by association. Pedro Sánchez Céspedes, Victor's papi. Ernesto Jimenez Almedo. Luís Molina Vargas. My father. At least four dead, then, from yesterday. My heart is a cramp inside my rib cage, but my eyes stay dry.

When it's our turn to talk to Padre Julio, I let Mami take the lead, standing beside her quietly like an obedient daughter should. Padre Julio tells her he's planning a joint funeral Mass for the fallen miners. *To lend the families the strength of their community in their time of sorrow,* he says. But I know that the real reason is that Padre Julio knows how poor our four families are. This way we can pool our donations for the Mass. Padre Julio is a good man.

When the arrangements are made, we walk to the coffin maker. It is a tiny, clean shop that smells of lumber and varnish, but the air in the room is filled with death anyway. When Mami pulls the roll of bills out of her skirt pocket, she ends up giving most of them to the coffin man. After all, we live on a barren rock far above the tree line. Even the cheapest, plainest box is not cheap when you have to get your trees from far away.

Our last stop is the miners' graveyard, at the foot of the Mountain That Eats Men. I've heard that, down in the valleys, they bury people underground. But up here, the ground is solid rock, so the dead are stacked in concrete sepulchers, one on top of the other. They stretch to the sky with each new disaster, bureau after bureau, where each drawer holds a corpse. If you come to visit your dead, kids with ladders will climb up and polish the plaques for a coin. While Mami negotiates rates with the graveyard man, I think how ironic it is that on this cursed mountain it's only when the men are alive that we bury them underground. They have to die to be allowed to lie down and stare at the sky.

It's dusk by the time Mami and I, finally finished, start the long trek up the mountain. Tomorrow will be another terrible day.

Wearily, I put one foot in front of the other and follow my mother's bent figure up the rocky road.

I should have worn my sneakers.

That night, I dream. It starts as it did before: with me standing barefoot outside El Rosario, the arched entrance to the mine looming dark in front of me. Beneath my feet, the mountain moves and a wave of air exhales out of the mouth of the mine and over me.

Rock dust on my face.

I lift a hand to wipe it off.

Sticky.

When I pull my hand away, I'm no longer alone. The watery light outlines a body at my feet. My breath hitches. Reaching down, I grab the material of his mining suit and turn him over. A stranger stares up at me sightlessly. I gasp in relief and straighten.

But instead of an empty entryway, the open space before the mine is now lined with the dead: tens of them, packed shoulder to shoulder. I step over the man at my feet and turn one after another, not even remembering who I'm searching for, or why, but gripped nonetheless with the certainty that I must look at each of them.

I turn body after body: some young, some old. Some paler than me, some darker than me, some who are eerily familiar. But none of them are who I seek, and I sob, wondering when I will be done. And I see body after body after body rolling out of the mine entrance, not tens now but hundreds, thousands, all slipping in the cold silt mud, piling in front of the mouth like heaps of mining slag. The mountain vomits them at me, one after another after another. Eight million of them. It is a never-ending cascade of death.

The bodies roll off each other and bump against me. I have to move quickly to avoid being buried by them.

"Your fault," the dead whisper in eight million shadowy voices. "You should have known better. This is your fault."

"Stop!" I shout, swimming against the torrent, trying to save myself. "Stop! No more!"

I wake up, a scream trapped in my throat, my breathing irregular and rapid.

Mami is moving through the predawn murk, putting on her best clothes.

Steadying my breathing, I get up and join her.

True to his word, Don Marcelino shows up at our house a little after dawn. With his help, we lift the cold, stiff thing that used to be my father and load it into the truck bed. Mami, Abuelita, and I pile into the heated cab, to start the slow drive down the mountain. Mami gets in first, angling her knees to make room for the gearshift. Abuelita wedges in next to her. With nowhere else to go, I climb onto Mami's lap. I'm far too tall for this to really work and I have to bend my neck at an angle, but it's the only way all four of us will fit in the cab. Don Marcelino gets in on the driver's side but says nothing. Perched awkwardly, I brace myself against the dashboard for the long, bumpy drive to the coffin shop. But surprisingly, Don Marcelino turns.

"I hope you don't mind, Doña," he says gently, "but another

one of my students lost a father. I said I would help him as well."

"Of course," Mami says.

We pass the school on our left and curve up the road toward El Rosario. I can feel Mami tense beneath me when she sees where we are.

At the edge of the entry lot, Don Marcelino hauls on the wheel, taking the truck up a steep slope to get to the ridge above the mine. Once there, he slowly rolls past a stretch where half a dozen one-room houses have been built against the cliffside out of mud bricks until he gets to a few solitary shacks off on their own, like ours. Don Marcelino stops the truck in front of the third one and gets out. Mami, Abuelita, and I wait in the cab. I realize I can see down into the entry lot of El Rosario. I know who we must be picking up.

A few minutes later, Don Marcelino backs out of the house, again supporting the head and shoulders of a corpse. The body comes out, horizontal, and then, carrying the feet, is Victor. His face is scrubbed and his hair is gelled aggressively into place. His dress clothes are clean, if a little too small. Though he's pale, his hands don't shake as he wedges what's left of his father into the truck bed beside what's left of mine.

I think about how awful it has been to have Papi's corpse in the house, even with Mami and Abuelita there with me. I can only imagine how Victor has managed these past two nights alone. Victor comes around and opens the passenger door, only then noticing us.

"I . . . I'll sit in the back," he says.

I imagine us, snug in the cab, while Victor sits alone with the corpses and can't bear the thought.

"No!" I say, before I even really think it through. "We can all fit . . ."

I trail off because it's obvious we all can't.

"It's okay," Victor says, and turns away from the door.

"Wait!" I scoot over Mami and Abuelita's laps and slide to the ground. "I'll sit with you."

The last thing I want to do is sit in the wind-whipped truck bed with our dead fathers, but I can't leave Victor to face that alone.

"Okay," he says, and we climb in together.

We crowd up near the cab to be able to hold on to the edge of the window. It also mostly blocks the dust kicked up by the tires. The rattling and cold make it so that we don't say anything. The corpses jostle with every bump. I'm afraid I'm going to be sick.

A warm hand grips my fingers. I look over. Victor won't meet my eyes, but he gives my fingers a small squeeze. Together, we stare at our joined fingers all the way down the mountain.

———

Only an hour later—a third of the time it would have taken us to walk to the city from El Rosario—we arrive at the coffin shop. I hop out of the truck bed, grateful the trip is over.

There are four plain pine boxes on the sidewalk in front of the shop. Victor and Don Marcelino put the contents of our truck into two of them and the coffin man comes out and nails them shut, then helps lift one of them into the truck.

"I'll drop the Águilars at the church," Don Marcelino says to Victor before he gets back in, "then I'll come back for you and your father."

Victor nods, his face very stiff.

I climb onto Mami's lap and we drive away.

———

Even on a normal Sunday, I have trouble finding God in this echoing stone space. Today, a Wednesday and my father's funeral, I find it even harder. My eyes keep wandering around the church, checking the faces again and again. Pretty much everybody I know has made it to the shared service. There are some people from the city, like Don Marcelino, but mostly it's mining families. My gaze roves over them. There are the families missing a mother: Susana, with her papi and her little brother; César, stiff and uncomfortable in a suit, his little daughter Belén beside him in crooked braids and a too-small dark dress. Then there are the families missing a father: mine now among them. When I see the families that still have both parents, I think: *Which will they lose first?* Because, even though the miners call it the Mountain That Eats Men, it doesn't just eat the men. It eats their wives with grief; it eats their children with poverty. I look at Victor, standing alone, his spine rigid. *And as soon as the men die, the mountain starts chewing on their sons.*

Mami pokes me gently in the side, and I face the front again and mumble along with the responses.

After Mass, I stand outside the church with Mami as people offering sympathy pool and eddy around us. I find I'm having trouble remembering who we've talked to. It feels like every time I blink, a new person is standing there. I blink again and it's César and Belén.

"Have you found Daniel?" I blurt out.

Abuelita *tsks* at me for being rude, but César answers me politely.

"Not yet. But I promise you, Doña Montaño," he says, holding Mami's hands in both of his, "and you, Ana, that I will do everything I can to find the boy or, at the very least, return you his body so you can properly mourn. I'm so sorry for your family's losses. As supervisor, I feel personally responsible. Please, if there's anything I can do . . ."

I stare at César's hands, unable to look at his face. I can't help but notice that his knuckles are raw from scrubbing, but that he wasn't able to fully get the dirt out of them either.

"Thank you for your kindness," says Mami, "but when the Tío decides to take a man, there is nothing anyone can do about it. Please don't blame yourself."

César doesn't contradict her. No miner would ever speak against the power of the devil of the mines, even standing on the steps of a church.

"Such a disaster," Abuelita murmurs. "Five dead and seven injured."

"You've counted wrong," I hear myself say. I'm surprised that my voice is clear and calm. Inside I'm boiling.

"Your grandmother is right, Ana," César says softly. "There are twelve slots I need to fill on that shift."

"You've both counted wrong." I can hear the steel creeping into my voice. Belén's eyes are wide at my tone. She always seems to catch me at my worst.

"Ana!" Mami snaps. "Don't be rude to Don César."

I close my mouth and stare angrily at my feet and stop listening to them.

Because they're wrong, wrong, wrong.

There are *four* dead.

Seven injured.

One missing.

———

When we get to the house that night, I collapse on my mat, feeling drained. Mami sits heavily on her bed, mechanically unbraiding her hair. Abuelita stands in the corner, staring into space. I watch Mami, too tired to move. Her fingers flex and weave. Her smooth black hair falls to her waist in waves, threaded with silver like the mountain.

"Mami?"

"Mmm?"

"What will we do now?"

Her fingers still.

"I don't know, Ana," she says finally. "But we'll find a way. We'll be all right."

The empty words make me think of something Abuelita says: *Promises set for a banquet, but rarely fill the plates.*

"How much money do we have left?" I ask, thinking about the roll in her skirt pocket.

She closes her eyes briefly.

"None. We'll need to work extra hard to pay off the burial. I still owe the cemetery some money."

"How much?" I ask. When I was little, I used to complain when Mami couldn't buy me the things I wanted. *I'm sorry,* mi hija, she would always say. *I have to buy the things we need before I buy the things we want. Living isn't free.* Now that I'm older, I know that living isn't free. Apparently dying isn't free either.

"Never mind," she says, her fingers moving again, double-time. "With a little hard work and a little luck, we'll be fine."

There's that word again. *Fine.* I'm learning not to trust *fine.*

I chew my lower lip, thinking. Hard work doesn't help you as a *palliri*. It's one of the things I hate most about the work: there's no way to do it better. You bash two rocks together and you either get lucky and find enough mineral in it to sell, or you don't. There's no smarter way to pick rocks; no faster way to get through them. The only way to have a better chance of finding the needle is to have more people searching through the haystack. I remember Don Marcelino's sad face yesterday when I said I wasn't staying at school. *This isn't forever,* I tell myself, and I make up my mind.

"I'll come to work with you and Abuelita tomorrow."

"What? No," Mami's response is automatic. "You need to go to school."

"With three of us working as *palliris* we'll be able to sort more. If we find some good ore, we'll be okay again, and then I'll go back to school."

"I don't like the idea of you missing any more school. I know your papi never had much good to say about it, but I still think an education could get you a better life."

"The older kids skip school all the time for work. It's not like dancing around and counting to ten in French are going to do me much good on this mountain anyway." I swallow against the burn in my throat and force the words out. "The price of mineral is high right now. School is for little kids."

Mami sighs.

"Just until we pay off your father's funeral," she finally agrees.

10

Mami shakes me awake before the sun rises. The day is cold and cheerless. When I fill the pot from the water barrel to make tea, Mami shakes her head.

"We need to get started," she says. "Just bring some coca leaves. We'll chew them as we work." She smiles to take the sting out of her words. "The sooner we pay off your father's funeral, the sooner we can get you back to school."

Mami, Abuelita, and I walk to a new slag heap, a little farther from home. This heap is by one of the active mines and Mami hopes it might have better metal than the one next to our house. All day long, carts loaded with crumbled rock will come out of the mouth of the mine and pour out their contents. Someone will sort the mineral-laden rocks from the ones that don't seem worth it. They will take the good ones to the mining cooperative, which will extract the metal and pay the miners. The trash they will throw down the hill.

The trash is for us.

I hunch beside Mami and reach for a rock. Breaking it open on the ground in front of me, I scan the inside for traces of minerals we can sell: something too small for the miners to bother using the machines to sort. Instead, we do it by hand. I peer carefully at the chunks.

Nothing. Just like the search for Daniel.

I throw the worthless halves over the cliff and reach for another. I smash the rocks against each other, again and again, thinking back to my conversation with Victor when he helped fix the air compressor and wishing I could do something that actually made a difference. Instead, I'm stuck here, bashing leftover rocks against each other hour after hour after hour.

Ten hours later, when it's too dark to see the colors striping the stones anymore, we stop. My fingers are sore, my nails are ripped, my mind is numbed by the repetition, and my heart is aching from having clocked another day without my brother.

"That was good work you did today, Ana," Mami says with a smile. "Thank you for your help."

I try to smile for her, but I'm not sure I manage it.

"Shh," she says, softly brushing a strand of hair off my chapped face. "Tomorrow will be better, you'll see."

But tomorrow won't be better. Because I know that, for all our work today, we weren't lucky enough. The little pile of rocks we'll bring to the smelter tomorrow has only the tiniest hints of metal in it. It's probably not even enough to buy dinner for a day, let alone repay the cost of Papi's burial.

Which means that tomorrow will not be any better than today. Tomorrow I will have to skip school again to work as a *palliri*.

I want to scream. Cry. Tear down this entire worthless mountain with my bleeding fingers and cast it into hell where it belongs.

But I don't say anything out loud.

Instead I follow Mami and Abuelita to our house through the gathering dark. When I look over my shoulder, in the direction of the El Rosario mine, I'm surprised to see someone wearing a miner's suit walking toward our house. For a split second I want to believe it could be Daniel, but even from this distance I can see that it's a large man, not a scrawny eleven-year-old boy.

"Who's that?" I blurt.

Mami squints at the road and Abuelita crosses herself as if she's seen a ghost. We all hurry into the house. We don't know who it is and there's no reason to take chances. He could be drunk or armed. Now that there's only the three of us and no man in the house, Mami stacks rocks in front of the closed door at night.

We're all inside when the knock comes.

"Doña Montaño? It's César Jansasoy."

We hurry to open it.

"Come in, come in!" says Mami, relief plain in her voice. She pulls over Papi's old stool and asks him to sit.

César sits stiffly on the stool, glancing around. He pulls off his helmet and sets it on his knees.

"Did you find Daniel?" I ask, echoing my earlier question.

134

César shakes his head. "Not yet. But, with your permission"—he glances at Mami—"I'll come by here on my way home after work and update you on the progress every day. That way you won't have to send Ana to the mine to ask after me."

I duck my head as Mami and Abuelita's twin glares settle on me. I know they'll scold me later for bothering César at work, but for now Mami just thanks him sincerely for his willingness to go out of his way for our family.

"No trouble, no trouble." César waves off the thanks.

"Ana, go make some tea for our guest," says Abuelita, and I scurry outside to do so. After all that César has done for me, the least I can offer him is a cup of tea.

As I sit by the pot, waiting for the water to boil, I think about how nice César is. I like that he always answers *not yet* when I ask about Daniel instead of *no*, and he always made sure to keep me safe in the mine.

He always made sure to keep me safe. My thoughts stutter to a stop. Is César still working to keep me safe from the miners who might do me harm? Is that why he's walking three hours out of his way, round-trip, to come talk to us? Do enough of the miners blame me for what happened that it's not safe for me to go back near El Rosario?

My thoughts drag up questions like an ore bin. And though I sift through the giant slag heap they make in my mind, I can't find answers anywhere.

Four days.

It's been four days since my father died and my brother

vanished into the Mountain That Eats Men like heat through an open door.

Two nights that César has come by and assured us that every man in the mine has been searching for him, and yet, has found nothing.

Today was my second day with Mami and Abuelita, spending every moment that there is enough light to see breaking rocks to try to earn enough money to cover the costs of Papi's funeral. Another day I've skipped school.

Four days, where without a man's income, we have slowly run out of food.

Of course we didn't buy meat, sugar, or any other luxuries. That wasn't so bad. But this evening, after two days of back-breaking work, we walked down to the base of the mountain and handed over so much of what we'd made to the cemetery man that we couldn't buy bread, just a few potatoes and some greens. And even that didn't pay off our debt all the way. After dinner tonight, all we will have left in the house is a big bag of coca leaves. It's true that chewing coca makes you less hungry, but that's not the same as being full.

Mami sends me out to the cookstove to wilt the few greens into a soup. She says the iron in the greens will keep us strong. Abuelita snorts and tells her that there is more iron in meat and that would keep us all stronger.

Four days with Daniel missing.

I've just taken the soup inside when César shows up, right on schedule. Mami offers him a bowl of soup. He sips it politely while he gives her the update: still no boy; still no body. I can't tell if he notices how thin the soup is. I can't focus on the conversation he's sharing with Mami and Abuelita. My thoughts keep twitching to Daniel, to the fact that they still haven't found him. As soon as I possibly can without being terribly rude, I grab the dirty dishes and head outside.

I plonk them angrily into a shallow plastic tub and slosh water from the barrel over the bowls and spoons. Then I add some soap flakes and scrub at them with sand. I'm taking all my frustration out on the bottom of a bowl when César comes out of the house.

"I'm heading home now, Ana," he says. "Good night."

I want to tell him I appreciate what he's done for us. I want to apologize for being rude. But when I open my mouth, what pops out is, "Do you think Daniel is dead?"

César lets his gaze drift away, over the edge of the mountain to the orange-and-rose-banded sky and the last hint of the setting sun.

"Like I told your mother: the men have cleared the rubble from the affected tunnels. The mining cooperative has closed the inquiry."

I scowl into the wash water and scrub even harder at the bowl. "So no one's searching for him? Everyone has given up on him?"

César considers me. "Your mother is worried about you," he says. "The mountain has taken her husband and her son. It would crush her to lose you too. She wasn't happy to hear that you went, alone, to the mine to ask about a boy who is likely dead. She knows how superstitious miners can be. You must promise me, Ana, not to come asking at the mine again."

This is all true. I nod. There's no point in asking the miners anything more. I know how they feel about me.

César turns to leave. I realize that he still never answered my question.

"Don César," I call after him. He pauses. "Are *you* still looking for Daniel?"

For a long moment there's a quiet where I stare at his shoulders and he stares off into the distance and I think he really isn't going to answer me after all. Then: "He disappeared on my watch," César says softly. "Even if I can only bring your mother a body to mourn, I look for Daniel every minute of every day I am in the mine."

Though it's the answer I wanted, it crushes something inside me to hear that even César is now thinking of the search in terms of a body, not a boy.

"Thank you," I whisper.

César nods once and then walks away.

He has only just vanished out of sight when Mami comes bustling out of the house.

"There you are!" she exclaims. "Aren't you done with those dishes yet?"

I glance down at the very, very clean bowl in my hands.

"I'm done," I say, and toss the wash water onto the rocks by the door.

———

That night I find I can't sleep.

I lie there, listening to the even breathing of my mother and grandmother, and I can't stop the angry, twitchy feeling that comes over me any time I think about Daniel being gone for so long. *Maybe they're not looking hard enough,* I think. *You don't try as hard when you think you're searching for a corpse.*

Then again, if they're not right about Daniel now, they will be soon. If he's in the mine, trapped, tomorrow he'll start his fifth day with no food or water. Even if he wasn't hurt at all by the initial cave-in, waiting will be enough to kill him. I can't leave the search to people who think he's beyond saving. I have to do something.

My eyes catch on the shadow of Papi's miner's suit, neatly folded in the corner with his helmet on top since the funeral. Getting to my feet, I run a finger over the stiff material. Slowly, barely believing I'm doing it, I pull it toward me. The suit slithers over me like a scaly second skin. I shiver, but lace the boots tightly. Then, setting the helmet on my head and putting some coca leaves and a bottle of water in a *manta*, I sling the bundle over my shoulder and sneak out of the house.

Just one quick look, I think as I start down the road.

Luckily, I only promised César I wouldn't ask questions at the mine.

He never thought to make me promise not to go into it.

———

The entry lot to El Rosario is deserted when I arrive. They still must not have found a *guarda* to replace Mariángela. Still, just because there's no official guard that I can see and it's not an official shift time doesn't mean that someone might not come by at any moment.

We call our twelve-hour day a "shift," but the hours are

hardly that official. The men who work in our cooperative decided to claim this entrance and its tunnels and work from six in the morning to six at night. But there are more than two hundred cooperatives on the mountain, and each of them organizes differently. Plus, there are thousands of men who work the mountain who aren't a member of any of the cooperatives. They hire out as laborers and they get paid by the day, not a fraction of the profits. Some men work sixteen-hour shifts. Some even work twenty-four, working deep in the mountain and fueling themselves with nothing but coca and alcohol. It can take six hours just to climb back to the surface from the lower tunnels, so it kind of makes sense, but I shudder to think what it must be like to routinely go that long in the heart of the rock.

Out of habit, I glance up at Victor's house on the ridge. There are no lights on, which strikes me as odd. I realize I haven't seen Victor at all in the crazy days since our fathers' funeral and make a mental note to go visit him soon. But I don't have time to think about that now. I need to get moving. Victor's isn't the only house within easy walking distance of the mine. César's house, I know, is only about fifteen minutes away. If he were to catch me here, that would be super-awkward. And if someone else were to catch me here . . . I have no idea what they'd say—or do—to me if they found me lurking when they think I'm to blame for what happened five days ago. I hurry my steps.

I take a deep breath and reach up, grasping the edges of my helmet. My fingers fumble the knob and the lighter. My hands feel like they belong to someone else. Then the lit helmet is on my head and I've crossed into the mine.

For the moment, I'm alone in the entry tunnel.

Breathing hard, I clomp forward. Papi's boots are far too big on me and the suit sags uncomfortably. I try to move as quickly and quietly as possible. By the time the moonlight from the outside world has shrunk to the size of a silver coin, I'm feeling a creeping panic. I had forgotten how much of a nightmare it is to be in the mines. And with every echoing step farther in, I'm super aware that the nightmare could easily get worse. Though I still haven't met anyone else, I have no guarantee that the mines are empty, or that I haven't been seen.

I turn the corner and find myself face-to-face with the devil that has haunted my dreams. He sits there in all his demonic glory, naked and aggressive, draped with strings of colored paper. Dark patches mark where he's been splashed with alcohol. On the walls around him are char-drawings: places where the miners have held their lamps right up to the rocks, burning prayers for safety or little drawings of the devil onto them to hopefully buy another day of life by pleasing him.

Forcing myself away, I shuffle quickly to the vertical shaft opposite the devil. César said the miners have cleared the rubble from the affected tunnels and searched the whole area around the cave-in, so I don't bother looking in or around zone two. Instead, I'm going to check the places the others haven't. When I begged César to tell me every detail of the cave-in, he had told me that Papi and Daniel had been working in zone seven that day, so that's where I'm heading first.

When I tip my head into the yawning hole in front of me, the weak light from my lamp bounces off the rough sides of the narrow shaft, but doesn't come anywhere close to showing me the bottom. A quick peek down the black hole shows me that the first foothold is much lower than I'd like. Taking a breath to steady myself, I sit on the edge and turn, straining my arms to hold my weight as I grope around with my feet for the little ledge. As I do, my eyes catch the devil's, right across from me. I consider making an offering to the Tío but decide not to. He's taken enough from me already. His light-bulb eyes and the broken glass in his mouth catch the light from my helmet, and for just a second, my flame flickers.

He knows I'm sneaking around his hell without permission, I think. My feet scrape against the ledge I was looking for. I turn away from the devil and let go.

The trip down the shaft is truly frightening. The handholds and footholds are shallow and smooth from years of miners using them. My fingers are sweaty and Papi's boots slide around on my feet. Half the time I have to support my weight by bracing my arms against opposite walls as my feet scramble for purchase on the worn outcroppings. Step by awful step I lower myself, fighting the pull of gravity and the will of the devil that wants me smashed in a red smear at the bottom. César rarely had me work these zones, and though I'm grateful he kept me to the more stable areas, at the same time I wish I had practiced this at least once or twice. Maybe with someone at the bottom to catch me if I slipped.

After what I know is only minutes, but feels like much longer, I see the floor of the zone five tunnel less than a meter below my feet. I let myself drop the rest of the way, and land in a crouch.

To my left, the floor plunges lower and winds out of sight.

At the bottom of the slope, I see the eerie reflected glow of acetylene lamps leaking around the corner of a wall and hear the pinging of spikes on stone. To my right, there is only darkness. I freeze. It's the middle of the night. There shouldn't be anyone down here. Who are they? What are they doing? For a brief second my curiosity tempts me to sneak closer. Then I remind myself that, down here, alone, with no César to protect me from them, those men are more dangerous to me than the dark. Should I give up on this whole crazy idea? No. I know if I leave, I'll never find the courage to come down here again, especially now that I know there are men working overnight.

Tiptoeing to prevent my boots from clomping and giving me away, I turn right.

The zone five floor slants steeply beneath my feet, and my lamp gives me nothing more than a small pool of light to walk in. I run my fingers against both sides of the passageway as I go, to remind myself that they're not closing in on me. I study the floor carefully and try to slow my breathing. I'm already sweating in my suit from the heat, and the farther I get from the entrance, the more frightened I feel.

It's a good thing I'm looking down, because suddenly, in the very center of the floor, a great hole gapes in front of me. A rope pulley has been rigged over it: it's not a random hole. It's the entrance to zone seven, where Daniel was last seen. I lean over it and tip my forehead, but the depth of the hole swallows my light as if it doesn't exist. I feel dizzy and lean away again, sitting down heavily.

Is the air harder to breathe here, or is it me? I can't tell. My light is still burning, so I tell myself I just need to keep going. *If the flame can breathe, there's enough oxygen for you too*, I remind myself, and scoot on my behind to the edge of the shaft.

It's wider than the one linking zones one and five, so I won't be able to brace myself against the walls. I sit on the edge for a moment, my feet dangling in open space. A torrent of hot air washes up at me from below, causing my headlamp to flicker again.

The breath of the devil.

Shaking off the thought, I reach out and grab the two ropes of the pulley and tug them toward me. I consider them for a moment. They carry buckets of ore up and down day after day. The full-grown men probably use them to steady themselves as they climb down. They should absolutely support my weight. Then again, ropes break all the time.

I take a deep breath and push off from the edge.

For one heart-stopping moment I swing in empty space. Then my back hits the opposite wall of the shaft. I twist around until my boots are scraping the sides and then lower myself down, hand over hand.

I have no idea how deep this shaft is and now I'm really regretting not telling anyone where I was going. If I vanish, I will never have said goodbye to Mami or Abuelita. And even if they guess that I came down here looking for Daniel when they see Papi's gear missing, no one, not even César, will have any idea where to start looking for me.

This is insane, I decide, and reach up instead of down, set to haul myself to the surface instead of continuing to risk my own death to prove someone else isn't dead.

I'm just tensing the muscles in my arm to pull myself out

of the shaft when the beam from my headlamp swishes past a dark patch on the tunnel wall. I let the spin of the rope pivot me around and stare. There, burned into the side of the tunnel with the flame from an acetylene lamp, is the letter D.

I have no idea whether it's my Daniel who has graffitied the wall or some other boy with the same initial who did it five, fifty, or four hundred years ago. Though he's a mischief-maker, I can't really picture my brother, with his weak arms and bad lungs, hanging from this rope like I'm doing now and deciding to scorch his initial onto a wall. It might not even be a D, come to think of it. It might be a lopsided O, or even a circle that was supposed to be part of a larger drawing. Still, I take it as a sign. I relax my grip again and slide farther down the rope.

When my feet land on the floor of zone seven, I prowl the dips and ridges like a hunter, swinging my light, searching for any clue of what happened to my brother, picking my way over the uneven floor. Climbing over a boulder, I trip in my too-big boots, landing heavily on my hands and knees. I'm about to heave myself onto my feet again when my light catches the edge of something caught in a crack at the base of the wall.

I reach in and, to my amazement, pull out a little mud angel. Fingers trembling, I turn it over in my hands. There's no doubt. It's the one I made for Daniel the day before he disappeared—I can still see the swells and dips of my thumbprints where I pinched the wings smooth.

My laugh is as shaky as my fingers. This little mud angel would never have held up in a cave-in. The fact that it's still in one piece lets me hope that maybe, just maybe, my brother is too. But what on earth is it doing all the way over here? This is nowhere near where cave-in occurred. Nowhere near where they've been looking for him.

There's a part of my brain that says he could have left this here before the disaster, but I shush it. For the first time in days I have real hope, and I can't wait to take this home and show Mami and Abuelita. At the very least, this should give César a direction to start a new search.

Then, from just beyond the curve of the tunnel up ahead of me, I hear the sound of a voice. *Miners!* More men who shouldn't be down here at this hour of the night, doing who-knows-what. And who knows what they'd do to me if they caught me down here alone. A vision of Mariángela's mangled body jumps into my mind.

Clasping the angel in my hand, I leap to my feet and take a step back toward the exit.

And that's when I feel the first of the explosions.

This deep in the mountain, it's not even a sound, it's a shiver I feel through the soles of my feet. I stop breathing, terrified. *They're blasting.* Whoever these unknown men are, they're using dynamite. I hold my breath, digging my fingers into the rock, trying to feel through the mountain.

Even though I have no idea how many charges were set, I find myself counting them anyway, out of habit.

One . . . two . . . Somewhere in the twisted web of tunnels, fire and explosives are ripping holes in the rock that weren't there before, further weakening the mountain.

Three . . . Abuelita said they've been mining in the Cerro Rico for over four hundred and seventy years. I wonder again how much more mining this one hill can take.

Four-five-six explode together . . . Whoever those mystery miners are, they'll be far away from the dynamite and safe.

Seven . . . My breath is coming in gasps as I panic, and I can feel tears mixing with the sweat dripping off my face onto the ground. *Please,* I pray to whoever might be listening. *Please take these tears instead of my blood. Don't let me die when I just found proof that Daniel might be alive. Please.*

Eight . . . I shove Daniel's tiny clay angel into a pocket, push myself to my feet, and make myself jog up the disused tunnel.

Nine . . . *ten* . . . Surely they're getting close to being done. I start to hope that I might not be buried alive today. Other than the irregular shudders, my tunnel is holding up well. If only my luck holds enough for the access tunnels to also be clear.

Eleven . . . *twelve* . . . Yes, it's going to be okay. I take a shaky breath.

Thirteen. I hear a clattering, caving, rending sound behind me. In a blind panic, I break into a run, as fast as my terror-weakened legs can carry me. My giant boots feel like they weigh a thousand kilograms each, the suit is choking me, and my helmet rattles around on my head, throwing its beam in wild patterns over the jagged tunnel walls as I run.

The rumbling behind me has stopped, but I can feel from the popping in my ears that something has changed. I scramble over the boulders, heading for the exit shaft, when I trip on a loose rock and go flying. Smashing to the ground, I feel both of my palms split open from the force, and my knee twists beneath me.

I cry out in pain, but what's the use of that? There's no one to help me down here. Sobbing, I heave into a sitting position and clutch my knee, sending shards of pain shooting up and down my leg and leaving bloody handprints on my suit. *Like when I first met the devil,* I think.

A cloud of rock dust billows out of the tunnel in my direction. I sit there, sobbing, and let it catch up to me.

A rolling wave of filthy, scorching air washes over me, stinging my eyes and filling my lungs. For a split second, I whisper a prayer of thanks that it's only dust, not tons of rock, that's hitting my face.

And then my light goes out.

11

I am plunged into darkness and a fear so complete that it's like falling down a mine shaft to the center of the earth. My breath is wheezing in and out, rapid-fire, and I can't get enough air, but whether that's from poison gas or my panic, I have no way to know. I claw at the neck of my suit, though I know it's not the problem, and force myself to scramble onto my feet. I lurch unsteadily, my twisted knee sending bolts of agony up my leg with every step. Somehow, in this complete blackness, I have to find that rope and get myself up it.

I stumble in what I hope is the correct direction, arms sweeping blindly in wide arcs in front of me. They beat at nothing but dust-filled darkness. I suck in lungfuls of silica-clogged air and cough them back out again violently. Spots dance in front of my eyes. I worry I'm going to pass out.

I slam into a hard surface and reel away. That should have

been open space. If the tunnel bent that sharply, then I'm not where I thought I was. I turn around, disoriented.

I stumble forward, agony lancing through my knee at each step, until I hit something else. Boulder? Dead end? No matter what it is, it shouldn't have been there either. I realize I have no idea where I am in relation to the way out anymore.

A distant part of my brain registers that if this area had filled with poison gas, I'd probably be dead by now, but I'm too afraid to be very happy about it. Thinking about gas does remind me of my lamp, though. I lower myself until I'm sitting with my shoulder blades pressed against the rock and reach up for my helmet.

Sobbing, my breathing raw and ragged, I turn the valve off and lean my head against the wall behind me. I pull the little lighter out of the band around the helmet. My first instinct is to instantly roll the little wheel under my thumb, but caution makes me pause. I force myself to think. Clearly the explosions, wherever they were, caused an instability here in zone seven. I have no idea whether other parts of the mine have collapsed as well, but I can't help but remember the overheard miner's theory that it was Daniel's open flame, added to a suddenly exposed pocket of gas, that vaporized him.

Vaporized.

I tuck the lighter back into the band of the helmet for the moment. I push my fingers gently against my knee, trying to gauge the damage. I gasp. In this murky world the pain is a crisp, bright thing I'm very sure of. But it's probably not broken. I sigh with relief. It will hurt, but my leg should be able to support me on my climb out.

I try to retrace my actions in my head; try to figure out which direction has the hole in the ceiling that leads to zone five and the way out. I stand up and take a step in the direction I think may be right when a horrifying thought occurs to me. What if there are openings in the floor of this tunnel too?

In a heartbeat, I'm on my hands and knees again. If I stumbled into a floor-access tunnel, they'd find my broken body at the bottom of it. I don't want to die. I scoot along the tunnel floor like a three-legged cat, holding my injured knee out stiffly as I climb over the rubble-strewn surface. I reach out a hand to trace along the wall and find nothing but open space.

There should be a wall there.

I'm sweating heavily and the suit sticks to my body, peeling off and slapping against me like terrible, slow applause as I crawl desperately around in the dark.

I reach up and touch the lighter again.

I need to know where I am.

Vaporized.

I let go and keep crawling.

———

I don't know how much later it is when I finally give in to temptation and light the lighter. I bury my face in my knees and hold the lighter high above my head. *One, two, three!* I tell myself, and hold my breath as I flick the wheel.

When I'm not instantly exploded into a million pieces, I lift my face.

I notice two things almost simultaneously.

First, the flame is a strange, unnatural color, which tells

me that, though the air might not have vaporized me, it's not so great for me to be breathing it and it's probably not a safe place to have an open flame either.

Second, the rock formations I can now see around me are completely strange. I'm at an intersection of four tunnels with no rubble on the ground. This isn't a part of the mountain I've ever been in before. There is no hole in the roof as far as the eye can see.

I let go of the little wheel. The flame snuffs out.

I drink half my bottle of water, put fresh coca leaves in my mouth, and try not to cry.

I'm lost.

———

I stumble in the direction I think I came, risking a flame periodically. When I'm convinced I've gone the wrong way, I retrace my steps. But that route dead ends in a wide, sheer chimney with no ladder or rope. Turning again, I find myself crawling up an incline I don't remember going down.

My lighter is running low on fluid.

My bottle is running low on water.

I'm hungry.

I'm thirsty.

I'm tired.

I'm scared.

My knee hurts.

When I can no longer stand being awake, I sleep.

When I can no longer stand my dreams, I wake.

How long have I been down here? Has it been a day? More than a day?

I puff my breath against the tunnel wall and try to lick the moisture off, but all I get is a mouthful of rock dust. I know better than to drink from the stagnant orange puddles, but the sound of my feet splashing through them is the worst of taunts. When I finish my water bottle, I do cry.

My lips crack and bleed.

I sleep.

I wake.

I wander.

I do it all again.

And again.

Eventually, I give up.

In my head I say my last goodbye to Daniel, wherever he is, and whisper an apology to Mami, who will now have lost all of us to the Mountain That Eats Men. I apologize to Abuelita that she will never know my story. I lean my head against the rough stone wall of the tunnel and pray to God that death will not be as terrible as living has become.

"Please," I whisper through split lips to the glowing stars above me, "please." I don't even know what I'm asking for anymore.

The stars twinkle and I close my eyes, satisfied that it's time for me to die.

The stars are so beautiful, I think sleepily.

Stars?

My eyes snap open.

I crane my head backward and stare up again. Sure enough, there, far above me, through a narrow shaft in the rock, is the sky.

I've found a way out of the mine.

Muscles shaking, I drag my body around until I'm standing, belly pressed to the wall, never letting the stars out of my sight, terrified that they'll vanish like a hallucination if I close my eyes even for a moment. But they don't, twinkling on high above me.

So high above me.

I reach and grab the rough edge of the steep shaft and start to pull myself toward the stars. It's hard going. This is a natural vent in the mountain, not a man-made tunnel, and it wasn't designed to allow people through. At times the shaft narrows so that I'm scraping my shoulders and hips to wedge through; other times it hollows out so I have no way to find purchase between the two walls and have to crawl up like a spider, taking my weight on my fingertips and toes, risking a broken neck if my aching knee or shaking arms give out.

But for all that, centimeter after painful centimeter, the stars are getting closer. I'm only three or four body lengths away from the opening, close enough to feel the cool waft of fresh air against my face and hear the otherworldly whistling of the wind across the entrance, when I find I can climb no farther. The space opens out around me, into a dome, the sides unscalable, the stars unreachable. I collapse on the floor of the cave under the opening and sob great dry sobs. I'm too dehydrated for real crying.

Only a few hours ago, when I was wandering in the dark, I

would have been content if you told me I could die under the stars instead of in darkness, but hope is a subtle poison. To be so close and not make it out lights a fury in me unlike any I've ever known. I shriek at the roof of the cave, shouting every curse word I know, screaming at my own echoes until I'm hoarse. Then, spent, I crumble to my knees. No more water for tears, no more voice for curses. Soon, there will be nothing left of me at all.

I tip my head and blow my frosty breath at the stars like smoke. Not far from my face, the dry air makes it vanish. *That is our lives,* I think. *One quick breath toward the stars, here only an instant before this mountain sucks it away.*

Since I'm slightly out of my mind, I find this fascinating, and breathe in and out in little puffs to amuse myself until death takes me.

Which is why when the first pebble hits my head, I ignore it. It's only after the third and fourth smack into me that I focus on the ceiling instead of my breath, wondering idly if I'll be killed by a rockslide after all, instead of lack of water.

"Oh good," says the boy framed in the opening above me, "I was beginning to think you were dead."

———

I stare up at the circle of starlight, struggling for a moment to understand how there is a boy in it. Then I reach toward him, my voice a croak.

"Help."

The boy puts down the handful of pebbles he was using to get my attention.

"Of course," he says. "But I have to go get some rope. Don't worry, I'll be back."

With that, he's gone; my circle of stars complete again. It all happened so quickly that I seriously wonder if it was something I imagined, but a while later, I hear voices drifting down from above me, and the end of a rope lands on the ground beside me.

I drag myself to it and loop it under my armpits, tying a clumsy knot at the front of my chest. I tug at it, hoping it will hold me. They must have been waiting for that signal, because suddenly I'm being pulled to my feet, then off them, the movements of the rope jerky. I cling to the rope, resting my cheek against it, holding my breath against the pain of it cutting into the soft skin under my arms. My feet dangle in empty space. I train my eyes on the knot, praying it will hold. Then, hands grab the material of my suit at my shoulders, and after scraping painfully against the lip of the opening, I find myself on the ground outside the mountain.

Fresh air hits my face, almost achingly cold after the heat of the mines, and the brilliance of a million stars is blinding. I heave with dehydrated sobs.

"Okay, that's enough, come on now." I'm surprised to hear a girl's voice behind me. Hands replace the rope under my armpits, and I'm lifted up and braced against my rescuers.

I glance at the hole, a dark crack in the hillside beneath our feet, and see a small boy with a round face and buckteeth, probably about eight or nine, looping the rope around and around his forearm in an efficient, practiced motion.

"See?" he says to the person behind me. "I told you I found someone."

"Help me carry her," says the girl holding me.

The boy trots over to us, rope coil slung over his shoulder.

"Her?"

He examines me from head to toe with curiosity. I can't imagine I'm looking very girlish at the moment, and I try not to contemplate what I must smell like after all that time in the mountain, but my braids are loose and long around my face, so I guess it's not too much of a stretch to imagine me as a her. He makes a noise that might be agreement and comes to my other side, lifting my arm over his shoulders. He's shorter than me, so I don't know how much he's really helping the girl, who's much taller, but I guess at least he's taking part of my weight.

"Water?" I manage to rasp.

"Sorry," says the girl. "I didn't bring any. When Santiago came in saying he found someone trapped in a cave, I just grabbed rope and ran. We'll get you water when we get home. I'm Yenni, by the way."

"Ana," I croak, and slump against her.

She nearly drops me.

"Ana? Oh my God, really? Ana Águilar?" Yenni sounds stunned. "The girl who went to work in that mine? They say you angered the devil and he killed your whole family and only you survived, but then the devil came and stole you away in the night."

It's not how I would have told the story, but there's no denying I'm *that* Ana. I shrug.

"Wow. You're not dead! I can't believe you're not dead. You've been missing for *two days*. What happened to you . . . ? No, actually, don't try to talk. Come on, let's get you home."

At first Santiago rattles on about how lucky I am that he found me—*Sometimes, when I can't sleep, I go for a walk, you know? And then suddenly I hear this noise and I'm like, what's that? So I go to where there's this hole in the ground, and I see you! It's a good thing you were cursing and shouting, or I would have maybe walked right by . . .* —but soon the effort of keeping their footing with me slung between them takes all their breath and we scrabble over the mountain in silence.

I slide in and out of consciousness, so I'm not sure how much later it is when Santiago and Yenni arrive at a small clump of mining houses and lead me into one.

There's a sleeping form in one of the beds.

Santiago drops his voice to a whisper.

"That's Papi. We don't want to wake him."

I nod in understanding.

There's a comforting similarity between Yenni and Santiago's house and mine. Same mud brick and rock walls, same earth floor, same jumble of belongings piled in the corner. I see a miner's suit and helmet laid out by the door. I wonder how long Santiago and Yenni's father has been in the mines and which mine he works in. It must be some mine other than El Rosario or I probably would have met them before now. I wonder when their door will have no suit in front of it too, or whether it will still be there, but it will be Santiago who belts it on every morning.

I see no sign of a woman.

Yenni and Santiago pull me to an overturned bucket. I collapse onto it, beyond grateful to be out of the cold and off my feet. Yenni stands beside me, a hand on my shoulder to keep me from tipping over onto the floor. Santiago vanishes, but a minute later, he's back.

"Here you go," he says, and a tall glass of water is pushed under my face.

My hands tremble as I reach for it, but he doesn't let go, so I don't have to support its weight. I sip slowly at the rim, water dribbling over my chin and tracing a freezing finger under my suit. It's almost painful: the coldness of the water hits my empty belly like a knife and my throat muscles cramp around the unfamiliar work of swallowing, but it tastes like life and I make myself drink it.

My stomach feels like it's going to explode when I'm only about halfway done with the glass. I pull away and Santiago takes the glass from me.

"Go bring me a basin with water, some soap, and a cloth, then sit facing the wall so I can clean her up," Yenni whispers.

He makes a face at her for giving orders, but does as she says. While Santiago bustles about getting the things she needs, Yenni smiles down at me.

"I still can't believe it's really you," she says. "Whatever happened?"

I feel so weak that my head is swimming. The water in my belly sloshes uncomfortably, and the edges of the room are starting to fuzz in my vision. I want to start at the beginning, string everything together in a way that makes sense and shows that I'm not crazy. I want to tell her about Papi, and

Daniel, and not being able to eat, and Mami, and Abuelita, and César, and the devil. But I only manage "Lost" before I pass out.

———

When I come to, I feel wetness against my face. My head lolls and my eyes open sluggishly to see a teenage girl holding a basin and a washcloth standing in front of me in a small, plain room. She has a wide, pretty face with arching eyebrows, and her cheeks dimple when she smiles at me.

Yenni, I remember.

"Well, now that you're awake again, we can do it right, hmm?" Her eyes sparkle with intelligence. She's at least five years older than me, so we wouldn't have gone to school together, but Santiago looks about nine: I would definitely know him from school. Since I don't recognize either of them, I'm definitely on the far side of the mountain. "Let's get you out of that disgusting suit and get you clean," Yenni goes on. Santiago sits across from us, studiously facing the wall. "Do you think you can stand?"

I nod, even though the idea of standing makes my knee scream and my legs tremble. Yenni helps me to my feet and strips me down to my underwear. When she pulls off the suit, Daniel's angel falls out and clunks to the floor.

Yenni bends over and picks it up.

"What's this?" she asks with interest.

Their papi rumbles a complaint in his sleep and they both drop their voices.

"What's what?" whispers Santiago, twitching with curiosity.

I shrug, too tired to talk.

Yenni lowers me onto the bucket and hands the angel to Santiago. He examines it while I sit there shivering, and Yenni scrubs my arms, legs, and torso with her wet cloth and a bar of lye soap. When she's done, she wraps me in a blanket and tells me to tip my head. She puts the basin on the floor behind me and attacks my filthy hair with energy. My eyes prickle when she hauls on the knots with a comb, but I sit there quietly until she announces she's done.

Yenni rinses my hair and wrings the water out of it, then braids it, still wet, with practiced hands. She considers me. "I don't think we're the same size, but now that I've done all that work to get you clean, I'm not going to put you into that suit again."

A relieved noise slips out of me. I was dreading putting that thing back on. If I have my way, I'm not touching it ever again.

Yenni kicks Papi's coveralls and the clothes I was wearing under it into a corner and reaches up to the rope slung across the wall behind the bed Santiago is sitting on. She pulls a pair of leggings, a sweater, and some clean underwear from where they were hanging on the rope and brings them over to me. It feels weird to change into someone else's underwear, but my clothes are all so gross that I slip everything on gratefully. My arms are longer than hers, we discover, but she's wider around the hips than I am. The clothes fit well enough.

"Thank you," I mumble up at her. It feels amazing to be clean again. Though I don't feel anywhere near healthy, I have started to feel human, not like some horrible, scummy creature dragged from a cave.

"You're welcome," says Yenni, wiping her hands on her skirt. "Santiago, you can turn around now," she says to her brother, then throws the basin of wash water out the front door. Santiago hands me Daniel's angel.

The sleeping form makes another grunt. Yenni drops her voice again.

"It's late," Yenni whispers. "Why don't you get some sleep and we'll talk in the morning? Do you think you could drink some more water first? Or maybe you need to go outside and go to the bathroom? My guess is you're too dehydrated, but if you need to go, there's a ravine you can use ten steps from the door."

I know I need to drink, but my stomach still feels stretched with what I already had. And as for going to the bathroom, Yenni's absolutely right—there's no way I have enough water in me to be able to pee.

I shake my head.

"Okay. You can share our bed for tonight." She points to where Santiago had sat while she cleaned me up.

And though there's much to say, I find that all I have the strength for is to take the two steps across the room and collapse onto the bed, Daniel's angel clutched to my chest.

I half wake to the sound of raised voices.

"Santiago!" A man's voice, gravelly and powerful. Though I don't open my eyes, I get the feeling that this is not someone I would like to be in trouble with. "Who is that? What's going on?"

"Um . . ." I hear Santiago, sounding slightly panicked. Then Yenni's smooth voice cuts in.

"This is Ana, Papi, the girl that went missing from the other side of the Cerro. She was trapped in a cave on the mountain, so we got some rope and pulled her out. She needed a place to rest, so we brought her here."

"She needs to go back to where she came from."

"Of course." Yenni's voice is soothing. "Don't even worry about it. She'll be gone before you get home tonight. Here, I've got your things all packed for the day. You'd better hurry. You don't want to be late first thing on Monday morning, and I have to get going, too, to make it to the city on time."

There's a grunt and the sound of the door closing. I drift back to sleep.

When I wake again, it's to bright midday sun hitting my face. I prop myself up on my elbows. I'm still in Yenni and Santiago's bed, and I have a blanket wrapped tightly around me. I'm alone in the house.

I untwist myself from the heavy wool and struggle to my feet. When I stand up, my head swims, and I sit down again quickly, light-headed. After a few steadying breaths, I try again, more slowly this time. I shuffle outside, my knee twinging at every step. I find the ravine Yenni had mentioned and am delighted to discover that I'm able to produce a tiny trickle of urine. It's really dark, but it means that my body has begun to process the water from last night.

Even though it's only about ten steps back to the door of the house, when I reach it, I'm winded. I take a moment leaning against the doorway to catch my breath before I head in and sit on the bed again. I see someone has left a glass of water near where I was sleeping, and I drink it. I can slowly feel myself coming to life.

Sitting there, drifting in and out of sleep, I lose track of time—my brain is still not working very well—but eventually I hear Santiago in the distance. In minutes, he's arrived, dusty and smiling and carrying a school satchel.

"You're awake!" Santiago bounces over to me. "How are you feeling?"

"Better." I smile at him without even thinking about it. "Thank you again for saving me. If you hadn't found me in that cave, I'd be dead by now."

Santiago beams, his wide smile showing off his buckteeth and the impressive gap between them.

"Can you walk?" he asks.

"Yes," I say, feeling proud of myself.

"Good! Let's get going." He slings his satchel into a corner.

I wobble to my feet. "Where?"

A frown pulls Santiago's eyebrows together. "Yenni said I needed to bring you to her before Papi gets home. She said if you woke up before school, I could walk you home, but that if you didn't wake up until after school, I needed to help you get to her."

Between my overall weakness and my hurt knee, I don't know if I can manage a long walk. Also, it kills me that, if I have to put in the effort of walking, I can't go home instead of to wherever Yenni is.

"Why can't you take me home now?"

"Yenni said you live way the other side of the Cerro," he says. "I wouldn't be home on time and Papi would be mad at me. Besides, it would be dangerous walking in the dark when neither of us really knows the way." He looks at me curiously. "Where do you live, exactly?" he asks.

"A little house off by itself. I'm about forty-five minutes downhill and an hour west of the El Rosario mine."

Santiago's face falls. He shakes his head. "That really is too far. It would take at least five hours to walk around the mountain to get you there."

"Don't worry about it," I say. Even though I really wish things were different, I owe Santiago my life. I'm not going to ask him to do ten hours of walking and get him in trouble. I take a few more swallows of water to fuel me for what's ahead. "Take me to Yenni. If you're sure I can stay with her, I'll find my way home from Potosí tomorrow morning when I can walk in daylight."

"Great!" He grabs my hand and starts towing me toward the door.

I smile. I really do like Santiago. He's so cheerful. So different from his dour father. I wonder what his mother is like.

"How far away is her work?" I grit my teeth against the discomfort of making my tired body move.

"Not too far," says Santiago, pulling me forward with a smile, "and it's all downhill. Come on!"

With a sigh, I follow him out the door.

12

Holding tight to Santiago's hand, I descend the scree-lined slope, my knee complaining the whole way. It was so strange to look out of Santiago and Yenni's house and see the crumpled brown rock blanket of the mountains stretching away into the distance instead of being able to see the city. We pick our way around the eastern face of the mountain and slowly, little by little, the city of Potosí fills our view again. It's the better part of three hours later when we're finally walking along the cobbled streets of the city. But to Santiago's credit, it is downhill to where Yenni works. Mostly.

We stop beside tall walls with a decorative wrought-iron gate. Through the gate there is a carefully tended garden courtyard and an imposing three-story house with big stone arches. My mouth goes dry. This is not the kind of place people like me are allowed.

"Come on," says Santiago, tugging on my hand. "The servants' entrance is this way."

The servants' gate is a heavy metal door set into the tall concrete wall. Santiago raps on it with his knuckles. "It's me—Santiago Quispe. Open up!"

I hear noise from within and then the door swings open. I stare and stare at the tended gardens. Potosí is so high up the Andes mountains that very little grows naturally there. This vibrant green is alien to my world of gray and brown and rusty red clay. I can only imagine how much work it must take the gardeners to create this little oasis.

Santiago points across the cobbled patio to a low, detached building.

"Servants' quarters," he explains over his shoulder. "This is where Yenni sleeps during the week. She comes home on the weekends. Today's Monday, so she'll be here until Friday night."

I blink to absorb this information. Yenni, the daughter of a miner, has landed herself a job as a maid in the city. I wonder how she did it.

"Let's try the kitchen first," he says.

I hope the kitchen isn't too far away. I need to sit down before I fall down.

The kitchen is in the main house and it is enormous, at least four times the size of my entire home. Its walls and floor are stone; the ceiling is white plaster. There are large surfaces for preparing foods, fancy metal appliances that I have only seen through shop windows on my walks to church and on TVs in public places, and two different sinks. An enormous fireplace takes up a third of one wall, and a huge black stove hunches in the far corner. Pots and pans of all sizes hang from the ceiling, and a heavy wooden table takes up the middle of the room. Three women wearing identical dresses are bustling around, cooking, cleaning, clattering.

If Santiago hadn't been steering me, I would have stopped in my tracks and stared. Instead, I'm plunked on one of the wooden benches at the table while Santiago goes over to one of the other girls and collects a bowl of soup and a spoon. He hands it to me.

"Eat this," he says. "I'll go find Yenni."

I take a sip, and flavor explodes in my mouth. After not eating for two days in the mine, this soup is something from another world. It's a salty broth with rice and potato and chicken and carrots. I find the cook, a woman twice as wide as any of the others, with my eyes.

"Thank you," I say. "This is delicious."

She grunts at me, and I sit and watch the workings of the kitchen while Santiago looks for Yenni. Honestly, I'm so happy to be off my feet, I don't even care how long it takes him. While I wait, I run my finger over the smooth grain of the wooden bench and table, marveling at them. Whoever owns this house must be really wealthy: a huge house, an impossible garden, and things made from wood even in the servants' areas.

A few minutes later, Santiago pops back into the kitchen, Yenni at his heels. She's wearing a neat black dress with a white apron just like everyone else in the kitchen. The fabric is even and heavy, better than either of us could afford. Clearly it's the uniform for the women who work here. Her kind face lights up with a smile when she sees me.

"Ana! You made it."

"Here I am," I agree.

"Thanks for bringing her," she says to her brother. "You'd better go now. You'll need to have dinner ready by the time Papi gets home."

"You cook?" I ask Santiago.

"Almost as well as Carmencita," he says, puffing up his chest and waggling his eyebrows at the dour cook.

She grunts at him, and I think she might be mad, but when he flits over to her, she swats his behind with a dish towel and hands him a small wrapped bundle. "That's because it *is* my cooking," she says. Santiago laughs and gives the big woman a peck on the cheek and a thank-you for the food and, with a wave to me and Yenni, heads out the door.

Yenni rolls her eyes.

"That boy," she says with enough feeling to make it a full sentence all by itself. Then she looks at me. "Go ahead and finish your supper. I've told Doña Arenal, the owner, that you're here. If she wants to talk to you, you should do all the getting better you can before she does." She winks at me and then leaves to help the other maids with their work.

I'm surprised to see so many of them working in the same place at the same time, but as I sit there and sip the salty broth, I can see that they're all busy. One of the cooks is making bread dough; another is washing and drying a massive stack of dirty dishes and pots. Yenni and the other young girl keep ducking in and out of the kitchen, taking folded cloths and clean dishes and glasses out, and bringing dirty ones in, adding them to the stack. The cook and the dishwasher work quietly, but the others chat as they work.

I find myself lulled by the heat and safety of the kitchen, and soon I'm struggling not to doze off over my soup. The brusque clop of heeled shoes on the stone floor and the sudden hush they bring with them makes me snap my head up. Doña Arenal has entered the kitchen and is staring straight at me.

Doña Arenal is a tall woman with a serious face. She wears modern clothes, and her silver-streaked hair is styled expensively around her face. Her eyes are piercing.

Nervously, I wipe my hands down the front of my borrowed clothes and stand up.

"Sit down," she snaps. "You look as if you're going to tip over in the first breeze." Part of me feels like I shouldn't be sitting in front of her, but I can tell she's not used to being contradicted. I sit.

"Thank you, Doña," I manage, though I'm not really sure what I'm thanking her for. For letting me come in the door, though I'm a dirty miner's kid? For letting me have some soup? I leave it at a simple thank-you and stick with a safe "God will bless you for your kindness."

Doña Arenal *humphs* and waves her hand dismissively as if God's blessing is no concern of hers.

"Now, tell me where you come from and how you came to be in my kitchen."

"My name is Ana Águilar Montaño," I say. Doña Arenal watches me with bright eyes. In the background, I can hear the rhythm of the dishwashing change, and I know that the maids are curious to hear my story too. "I lived with my mother, father, brother, and grandmother on the Mountain That Eats Men." There's a pause in the kitchen noise when I say this, quickly covered up by a fresh wash of activity. I try not to let their judgment sting. I know how cruel the city kids are to mining kids. "Dust-suckers," they call the boys whenever we come into town for church or the market, and "rocks for brains." I meet Yenni's eyes and she gives me a small, encouraging smile. I'm glad Yenni, at least, doesn't think less of me. She's a mountain girl too. "There was a mine disaster about a week ago. My father died and my brother disappeared." I wish I knew what was going on inside Doña Arenal's head, but I have no idea how the rich think. If she doesn't believe me, will she kick me out? I know I'm not strong enough to walk up the mountain now. I need her to let me stay the night with Yenni.

I swallow and go on with my story. "My brother just vanished, Doña. Everyone thought he was dead even though we didn't have a body to bury." I leave out the fact that everyone blames me for the disaster, and I feel dirty for it. "I went into the mine to look for my brother." I decide to also skip the mystery men in the tunnels because I have no explanation for why they were there at midnight using dynamite. "My tunnel collapsed, my light went out, and I lost my way in the darkness. I was down there for two days. Finally, I found myself in a cave with no way out, ready to die . . . and then . . . then Yenni's brother, Santiago, heard me calling out, and threw me a rope, and they pulled me up and brought me here." Tears are choking my voice, but my story is finished anyway, so I stop talking.

There's a long pause where no one says anything. Doña Arenal's piercing gaze rests on me. A lifetime of being seen as lesser makes me wilt a little inside, but I keep my shoulders back and my head up. *You faced down the devil in the mines,* I tell myself. *She can't be worse than that.*

"Well," says Doña Arenal, breaking the silence. "Well." She smooths the front of her severe black dress and seems to change what she was about to say. "You can stay in the maids' quarters tonight, but then you must leave. Say your prayers and thank God you're alive, child. The rest of you, get back to work." With that, she turns and sails out of the kitchen like a giant warship in a time of peace.

I hear the collective sigh as the maids and I let out a breath. Then Yenni giggles.

"What a story, eh?" she asks me, eyes sparkling. "You went down into the mines to search for your brother. Really? *That's* why you were in there?"

"Yeah."

"Well?" She pulls over a basket of laundry to fold and sits across from me at the table. "Did you find him?"

I glance from her to the three maids behind her, all openly curious. I reach into my borrowed pocket and pull out Daniel's clay angel. It's the worse for wear after all it's been through, with the tips gone off both of the wings and chips out of the hem of its dress.

"No," I say, putting the clay figurine on the table between us. "But I found this little angel he had with him." I feel the hot prickling of tears behind my eyes and take another spoonful of broth to cover it. Having spent two days lost in the mine, I realize just how impossible it is that Daniel could still be alive after—what would it be now? Six? Seven days?

Across the table from me, Yenni is folding small squares

of black cloth into fancy shapes, lining them up on the table between us. I appreciate Doña Arenal allowing me to stay here, but Mami will be terribly worried about me. Now that I'm her only child, I need to get home to her as quickly as possible.

But just then, the dishwashing girl speaks up. Her voice is so soft we would never have heard it if anyone else had been talking.

"My brother said there's a mining boy who showed up in town a few days ago who's fighting for cash. Do you think that might be him?" she asks the room.

"What?" I ask, my heart pounding in my chest. I can't imagine Daniel fighting for money . . . He was never very strong. But still . . . a miner boy showing up just a few days ago? It's too much of a coincidence. Could it be?

"When was that, Juana?" Yenni asks.

"The day the boy was first seen in the city," Juana whispers to the wall, never pausing her washing, "was three days after the cave-in."

"The cave-in that killed your uncle?" asks Yenni softly.

Juana nods. I feel nausea roll through my belly. Does she know that people blame me for that cave-in? Does *she* now blame me for her uncle's death? I find I can't make myself eat any more.

But then my brain jumps to what she's saying. My hands start to shake and I curl them into my lap.

Could it be? Could it really be that Daniel is *alive*? And not only alive but here in the city instead of trapped in the mountain somewhere? Having just given up on him, it feels almost painful to hope again. But it's possible, isn't it? After all, I found a way out. Maybe Daniel did too.

I frown. If he *is* alive, why on earth hasn't he come home? Why didn't he send word? He must have known that Mami, Abuelita, and I would be frantic, that César would have the men tearing the mine apart searching for him.

Then I remember the last conversation we had together. *I don't know how much longer I can take it,* he had said, and I had joked, *You planning to run away to a green valley or a sparkling city?* He hadn't answered. My stomach drops.

Would he actually have done that to us?

———

I wake up the next morning to hard sunlight coming through a glass window. I had spent a few hours last night with the maids in the kitchen but had gotten so sleepy that Yenni packed me off to bed ridiculously early. After my difficult hike down the mountain, I fell right to sleep.

I prop myself up on my elbows and consider my surroundings. I'm in Yenni's room in the maids' quarters, with a plain wool blanket wrapped tightly around me. I untwist myself and struggle to my feet. After water and food yesterday I'm much better today, but my body still feels weak from my time lost in the mines and my twisted knee is killing me.

I limp across the gardens to the kitchen. I see the cook and Juana, the quiet dishwashing maid from last night, but Yenni and the other maid aren't there at the moment. Yenni must have gotten up before dawn to start work.

"Sit down," barks the cook. "I'll get you something to eat."

"Thank you, Carmencita," I say, pleased I remember her name. I take my place from last night, at the wooden table. The smells of the kitchen are amazing, and I find my stomach pinching painfully as I wait for the cook to finish what she's making and bring it over to me. My stomach grumbles, embarrassingly loud. The stocky woman glares at me from across the room, as if hunger in her kitchen were an unforgivable offense.

"Here." She marches over and plunks a tin mug in front of me. "The tourists drink coffee, but I've poured you a cup of *api*."

I sniff the thick purple liquid in front of me. In our house we never had anything for breakfast other than coca tea. Food is so expensive we usually only eat once a day—sometimes twice if the price of mineral is high. I've never had *api*. I take a cautious sip.

For someone used to clear tea, *api* is overwhelmingly rich: sweet, spicy, thick. I sigh with pleasure. Carmencita levels a glare at me from across the room. I worry she might have thought that was a criticism.

"It's wonderful," I say sincerely. "What is it?"

Her face softens.

"You make it from ground purple corn, water, and pineapple. Some people make it with oranges, but that's no good." Her words are terse, but she seems pleased. "Then you add cinnamon, sugar, and cloves." She turns away from me again, but her shoulders are relaxed and I can see she's not angry with me.

Pineapple? Cinnamon? It sounds like a lowland drink. They would have to truck all that stuff up here from the edges of the Amazon rain forest where it grows. No wonder I've never had it before. I relax and sip my *api* happily. I can feel my belly filling, so I am stunned when Carmencita turns around and places a plate in front of me.

"More?" I goggle at her.

She gives me a satisfied look and walks away.

I stare at the plate. An entire roll of soft white bread and three squares of homemade cheese. It's a feast. I can't believe my luck and dig in hungrily. Of course, soon I have to slow down, but I force my near-starved stomach to hold as much as it possibly can. I'm not going to throw out the best breakfast of my life.

I chew slowly and take in the kitchen around me.

"Where's Yenni?" I ask. "And the other maid?"

"Out," answers Carmencita. "Yenni and Gisele are at the market buying meat and vegetables for dinner."

Meat, I think, and try not to let my greed show on my face. Cheese for breakfast and meat for dinner? I'm in heaven. *Stop dreaming about food and focus!* I scold myself. I have a job to do: go into the city, find Daniel, and then get home to Mami as fast as I can.

"Thank you for the food," I say, finishing up the bread and cheese and drinking the last of the *api*.

She takes my plate, stacking it by the sink where the quiet Juana is already elbow-deep in soap suds.

I sit for a minute or two more, but then I start to get twitchy. Never in my life have I sat around while other people do work for me. I clear my throat.

"I don't know what I can do," I say quietly, "but until Yenni gets back and can take me into town, I'd like to be useful, if I can. Is there anything I can help you with?"

And I might be wrong, but I think I see a tiny smile on Carmencita's face before she turns away.

———

Two hours later, chapped to the elbows in a giant tub of washing, I'm reconsidering that smile.

I rub at a stubborn stain on the white tablecloth in the sudsy water in front of me, shoving it under the water and attacking it with the hard corner of the big brick of lye soap. Carmencita had given it to me when she set me up in this tiled room with a waist-high pile of dirty linens. *How many people live here?* The question was out of my mouth before I really had a chance to think about whether I wanted to say it or not. And that's when Carmencita told me that Doña Arenal's home was a *posada*—a place where travelers, like the Americans who were here right now, could come and stay. They paid for clean sheets every day and clean tablecloths and napkins every time they sat down at a table. She indicated the pile with her chin. *So get to work,* she had said.

I'm glad of the work, really, though my arms are killing me and I tire much more easily than I should. It puts my body into a pattern, which leaves my mind free for thinking. And so I wash. And think.

I think about Mami and Abuelita, far away, up the mountain. I think about Yenni's kindness, and Carmencita's prickliness, and Juana's shyness. I think about little Santiago, off at school. I wonder about Doña Arenal, and the secret life of rich people.

But mostly, I think about Daniel. I think about the way he'd make fun of me for being too weak to wash napkins, and then plunge his hands in beside me to make the work go faster; the way his eyes would have sparkled if he'd been served a breakfast like I was this morning; the stories he would make up about the people who lived here. I think about the angel that presses into my thigh every time my pocket bumps the tub.

"*Ana!*"

I whip my head around. Yenni is standing behind me.

"You dreamer," she says with a smile. "I called you three times."

"Sorry," I say, hauling the last tablecloth out of the water and wringing it between my hands. "I guess I was caught up in the work."

Yenni makes a face.

"I hate laundry," she says, but she rolls up her sleeves and grabs the other end of the cloth. Between us, we twist the water out of it much faster. Yenni helps me heave the damp, heavy fabric over a line. She raises an eyebrow at the eleven tablecloths and half a hundred napkins hung on the various lines crisscrossing the little washroom. "You, on the other hand, seem to like it?"

"*Like* is too strong a word for what I feel about this," I say, making a face at her. Still, I swell with the praise. I had figured out how to get it done quickly and well. I'm pleased that I've impressed Yenni.

Yenni laughs.

"Well, okay, maybe you don't *like* it," she amends. "But you are good at it. It would have taken me all day to get this done, and you finished it in barely a morning. Come on." She holds out a hand to me. "It's time for lunch. Carmencita gives you extras when she's pleased."

I wipe my hands and raise an eyebrow at Yenni. She laughs again. I like how much she laughs. I don't think I've ever known anyone to laugh as much as she and her brother do.

"You won't be able to *tell* she's pleased," Yenni admits with a grin, "but she will be, all the same. Come on."

Pushing my way through the forest of clean-smelling damp cloth, I follow Yenni to the kitchen.

When we get there, I can see that Carmencita and Juana have been working the whole time I've been in the laundry. The kitchen is a confusion of steam, smells, and loud clanging noises. I sit down at what I'm rapidly beginning to think of as "my" spot at the table and watch in awe as Carmencita sends plate after plate of steaming food out the door to be served in the restaurant. Gisele carries the trays; Juana is working away ferociously at the sink again. Yenni gives me a wink and slips into the chaos, emerging a few minutes later with two plates of food. Handing me one, heaped high with meat, rice, and potatoes, she folds her slender form onto the bench and sits beside me.

"So," she says, digging in to her food, "how are you feeling?"

I'm staring at the food in front of me, struggling to believe that it's real. I've only eaten this well at weddings, and I'm ashamed to feel tears prickling at the corners of my eyes. I hope Yenni doesn't notice.

"Better," I say, sounding only a little froggy. I pick up my knife and fork and clear my throat. "Thank you."

"Good," says Yenni, "because later, I'm taking you into town."

I smile at her tentatively and wonder whether, despite the difference in our ages and despite the fact that she's found a choice better than I can dream of, Yenni and I could be friends.

———

It's midafternoon by the time the napkins have all been ironed and folded into the pretty shapes Doña Arenal likes, and then the tablecloths that I washed in the morning are dry enough that they can be ironed and folded too. Throughout the day, Yenni has flitted in and out of my working space like a friendly moth, smiling and offering words of encouragement.

When the laundry is done, I say goodbye to Juana and Carmencita. I ask the women to say my goodbyes to the rest of the staff I've gotten to know. Carmencita gives me a small wrapped bundle to take with me and puffs up like a bird that's been poked when I thank her for it. I don't open it right away because I don't want to be rude, but I hope she packed me a dinner like she did for Santiago. Then Yenni and I head into the main rooms of the *posada* to find Doña Arenal.

It's odd to walk through the echoing stone hallways. In my time here, I've kept to the servants' areas. There, the rooms are clean, but plain. Out in the main areas of the *posada*, every wall has a painting or a woven cloth hanging on it, and there are statues and vases with flowers on the tables and in the alcoves of the walls. The floors are intricately tiled, the vaulted mosaic ceiling stretches high above my head, and there are lush green plants in ceramic pots surprising me in the corners. I wonder at the plants. I reach out a finger and trace it gently along the edge of a leaf.

"Ana?"

I whirl, an apology already forming on my lips. Thankfully it's only Yenni.

"There." She points with her chin. "The *doña* is in the dining room."

Doña Arenal is working on a thick ledger at one of the far tables. It's between mealtimes, so the tourists aren't here, but even without it being filled with fancy people and foreigners, the dining room makes me catch my breath. It's on the second floor of the *posada*, and one whole wall of it is windows. Through them, you can see right over the outer wall. To one side, the city of Potosí stretches off into the distance. To the other, the Mountain That Eats Men looms like a hunchbacked giant.

"It's a great view, isn't it?" Yenni whispers.

"Um . . . absolutely," I manage. I don't want to disagree with her, but seeing the mountain on one side and the city on the other makes me feel like they're two different worlds, with no bridge between them. It makes me feel even more like I will never have a future anywhere else.

If I'm honest with myself, I'm going to miss the *posada* terribly. It's been warm, comfortable, and safe, and I had easy work to do. Yes, Carmencita is prickly and Doña Arenal is stern, but Santiago and Yenni have been nothing but kind to me and no one has judged me for having gone into the mines. I know that none of that will be true once I get home. Though I feel stupid to admit it, it's hard to leave.

Doña Arenal has seen us come in and is walking over, her face severe.

"Doña," I say politely when she reaches us.

"What is it?"

"I just wanted to come and say thank you again for all you've done." I practiced this speech in my head all morning. "You opened your doors and fed me. I know that God will reward you for your mercy and kindness, and you will be forever in my prayers. I wanted to let you know I was leaving."

She softens. "I'm glad you're better," she says, "and I'm sure your mother will be relieved to see you. Safe journey home."

I don't correct her. I don't tell her that I'm leaving the posada not to head straight home to my mother but to go into the city of Potosí to search for a street fighter who might be my brother.

"Thank you, Doña," is all I say.

13

Yenni hustles along the streets of Potosí. I have to almost jog to keep up with her.

"We have to go quickly," she says. "I need to get back in time to help with the dinner rush."

"Okay." I don't want to get her fired, but in the past I've only come to Potosí for church and festivals. I wouldn't know how to find my way around this maze of cobblestoned streets without her.

My knee throbs with every step. My brain whirs—*Am I about to find Daniel? Is he okay?*

I swallow my questions and stick to Yenni like a shadow.

We walk through the streets of the mining neighborhoods of Potosí that I'm a little familiar with. Then Yenni takes me through neighborhoods I haven't been to before, ones where I don't feel comfortable. The streets are dirtier here than in the rest of the city, the houses shabbier. From a shadowed doorway a man whistles at us. Yenni ignores the man, her mouth a tight line.

I scoot closer to Yenni and we hurry onward, arm in arm.

We trace through the filthy streets of this battered neighborhood for another ten minutes until we come to a squat, ugly building made out of concrete slabs. Men crowd the door and waves of muffled cheering filter onto the street from inside.

"Yenni!" I whisper. "Where are we?"

Yenni takes my hand and pulls me to the door of the horrible building.

"Excuse us," she says, shouldering her way through the men there.

I suck in a breath, shocked, but though they grumble and growl, the men let us through.

Inside, the press and heat of the crowd is suffocating. The stale air is a choking mix of the smells of sweat and dirt, roasted peanuts and stale alcohol, with a nauseating metallic hint of blood. Yenni pulls me forward. The world closes in around me; my breath comes in pants. My vision blurs and the push of shouting bodies vanishes. Instead, I feel the press of rock, the mine collapsing, suffocating me. *You're not in the mountain*, I tell myself sternly. *You're in the city, with Yenni. Stop panicking.*

"There," says Yenni, pushing me up to the edge of the rope in front of us. "Is that your brother?"

My heart sinks into the pit of my stomach and stays there. I shake my head. Because no, the boy in the ring is not Daniel. But he's not a stranger either.

Victor and another boy about his age are stripped to the

waist in a dirt ring; a grimy rope cordon holds off the crowd that surges and roars whenever either one of them lands a hit on the other. They're drenched in sweat and both are bleeding freely from nose and mouth, but neither stops. I stare at them.

Of all the places and ways I expected to see Victor again, this would never have been one of them. The last time I saw my friend was at our fathers' funeral last week. With everything that's been going on in my family, I hadn't checked on him. I figured he was still working in the mine.

The boys circle each other, searching for an advantage. I stare at the bare back, the sweaty shoulders, the ragged bangs spattered with blood half covering his eyes. Victor is my best friend. And yet the boy in front of me is someone I don't recognize.

Just then, Victor glances into the crowd and sees me. His hands drop in surprise as he gapes at me and the other boy takes advantage of his inattention and lands a brutal hit to his jaw. I hear the clack of his teeth as his head snaps from the blow, and then the light goes out of my friend's eyes as he crumples to the ground in a faint.

The crowd hollers and roils around us and I clutch at Yenni's arm, not wanting to lose her, my one tether to things that make sense in this world. Around me, I see money changing hands and hear men shouting to each other, but somehow I can't get meaning out of it. I'm used to the quiet, lonely poverty of our little house. This loud, aggressive poverty is new to me, and I find it upsetting. I realize I'm shaking. Yenni points toward the other side of the ring. I see one man is holding up the arms of the winner, calling for cheers, and another is dragging Victor's body out of the dusty ring. His head lolls over his shoulder and the dirt of the floor sticks to his sweat. The man pulls him out a back door.

I'm walking that way before I even realize I'm doing it. This time Yenni is my shadow as I push through the herd of men. My eyes don't leave that door. I haven't managed to find my brother. I'm not about to lose my best friend too.

———

When Yenni and I make it to the far side of the room, the man who pulled Victor out of the ring blocks our way. I try not to cringe under his piggy-eyed gaze.

"You can't come through here," he says. His face is wide and puffy, and his nose is crooked from having been broken many times. "No one is allowed to see the fighters when they're not in the ring."

I can tell he's not going to change his mind. All of the kindness has been punched out of that face. Turning away, I push my way through the sweaty crush of bodies. They're cheering again for some other blood match. Shoulders shove me, but I ignore the men and make my way out the door into the startling brightness of the open street beyond.

I stand there for a moment, grappling with the impossibility that this is still Tuesday afternoon; that the sun is still shining. My friend is lying, sweaty and bloody, inside the dark building behind me. My brother is still missing, maybe dead. And out here, the world is going on exactly as it has been, without a change, without noticing the giant black void that has opened up inside me.

"Ana. Ana! Are you okay?" Yenni puts a hand on my arm and peers into my face.

I blink at her. No, I'm not okay. Everything is falling apart and I have no idea what to do about it.

"I'm fine," I manage to choke out. I take a deep, steadying breath. "Thank you for helping me so much, Yenni. You should go back to the *posada* now so you don't get in trouble. I know my way home from here," I lie. "As soon as I get home, I'll wash these clothes and get them back to you."

"You'd better," says Yenni, swallowing my candy-coated lie without even pausing to taste it. "That ratty old thing is my favorite." She gives me a quick hug. "Be careful," she says. "This is not a good part of town. Hurry home."

With a final squeeze, she leaves me. I watch her until she turns a corner and is lost to sight, then I face the still-crowded door of the fighting den. I can't just stand, waiting, in the middle of the road in front of the building, so I move up the street a little way and find a shadowed doorway to lean in. It smells like pee, but I ignore it, keeping my eyes fixed on the last place I saw my friend.

That piggy-eyed door guard has no idea how stubborn I can be. He may not let me *in* to see Victor, but he can't stop me from meeting him when he comes *out*.

I watch the sun creep its way across the spit-colored sky. I ignore my body asking for food, for water, for the chance to sit down, to doze, to pee. I ignore the leering men, stinking of alcohol, my heart pounding in my chest but my face flat. Through it all, I watch that door, carefully examining anyone who goes in or out.

It's almost full dark and I'm starting to worry about safety when I finally recognize the hunched shadow of Victor leaving the building. He turns and starts limping up the street away from me.

"Victor!" I call.

"Ana!" He laughs disbelievingly, rubbing the back of his neck with a split-knuckled hand. "I thought that was you I saw earlier. How do you always manage to show up in the worst places?"

I jog up to him.

"You're one to talk," I say, forcing a smile. "You're always in the worst places first."

Victor huffs another laugh. "I suppose you're right about that. Seriously, though, what are you doing in this part of town?"

"It's a long story," I dodge. "What about you? Why are you here, doing this?"

Night is falling fast, and Victor's features blur in the dim light, so I can't see his expression when he answers.

"You know what happened, Ana. Your papi died too."

"Yeah, but . . . you just, what? Ditched home and came to the city?"

"What was left for me up there? The mines?" Victor's eyes are hollowed out by the lengthening shadows. "I don't have anyone else, like you do. I had to leave."

"But fighting . . . ?"

Victor's shoulders stiffen. "What else am I good for? The only thing I know how to do is mining, and I'm never going back to that. There's no way out of the mines unless you leave them in a pine box, just like my papi." He turns his face away again. "Fighting's not so bad, compared to that."

He's not wrong. If he had stayed on the mountain, his fate would have been to live and die in the mines. But I can't believe that the best choice that's left for him is to let himself get beaten up for money. Still, I shouldn't judge him.

"Sorry," I say. "Forgive me?"

"Of course." His tired smile reopens his split lip and blood trickles down his chin. "What are friends for?"

For a moment we stand there looking at each other, noticing the differences the last week has brought about in each of us. Then the wind whistles over us and I shiver. That breaks Victor out of his thoughts.

"You should get out of the cold," he says. "Do you have somewhere in town where you're staying that I can walk you to?"

For a second I think about the *posada* with its clean sheets and good food. But Doña Arenal was very specific about me only being allowed to stay the one night. I know I can't go back there, especially with a bloodied boy at my heels. I'd get Yenni fired for sure. I also can't go home: it's dusk now and I'd never find my way safely up the mountain in the dark, even if I had the energy to attempt it. I shake my head. Victor reaches a battered hand to my face and wipes a tear from it with one grubby finger. I didn't know I was crying.

"Can I stay with you?" The words leave my mouth without my permission.

Victor bites his lower lip. "That's not ... the best idea ..."

"Please?" I feel more tears tracing their way down my face, but I don't make a move to stop them. I'm tired and overwhelmed and heartsick over not finding Daniel. I feel like I can't take any more right now. "I don't know anyone else in the city. I don't have anywhere else to go tonight. I'll go home first thing tomorrow, I promise."

Victor sighs, clearly not happy about the idea.

"Come on," he says.

I walk at his elbow as he heads into the darkening alley and down a warren of twisting streets. Victor stops in front of a stained door in a filthy, stucco-walled building.

"This is it," he mumbles, so quietly I can barely hear even though I'm standing practically on top of him. "This is where I live now."

Victor's split-knuckled hand rests on the peeling paint of the door. He pauses, giving me one last chance to change my mind. The dark buildings loom over us. I glance up the alley and decide that whatever it is that's waiting inside the building in front of us, it can't be as bad as walking through this neighborhood by myself after dark, leaving him alone.

"Great," I say. "Let's go in."

Victor pushes the door open and I follow him into the building. When the door shuts behind us, the darkness of the interior takes over and I stumble blindly in his wake. I can tell where he is less by sight than by the warmth of his body, as the inky hallway we're in is just as cold as outside. The hallway reeks of old sweat, dried vomit, and urine, and I try not to identify the trash on the floor and piled against the walls as I stumble over it to keep up with Victor.

At the end of the hallway, he turns left, into a windowless room. It's not large, but there are already five other young men and boys in it. One of them has a flashlight and is staring at a photo in his hands. In the darkness, his face glows like a moon.

Maybe this wasn't such a good idea, I think. But it's too late to make a different choice now. *You have no good choices,* I remind myself.

Victor walks to the back corner, but says to the room as a whole, "This is my friend Ana. Everyone leave her alone."

One by one, the boys peel their dark gazes off me. Victor collapses to the floor and lets his head fall against the wall. I lower myself gingerly down the other wall, our feet and the corner of the room making a rough square around a small, filthy pile of belongings I assume are his.

"Sorry," he says in a low voice. "This is all there is."

I stare around at the grimy walls, at the other hungry-looking boys and their miserable piles of stuff.

I find him studying me.

"This is where you live now?" I ask.

He nods.

"What happened to your house?"

"I couldn't make rent on kid's pay."

"No one could help you?" I ask. Though, given that he's here, I already know the answer to that. Victor's papi had come to the Cerro from the lowlands when the price of aluminum went up only five years ago. I remember Victor standing alone at the funeral. With his mami dead too and no family around here, he really is all alone.

"It's not so bad, really." It sounds like he's trying to convince himself. "Not as bad as being in the mines."

"It's so dark." My voice is almost a whisper.

He shrugs. "It's not as dark as the mines either."

I shudder, remembering my days stumbling through the bowels of the Cerro Rico. As if on cue, the boy with the flashlight turns it off and the darkness closes over us like a fist. I find my breathing coming faster and try to control my panic, but it's like I can feel the mountain around me again, the devil's hot breath at the nape of my neck. A tiny sob escapes me.

Next to me I hear a small rasp. A match whooshes to life in Victor's fingers. He digs through the pile between us with his other hand and comes out with a filthy stub of a candle. He holds the match to it, then sets the tiny flame on the ground, shaking the match out. I heave a shuddering breath.

"Thank you," I whisper.

"Not the end of the world to be afraid of the dark," he says without judgment.

I feel like I owe him a better answer.

"After the funerals, I went into the mountain to see if I could find Daniel," I say. "The tunnel collapsed. I spent two days trying to find my way out."

"God, Ana!" He sounds horrified.

My eyes pull to the candle as if drawn by magnets. I realize I'm shaking and curl my hands into fists so he won't see them. "When I was a baby, I was scared of the dark because I imagined it was full of monsters. But now I've lived and almost died in the dark, and I know that it's not full; it's empty. Completely empty. And I'm more afraid of it than ever."

I examine the tiny candle and try to calculate how long the stub will last before it gutters.

"I'm sorry," he whispers.

"Not your fault," I say with a shrug.

"Actually"—Victor's voice is strained—"it is."

That's enough to pull my eyes from the candle to his face. "What? Don't be ridiculous."

Victor won't meet my eyes. He's staring at the candle flame so intently it's like the world might end if he blinks. Even in the flickering light I can see stress lines on his face that weren't there before.

"Victor . . . ?"

For a long moment Victor is quiet. Then, in a voice almost too low to hear, he starts talking.

"I . . . I was there," Victor starts, "the day of the disaster. I know everyone is calling it a cave-in, but I was working in an old section of zone two, laying dynamite. I was"—he pauses, searching for the right word—"sloppy. I laid them badly." He shuts his eyes against the pain of the memory. "I only had the fuse partially out of the mine when they started going off." He lifts his eyes to mine, begging me to understand. "I made it out okay, but then I saw my papi's body and all the others. It was my fault, Ana. That's why I can't go back. The miners that died there that day, Daniel . . . I killed them." Victor starts to cry. "I'm sorry, Ana. I'm so, so sorry."

I sit, stunned, struggling to imagine the guilt he's been carrying. Victor has always had a tender heart, shooing stray dogs away gently when other boys would have hit them with sticks. I can't imagine how he must feel, thinking he was responsible for the deaths of multiple men. I remember how he wouldn't meet my eyes the day of the funerals. Now I know why.

"The mines are dangerous," I say, my voice as soft as I can

make it. "Things go wrong there all the time. It's not easy to lay dynamite right, and even when you do, you risk the mountain coming down on your head because of hundreds of years of people digging tunnels without a plan. It happens. No one would have blamed you. No one does blame you." My gaze drops to my hands in my lap and I admit the truth that has been eating holes through me like acid rain boring slowly through rock. "They blame me."

"You?" That startles Victor into looking at me again. "But you weren't even working there the day of the disaster."

I shrug. "I'm a girl. They say I should never have gone into the mine. That I called down the anger of the Pachamama . . . or the devil . . . whoever."

Victor snorts. "Seriously?"

"Seriously. When I went there to ask questions about Daniel, they spat at me and told me to stay away."

Victor shakes his head. "It's not your fault. That's just silly."

I reach over and take his hand, careful not to press on his split knuckles.

"It's not your fault either. Those deaths," I say, and it breaks my heart inside to realize I've finally added Daniel to that number, "were accidents."

Victor looks at our hands and doesn't say anything. The candle stub flickers between us, throwing our faces into light and then shadow and then light again.

Then my stomach growls loudly, breaking the moment.

"Hungry?" Victor asks, a sideways smile on his face.

"I guess," I say, embarrassed.

"Well, then, sorry again," he says. "I lost today, so I didn't get paid. I don't have any food on days I don't win."

Suddenly I remember the bundle that Carmencita gave me. I had tied my *manta* into a quick sling and pulled it over my shoulder. Now I rummage through it and find she packed me a few loaves of flat sweet bread and some cheese.

Smiling, I hold up the feast so Victor can see it.

He's stunned for a moment, then he breaks into a huge grin.

"Anyone who says you're unlucky is an idiot."

I laugh and hand him half the food.

And with that, the candle gutters out, leaving us in the dark. This time, though, the darkness doesn't feel as awful as it did before.

We sit like that for a while, a friendly silence filling the space between us. Then I hear Victor shift, his shirt scraping down the wall. His legs pull away from mine and I realize that he's lying down to go to sleep. I consider the bare concrete floor beneath us. It won't be comfortable, but I've slept on worse.

Gingerly, I lower myself to the ground, keeping the wall behind me. I fold an arm under my head and stare into the blackness, wishing it held the answers we both so desperately need.

14

For the first time since Santiago pulled me from the cave, the devil is waiting for me in my dreams.

I'm walking back and forth in front of the entrance to El Rosario in my dream, the moon high above me, unreachable, the rock lot empty. The whole scene has the flavor of deep night and, other than my footsteps, nothing disturbs the quiet but the sighing of wind over the holes in the rock.

I'm startled to realize I'm wearing a helmet but not my miner's suit. I can't figure out why I'm at the mine in the middle of the night. I scan the empty lot in front of me, the barren crags surrounding me. Nothing. But I can't shake the feeling that there's a danger I'm not seeing.

Then, finally, I turn and see an unmistakable glow coming from inside the mine. Just like the night I went looking for Daniel, someone is in there when they're not supposed to be.

And then, in the way of dreams, I'm deep inside the mine, in the choking heat of zone seven, and I come around a corner and find Daniel, wearing his miner's suit, sitting cross-legged in front of the devil. The glow I had seen was the reflection of his gas flame in the bloodshot light-bulb eyes of the Tío. I run over and shake my brother, but he doesn't respond. He sits there, staring glassily, not moving.

The devil looks from my brother to me.

"What have you brought me, that I should spare his life?" he asks.

I think frantically, but nothing occurs to me. Like the last time I faced the devil, I haven't brought anything to offer him. I grab a stick of dynamite from Daniel's belt and hold it out to him.

"Here," I say. "Take this."

The devil doesn't take it. I see the coca leaves sifting over him, see the burning cigarettes and streams of alcohol dripping out of his mouth. See my own pale face reflected in his painted light-bulb eyes.

"Not good enough," he snarls. And wetting his fingers with the tobacco-alcohol drool slavering his jaws, he reaches his damp fingers toward my brother. Before I can move, he closes them over the flame on Daniel's helmet and it goes out. From the light of my own helmet, I see the darkness overtake him. My brother's body hits the floor.

When I scream, it brings the devil's attention to me.

He grins.

"And what have you brought me, that I should spare yours?" he asks, reaching his still-dripping fingers toward my head.

Without thinking, I touch the fuse to the flame on my helmet. I hold the stick firmly between us and I have the satisfaction of seeing the devil's eyes widen slightly in surprise before the dynamite explodes in my hand.

I wake up with a gasp, and a sound stops abruptly.

I lie there in the dark, trying to figure out what the sound was. I focus on it with all my energy, trying to push the nightmare from my head; trying not to imagine the devil hunkering in the darkness, leaning toward me.

Stiff from lying on the concrete, I shift around a little until I find places on my hip and shoulder that aren't sore yet, and then I lie still. In the pitch blackness, I count my heartbeats and the snores of the boys in the room around me, each an island in a stale black sea. I try to think about happy things. Slowly, my panicked breathing settles and my muscles unclench. But still I can't figure out what the sound was that woke me.

In the end, it's not the sound but the smell that gives him away. As he leans over to push the bottle back into the pile of dirty clothes in the corner, I hear no sound of sloshing liquid; no sound of glass clinking against concrete. But my best friend's breath washes over me, heavy with alcohol, just like the breath of the devil.

Victor's drinking! I think. And between that and the horrible dream where I watch the devil of the mines kill Daniel, it's good that growing up with Papi taught me how to cry without making a single sound. It allows me to weep silently without disturbing the boys around me until I fall asleep.

———

The next time I wake, I can tell it's no longer night because the light leaking into our windowless room from the hallway allows me to see the space around me. I uncurl stiffly. Some of the boys have already left; some are still asleep. I have no idea what time it is. The ones who are awake are looking at me again with those slightly hungry eyes. I hurry to straighten my clothes and sit up. Victor is passed out beside me, arms thrown out to the side, boneless as a fish in a stall at the market.

I stare at him. When did my caring, sweet friend start trying to lose himself in a bottle? I had always assumed that the Mountain That Eats Men was named for the men who died in its mines. Now I see Victor and realize that the mountain is eating him too, as surely as if he had been killed in the rubble along with the other victims of the cave-in.

To distract myself from my thoughts, I take Daniel's little clay angel out of my pocket and turn it over in my hands. It hasn't held up very well to being carted around for so many days on end: its face is worn smooth where it's been rubbing against the fabric, and its remaining wing is half chipped off. It occurs to me that if the wings crumble off entirely, then it will only be a little clay man, not a little clay angel, and for some reason this makes me sad all over again.

"Hey, Victor's friend."

I turn to the young man who's trying to get my attention. I may be wrong, but I think it might be the one who had the photo and the flashlight last night.

"Yes?"

"Do you have any money?"

I shake my head.

"Any food?"

"Not anymore."

"Coca? Cigarettes?"

"I don't have anything," I tell him, and hear the truth in my own words.

"Oh." He heaves himself into a sitting position. "Are you staying or leaving?"

My eyes flick to Victor.

I need to go home. I've already put it off long enough. Now that I haven't found Daniel, I need to get home to Mami. But I hate to leave my best friend like this. In the murky un-dark of the room I can see older bruises beneath the fresh purpling from yesterday's beating.

There has to be a better way, I think.

I hate to leave him here battering himself for money and drinking to drown his feelings. Guilt has hollowed him out like four and a half centuries of mining have hollowed out the Cerro Rico. And like the mountain, if I put pressure in the wrong place, I'm afraid he'll collapse entirely. No, I need to be smart about this. If I'm going to help Victor, I need more than good intentions.

"Leaving," I tell photo boy. "I'm going home now. Will you tell him, when he wakes up, that I had to go home, but I'll come back and visit again when I can?"

"Sure," says the boy with a shrug. He doesn't seem to care much one way or the other now that it's clear there's nothing in it for him.

I pull myself to my feet as quietly as I can, though that's silly: if the noise of half a dozen people leaving for the day didn't wake Victor, it's unlikely that my quiet rustle will. The knee I twisted in the mine still aches in the mornings when I wake up, although once it loosens up, I can mostly walk normally now.

I limp out the door, down the dark, filthy hallway, and onto the street. When I step into daylight, I'm shocked to see the sun straight above me. In the darkness of that cinder-block box, without dawn to cue me, I slept through half a day! Angry at myself for wasting more time when I should have been home already, I hurry the best I can through the dingier sections of town, toward the areas I know and feel safe in. When I reach the familiar streets of San Cristobal, the miners' neighborhood, I turn under the big stone arch and cross the bridge by the miners' health center.

For a moment, I stare at the hulking red mountain before me. I let the big, heavy thoughts pile up in me: that I didn't find Daniel, that Victor is hurting, that Mami and Abuelita will either be frantic with worry if they think I'm alive, or completely filled by misery if they think I'm dead. That I have no plan for any of us.

My feelings swirl through me like ashes on the wind.

Staring at my feet instead of the horizon, I start walking.

The difficult work of walking uphill sucks away my energy, and instead of the usual three hours it takes to walk to my house from Potosí, with my wonky knee today it takes me more than five. By the time I'm turning the last cliff corner, the long shadows of late afternoon stretch over everything.

When I finally see our little house and the light spilling out the open front door, I feel relief surge inside me, a hot pressure against the backs of my eyes. I'm home. I hurry my limping steps as much as I can. But when I get to the open door, I see not just Mami and Abuelita inside, but also César. That alone wouldn't have confused me so deeply—César had been coming by every evening to update us on the search for Daniel, after all—but he's not sitting and drinking a cup of coca tea or talking. Instead, he's helping Mami and Abuelita pack all of our things into a pushcart.

Abuelita is facing away from me, folding our clothes and tying them into bundles. Mami and César are breaking down the bed frame. Mami's face is lined and drawn, and César is moving slowly, as though he were carrying a heavy load or a great sadness. The two of them move smoothly around the small space, and it strikes me that, for so little time having known each other, they work together easily. When Abuelita turns around to place a bundle in the pushcart, she is the first to see me.

She makes a strangled sound and drops the clothes, covering her mouth with her hands. Mami and César spin to see if she's all right, then turn to see what made her cry out. For a split second they all stare at me, faces pale and stunned. And then Mami is throwing her arms around me, sobbing hysterically, while Abuelita strokes my face with her knobby fingers. César pats me awkwardly on the shoulder.

"Ana!" Mami sobs. "*Mi hija!* You're alive! How are you alive? Oh, praise God!"

I hug her tightly, never wanting to leave this moment when I feel safe and loved and wanted.

Eventually the hugging ends.

"Here, sit here and tell us everything." Mami makes me sit down on the tied bundle of folded clothes. "When you vanished the same day Daniel was found, it broke my heart."

"Wait, what?" I'm glad I'm sitting down because suddenly it feels like the room is spinning around me. "You found Daniel? Where? Is he okay?" The questions tumble out, one after the other, so quickly I don't even know what I'm asking.

"The night you disappeared, a tunnel collapsed at the mine," César says, his rumbly voice cutting through my noise. "When we went to clear the rubble, we found Daniel behind it. He had run, the day of the disaster, away from the blast zone and deeper into the mine, trying to get clear once he realized that the explosions were wrong."

"Why didn't he come back up when the blasting settled?" I ask. "Where has he been all this time? Why did no one find him?"

César looks down at his hands.

"He didn't come back because he fell down a shaft in the darkness and wasn't able to climb out. We didn't find him because of how far he'd run: he was in a section we weren't working in anymore. There had been reports of bad air."

I stare at César, horror written on my face. In my mind I'm back in the dark and I can feel the cloud of poison dust wrap around me, making my voice tight. I swallow. "He was trapped there the whole time?"

César nods. "He had his lunch sack with him still, and your papi's. The food and water in them kept him alive, but he was alone in the dark for over four days." César's face tightens when he says this, as if thinking about it physically pains him.

"Where is he now?"

"At the hospital," Mami says when César doesn't answer right away.

The hospital! We never go to the hospital if we can avoid it—it's far too expensive, for one thing. Though our government's socialism means that the bed and the doctor's time is free, you still have to pay for all the medicine and supplies they use. By the time anyone we know finally has no choice but to go there, they usually die soon after. It's not a happy place.

"Oh no . . ." I manage. "How . . . What . . ." I don't even know what I need to ask, but César comes to my rescue.

"He had only sprained an ankle running from the first blast. Maybe a concussion too, but nothing too bad. But that second tunnel failure dumped rubble over him." I can tell by the tight lines bracketing his mouth that César considers it a personal failure he didn't find Daniel before this happened. "The rocks collapsed his rib cage. We just got him to the hospital in time for the doctors to save his life."

Tears leak down my face. I know how frightening it is to be hurt and lost in those tunnels. But to be crushed . . . I shudder. Poor Daniel.

"Will he be okay?"

"Yes," says Mami quickly, hugging me to her again. "The doctors have fixed him up. They're releasing him tomorrow. That's why we're packing up here."

I frown at the reminder of what's been confusing me ever since I walked in the door.

"Yeah . . . why exactly are you doing that?"

I feel Mami freeze where she's holding me.

"Well, just because you've been gone doesn't mean that everyone else's stories stopped." Abuelita chuckles.

I pull away from Mami and stare at Abuelita. "What?"

Abuelita snickers again and pats my cheek.

"Ask your mother," she says, and returns to her folding, smiling secretively to herself. I flick a glance over to César. Is he *blushing*? Now I'm really curious.

"Mami?"

Mami clears her throat, not meeting my eyes.

"Well," she says, "César and I are married now."

"César?" I ask, stunned. Then, in a show of deep insight, I add, "You?"

Mami smacks me gently on the side of the head.

"Yes, rocks for brains! Aren't you listening?" She finally meets my eyes and takes my hand in hers. "After they found Daniel, César asked me to marry him. I've stayed at the hospital with Daniel for the past five days, but now that they're releasing him, we're moving our stuff out of this house and into César's, over by El Rosario."

I think my jaw may be hanging open. I can't believe we're having this conversation. I mean, I suppose I noticed how comfortable she was talking with César when he came to our house in the evenings to report on the search for Daniel. And Mami was beautiful in her youth, with shiny hair and thick-lashed eyes, a face wide and flat like the moon, and a round figure that showed she had grown up with enough to eat. Even now, thinner, and with silver in her hair and worry lines on her face, she's beautiful. She even still has most of her teeth. But *marriage*? Again? It's only been a week since Papi's death.

I realize that there is a silence in the room and everyone is waiting for me to respond. I snap my mouth shut. What is there to say, really? What's done is done. I don't know if César drinks, but at least he's kind when he's sober.

"Congratulations," I say, my voice stiff. "I hope you'll be very happy together."

I feel a little of the tension go out of Mami's fingers.

"Thank you," she says. "Now, tell us about you. Where have you been? Are you okay?"

Mami and Abuelita settle themselves on the edge of the pushcart, close enough that they can both reach for me every few seconds, like they need to remind themselves that I'm still there and not a ghost who visits and then leaves. César leans against the wall, arms crossed in front of his wide chest as if he's bracing to hear more things he can blame himself for.

Taking a deep breath to steady myself, I tell them everything. I tell them about deciding to go into the mine. I tell them about hearing mystery men and choosing a different route. César scowls at that information but doesn't interrupt me. I tell them about climbing down into zone seven and finding Daniel's angel. I realize, with a start, that I was close to Daniel when I found it. He had probably been the voice just around the corner that I heard before the tunnel collapsed. Had I kept walking, instead of turning around, I might have found him. Then again, I tell myself, if I had continued down the tunnel, the blast that crushed Daniel would have caught me too, and Mami would have two kids in the hospital instead of one.

I tell them about the explosion and wandering lost for two days. I tell them about Santiago and Yenni and my time in the *posada*. I tell them I went into the city instead of coming straight home because I thought Daniel was there. I tell them I found Victor instead, though I don't tell them what he is doing.

César goes back to quietly packing in the background, as if he can't stand for his hands to be idle.

"How could you?" Mami demands, her hands cupping my face gently, the opposite of the hard words. "To go down there all alone, without telling anyone . . . It's a wonder you made it out alive!"

"I know," I say. "I thought I was going to die. But I made it out. I'm sorry, Mami."

She shakes her head.

"No more apologies," she says firmly.

"You are both given back to us from the dead," Abuelita agrees, pulling me into a bony hug. "This is a time for gratitude. A time of celebration."

I sag into their embrace, glad they've forgiven me. After a few minutes, Mami gets to her feet. "Now, let's finish packing so we can get home before full dark."

And I want to say that we *are* home, but I realize this isn't true anymore, so I get up from where I've been sitting and help Mami, César, and Abuelita pack.

For a little while, I feel uncomfortable, trying to process everything they've told me. But eventually their happiness at having me back and my happiness at finally being home safe and knowing that Daniel is alive covers over the awkwardness like clouds covering the moon. We all know it's still there, but, for the moment at least, none of us can see it.

With four of us working, we manage to empty our old house in under an hour. Then, Abuelita and I carrying packs balanced on our shoulders and César and Mami maneuvering the heavy pushcart, we walk together through the deepening dusk across the mountain to César's house and our new home.

—

When I see it in the distance, one lighted window in a row of mining houses, not off by itself like our old house, I get a strange feeling inside. The lights are welcome, and the fact that it has a good tile roof instead of just a flimsy sheet of tin leaning into an overhang of the mountain makes me happy. But knowing that from now on I will have to call this unfamiliar house my home leaves me feeling strange.

You'll get used to it, I tell myself.

But I know it's not only the house I'm going to have to get used to.

It's a nice house, I think as we walk in the door. With two rooms, it's bigger than ours, and better made too. I get the feeling that this is the kind of house that the wind will go around when it howls across the mountain at night, instead of whistling through it by a hundred tiny holes. César looks a little sheepish as he moves Mami's things into the one bedroom. I try not to notice. Then he points to the far corner of the main room. There's a cot along one wall that I assume is for Abuelita and a pile of blankets in an alcove. I move to put my stuff there, figuring it's where I'm going to sleep. But when I get there, I see that the alcove already has someone in it. When I see the little figure sleeping there, rolled up in the alpaca wool blankets, I drop my things on the floor and have to walk outside.

Standing in the freezing night air, I take gulping breaths to calm myself.

Somehow, I've been able to manage the thought of César being my new father: my father is dead, after all. But I had forgotten, on the walk across the mountain, and in hearing all about Mami's marriage, that César has a daughter too. Daniel is alive. The thought of suddenly having Belén as a younger sister is, for some reason, too much for me to bear.

I stand out there in the dark, clutching my stomach. After a few minutes, César comes out of the house and stands beside me.

"Ana," he says softly, "I know this must be hard for you."

I stare down at my hands. I refuse to cry in front of my former boss.

"This all happened very quickly," he goes on in his low, gravelly voice. "When we brought your brother to the hospital, at first they wouldn't admit him because your mami was already in debt and they didn't think she could pay. I tried to vouch for her, but they would only let me be a guarantor for the payment if I was legally connected to Daniel." César puffs out his cheeks. "Moving him down the mountain jostled his wounds. He was bleeding, turning blue. We thought he was going to die. Your mami and I found the hospital chaplain and had him marry us on the spot."

I stare at César.

"I felt responsible for not finding Daniel in time," César

goes on. "I needed to make it right. I know the proper way to do these things is to take them slowly. For there to be a plan and a party. To involve family and friends. But there just wasn't time for any of that."

He reaches out a hand. Instinctively, I flinch away.

César lowers his hand without touching me.

I feel terrible. César has never been anything but kind. It's not his fault men's hands scare me. I want to apologize, but the words can't make it out around the lump in my throat.

"You were only gone for a few days," César finishes gently, "and you came home to find your whole life changed. I know it's a lot to get used to. But it's going to be okay now, Ana. Your family is safe with me, and so are you. I promise."

15

I believe César's promise for about two hours. Then I wake up in the middle of the night and I hear him and Mami whispering about Daniel.

"...you're sure your cousin can take him?" Mami is saying.

"I called her from the hospital phone," César's low rumble answers her. "It's all set up. She can't catch the bus until Friday, but then she'll take him with her right away. He'll only have to be here tomorrow night."

Their conversation continues, but I have trouble hearing them over the rushing of blood in my ears. I'm furious. I feel betrayed. We've only just gotten Daniel back, and now they're sending him away? César said my family would be safe here, and then the first thing he does is kick Daniel out of his house? Why? And why is Mami going along with it? Is César abusive, like Papi was? Does she feel like she has no choice? Rage is a fire inside me, and long after their voices settle out into even breathing, I lie awake, hating the world.

Next morning, Mami and César leave before dawn so that they will get to the hospital as soon as it opens. I pretended to be asleep until after they had gone. I'm too angry to talk to either of them.

Standing by the cook fire, I find myself staring over the mountain in the dawn light, thinking back to that morning, which seems like forever ago now, when I joked with Abuelita about God's view. Though His view hasn't changed, mine certainly has. Before, our house sat alone on a barren crag by a used-up mine shaft. Now it's in a long row of miners' houses just a fifteen-minute walk from El Rosario. Before, there was total silence unless I decided to break it. Now there is a cheery bustle of half a dozen families starting their day. Before, I lived with my old family. Now I live with my new one. In some ways, it's as exciting as getting new shoes. But just like getting new shoes, it doesn't fit yet. I wonder how long it will take to break me in to this new reality.

I turn when I hear a clatter of rocks. Belén comes up beside me. She's still rumpled from sleep and rubbing her eyes. I remember the first day I met the little unicorn who dreamed so big and wanted to be so helpful when I was crying outside of school. I realize it must be a lot for her to take in too: a few days ago it was just her and César in the house. Now, suddenly, there are all these extra people filling her world, demanding to be a part of it.

"Hi," I say. *Brilliant. Super friendly.* I paste on a smile and try harder. "I hear we're sisters now."

"Yeah," she says, seeming a little unsure of herself. Her eyes meet mine. "Are you okay?"

My smile freezes. Is it obvious, even to an eight-year-old, that it's hard for me to be here?

"Why wouldn't I be okay?" I stall.

"You were trapped in the mine. You were lost. Everyone thought you were dead."

Oh. That makes sense. "Yeah, I'm okay now, thanks."

Belén squats down on her haunches beside me, and for a few minutes we just look over the horizon together.

I decide to change the subject. "Come on," I say, taking her hand and pulling her toward the house, "show me where everything is, and then you need to get ready for school."

Luckily, that's all the invitation Belén needs to start zipping around like a hummingbird, telling me all about my new home. On our second lap, I lift the pot off the cookstove and bring it in with us, plonking it on the table.

I let Belén chatter while I set the table with bowls and spoons because it's easier than finding the words inside myself to grapple with all of this. I'm happy that my mother has found a safer, bigger place to live. I'm glad there will be enough money so that Abuelita won't skip meals so I can eat. I'm so relieved that Daniel has been found. And yet . . . Daniel is injured, and they're sending him away. I can't quite see this place as my home, and it's just too strange to think of calling César "Papi." All my feelings, the good and the bad, mix inside me until I don't know what I feel anymore.

I wonder whether Mami's smiles are real or whether she feels mixed-up inside too. It's hard to tell. She's always had a thick shell covering whatever's underneath that I've rarely been able to see through. I'll have to ask her later, when we're alone.

When I lift the lid and take a sniff, I discover it's a salty broth with potatoes and carrots. It smells amazing, but even as my mouth waters, a frown knots my eyebrows as I ladle it into three bowls. Is César so much richer than we were that he can have more than coca tea in the mornings?

With a pang, I remember the huge breakfast at the *posada*. But thinking of the *posada* is dangerous in all directions: think forward, and I remember Victor and feel guilty for leaving him, hopeless and alone in that hovel; think back, and I remember Daniel and how I failed to find him in the mine before he was injured; stay put on the memory of the *posada*, and I wish I were there in that warm kitchen filled with familiar strangers instead of in this kitchen filled with strange family. No matter what direction my thoughts go, they lead to guilt.

"Good morning, Abuelita." I wake her.

"Ah, good morning, Ana." She pats my hand with her wrinkly one and fixes me with her knowing eyes. "Are you feeling better today?"

My smile curdles on my face. "Maybe I will after breakfast," I manage, and turn again to the table. *You're just going to have to get used to this*, I tell myself severely. *This is your life now.*

Abuelita gets up from her pallet and limps over to the table. She's always creaky first thing in the morning. I hand her a bowl of soup. Belén hops onto an overturned bucket and I take the folding chair at the head of the table.

"That's Papi's seat," Belén tells me.

I feel awkward sitting in César's place, but I try not to let it show.

"I won't sit in it when he's here," I say cheerfully.

Belén tears a small loaf of bread into sections and passes it around. I lift my spoon and take a sip. After not eating for two days underground, I don't think I will ever take food for granted again. And yet, even though it's delicious, eating like this, as a family, is putting me on edge.

Memories of eating with *my* family, before it fell to pieces, flood me. Papi and Mami sitting together on the edge of their bed, eating and laughing as Mami teased him about getting dust in the house; Daniel, Abuelita, and me facing them, sitting on cinder blocks stacked against the wall. Our house was far too small for a table, so each of us ate with our plate in our lap. There had been bad nights, but there had been good nights too. Nights when Papi was sober and the price of mineral was high enough that he wasn't worried. Those nights, he would tell us stories about his day, contradict Abuelita with science when she told her stories of ghosts and angels, and make Daniel and me recite something we'd learned at school.

I always took this very seriously, paying close attention to the teacher and, as soon as he or she shared a fact I thought would be good to share, repeating it in my head the rest of the day so as not to forget.

An equilateral triangle has three equal sides and three equal angles.

There are four oceans: the Pacific, the Atlantic, the Arctic, and the Indian.

Our first president was Simón Bolívar, and our country is named after him.

Daniel never took it seriously. He would summarize something his teacher had said or, more often than not, make something up on the spot. *I learned today that the earth is one million, five hundred, and twenty-three kilometers around the middle*, he would say, lying with the straightest of faces.

It took me a long time to realize that was what he was doing.

Usually Daniel was the one to get sick, but I remember one day in particular, when we were about seven, that I had caught a fever. The walls of the schoolroom seemed to pulse in and out with my headache, and the light from the windows stabbed at my brain. By the closing bell I was sweating and weak and Daniel had to support me as we stumbled home. We were halfway there when I realized that I hadn't learned anything and wouldn't have anything to say when Papi asked me for a fact.

In my fevered state, this seemed like the most horrible thing in the world, and I started bawling. Daniel held my burning hands in his cool ones, worry written all over his face, and asked me what was wrong. When I told him, he just shook his head.

Don't worry, Ana, he said, *we'll make something up together, and they'll never know any better.* I had stared at him, not knowing what to say. Daniel had winked at me. *First lesson from Professor Daniel*, he said, throwing one of my arms over his shoulders so that he could take most of my weight and get us moving again, *always lie in odd numbers. They're more believable.*

That night, when Daniel shared that he had learned that the

temperature on the moon was negative 13.7 degrees Celsius, I knew why.

"Ana?"

My head snaps up at Abuelita's voice.

"What's wrong, love?"

Whatever is showing on my face is too much. Both of them are staring at me.

"I'm sorry," I say quickly, pasting on a smile. *Always lie in odd numbers.* "That's the third time I bit my tongue this morning."

———

When breakfast is finally over, I stack the dishes in a shallow basin and leave them to one side to wash later.

"Come on," I tell Belén, "get dressed for school."

She bustles around the house, pulling on a colorful T-shirt and corduroy pants. When she reaches for her comb, I decide to make an effort at this big-sister thing.

"Here," I say, "let me help."

Belén shoots me a funny look but sits where I point and hands me the comb. I comb out her hair in long, smooth strokes and braid it into two plaits, like Mami used to do for me when I was little. *She won't be the little girl with crooked braids today,* I think as I finish, a bittersweet feeling in my belly.

Belén finds her notebook and together we walk toward the door.

Abuelita pulls me into a quick hug as I walk out. "Now that we have a man's salary again," she whispers into my ear, "there's no need for you to keep missing school. They won't be back here with Daniel for at least another three or four hours.

Stay at school if you like; I can tidy up here. You can help your mami and me as a *palliri* for a few hours every day when you're done with your lessons, but you don't have to work all day anymore."

I stare at her for a moment, stunned by the idea. Abuelita tucks a loose strand of hair behind my ear and gives me a big smile. "Go on now," she says.

Ten minutes later, in clean clothes, face washed, and hair freshly braided, I'm ready to go. I fold Yenni's borrowed clothes carefully and put them in a bag, planning to return them this afternoon. The school is about an hour closer to her house than César's house is.

Belén is waiting for me outside the door, smiling cheerfully. "Ready?" she asks.

"Off we go," I say, butterflies in my stomach.

I fall into step beside Belén. As we walk, kids bubble out of the other houses and join us. Belén is soon surrounded by a small pack of friends, the older ones towing or carrying their younger siblings. It must be nice for Belén to always have a group of kids her own age around. Daniel and I always lived so far away that we walked to school by ourselves. I imagine Daniel, lying against the white, white sheets of the hospital, and remember the thing I overheard Mami and César whispering about last night when I was supposed to be asleep. It sours my joy, and I walk a little faster to outpace the feeling.

I'm the tallest by far and I feel like the one grumpy old llama in a herd of happy sheep. *It'll be better when you get to school,* I tell myself. *Then the little kids will go do their thing and you'll be with your friends too.*

When we finally arrive, Belén picks up a stone and bangs on the door for us to be let in. When Doña Inés cracks the door open, the kids surge through in a chattering tide.

I'm carried in with them and find myself standing in the courtyard. We're barely in time for the morning scramble to get into lines for the anthem. I watch Belén and her friends find their places, then search for mine.

But my line, Daniel's line, is gone.

My eyebrows pull together as I scan and re-scan the courtyard. But no matter how hard I look, I don't find anyone older than eleven.

"Where are all the older kids?" I ask Doña Inés, who's latching the door behind me.

"Oh," she says sadly, "after the disaster at El Rosario, a bunch of work slots opened up. The older boys took them. I'm not sure what happened to the girls. They tend not to say. They just don't come back."

I thank her absently, and glance over the schoolyard again.

There is no one here older than me anymore. There isn't even anyone here my age.

The little kids jostle in their lines. It seems like a big game to me all of a sudden, and I see the school through old eyes. It seems like babysitting, not like an important step toward a better life. The teachers with their wide smiles that tarnish over time, every false comfort that slips past their lips corroding them further. The classrooms with their brightly colored posters that are fading day by day in the harsh light of the Cerro Rico. The kids, row after row of them, slowly getting older, slowly vanishing.

I swallow hard. How had I ever believed that school was really a good way to get off the mountain? I always knew I was just buying time, that I'd never make it to secondary school in Potosí. I always knew that girls like me don't really have choices. But it took seeing my line disappear to realize that I truly don't have a place here.

Don Marcelino sees me from across the courtyard. He breaks into a big, beaming smile and hurries over to me.

"Ana!" he says. "It's so good to see you. I visited your mami at the hospital when I heard you had disappeared and your brother was hurt. Everyone thought you must be dead. Yet, here you are, safe and sound. It's wonderful!"

I try to smile for him, but I'm not sure I manage it.

"And welcome back," he adds, but his tone goes up at the end, betraying it for the question it really is.

My eyes rove once more over the lines of little kids.

"Thank you, Don Marcelino," I hear myself say softly, "but I'm just dropping off my sister. I have some errands to run. I'm not here to stay."

And before I can second-guess myself, or decide whether I mean that answer to be for today or for forever, I turn away from the disappointment on his face and let myself out the big blue metal gate.

16

I lean against the peeling blue paint and let the cold of the metal seep into my shoulder blades. I have no idea why being the oldest kid in the school unsettled me so much. No idea why I felt like I had to run. But here I am. I can't go inside now. Better if I just take the day off, figure out what's wrong with me, and come back when I've sorted things through.

A clatter to my right makes me turn. At the small mine entrance a few hundred meters from the school, ore carts roll in and out of the mouth, pushed by sweating boys not much older than I am. How did we ever think—Victor, Daniel, me, any of us—that we could escape this?

I let my gaze rove up the drab cliffs in front of me. My future looks as bleak as the rocks. When I was younger, I thought about that future all the time: what I would do, where I would live. But in the past few weeks I've grown up: I've buried my father and survived the hellish mines of El Rosario only to crawl out and find that my world has changed in ways I can't control. I feel out of place in my new family; without a place at my old school.

Behind me, I hear the opening bars of the national anthem sung by an off-key chorus of high-pitched voices, led by Don Marcelino's booming bass. The impossible weight of all the days stacked between my childhood and death feels heavier than a fully loaded ore bin pushed uphill.

For a few minutes I let myself stand there and wallow in sadness and aloneness. Then, as the scratchy blare of the anthem winds down, I push myself away from the gate and start walking.

I pause as I reach a fork in the road. One direction will lead me to my new home. The other will take me down and around the Cerro Rico, to Yenni's house. I know I should go help Abuelita, but for just a few moments, I'm desperate to talk to someone whose life is working out and breathe air not laced with rock dust and regrets.

I turn left and start downhill to Yenni's.

I have the parcel in my hands and a smile on my face when the door opens, but it's not Yenni who answers the door, it's Santiago.

"Ana!" He breaks into a beaming smile. "What are you doing here?"

"I—I've come to see Yenni," I say. "I've brought the clothes she loaned me."

"Oh, yeah, I washed your stuff for you too," he says, pointing to a corner where Papi's suit and my clothes are clean and folded, the helmet stacked neatly on top. "But Yenni's not here. She's working."

I could smack myself. Of course Yenni's not sitting at home waiting for me to return her second-favorite leggings. It's Thursday. She has a good job in the city, working weekdays. So much has happened that it's hard to believe we're still in the same week that she found me. On Monday I was here, and she left early for work, and Santiago . . .

"What are you doing home? Shouldn't you be in school?" I feel like a hypocrite, but I ask anyway.

Santiago makes a face.

"I'm sick," he informs me. "Papi wouldn't let me go today."

I reach out and press my hand against his forehead, a reflex after so many years of worrying about Daniel.

"Stop it! One big sister is enough." Santiago swats my hand away, but not before I feel how hot he is. He's not faking it: he really is sick.

"Get into bed," I say, ignoring his sass. "We can talk with the door closed and you lying down."

Santiago climbs into bed without too much of an argument, a clear sign from any young boy that he's not feeling well, and lies against the pillows with a grumble. I put Yenni's folded clothes at the end of the bed.

"Was your mami happy to have you home?" he asks.

"Yes." I smile.

While Santiago settles back into his blankets, I tell him how, after my adventures in the city, I got home to Mami and how I'm suddenly living in a new house with a man who used to be my boss but is now my stepfather. "I have a new stepsister too," I tell him, "a little younger than you."

"And what about your brother?" Santiago mumbles, tired

after even that short time out of bed. His papi was right to make him stay home.

"Yenni thought she found him for me." I get up and get him a glass of water from the barrel outside. "But it wasn't the right boy. They did find my brother, though, back in the mine, while I was gone. You need to drink," I say, holding the cup out to him.

Santiago makes another face.

"Now you know what it felt like to be me the day you pulled me out of the cave."

I'm rewarded with a smile. He takes a sip of water.

"Happy?" he grouses.

"Soooo happy," I joke, putting on a big clown smile.

Santiago snorts and curls up in the blankets. "Well?" he asks once he's settled, showing I haven't managed to distract him.

"The boy in town wasn't my brother," I start, "but he was a friend. He's in trouble . . ." I trail off, not sure how to explain Victor's situation to a sunny nine-year-old. "And my brother, they found him too, but he's hurt. Really hurt. I . . . I wish I could make things better for both of them."

Santiago hears the catch in my voice. "But . . . ?"

I want to pour all my worry and heartache out at someone's feet—anyone's feet, even Santiago's—to not feel so alone with my problems. But seeing his young, feverish body hunched in the bed, I refuse to give him one more thing to carry.

"But life is hard and people are complicated," I say, "and I'm not sure how."

Santiago nods, as if that makes perfect sense.

I hesitate for a moment, but then I force the words out, admitting the terrible thing I overheard in the middle of the night. "And they're talking about sending Daniel away, down to the lowlands, to some cousin of César's."

Santiago considers me for a long moment.

"Sometimes people can't stay with you," he says softly, "but they still love you and they're still okay."

I glance at him, startled, but Santiago is looking at his hands, twisting the blanket between them.

"My mami left us to go work in the capital because she couldn't stand it up here anymore," he says.

"Oh." I put my hand over his. "I'm sorry." I had wondered where their mother was.

Santiago shrugs.

"I was little," he says, dismissing the old pain. "Yenni says she hates Mami for leaving us. But Yenni goes down to Potosí to make money at the *posada* and only comes home on weekends. She says she's trying to get enough so that she can get a little place in the city and I can come with her. But most of the time I'm here, and she's gone, just like Mami." He sighs. "I mean, I get it. It's bad up here. Sometimes the only way to survive is to get away."

I have no idea what to say to all that. I know how it feels to lose someone. My life used to be like a three-legged stool: I was supported, in different ways, by Mami and Papi and Abuelita. Then, suddenly, Papi was gone. Now it feels like my whole life is wobbling, unbalanced, likely to tip over at any moment and crash into a million pieces. Santiago's mother and sister have gone to work in different cities. My papi is dead and my brother is being sent away. We're both being left behind here.

I take Daniel's little angel out of my pocket, where I put it this morning, and run my fingers over its cracked edges. Just like the rock dust clinging to the lines of César's hands, the belief that my brother was going to be okay and that everything could go back to normal wasn't something I could scrub away easily. But in the week and a half since the mine disaster, that hope has flecked off me, a speck at a time, without my even noticing. I realize, as I sit here with Santiago, that there's none left. I know things will never go back to the way they were before. I will have to find a new way forward.

"You should get some sleep," I whisper. "If you like, I'll stay here and keep you company until you drift off."

Santiago, tired from all the talking, lets the conversation drop. Not much later, he's asleep, his fevered face flushed in the low light.

Leaving Santiago with a full glass of water by his head and Yenni's folded clothes at his feet, I close the door behind me and walk slowly home, Papi's helmet and suit tucked under my arm.

———

It's early afternoon when César and Mami come into view. César is carrying Daniel on his back and Mami is one step behind them, supporting Daniel. I can't help it. As soon as they crest the rise, I race out of the house.

"Daniel!"

I screech to a stop just in front of them, not sure what to do with my body. I want to throw myself at him and give him a giant hug. But I can see the strain on César's neck from carrying him up the mountain and I don't want to topple them all over. Besides, Daniel doesn't look up for giant hugs. His arms are limp by his sides, and even though he hasn't been walking, he looks as exhausted and sweaty as they are. His face is lined and pale and his eyes are half rolled back in his head. If Mami wasn't holding him against César's back, it looks like he'd fall to the ground.

"Is he . . . is he okay?" I ask, scrambling out of their way.

César grunts.

"Let's just get him in the house," says Mami.

I run and open the door wider. Abuelita stands by her cot, which she has cleared off for Daniel. Belén, home from school, stands well clear. César carries Daniel over to the cot and Mami helps lay him down. Daniel gasps in pain and slumps against the blanket. When César steps away, I can see the extent of his injuries. Daniel's torso is mostly covered in gauze bandages. Huge bruises blossom under the edges and there are rusty spots on the white where he's bled through. Worse, Daniel's making far too much noise as he breathes, like a broken air compressor.

Abuelita hands Mami and César cups of water. For a long moment, none of us says anything.

"The surgery to fix his punctured lung went well," Mami says into the silence. "They took out the chest tube yesterday. His lung has reinflated and they've reset his ribs. He's to breathe as deeply as he can, and sleep propped up. It will take two to three months for him to heal all the way." She recites these things robotically, as if she has been repeating them to herself all the way up the mountain like I used to with my memorized facts.

I rub tears out of the corners of my eyes. Daniel's breath is fast and shallow. Mami goes over and wedges a blanket under his head and shoulders, lifting him at an angle. It doesn't seem to help. Her shoulders slump.

"Ana," Mami says softly. "Come outside with me. We need to talk."

Abuelita takes her place at Daniel's side and wipes his face gently with a wet cloth. He squeezes his eyes shut and wheezes. His lips aren't the right color.

Numbly, I follow Mami out the door.

Mami finds a ledge away from the miners' houses. She sits and waits for me to join her. Below us, the city of Potosí is laid out like a blanket, stretching to fill the valley at the base of the Cerro.

"Ana—" she starts.

"You're sending him away," I break in.

Mami shoots me a sharp look.

"I couldn't sleep last night. I overheard you and César talking." I glare at her. "How could you? We only just got him back!"

"I've spent the last five days at the hospital with him," Mami says slowly. "When his breathing slows naturally overnight, it suffocates him, and he wakes up. He hasn't been able to sleep in a week except for when they gave him pain medication and put an oxygen mask on his face." She looks down at her hands, her face lined with sorrow. "We don't have pain medication," she says. "We don't have an oxygen tank. I can't watch him struggle for every breath, in agony for the next three months."

Tears drip off my chin into my lap. This morning I was angry at her for even thinking of sending Daniel away. But that was before I had seen him. Now all I want is for him to hurt less.

"The hospital won't keep him any longer," Mami is saying, "and it will be months before he's back to normal—and that's assuming he doesn't get bronchitis or pneumonia like he tends to. His lungs were so weak and scarred even before this. Now . . ." She trails off. Then she straightens her spine and continues. "César has a cousin who lives down near Sucre. That's half the altitude of the Cerro Rico, only 2,800 meters above sea level. There's much more oxygen in the air there. It's like putting a free oxygen mask on his face all the time. I can't get him more pain medication, but at least he'll have an easier time breathing while he gets better. César contacted them from the hospital. They've agreed to take Daniel for the next few months, until his ribs heal."

I don't say anything, remembering all the times I wished that I could get Daniel better air to breathe. Now, because of César, we're able to do exactly that.

Even though I know it's the only thing that makes sense, the hurt feels real. Mami wraps an arm around me and holds me until my sobs still. I know we should head straight back inside, but there's nothing we can do for Daniel at the moment, and I can't quite face everyone else right now. I realize this is the first time, since I got home, that it's been just Mami and me. I sit back and look at her.

"César told me why you got married," I say. "He said you did it because you had to. To save Daniel."

She smooths my hair out of my face and nods, waiting for me to go on.

"I get it," I say, "and I'm glad he was able to help Daniel, but are you really okay with this? Papi only died a week ago. Did you even want to be married again?"

Mami lets out a slow breath. "I am very grateful to César. He put forward the money that saved my son's life. He connected me with someone who can give him a safe place to heal. He has taken on the burden of caring for me, my mother-in-law, and my daughter. He is kind, and generous, and patient. He listens to me when I have something to say."

I wait, but she doesn't answer my question about whether she wanted to be married again after Papi.

"Is that enough?" I ask finally.

Mami looks at the house where César, Abuelita, and Belén are caring for Daniel.

"No," she says, a small smile softening her face, "but it's a good place to start."

───

That night, even though we all pretend to, none of us sleep. Instead, we lie where we are and listen to Daniel fight to get enough air to make it to morning.

Since Daniel took her place, Abuelita is sharing the big bed with Mami. César is on the floor next to it, lying on a pile of folded blankets. Their door is open so they can hear if Daniel needs them. Belén and I are in our usual alcove, and Daniel is on the cot. Just like Mami described, whenever his breathing starts to even into sleep, he jerks awake, gasping and coughing. The pain from that on his healing ribs keeps him awake and panting shallowly for the better part of an hour. Then, when he finally settles down, the whole process starts again. It's awful and it convinces me, like nothing else could, that he has to leave.

The next morning dawns bright and cold, just like so many others. I feel like there should be some way to mark it, something to make it stick out in our memories. It should be raining, or snowing, even! Some kind of freak weather should mark this day as different. Instead, it's just another mid-March day, as if Daniel leaving didn't matter to the universe one way or the other.

As soon as it's light enough to see, we all stop pretending to sleep and get ready to walk into town. The trip from Sucre to Potosí takes over three hours by bus, so César's cousin won't arrive before midmorning. We need to be ready to settle Daniel next to her for the immediate return trip to Sucre.

Abuelita says a murmured goodbye to Daniel while Mami packs his schoolbag with his clothes and things to send with him. After a quick breakfast, we're ready to head out. Abuelita puts her hands on Belén's shoulders. Belén gives us a weak wave. It's Friday, so she's off to school. Abuelita will stay home in case she's needed.

Mami and I are going along so we can be with Daniel until the last possible minute. César will carry him. César boosts my brother onto his back and the four of us set off. With gravity pushing Daniel onto César instead of away from him, Mami doesn't have to support him on the downhill walk. Instead, she carries his things. I feel useless with nothing to carry, but I walk next to Daniel the whole way down the mountain. I tried a couple of times last night to talk to him, but conversation was too tiring when he had to fight for every breath. Pretty soon, we gave up. Now I hang on to the laces of his tennis shoe like a three-year-old, wishing he didn't have to leave us.

We need to stop a bunch of times to let both Daniel and César rest, but we make it to the bus station with twenty minutes to spare. César finds a bench against a wall and sets Daniel on it. I perch beside him while César and Mami head off to buy him a ticket.

After the jostling of being carried down the mountain, Daniel's face is almost gray and his sweat has soaked through the collar of his shirt.

"It's going to be okay," I tell him.

"How"—Daniel scowls at me between gasps—"is any—of this—okay?"

I look at his eyes and realize they're wide not just from the pain.

"Are you scared?" I ask.

Daniel hesitates, then nods.

"Don't be," I say softly. "You're getting away. Far away from here. Far away from the mountain and the mines. Far away from the rocks and the cold. You're going to a green valley, and you're going to sink your toes into the soft black soil. You're going to breathe air full of oxygen and grow strong and healthy."

I see tears gather in the corners of Daniel's eyes.

"We were—supposed—to do that—together," he manages.

"Maybe it's not quite like we planned," I admit. "But having you alive is still a dream."

With a screeching of brakes, César's cousin's bus arrives.

She's extra short and round with very bright eyes and a high, clear laugh. She reminds me of a bird in her bright colors and with her quick ways. César greets her with a hug and introduces her to Mami. As the women go over Daniel's care and how they'll stay in contact, César walks over to where we're sitting.

"Time to get on the bus," he says to Daniel. "Are you ready?"

Daniel looks at me. I squeeze his fingers and give him an encouraging smile.

"Better air is waiting," I say, tucking what's left of the little mud angel into his hand.

Daniel's fingers wrap around the angel, and giving me the ghost of a smile, he turns to César.

"I'm ready," he says.

17

I'm amazed at how easily my days fall into a new routine. Mami and I get up before dawn, like we always did, and prepare breakfast. After that first day we don't have soup anymore, but it's a refreshing treat to always be able to lay out loaves of flatbread to eat with our coca tea. Once the tea is ready, Mami wakes César, and I help Belén brush and braid her hair. After breakfast, César heads off to the mine, and Belén meets up with her friends from the neighboring houses and walks down the mountain to attend half-day school.

So far, in the two weeks since Daniel left us, I've found an excuse every day to avoid going back to school. And every day that I've let it slide has made it easier to skip the next day.

There's plenty to do: merging two houses means that there's lots of laundry, cleaning, preparing food, and thinking about what we need to buy and what will have to wait. I'm kind of surprised that Mami hasn't made a bigger fuss about me going back to school since, as a supervisor for the cooperative,

César must make more than Papi did, but she's let me work as a *palliri* with her and Abuelita every day without comment.

Though there are times I miss the quiet, it's nice being near other people. I hadn't realized how lonely our life was before. I like seeing the glow of other windows when I'm working outside past nightfall, and it's cheerful to say hello to people during the day. It's also nice to see Mami and Abuelita start to make friends. Instead of breaking rock alone, we all now sit on the slag heap down the road from El Rosario with the other mining wives. They're mostly women Mami and Abuelita knew from before, but never had the time to talk with. Now that they're three minutes away instead of the better part of two hours, Mami and Abuelita are rekindling all kinds of old friendships.

And though it's hard to have new people inside the house too, I do like Belén. And César is still nice. He doesn't drink too much and, so far, he hasn't hit Mami.

Yet, for all the good in my new life, there are times when I miss the life that fit me more comfortably. Times I even find myself missing Papi, just because I knew how to live the life that he was part of and now I feel so unsure of myself. Times I still wake up, haunted by dreams of the devil, as if nothing had changed at all. Most of all, though, I miss Daniel. I don't remember life when he wasn't one step behind me. I keep turning around, expecting to share something with him, and not seeing him there. I miss the way he could make me laugh. I miss having someone who knows what life used to be like. I even miss his mischief and the way he used to tease me.

Every few days, one of us makes the effort to go to the post office in Potosí. We send letters to Daniel, money to César's cousin, and pick up any letters they've sent us.

Dear Mami, his last letter said. *You were right. It is so much easier to breathe down here. I don't feel like I'm choking all the time. Everyone is nice to me and I'm learning about farming by watching them. Someday soon maybe I can start to help out for real. Yours, Daniel.*

His letters are positive, encouraging. It still hurts to have him gone.

This morning, though, doesn't follow the pattern. Instead of his standard mining gear, César comes out of the bedroom in dark trousers and a knitted alpaca-wool sweater. I blurt out the question before I can stop myself.

"Why are you all dressed up?"

"We're off to the city," César says, as if that explains it all. "Your grandmother wants to catch Mass."

I raise an eyebrow at him. We're not that religious and today's not even a Sunday. We only go to Potosí if we need something or when we're getting Daniel's letters. In fact, now that I think about it, the last time I sat in a church was for my father's funeral.

"It's a Friday," I manage, still not entirely able to decipher the sparkle in his eyes.

"Well," he says, straight-faced, "no time like the present to get more devout."

I can tell he's teasing me, but I still haven't figured out the joke when Belén comes shrieking into the house, bouncing up and down on the balls of her feet.

"It's the first of April! It's the first of April!"

César scoops her into a hug.

"Is it?" he asks, pretend confusion on his face. "So what?"

"Pa-*pi*!" she groans, making the second syllable go on forever. "They've been talking about it in school all week. I had to practice a special dance and everything! Tell me we're going into town, pleeeeeease?"

"We're going into town," he says, and puts her down.

Belén shrieks with joy and runs off to change into something fancier.

Now I'm in on the joke. The first of April is the anniversary of when the Spanish first found silver in the Cerro Rico in 1545. It's a festival day, and down in the city there will be speeches and parades all day long.

"The first of April, huh?" I say to César, who managed to keep a straight face through all of Belén's ruckus. "I suppose it's as good a day as any to get holy."

I hadn't noticed before, but César's eyes crinkle in the corners when he smiles.

———

We head out as a family: Mami and Abuelita in their many-layered skirts and bowler hats, César in his slacks and sweater, Belén in a frilly pink disaster of a dress with bows in her hair. I'm in a knee-length skirt I saved from my school days and a pretty blouse with embroidered flowers on it. Even though they make my toes cold, I'm wearing strappy sandals with little heels that were hand-me-downs from Susana because I like the way they look, and a cardigan to keep me warm. The adults walk in front and Belén and I follow half a dozen steps behind.

That's the way it is here, I think. *Girls follow in their mothers' footsteps; boys in their fathers'.* It wasn't something I had ever really thought about before, like you don't think about having two hands or one nose. It just always was. But now, with Daniel off in the lowlands instead of in the mines, and Victor swearing to never come back, I wonder if there might be other paths for me too. It's a surprising thought, like wondering what life would be like with two noses.

When we get to church, we shuffle into a spot—off to the right, toward the back, where no one will give us dirty looks for being miners—and sit down. Mami and Abuelita smile when they see women they know. I'm sandwiched in between Mami and Belén. Abuelita and César sit on the edges.

As the opening song starts, César gives Mami a soft look and she smiles back at him. I know they both entered into this marriage because they felt they had to, but more and more, I catch them in moments like these and I wonder whether they're starting to like each other too. I feel like a spy and focus on the rounded shoulders of the woman in front of me.

My mind wanders through the opening prayers and the readings, but when we stand to hear Padre Julio read the Gospel, I pay attention again. I've always liked Padre Julio. He's an old man, so old you sometimes wonder how much of anyone's confession he hears before he absolves them, but he's kind. For a moment before he starts reading, he lets his rheumy eyes wander around the church.

"A reading," Padre Julio starts, "from the Gospel According to Matthew."

We all mumble the response, each one a little faster or slower than everyone else, so that, if you didn't know the words, it would be an unintelligible murmur.

"*Then Jesus was led up by the Spirit into the wilderness to be tempted by the devil.*"

Cold washes over me as Padre Julio's reedy voice begins the passage. Ever since my first day working in El Rosario, I've paid a lot more attention to mentions of the devil than I did before. He still stalks my dreams, though most nights I wake and don't remember what happened in them.

"*When he had fasted forty days and forty nights,*" Padre Julio goes on, "*he was hungry afterward. The tempter came and said to him, 'If you are the Son of God, command that these stones become bread.' But he answered, 'It is written: Man shall not live by bread alone, but by every word that proceeds out of God's mouth.'*"

An icy trickle of sweat traces its way between my shoulder blades. I went into the mountain with Papi because the price of zinc and tin was high and we needed more money for food. Is God telling me I was wrong to do that?

"*Then the devil took him into the holy city. He set him on the pinnacle of the temple, and said to him, 'If you are the Son of God, throw yourself down, for it is written: He will command his angels concerning you, and on their hands they will bear you up, so that you don't dash your foot against a stone.' Jesus said to him, 'Again, it is written: You shall not test the Lord your God.'*"

I think of my brother, struck down by stones. When had Daniel ever put God to the test? And if he did, God failed that test: Daniel was so badly hurt he had to leave us. Moments like this, standing in the middle of my new family, make me miss my brother even more than usual.

"Again, the devil took him to an exceedingly high mountain, and showed him all the kingdoms of the world and their glory. He said to him, 'I will give you all of these things, if you will fall down and worship me.' Then Jesus said to him, 'Get behind me, Satan! For it is written: You shall worship the Lord your God, and you shall serve him only.' Then the devil left him, and behold, angels came and served him."

I think about all the times I've gazed down at Potosí and wished for all it contained, and I cringe. What is the passage trying to say? Why is it so bad to want better things? Religion is confusing.

Padre Julio looks up from the book in front of him. "The word of the Lord," he proclaims, and his voice has lost all its weakness.

"Glory to you, Lord Jesus," I manage, then I collapse into the pew, relieved that the reading is over. It feels too close to home.

I try to focus on Padre Julio's homily, but my thoughts are like the dust motes swirling in the colored light coming through the stained-glass windows—directionless, spinning.

It's time for the presentation of the gifts, and I think about how the same men who bring up the bread and the wine to the priest will bring coca and cigarettes to the devil in just a few hours, when the feast day is over and they head back to the mine.

We shuffle up to Padre Julio in a line for communion, like miners shuffling into the mouth of the mine at the beginning of a shift. Then we're back in our seats, heads bowed, eyes closed.

I must have made a noise, because beside me, Belén whispers, "Shh, or we'll get in trouble!"

I raise my head off my hands. I am not in the mine, I remind myself—I'm kneeling in a pew. Padre Julio is cleaning up the altar. Belén gives me a look that begs me not to wreck this special day by getting us in trouble. When we sit back, my eyes catch César's, and hiding a smile behind one of his battered hands, he gives me a small wink.

I give him a tiny ghost of a smile and then stand with my family for the last blessing.

———

I'm worried we're going to be stuck near the church forever while Mami and Abuelita talk to everyone they've ever known, but César says we should get going if we want to find a good spot to watch the parade. The streets are packed with people, but I don't see Yenni or Santiago or Victor. Not that I'm really expecting to see any of them at the parade, of course. But still.

We find a spot on the steps of the cathedral, high enough above the street to be able to see the marching groups as they enter the plaza before they loop around in front of the bishop's residence and the Municipality. César steps away from us, and I see him bend double in the shadow of one of the cathedral's pillars, coughing. But then he straightens and finds a food vendor. When he comes back, he hands me a sleeve of popcorn and gives a big pink puff of cotton candy on a paper stick to Belén. If I hadn't been watching him instead of the parade, I would never have known he had gone away for any reason other than to find us snacks. I want to ask him if he's okay, but then the music cranks up and none of us would hear each other anyway. I smile to thank him for the popcorn and settle in to watch the groups.

There are hundreds and hundreds of people in the parade. All the divisions of society are represented there—from neat rows of government workers in suits to secretaries wearing makeup and high heels to construction workers holding their banners in thick-knuckled hands to blocks of kids in matching uniforms representing the different schools of the city. Belén squeals with delight when the traditional dancers passed us, dressed in short skirts and bright blouses, twisting and twirling to the music. My favorite are the crossing guards because of their silly white tiger costumes. Though I would never admit it to anyone, one of my favorite things about coming into the center of downtown Potosí is having the tigers take my arm and escort me across the crosswalks.

"Today is the day," booms the mayor over the dance music, "that we commemorate the discovery of silver in our mighty mountain in 1545. Think of the glory," he goes on. "A city built at the foot of a richness that changed the world. The great city of Potosí was larger than London, Paris, Rome, or Madrid. It was the hub of wealth of the Spanish empire; it was called the eighth wonder of the world. Is it any surprise that the first coat of arms of our city read: *I am rich Potosí; I am the treasure of the world; I am the king of all mountains and the envy of all kings?* No, because it was all that, and more."

I lift my eyes from the mayor to the brick-colored beast looming behind the Municipality. Someone has put lights along its outline so that, even after dusk, people down here in the city can see the silhouette of the marvelous hill that has gifted the world with its treasure.

I live on that mountain. I walk its slopes and live in a house made with bricks and rocks from its sides. My father died on it; my brother was crushed in it. It has ruled my days and my nights for my entire life. And for all that, listening to the mayor as he drones on about the wealth of nations and the glories of the world, I don't recognize it at all.

Worst of all, the music is no longer loud enough to cover the sound of César coughing.

I find I've lost my taste for popcorn.

Though we usually stay as long as possible to make the most of our trips to town, today we end up leaving early. When the parade ends and the mayor finishes his speech, even Mami and Abuelita notice that César isn't feeling well. So, step after slow step, we all trudge home, onto the mountain that seems less and less of a thing to celebrate.

18

By the time we get home, César is having trouble walking more than a dozen steps without pausing to cough. And the cough is everything a cough should never be: a barking, wet, wrenching sound, followed by a rattling inhale. And then another. And another.

As soon as we get to the house, Mami hurries him into their bedroom and closes the door. Abuelita, Belén, and I trail in and stand awkwardly in the main room, unsure how to help.

"Ana, go put on some tea," Abuelita says as she starts to loosen Belén's braids. I move quickly, grateful to have something useful to do.

When I bring in the tea, Abuelita has managed to get Belén sitting in a corner, reading from her schoolbook, so I walk up to the bedroom door and knock. Mami lets me in and I hand her the pot and a cup. When she turns to set it by the bed, my gaze snags on César. He's hunched over on the mattress as a coughing fit grips him, fighting to breathe. I notice he's changed out of his church clothes into a plain T-shirt and sweatpants.

That's the detail I latch on to: his clothing. It helps me ignore the waxy sheen of his face, the way his huge hands clench the sheets, and the bright red speckles staining the pillowcase. Mami is shushing and muttering gentle nothings like she would when Daniel was sick, wiping his face with a cloth and trying to coax him to sip from the cup. I feel shaky and, not sure my legs are going to hold me up, lean against the door-frame and watch them.

Not César, I beg no one in particular. *Please, not César.*

Not Mami's new happiness. Not the paycheck keeping Belén fed. Not our one connection to a cousin in the lowlands for Daniel. Not the strong arms between all of us and the next group of drunken miners with mischief on their minds. Not the mountain of a man who has never been anything but kind to me.

After an eternity, the fit passes and César collapses onto the mattress. Mami dabs his forehead. When he breathes, the air enters his lungs with the same hissing and whispering that the air tubes make snaking into the mine.

Both are filled with too much rock dust, I think numbly.

Mami shoos me into the main room and closes the door behind me.

"How can he be this bad this quickly?" I ask Abuelita. "He was fine yesterday. He was fine this morning!"

"It doesn't sound good," she agrees, her face seeming older than usual. "It might turn into something serious."

I think of the miners' hospital with its mint-green walls and

cold metal gurneys and the word she's not saying—*la silicosis.*
Sometimes, like when Daniel was just there, the wards are
empty. Sometimes they're full of men and boys, slowly suffocating. When my grandfather died of silicosis, I remember
what Papi said: *It's only fair. We take the rock out of the mountain. Its revenge is to fill us with it.* He was deeply drunk at the
time, but even so, I didn't talk to him for a week after that. It
was just too horrible.

I realize that Abuelita's been speaking and I haven't heard a
word she's said.

"I'm sorry." I force myself to focus on her. "What?"

"I said, someone should buy more cough medicine." She
motions toward a green plastic bottle on the edge of the table.
"We gave the last of it to Daniel and never bought more."

"I can go," I say, jumping to my feet, glad again to have some
useful task. Glad to be able to leave.

Abuelita knows me so well.

"Get some money and go to the pharmacy in San Cristobal,"
she says. "They're likely to give you a better price than one of
the fancy pharmacies in a non-mining neighborhood."

I walk over to the small ceramic jar on the shelf where
we keep our money. Opening it, I frown. There is one fifty-
boliviano bill and a few small coins. Why is there so little
money? I know César puts his salary in there every time he
gets paid.

I hear César cough again in the far room, and I shelve the
mystery of the missing money for later. I shove the fifty into
my pocket. I think about the four-hour walk we all just took
back from town and how, even if I hurry, it will be at least

246

seven more hours before I can get César the medicine—two and a half downhill if I rush, at least three and a half uphill. It's the middle of the afternoon. I don't know if I can make it to Potosí before the shops close. Even if I do, I'll be walking the last hour and a half home in the dark.

Abuelita must have done the same math.

"Do you think you can stay with your fancy friend, the maid, again tonight?" she asks. "You can get the medicine, stay with her, and then come home first thing in the morning."

"I'm sure that would be fine," I say, though I have no idea whether it's true. Besides, if I *can* make it in time to get the medicine today, then I will come straight home. Yes, I'll likely have a bit of a walk in the dark, but it seems worth it to help César. Getting yelled at by Abuelita for taking a risk after I'm already home safe is better than having him get sicker overnight. "Will he be all right until then?" I ask.

"It's all in God's hands." Abuelita passes me the empty bottle but won't meet my eyes. "Make sure you get the same kind."

When she turns to go sit with Belén, I grab a battery-powered flashlight for the walk home and slip it into my *manta*. I take a moment to shuck out of my fancy clothes and put on some sweatpants, a sweatshirt, and comfortable shoes. I tuck the money, the empty bottle, and a loaf of bread to serve as dinner into my *manta* along with the flashlight, and head out the door.

———

One trip down and back up the mountain is plenty. Starting out on yet another lap in one day, my calves and hamstrings wail at me. I ignore them. All I can think about is César and how desperate I am not to lose him. Three hours is a lot of time to think, even when you tell yourself to pay attention to where you're walking, even if you slide down the scree hills to make it go faster instead of taking the path. I think about all the things being in César's family gets for us: safety, food, a bigger house, a place in the community. But if I'm honest, it's not these things that make me hustle. It's that, despite my mixed-up feelings about how much my life has changed, I think I might be starting to care about César just for him.

Though I hurry, by the time I make it to the pharmacy, the shop is closed. I bang on the wrought-iron grille pulled over the doorway, but no one comes to let me in. Now that I think about it, given that today was a holiday, it might not have been open even if I had gotten here earlier.

I thread my fingers through the grille and rest my forehead against the cold ironwork. I need the medicine. I refuse to go home without it. I won't show up in César's doorway until there's something I can do to help him. Sighing in frustration, I turn away from the pharmacy and follow Abuelita's suggestion.

It's a Friday, so Yenni should still be at the *posada*. Remembering Doña Arenal's command that I only be there the one night when I was at death's door, I'm not sure of my welcome. Even so, thoughts of warm rooms and good food point my feet in the direction of the inn. Outside the servants' gate, however, I pause.

Deep, deep in my heart, so deep the cold Andean winds haven't managed to snuff it out yet, I've been holding a hope that I might someday get a job at the *posada* too, like Yenni. I have no idea how she managed to get a choice like this, but I want a way off the mountain desperately. And, as much as I want a meal from Carmencita and a safe bed for tonight, I hate to gamble with my chances of a future job. I'm still debating whether it's worth making them mad at me by showing up and begging for a roof for another night when the door opens suddenly and Yenni is standing in front of me.

"Ana? What are you doing here?"

"Yenni? Oh, hi," I say awkwardly, covering my surprise with an overly-bright smile. "Are you done for the week?" She's still wearing her maid's uniform.

"Usually I would be, but with the parade and everything, there's more to do." Yenni shuts the heavy door behind her. "Carmencita didn't have enough sugar to finish the breakfast breads for the morning. I need to run out and get some more. The little corner store should still be open, but only for another fifteen minutes or so. Want to keep me company?"

"Sure," I say, falling into step beside her as she jogs down the street.

"So," she says, "what brings you to the door of the *posada* at this hour?"

I tell Yenni all about the parade, since she missed it, and César getting sick, and the pharmacy being closed. Yenni shakes her head in sympathy.

"They definitely won't be open until tomorrow," she agrees.

As we walk, we update each other on our brothers: I tell Yenni about everything that has happened with Daniel, and she tells me Santiago is feeling better and is back to school.

We get to the little corner shop. It's tiny really: only a room in a woman's house. There's not even a door to get in: it's a barred window that opens onto the street. You can look through the bars into the small room and see the items on the shelves along the walls. It's basic stuff: sugar and rice in little plastic twist-tie bags, cans of Inca Kola, batteries, pencils, single-use shampoo pods. The woman sits just inside the window, and you ask for what you want. You give her your money and she hands you the item and your change. It's a good system. She can stay open late and still be safe because she's behind the heavy iron bars, inside her house.

Yenni puts her purse on the windowsill and counts out the coins. She pays the woman, and the woman hands her two of the plastic bags of sugar and shuts the wooden shutters inside the window. We barely made it in time before she closed up for the night. When a motorcycle backfires behind us, we both jump in surprise and whip around to face the street. When we see the cause of the noise, we laugh shakily. Yenni smiles at me, about to head back to the *posada*. I decide now is the time to ask.

"So, Yenni . . . I was wondering . . . is there any chance I could spend the night with you?"

Yenni, looking uncomfortable, shakes her head.

"No, sorry. I can't bring you with me like before. I know Doña Arenal let you stay the last time, but afterward I overheard her talking with one of her lady friends, saying she regretted it. That she was running an inn, not a charity. If I brought you back, I'm afraid I'd lose my job."

"Oh, Yenni, I'm so sorry."

She shrugs. "Not your fault. The *doña* changed her mind, is all."

I try not to let my disappointment show on my face. Not just for tonight, but also for the future. If the *doña* changed her mind about me, it means she probably won't ever hire me.

"Do you need a place to stay? Are you alone?" Yenni seems worried.

I can't put my problems onto her. She needs to get back with the sugar so that Carmencita can finish the baking for tomorrow. She needs to keep her job and get her brother off the mountain.

"No, I'm fine," I lie. "I can stay with my cousin. I just missed Carmencita's cooking."

Yenni dimples.

"Well, come around the back door tomorrow morning and I'll sneak you out a piece of the sweet bread," she says.

"Okay," I say. "See you later."

"Bye, Ana!" Yenni waves over her shoulder and hurries off in the direction of the *posada*. For a few minutes I stand there, leaning against the peeling paint of the concrete wall, resting my forehead against the iron bars of the closed shop window. Finally, I huff out a breath and straighten. The night is only getting later, the streets more dangerous. I need to figure out another plan as quickly as possible.

As I step away from the window, my toe catches on something. Bending down in the dim light, I see that it's Yenni's coin purse. She must have missed putting it in the pocket of her apron when she startled at the motorcycle's noise. I pick it up and open it to be sure. I gasp at the money inside: forty-eight bolivianos and fifteen centavos! That's a lot to drop. I jog after her, but when I get there, the *posada* is shut down for the night, the door bolted. I tuck Yenni's purse carefully into my *manta*. I'll keep it safe for her tonight and give it back to her tomorrow, since she already invited me to come by and get some sweet bread.

Then, out of options, I head to the only other place where I know someone in Potosí: I go to see Victor.

I find the right building, push open the door, and click on my flashlight so I don't stumble in the littered hallway. But when I get to the room at the back, two of the other young men are there, but Victor's not. My eyes fly to his corner. I see the small pile of his things and breathe again. He's not here now, but he hasn't left forever. When you have very little, you don't leave it behind if you can help it.

"Hey there," says one of the guys, leering at me. I instinctively don't like him.

"Hello," I say, willing my voice to stay steady over the fearful thudding of my heart. There are no other doors in this room; no windows. I have no idea when Victor will be back. I begin to rethink the wisdom of coming here. At the time, I wanted nothing more than to get off the dangerous streets. Now I glance around this dark, cramped room and wonder whether the street would have been the safer option. The beam of the flashlight wavers slightly. I realize my hands are trembling and tense the muscles in my arm, refusing to show my fear.

"Leave her alone, Osvaldo," comes a voice from the far corner of the room. The other guy pushes himself up on an elbow. "She's the fighter's friend, remember?"

"As if I were afraid of him." Osvaldo snorts.

"Of course not," the other one says soothingly, "but a friend of a friend, right? Let's be nice to her, eh?"

"Shut up, Joaquín," he grumbles, but he turns away from me and walks over to his corner.

I give Joaquín a grateful nod. He winks at me and then goes back to what he was doing. I force myself to relax, sit, and wait for Victor.

It seems like it's hours later, though in the windowless space it's difficult to tell the passing of time, when he finally walks in. His eyes go first to the light: I've put the flashlight on the floor beside me, pointed at the ceiling. The small circle of white light isn't much, but in the otherwise dark room, it's a beacon. From there, Victor's eyes move to me and go wide.

I let out a breath I didn't realize I was holding. It has been nerve-racking, waiting as the shadowy room around me filled with the shapes of strangers. My old terror from the mines clung to me like stale sweat, and I alternated between trying to be invisible and trying to appear fierce. Neither worked very well. Now, with Victor here, I feel safer. Though, looking at my shield, I wonder just how much he could stand up to before breaking.

Victor plonks onto the floor across from me. I pull the loaf of bread out of my folded *manta* and rip it in half.

"Here," I say. "I brought you dinner. Again." I put the larger half in his lap.

"Ana, what on earth are you doing here?"

"Bringing you dinner," I repeat. "I said I'd be back to visit. Oh, and some light." I point at the flashlight by my hip. "This way I won't freak out in the dark tonight, and you don't have to waste any more candles."

Victor stares at the flashlight as if it he had never seen one before. He tries again.

"No, really," he says, seeming to struggle for words, "why are you here? This isn't a safe place. You went home. You've been gone for weeks. You're supposed to be *home*. You're supposed to be back to normal."

"Eat," I say, pointing to the food in his hands. I rip off a small piece of bread and put it in my mouth to show him how. He glowers at me, then bites off a corner and chews. Only then do I answer him. "I did go home," I say, "but nothing is back to normal."

I tell him about Daniel, my new family, and about César being sick. I whisper when I tell him about being too late to get the medicine because I don't want the other boys in the room overhearing that I have money. I explain why I needed to spend the night.

Victor laughs softly.

"You know you're in trouble when visiting me is your best bet and this place is your best option for a hotel," he says.

"This is a terrible hotel," I agree. "But you've always been my best friend."

Victor gets quiet when I say that. "Thanks, Ana," he whispers.

"So what did you do today?" I ask. "Did you fight again?" I can't believe that I'm making small talk about him volunteering to get beat up in exchange for money, but I have to do something to get that sad, lost look off his face, and it's the first thing that pops out of my mouth.

Victor moves his bloodshot gaze to me.

"Yes."

"Did you win?"

"Yes."

He's not making this easy.

"Are you hurt?"

"Yes."

I huff in frustration and watch Victor finish his food. He seems sadder than usual, more on edge. Two and half more weeks of living this life have aged him even more than working in the mines did. I wish I had come up with something to offer him—wish I could have brought him hope instead of bread. But I didn't, and clearly he doesn't feel like chatting.

"Never mind," I say. "We can talk more in the morning. I want to be at the pharmacy as soon as they open, so I'm going to sleep now. Good night." I stretch myself out on the floor, my head resting on my folded *manta*. But I don't fall asleep right away. Instead I lie there pretending to sleep while I watch him between my lashes.

He sits, not doing anything, for a long time. I see his hands clench and unclench, but he doesn't go to sleep.

A boy comes over and stands behind him. It's the boy from before, who made Osvaldo, the creep, leave me alone. He looks at me and then at Victor.

"Can't figure out what to do about the problem of Sleeping Beauty?" He chuckles.

"Go away, Joaquín," Victor grumbles.

"I could kiss her," Joaquín suggests. "That usually fixes things in fairy tales."

"This is no fairy tale. And she wouldn't thank you for getting engine grease all over her clothes if you touched her," he says, but there's no venom in it. I don't really think I'm in any danger from Joaquín.

"Hey! Not my fault I spend all day working with cars. You'd be oily too if you were training as a mechanic." Joaquín laughs. "Seriously, though, Victor"—his voice loses its laugh—"she can't keep coming here. It's not safe. I got Osvaldo to leave her alone earlier, but next time he might not listen to me."

Victor rubs a hand over his face roughly, deepening the lines of exhaustion there.

"I know," he agrees tiredly. "I'll talk to her in the morning."

Then, as though they both agree to it without discussing it, Victor and Joaquín move their blankets so that they've boxed me into the corner with their bodies. Anyone wanting to get to me would have to walk over them to do so. And though this should make me feel even more strongly that I'm in danger here, instead it makes me feel taken care of. I fall asleep before the batteries in the flashlight die.

The next morning, Victor walks with me to the pharmacy and we sit together on the stoop, waiting for them to open. I'm glad they don't open late on Saturdays. I don't think I could stand to wait much longer to get this medicine to César.

"So," says Victor casually, "as much as I love your visits, you really need to stop staying over. Some of the other guys . . . they're not so nice. I don't want you to get hurt."

"Okay," I agree, because I'd realized that myself. "If I come to visit you again, I'll make sure to leave enough time to get home before dark."

"Good."

"So"—I mimic his tone—"are you still drinking?"

Victor is quiet for a moment, but beside me his shoulders have gone as rigid as the mountain, so I know he heard me.

"Who told you?" he asks finally.

"No one," I say honestly.

Victor doesn't press.

"I'm not judging you," I say softly, "but my papi was a drunk and it didn't help him—or us—ever. Does drinking make anything better for you?"

Victor sits up and scrubs his hand over his face.

"Not for very long," he admits with a wry smile.

I'm about to press him for more, but just then, I hear the metallic clank of a key and the rattle of the shop opening. I slip under the wrought-iron grille as it lifts and I'm showing the bottle to the pharmacist before he even has a chance to polish his glasses.

He pulls out a bottle identical to my empty one from a shelf behind the counter. But he won't hand it to me until I've paid. It makes me angry, but I suppose I look pretty rough and dirty right now, so I try not to judge him too harshly. I put the fifty-boliviano bill on the counter.

"You're short fifty-two bolivianos, eighty centavos," he says in a bored voice.

I gape at him. Panic twists my insides. Not once did it occur to me that I wouldn't have enough to pay for the medicine. I reach into my *manta*, as though willing more money to appear out of thin air. My fingers brush against Yenni's coin purse.

I pause. I can't. I *can't* spend Yenni's money. And yet . . . César needs this medicine.

She'll never miss it, says a voice in my head. But the voice hisses like the air tubes choking the entrance to the mine, and I know it's the voice of the devil.

"Well?" says the man, yawning.

I'm not stealing, I tell myself. *I'm borrowing. I'll pay her back right away.* The devil inside me only laughs.

Slowly, not believing I'm doing it, I pull the coin purse out and empty it onto the counter. The man's fingers flick over my friend's money, tallying my sin. I feel like Judas from the Bible, betraying a friend for a handful of coins.

Victor joins me at the counter. "What's wrong?" he asks, seeing my face.

"You're still short," the man says. He's getting annoyed now.

"How much?" asks Victor.

"Four sixty-five."

"I've got you," says Victor, and he puts a five-boliviano coin on the counter. I couldn't feel worse. Not only have I borrowed money from Yenni without asking, but now I'm taking money from Victor too. Knowing that he literally bled for that money makes my stomach churn. But César needs the medicine, and my whole family needs César. I nod at the man.

As the man hands Victor thirty-five centavos and puts the bottle on the counter, I wonder what I would have done if

Victor hadn't been here. Would I have stolen the medicine? The bitter irony of how poor we are when the mayor says we live on a mountain that was practically made of money burns inside me.

Clutching the bottle like it's made of silver itself, I walk out of the store.

"Thank you," I say to Victor once we're outside.

"Anytime," he says breezily.

I snort.

"Yes. Anytime I'm in desperate need of super-expensive medication to keep my stepfather breathing, I should shake you down for your blood money to make up the difference of what I can't pay."

Victor breaks into a lopsided grin.

"Exactly," he says. "Catch you later, Ana." And with that, he turns and starts to walk off in the direction of his hovel.

"Victor!" I call after him.

He turns, looking wary.

"Yes?"

"I'm sorry for nagging you earlier," I say. "I just hate to see you hurting yourself."

Victor sighs.

"Yeah," he says softly. "But sometimes life feels like such a trap, you know? Like there's no way out. I don't *like* getting beat up. I just don't know what else to do. I'm no good at anything other than mining, and I won't do that. I'm not going to beg either. At least when I drink, I forget about all that for a bit."

"You don't have to beg," I say, thinking furiously, trying

to come up with an answer that makes sense. Surely there's something else he could do—I get that he can't go back to school when he has to cover his own rent and food, but there must be some skill from when he was a miner that he could use now to get a job. "You're strong, you know how to use dynamite and tools. You could do construction!"

Victor is shaking his head.

"You don't use dynamite to build a house, silly."

"You do in demolition," I counter. "Like when you build a road."

"I don't think they let kids play with dynamite outside the mine. Besides"—he looks away—"I don't want to work with dynamite anymore. I know you say it's not my fault, but I just . . . I just don't want to, okay?"

I get it. I was terrified of working with dynamite in the mines, and that's not even counting the guilt I know he still carries from the accident he believes he caused. I can understand why he would never want to touch dynamite or mining gear again. It would remind him of that terrible day every single time he used it.

"Okay." Then I remember a different day from our time in the mines and the conversation I overheard last night. "What about Joaquín?" I blurt out.

Victor raises an eyebrow in my direction. "What about him?"

"He said last night he was training to be a mechanic."

"I knew you weren't asleep," Victor teases.

"Okay, okay, I was faking," I agree. "But seriously, he's a nice guy, right? If he knows about how to fix cars, maybe he could show you how? Introduce you to his teacher?"

"I don't know anything about cars!"

I can tell he's laughing this off, but I have to make him see.

"So what? You love to learn about machines! Remember that air compressor you fixed with César?" Victor blinks at me. I race on. "You were so interested in learning how that dumb thing worked. You got it working again with him, and later you told me how good it felt to actually fix something. Imagine if you could do that with your whole life?"

Victor stares at me a moment, considering. He doesn't say anything, but he's not laughing me off anymore either.

"It's got to be better than getting beat up every day," I add. "Think about it, at least?"

"Yeah," he says slowly. "I guess it would be. I'll think about it." Then his face clears and his usual smile pops back into place. "Now get home and put my 'blood money' to good use." And with a wave over his shoulder, he turns the corner and is gone.

"Bye, Victor," I say softly to the empty street.

Clutching the precious bottle of medicine to my chest, I head toward the tall stone arch that leads out of the city.

I don't go anywhere near the *posada*. I couldn't eat Carmencita's sweet bread even if they gave me a whole loaf of it. I stumble up the rocky incline, head bent against the wind, a wreck inside. I feel horrible having taken Yenni's money.

César, I remind myself. *It's for César. Your family needs you right now.*

But even though I'm nowhere near the mines, I feel like I've finally let the devil inside. It makes me feel dirty and bad. The cathedral's bells clang hollowly behind me, a taunting reminder from God.

I have to find a way to repay Yenni.

19

The look on Mami's face when I walk in the door and hand her the bottle of cough medicine is a beautiful thing, no matter the cost it took to put it there. She rushes at once to give some to César.

Since it's a Saturday, Belén and Abuelita are out at the slag heap, so for a moment I'm alone in the main room. I sink onto the bucket seat and take a moment to savor how good it feels to be warm and off my feet. Through the closed bedroom door I can hear the rustle of Mami tending to César, and I sit there with my eyes closed, letting my body relax, listening to their quiet murmur.

Ten minutes later, Mami comes out.

"Would you like some soup?" she asks.

"Yes, please," I say. Other than the loaf of bread I shared with Victor last night, I haven't eaten anything since yesterday's popcorn. The last time I had a hot meal was the night before that.

Mami gets down a bowl and serves me from a pot that she had wrapped in a blanket on the counter to keep it warm. Gratefully, I take it from her and sip it, breathing in the savory steam and breathing out my frustrations. Too quickly it's gone, but I know not to ask for more. Even in César's house, money doesn't stretch to second helpings.

"Thank you," I say, putting the bowl down.

"Thank *you*," Mami says. "Maybe with the medicine he'll be able to get some sleep. Did you have any trouble getting it? How was your night at the *posada*?"

Briefly, I consider telling her that I didn't spend the night at the *posada* and that there wasn't enough money to cover the cost of the medicine. But I don't know how I'd answer her questions about Victor, and I'm ashamed I took Yenni's money. I'm too tired right now to get into the conversations those facts will lead to.

"My night wasn't so bad," I say, dodging the question. "The biggest problem was that I had to wait the extra day for the pharmacy to be open. I was worried about César the whole time."

Mami nods slowly, her face drawn with concern.

After a pause, I ask, "Mami . . . is he very sick?"

"I just don't know," she says quietly. "I'm not a doctor, but I've spent a lot of time listening to coughs with your brother. I don't like the sound of this one. He needs to rest, but I don't know if he can take the time off work . . ." Her voice trails off.

The mention of work gets me thinking.

"Do you want me to sit with him so you can work, or do you want me to take your place as a *palliri* today?" I don't really want to spend my day in a sickroom, but I give her the choice because she's been locked up with him for a whole day already.

"Actually," Mami says, shaking off her mood, "I need you to go find Don Carmelo, the head of the mining cooperative, and tell him that César's sick and won't be able to work for a few days. They'll need to assign someone else to cover his shift."

My legs ache when I stand, but all I say is, "Okay," and I head out the door.

———

I haven't been near El Rosario since I snuck in and got trapped, and I'm in no hurry to go there now. Since it's a Saturday, I decide to check Don Carmelo's house first to see if he's home before I go looking for him at the mine.

When I knock on the door, he answers.

"What do you want?" he barks.

Don Carmelo is a thin, wiry man not much taller than me. I've never liked him. Once, when Daniel and I were about nine, we came around a corner of the Cerro quickly and surprised a condor that was eating something dead in the rocks. Before it took to the skies, flapping its enormous wings, each one bigger than we were, it looked at us. And even though I knew I had nothing to fear from the bird, it creeped me out. For weeks afterward I saw those eyes whenever I slept. Don Carmelo has those same eyes. I wonder to myself, briefly, if they'll be in my dreams tonight.

"Don Carmelo," I say politely, staring at his shoulder so I can avoid his condor eyes, "I came to tell you that my stepfather, César Jansasoy Herrera, is sick. My mother asked me to tell you so that you could make sure his shift is covered. Six to six, at El Rosario," I add, trying to be helpful.

"I know what shift he works," Don Carmelo snaps.

I close my mouth.

"How long will he be gone?"

"A few days, maybe. Not long." I pray I'm right. César's cough does not sound like it will be gone in a few days, but I don't want to get him in trouble.

Don Carmelo humphs. "And I suppose this means that he would like an extension on his loan as well?" he growls.

"His loan . . . ?" I'm lost.

"Yes," he grumbles. "The idiot took a giant advance on his wages to pay off the medical debts for that new cripple stepkid of his." His gaze sharpens on me. "I guess that would be your brother, then. Well, I hope he's worth it."

My mouth has gone completely dry. I had no idea César had gone into debt to help Daniel. That would explain why there was so little money in the jar and why we don't have soup for breakfast anymore.

"Yes," I manage. "He would also like an extension on the loan."

"Very well," he says brusquely. Clearly he thinks we're done.

My head swims. We don't have more money at the house—I know because I took it to pay for the medicine. We still need to eat while César gets better. Plus, I need forty-eight bolivianos and fifteen centavos to give to Yenni. And now, apparently, we're also in debt to this carrion-eater. If we default on a loan to the cooperative, César could lose his house. Our house.

Don Carmelo is turning away, closing the door, when I speak up.

"Don Carmelo!"

He pauses, his predator eyes considering me from the shadows of his house.

"What?"

"Is there"—I have to swallow a few times to work up the nerve—"is there any work I could do for the cooperative?" My mind flashes back to that day, all those mornings ago, when I stood with Papi in front of César and asked a similar question. "I know I can't work *in* the mine," I rush to add, not wanting to think about what it would be like to head into that hellhole when everyone blames me for the collapse and César's not there to protect me, "but is there anything I can do around it? For it?"

Don Carmelo stares at me for a beat. He sucks on his teeth like he's tasted something sour. "Yes," he says, "I suppose there is something you could do for the cooperative."

I wait while he considers.

Don Carmelo gives me an oily smile. "There is an opening for a *guarda*."

I blink at him.

Of course they have an opening for a *guarda* and of course they still need one. I snuck into the mine just fine three weeks ago. Who knows who else has managed to sneak in? I shudder thinking of the mystery men. Yes, the mine needs a guard. But to actually be the one doing the work . . . ? Cold washes over me as I remember Mariángela. Being a *guarda* is a scary job, and you don't get paid much to do it. But . . . if I can add to what Mami and Abuelita already make picking rock . . . maybe it will be enough to buy César the time he needs to get better. It will certainly give me enough that I can pay Yenni back. I can figure out a way to manage the danger. It's not great, but it's the best option I have right now.

I sigh. No good choices.

"I'll take it," I say, pulling the words out of myself like the dentist pulls rotten molars.

As I try not to think too hard about what I'm signing myself up for, we agree on the details. I'm expected at the mouth of the mine tonight at sunset. I'll make thirty-five bolivianos for every night of fear and loneliness I put in. It's not much. *But, I remind myself, it's something.* And it's guaranteed. Even the men who work in the mining cooperative aren't guaranteed their pay. They only get paid a portion of what they can bring out. If they don't manage to bring out much, like on the day of the disaster when Papi was killed, or if what they bring out is mostly poor-quality rock, low in the ores that the manufacturing plants want, then they don't get paid much. If they're sick, or hurt, or don't work for whatever reason, they don't get paid at all.

It's something. And something is more than nothing.

"Well then," says Don Carmelo, "I guess I'll see you tonight."

"I'll be there," I hear myself saying. "Thank you, Don Carmelo."

After leaving the condor's house, I walk until I get to the slag heap where Mami and Abuelita are working with half a dozen other women. Belén's not with them. She must have run off to play with friends. I think wistfully to the days when I was young enough that I could run away from work. I am not that young anymore. I tuck my shaking hands behind my back so the women won't see my fear.

"Ana!" Abuelita calls. "It's good to see you. Mónica told us the whole story of how you waited overnight to make sure you got the medicine. Good job."

I smile at her, wondering what that story will be embroidered into by the end of the day.

"Come," Mami says, indicating a boulder near her for me to sit and work with them. "Belén's at home in case César needs anything. You can sit here and work with us."

I feel a twinge of sadness that I was wrong about Belén still being allowed to play. It makes me feel even less like listening to Doña Elena complain about her aching hip and Doña Marisol talk about her daughter's upcoming wedding. But I fold onto my knees at the edge of the group and start breaking rocks anyway because I'm not quite sure how to say what I need to.

It turns out the women are in the middle of a fairly intense conversation. It seems rude to interrupt them with my news, so I sit quietly and wait for an opening.

". . . I still say the government should nationalize the mines again," Doña Marisol is saying. "This switch to little cooperatives leaves us all vulnerable."

Some of the women nod. Despite myself, I find I'm paying attention. Our whole lives change every time the price of *mineral* goes up or down. Would we be better off if things were different?

But Mami is shaking her head. "Prices for metals are set by international markets. There's no way for the government to control that."

"The government would find a way," Doña Elena huffs, "and I'd rather have one of us running things than some international power. Give them a hand and they'll take your whole arm. Remember the Water Wars of 2000?"

Even I know what she's talking about. It was four years before I was born, but they teach it in school and lots of people still talk about it. Years before Evo Morales got elected president, the Bolivian government needed a loan from the World Bank to improve the waterworks for our third-largest city. But one of the terms of the loan was that they had to privatize it: sell the public water service to a foreign company. Bechtel, the largest construction company in the United States of America, ended up owning all the water in Cochabamba—a city of 800,000 people—even the water that fell from the sky. When they doubled the price of water overnight and padlocked the public taps, a huge protest broke out. Protesters were met with tear gas and bullets. Six people were killed and 175 were wounded. It was partially the anger over this Water War that helped Morales become president.

"Corporations, *pah*!" adds Abuelita. "How is what they do any different from the way the Spaniards enslaved the Inca and took the silver out of this very hill to make themselves rich?"

"Not the Spaniards again," mutters Doña Elena under her breath.

Abuelita bristles. "Yes, the Spaniards! Our rulers were always Europeans, all the way back to the colonial times. Even

Simón Bolívar, the great liberator, was just another European. We indigenous—Quechua, Aymara, Chiquitano, the Guaraní down in the Amazon—we've always been the majority. It's about time we keep our wealth here instead of sending it off to make others rich. Tell me," she goes on, fixing Doña Elena with a glare, "how can a corporation in San Francisco own the rain that falls in Bolivia? Rain belongs to God."

I love the fact that, even though Abuelita and Doña Elena are basically agreeing with each other, they're still fighting.

"Yes, well, everyone's a good socialist until they get a taste of power," says Mami. It's interesting to see Mami participate in political conversations. She never offered opinions when Papi was still with us, but out here, surrounded by no one but other women, she speaks freely. I wonder whether she would voice these opinions around César and how he would react if she did. "Then they hoard money for themselves as much as anyone. Look at the Morales government now—as corrupt as any government ever was."

"How so?" asks Doña Marisol. "He took power away from the U.S. corporations and the World Bank. He gave us a new constitution, a new, indigenous flag. He brought women into the government and protects the environment."

"Such an environmentalist," says Mami, practically rolling her eyes, "putting roads through our national parks and indigenous spaces to dig for natural gas."

"He reduced poverty," counters Doña Marisol. "You can't deny that. He raised the minimum wage."

"He's also breaking ground, right now, to raise a two-hundred-and-thirty-million-boliviano presidential palace." Mami gestures emphatically. "Oh, and of course he's trying to abolish term limits to keep power for himself forever."

"All I'm saying," says Abuelita, "is that we are a country where valuable things have always been taken away from us, from silver for the Spaniards to lithium for mobile phones; from water to natural gas. It's time we stopped making deals with the devil to be modern."

"Some good things come from outside," says Mami, refusing to back down. "You can't just ignore the rest of the world or throw out the good with the bad. Okay, Morales kicked out some of the corporations, but he also kicked out foreign aid."

"Why do we need it?" scoffs Doña Elena.

"Because sometimes outside help is the only help to be had. Do you remember Rosaura? She was able to get a divorce from her husband when he beat her because of that Danish legal aid clinic. And, Marisol, your own daughter was able to get into a training program so she could become a preschool teacher because of that other charity. You can't say that her life isn't better because of it. Now those organizations are gone. Where will my Ana go to get help finding a better future?"

As one, all their gazes swing to me. I swallow. I wasn't planning on being an exhibit in their argument.

But Mami has given me the opening I need.

"I don't need a charity," I say, not quite able to meet Mami's eyes. "I've taken a job. At the El Rosario mine. As a *guarda*."

Deafening silence meets my announcement. Even the ping and crack of rocks in the background vanishes. The other women have stopped work completely to listen in.

Mami's eyebrows shoot up. "You what?"

I stare at the worthless hunk of rock in my hand, wishing we weren't having this conversation.

"El Rosario needs a *guarda*. We need the money." I do some quick math to make the number seem more impressive. "I'll make eight hundred and fifty bolivianos a month."

"So," Mami says. Tears roughen her voice, and whatever hope I had that my news wouldn't make her angry vanishes like clouds in the dry season. "You thought it wasn't enough that I lose a son and a husband to the mountain. You decided I should lose my daughter too."

"I'm trying to help." It comes out as a whisper.

"Do you think that getting yourself killed is going to help me?" she snaps. "What's your logic? That I'll have one less mouth to feed when you're found dead in a ditch?"

Tears are running down her face, and I know that her sharp words are coming from worry, not meanness, so I don't let her see how much they frighten me.

"There was a job open. This"—I wave my hand at the piles of slag around us—"isn't going to be enough. We need to eat. César needs time to get better. This is a way to do that. I'll be careful."

"There are other ways," Mami says in a clipped tone.

"What other ways?" I ask, my voice rising in frustration. This isn't something I've decided on a whim. I've thought and thought about this. There are no better choices available to us.

Mami doesn't get a chance to answer because that's when Doña Elena decides to join our conversation.

"A better way would be to get her a man," she states with complete certainty.

Mami and I stare at her, struck dumb.

Abuelita has no such problem. "Don't be stupid, Elena," Abuelita growls at the other woman. She glares daggers at the eavesdroppers until they go back to cracking rocks. The noise of their work underlines Abuelita's words to Doña Elena. "She's far too young."

"Nonsense!" barks Doña Elena. "I was fourteen when I got married. How old were you, Elvira? Fifteen? Sixteen? Besides, the girl wouldn't even really have to marry. Even if she just got engaged, his family would take care of you all until César is healthy again."

"No."

Mami's eyebrows rise at the tone in my voice. "Ana," she whispers. "Manners." Abuelita can sass Doña Elena all she wants because they're the same age, but Mami and I need to be polite to her.

I shake my head, no longer trusting my own voice.

Doña Elena turns on me. "Stubborn girl," she scolds. "Look at how hard your mother and grandmother are working now to take care of you. If you were a good daughter, you'd be thinking of ways you could take care of them. A husband would be responsible for making sure you all have enough to eat." Her eyes travel over me much like the miners' did. "You're pretty enough..."

"I'm not going to get married! Ever!"

"Don't shout at your elders," Mami says, a hint of heat creeping into her voice. She turns to Doña Elena. "She's young still. She doesn't know what she's saying."

"I know exactly what I'm saying," I grind out. I've lived in a one-room house most of my life. I do not want to get married.

"Ana, stop being so melodramatic." Mami sighs. "No one is saying you have to get married at twelve, but of course you'll get married eventually. It's not good to be alone. Remember those days after your father died? Barring the door every night? You, having to leave school to help us sort rocks?"

Having to leave school is a wound I still can't stand to have poked. "Yes, I remember those days," I snap. "There was a whole week when no one hit you."

I realize, in the stunned quiet that follows, that I have embarrassed my mother in front of her friends. I feel slimy inside. I clear my throat and force my voice to be less ugly. I can't meet her eyes again.

"I've made up my mind," I say loud enough for Mami, Doña Elena, and all the other women and their worthless rocks to hear me. "Tonight, I'm going to work as a *guarda* for the mine." I stare at the anemic blue sky and let out a shaky breath, trying to let go of my anger with it. "I'm going to go home and sleep now. It'll be fine."

And with that, I turn and walk away.

I really hate the word *fine*.

Even though I'm tired, I can't fall asleep. First of all, I'm not used to sleeping in the middle of the day. It feels wasteful. Also, even though I manage to still my body, I can't get my mind to stop whirling around and around. Tonight will not find me safely behind a latched door with my family, nestled under blankets. Tonight will find me walking around the mine, guarding it from who knows what. I know I'll need my wits about me. I will myself to sleep, but I don't manage it. Plus, guilt over how nasty I was to Mami eats at me.

For over an hour I stare at the ceiling, listening to César cough, wasting my precious rest time. But then I must have dozed off, because suddenly I hear Mami calling from outside.

"Ana? Ana! Get up! It's time for you to go."

I force myself to get out of my blankets. The evening air cuts like a knife through my clothes. I can tell tonight is going to be the type of end-of-summer night that feels more like the start of winter.

"I'm awake," I call, surprised to hear her. It's still light out. She should still be working with the *palliris*.

I walk outside and find her laying things on a flat rock. I see a bag of coca leaves, two blankets, Papi's old helmet with its attached acetylene lamp, and seven sticks of dynamite. Three of them are full length, like the ones that the miners use for blasting, but the other four look like they've been sawed in half.

I hug her, burying my face in her shoulder.

"I'm sorry, Mami," I mumble into the scratchy fabric. "I'm so sorry for what I said earlier about you and Papi."

Mami turns me in her arms and hugs me.

"It was never that much of a secret, I suppose," she says.

"Still. You don't deserve to have me throwing it around like that. Please forgive me?"

"There' s nothing to forgive," she whispers. "We all say ugly things when we're upset. I'm sorry that I yelled at you for trying to help."

"I found out about the debt," I say, looking up at her.

Mami's face is lined with exhaustion when she looks down at me.

"I wondered," she says. "You're so smart. And too curious by half."

"You can tell me things," I say. "I'm old enough to help."

Mami sighs. "I wish you didn't have to. I'm worried about you, *mi hija*."

I'm worried about me too, so I don't answer that. Instead, I look over the things she's assembled.

"What's all this?" I ask.

"Watch," she commands, letting me go. She takes one of the three big sticks of dynamite and pulls out the fuse. She then cuts both the stick of explosives and the fuse in half with a knife and reassembles them into two mini-sticks. "You don't want to detonate so much dynamite that you can't outrun the blast," she says. "But if a group of men comes after you like they did poor Mariángela, you light these, and throw them at them, and run. Promise me."

I imagine myself hurling dynamite at shadows and bringing the whole mountain down on top of myself. Then I imagine being caught alone and unarmed by a group of men. I remember Mariángela's smiling face.

"I promise," I hear myself say.

"Well," she says, her voice gruff, "there you go, then, that's all you need. Keep your eyes open and be safe. You can't fall asleep when you're a *guarda*. You'll have to stay up all night, eyes sharp! And don't dawdle coming home. I won't breathe easy until I see your face tomorrow morning."

She puts everything onto the *manta* and ties it into a pack that she slings around my shoulders. Tying the two ends into a knot over my collarbone, she rests her hands gently on my shoulders for a second. In the quiet between us I hear her regret, her sadness.

"Thank you, Mami," I manage, my voice thick with tears. I lean forward and kiss her on the cheek. "I'll see you in the morning."

Giving my shoulder a quick squeeze, she walks away from me without another word, back to the slag heap and the never-ending task of sorting good rock from worthless. I square my shoulders and face the other way, toward El Rosario and my new job.

20

I get to El Rosario just as the last light of day is purpling the sky. Small circles of light bob toward me and I realize that they're the headlamps of the miners coming out of the tunnels. I step out of the way as the men walk past me, all dirt-streaked faces, grime-encrusted suits, and sweaty bodies. Remembering the last time I was in this entry lot, I duck my head and try not to get noticed. Luckily, this time none of them pay me any attention, and soon they've left and I'm facing the mouth of the mine in the gathering gloom.

In some ways, not knowing if I'm alone yet is creepier than actually being alone.

A few minutes later, I see another glow from deep within the tunnel. It seems to take forever for it to get to me. At last, Don Carmelo steps out of the mine. He takes his time locking up the toolshed, then walks over to where I'm standing.

"I didn't think you'd come," he says.

"Here I am," I say, trying to sound brave.

"Do you need anything before I leave?"

A ferocious pack of guard dogs to keep me safe overnight. A five-course meal for my family. A miracle cure for miner's lungs. Enough money to be safe forever.

"No. Thank you."

"Very well. See you first thing in the morning."

"Good night," I say. It's odd saying it knowing I'm about to start work, not end it.

"Good night," he says. And with that, I'm truly alone.

For the first half hour I distract myself by walking around the mine, checking behind the coils of rope, piles of slag, and wheeled metal bins. When I'm positive that there are no monsters lurking in any of the shadows, I walk over to the tin-roofed adobe shed. Looking through the iron bars on the window, I see the mining equipment—spikes, cables, rolled-up air hoses, the air compressor, a single, precious pneumatic drill, parts of broken track, plastic jugs filled with I'm not sure what, and all kinds of other stuff I can't even identify. I test the bolt on the door. It holds.

Satisfied, I hunt for a good place to spend the rest of the night. I want it to be comfortable enough, but not so comfortable that I fall asleep—not that there's much danger of that. The sun has only just gone down and already my fingers and toes are numb with the cold. I also want somewhere that I have a good view of the things I need to guard and the surrounding area, but where no one can sneak up on me. I eventually settle on an outcropping of stone about a man's height above the ground to the right of the mouth of the mine. I'm next to the mouth and facing the shed, and with the cliff behind me, I'll feel safe enough.

Pleased with my choice, I haul myself onto the little ledge and open the bundle Mami made for me. I fold one of the blankets as many times as I can and put it on the ground. Then, sitting on it, I wrap the other one around me. I pull a small handful of coca leaves out of the bag and tuck them into my cheek. I lay the sticks of dynamite on the ground beside me, within easy reach. The helmet I'm not sure what to do with, so I wind my braids around my head like I used to when I worked with Papi in the mines, and put it on, belting the acetylene around my waist.

I decide that I should turn on the lamp, just to make sure it works if I need it. Rubbing my fingers along the band, I find the lighter tucked in there and flick it a few times with my thumb, letting the tiny flame steal my night vision. I smile sadly, remembering when Abuelita gave the helmet to me to light a dung fire so I could make dinner, for no reason other than to stop me from crying. Back in the days when wet matches felt like something worth crying over. In that moment, I miss my old life so badly it hurts.

I tip my head and stare at the stars until the dry wind pulls the tears from my eyes, never letting them fall.

A shadow flits by the mine entrance and I jump to my feet, brandishing a stick of dynamite, ready to repel a robber. But when I look more closely at the intruder, I see that it's nothing but a stray dog, sniffing around, hoping for something to eat. *I know how you feel*, I think, and relax again.

For a while I distract myself by staring down at the city of Potosí, a lake of lights at the base of the mountain. It still represents everything I want from life. The solid houses made of brick and painted concrete; the roads paved and cobbled. The shops full of things to buy; people bustling around purposefully. Most everyone wearing clothes that fit them and all the schoolkids in clean, matching uniforms.

Shivering on my rock ledge, I let myself imagine living down in the city, wearing clothes that are warm and stylish, laughing with a group of friends. I imagine myself in a secondary school, learning math and science, and reading about all the wonders of the world. With my fancy education I'll have a job waiting for me, and my family and I—since I'm dreaming, I go ahead and put Daniel in my new house too, relaxing in a comfortable chair and laughing at me with bright eyes and normal lungs—live in the city and are happy for the rest of our lives, not a speck of rock dust anywhere. I hesitate for a moment when I remember Papi and Belén and César, but everything in my dream world is free, so I make Papi alive again and toss them all in too, filling the imagined world below me with wonders for us all.

As lovely as the wish is, though, I find that I quickly wear it threadbare with too much touching. Besides, I know there's nothing left for me in the city now, not even the hope of working at the *posada*. Not after I've stolen from one of their employees.

I'm just shifting my position to get more comfortable when a shadow approaches along the road that is definitely not a dog. I jump to my feet, grip a stick of dynamite, and call out.

"Who's there?"

The figure puts both of its hands up and continues to shuffle toward me. I keep an eye on it, my heart pounding. I light the acetylene lamp on my forehead in case I need the dynamite in a hurry. When the shadow is a few meters away, it finally speaks.

"Ana, dear, put down the dynamite."

"Abuelita?" I'm stunned, but I do as she says. I jog over to where my grandmother is standing in the entry lot and take her cold, knobby hand in one of mine. She's wearing a knit hat pulled low over her ears and has a bundle tied to her back that made her shadow unrecognizable, but now that I'm up close, with the light of the lamp shining on her, there's no doubt who it is.

"What are you doing here?" I ask.

She gives me a wrinkled smile.

"I came to keep you company. Nights alone are long."

"But you shouldn't be out in the cold . . . you'll get sick . . ."

"*Pah!* These old bones never sleep through the night anyway. Might as well put them to good use. Now, where were you sitting? Was it out of the wind? Take me there."

Though I still feel like I should make Abuelita go home and rest, I'm grateful that I don't have to be alone anymore, so I show her where I've been sitting. Using the blankets Abuelita brought, I make her a warm little nest, hand her some coca leaves, and we settle down together in an easy silence.

"The city is so beautiful," murmurs Abuelita after a while. "It sparkles like a rich person's Christmas tree."

Whenever we go into the city near Christmas, Abuelita and

I always love the decorations in the shops. Sometimes you can even see through windows into people's houses. The trees with their fairy lights are so pretty. Then my smile fades.

"Just like a rich person's Christmas tree, none of the gifts there are for us."

For a moment Abuelita is quiet. "What's wrong, Ana?" she asks at last.

I wave my hand, half brushing off the question, half pointing to everything around me. "I . . ." I struggle for a moment. "Doña Elena wanted to marry me off."

Abuelita snorts. "Elena is an idiot. Ignore her."

I smile at my grandmother's support, but the feeling doesn't go away so easily. "I won't be able to ignore her forever," I say. "I mean, maybe Mami and César won't force me to get married anytime soon, but eventually . . . ? No matter how long I manage to put it off, my life will always be to marry a miner, have his children, and be his widow. I'm supposed to break rocks and keep house and send my sons into the mine."

Abuelita is watching me carefully.

"And I just . . . I don't want that. You're always telling me stories of the Inca—look at us! We've been doing this for centuries, trapped on this mountain for hundreds of years, no one ever doing anything different than their parents or their parents' parents. I wish . . . I wish I could do something else with my life . . ." I trail off and drop my head onto my crossed arms. "But girls like me don't have choices. There are good things out there, but we'll never have enough money to buy them. Everything is just too hard."

For a long moment Abuelita is quiet, considering me. I

finally lift my face, feeling rude and ungrateful that I've told her I want a life that is nothing like the life she lived.

"Abuelita—" I start to apologize, but she cuts me off.

"All this talk of gifts and buying," she says, "you're thinking like the Spaniards."

I roll my eyes, not wanting another history lesson. I'm talking about my life now. I don't care about any epic clash between Andean and Spanish cultures in the 1500s. But either Abuelita doesn't see my eyes or doesn't care, because she keeps talking.

"The Spaniards came here searching for El Dorado, a mythical city made all of gold. They wanted to melt it down and turn it into coins and buy better lives for themselves, just like you're saying. Do you know what the Inca called gold and silver?"

"No," I mumble into my knees. Once Abuelita gets started, you can't cut her off. You have to let her finish.

"They called gold 'the sweat of the sun,' and silver 'the tears of the moon,'" she says. "They thought they belonged to the gods and used them for religious artifacts because they were beautiful. They never gave them value beyond that. Do you know what the currency of the Inca empire was?"

I shrug.

"Work."

I look up at her.

"You were wealthy in those times if you had good lands to farm for food, or herds of llama, alpaca, or vicuña that you could shear for fine wool to make cloth. People worked in family units and everyone contributed to help make life good for the whole family. The Inca took that model to the level of an empire. They made the people they conquered work for them two months out of the year, and in exchange they fed and defended them. With this model, they built everything they needed, from over forty thousand kilometers of paved roads to cities, fortresses, way stations, and storehouses."

I'm not sure where she's going with this. "So?" I say. "They were defeated by people that had horses and guns and new germs. They were squashed by Spain and forced to work like slaves. Who cares what the Inca did?"

"You"—Abuelita's voice is fierce, and she pokes me in the middle of the chest with a bony finger—"are Inca. You are a child of that heritage. If you want a different future, it will never be yours if you chase it like a daughter of Spaniards. Money, *pah!* When does anyone ever have enough of it?"

"Never," I grumble.

"Exactly. It's the wrong currency. Up here, if you measure your future in coin, you will always be poor. Remember your ancestors. *Work*, Ana. If you want a different future, don't wish for it. Work for it."

And with that, Abuelita wraps herself in her *manta* and leaves me to my thoughts.

By the tiny hours of the morning, Abuelita has dozed off and not even the sparkle of Potosí is enough to keep me warm. I try staring up at the stars instead, but they're far away and just as cold as I am. Besides, looking at heaven makes me think about dead people, and I don't want to think about them either. I realize that I had no idea how long a night could be, cold, and awake, and alone. *It's not good to be alone,* whispers an echo of

Mami's voice. I hunch into my blankets, trying to block everything out, willing the night to be over.

My head bobs.

You're getting sleepy, I think. *You should get up and walk around for a bit.*

But that realization comes a little bit too late and I nod off.

Seconds—minutes? hours?—later, a formless fear washes over me, coupled with the feeling of falling and I startle awake with a gasp. I nearly wake Abuelita, but I can't bring myself to be that selfish, so I let her sleep. She's here to help me in case of an emergency, not just when I get scared by a nightmare.

If only I could see the line between the nightmare and my life more easily. Like the devil in the mines, unless you find the right tribute, fate catches you eventually and savages your dreams with its broken-glass teeth. Perhaps I was a fool to ever think to look for a different future from the one I was born to.

I push to my feet and force myself to do a lap. As I walk, the cold wind whistles around me and I bend my head against it. Unable to shake the feeling that the Tío knows that I'm here, I stumble up to the edge of the darkness at the mouth of the mine and sprinkle a few of my precious coca leaves onto the mud.

"An offering," I whisper, and climb back to my lonely perch.

Finally, long past the point where I'm sure I can't bear it any longer, dawn arrives. And with the dawn, trudging up the slope, is Don Carmelo. I never thought I'd long to see his sour face, but the feeling of relief that washes over me when I see him is huge.

Stiffly, I get to my feet and wake Abuelita. She gathers our things while I clamber awkwardly off my perch to talk to Don Carmelo.

He considers me for a few moments, then holds out two paper bills and a five-boliviano coin. I take them from him with hands made clumsy by a night in the cold.

"I get paid every day?" I ask, wedging the thirty-five bolivianos into my pocket.

"No," he says. "But I thought, for the first few days, maybe we'd do it this way." He scratches his nose. "I'm paying you for just last night because maybe you've decided you're not coming back tonight."

Thirty-five bolivianos is not enough to repay Yenni, let alone feed my family or pay down our debt. I lift my chin.

"I'm coming back," I say. "Have a good day, Don Carmelo."

He shrugs as if it doesn't matter to him one way or the other. Which I guess it probably doesn't.

"Until later, then," he says, and plods into the mine, starting the morning shift.

21

When Abuelita and I get home, a wave of exhaustion crashes over me, and I collapse into bed. The devil is waiting for me, as I knew he would be.

"So," he says, standing. "You're just like all the others." The coca leaves and offerings slide off him to drift around my feet. He towers above me.

When I tip my head to meet his eyes, I reach reflexively for my helmet to keep it from slipping off. But my hand touches nothing but my hair.

Risking a quick glance at myself, I see that I'm wearing my outfit from today, right down to my ratty tennis shoes.

"Like who?"

The devil ticks off a list on his cracked red clay fingers.

"The conquistadores, the viceroys of Spain, the bishops, the mint masters, the pirates, the kings, the emperors, the governments, the multinational corporations, the mining cooperatives."

"What do you mean?" I demand. "How am I like all of them?"

The devil of the mines leers down at me and his tone is possessive when he answers, "You're a thief."

When I wake, I find that I've clenched the thirty-five bolivianos I earned last night so hard in my fist that I can read the imprint of the metal coin on my palm.

I carefully put the money in the little jar on the shelf and force my stiff fingers to relax, refusing to cry. *You only borrowed it,* I tell myself, over and over again like a prayer. *You're earning it back.*

I sleep most of the rest of the day. Though Abuelita tells me she's fine and works outside with the *palliri,* after our midday meal I notice that it takes her a couple of tries to get up from sitting, like her whole body is hurting her. Belén rushes over to help her before I can, and Mami gives them a worried look.

That night, when I layer on all my extra sweaters and pack my *manta,* Mami appears at my elbow.

"I've told Elvira not to sit with you every night," she says, helping me settle my bundle over my shoulder. "It's too much for her old bones."

"I didn't ask her to come with me last night," I rush to clarify, trying to keep my voice even. I knew it was too much to ask, but even with Abuelita getting on my case, it was nice not to have to face the unending dark hours alone. "Of course she shouldn't come. We don't want her getting sick too."

"Exactly," says Mami. "She can come with you every few days maybe, when she's had a good rest in between. The other nights I'll come with you."

I feel a wave of relief, remembering the terror of the empty hours before Abuelita showed up last night; hours so lonely I would have done anything to see another living soul, and yet terrified that I might see someone at the same time. Then I think about what Mami is offering.

"No," I say. "You didn't sleep all day like I did. You worked as a *palliri*. You still have to cook, and clean, and take care of Belén and César. We can't afford for you to get sick either. I can do this."

Abuelita and Belén are listening in as we talk. Abuelita's mouth is a thin line, but I guess Mami talked to her earlier, because she doesn't say anything.

"I'm used to being by myself," Belén breaks in. "When it was just me and Papi, he had to leave me alone a bunch. I'll be fine. Doña Elvira and I can take care of things here."

Abuelita gives Belén a fond look. "Yes, we can. Do whatever you need to do, Mónica," she says to Mami.

And so it's settled: the plan is for Mami to come with me to the mines.

But, like so many plans, it doesn't work out.

We're just getting to the door when Doña Elena comes running up in spite of the aching hip she was complaining about earlier.

"Mónica!" she says. "Inés is having her baby, but something's not right. Please, can you come?"

Mami jerks as though she's been electrocuted. She's not a doctor or a nurse, but she has helped deliver many babies. Her eyes flash to mine, and I can see her gathering her courage to say no. I know that, given the choice, she will protect me over Doña Inés's child. I'm hers, after all.

But I am no longer a baby.

I straighten my spine. "Go," I tell her. "It's just one night. I'll be fine. Abuelita can stay here with César and Belén. If the birth goes quickly, you can join me later."

Mami opens her mouth to argue with me, but I cut her off.

"It's not worth a baby's life just to keep me company."

For a moment more, Mami stands there, torn. I keep my back straight and my face clear, showing her how strong I am. Finally, she nods. "Okay," she tells Doña Elena. "Tell Inés I'm on my way."

The woman bolts from the room, and Mami, after gathering some things she might need, turns to go as well. Just before she leaves, she pulls me into a hug. "You're so brave, Ana," she whispers into my ear. "I'm so proud of you. Thank you." Then she gives me a quick kiss and hurries after Doña Elena into the night.

I heave a sigh. Being brave is the worst.

"Okay," I say to Abuelita and Belén, "have a good night. Take care of César. I'll see you in the morning."

Abuelita pats my cheek. "Take care of yourself tonight, Ana. I'll pray for your safety."

"Good night," I say to Belén, who's giving me a funny look I can't figure out.

"Good night," she says.

I wave over my shoulder and head out.

———

I get to the mouth of the mine just in time to check in with Don Carmelo before I climb up to my perch and settle in for a cold and lonely night.

The moon is barely a hand's width above the edge of the mountain when I see a small figure creeping through the shadows toward me.

That can't be . . .

But when she gets closer, I see that yes, it is.

"Belén? What are you doing here?" A thought occurs to me: the only reason they would have sent her to come get me is if something truly terrible had happened. "Is Abuelita okay—is César—did Mami—" I don't know how to organize my thoughts, but Belén cuts me off.

"Everyone's fine. Your mami is still out helping with Doña Inés, your abuelita is sleeping, and Papi's breathing settled a bit. I left a note saying where I went so they won't worry." Belén bounces over to join me.

"So they won't worry . . . about what?"

"Me staying here with you, of course!" She smiles brightly.

I stare at her blankly. Then I snap out of my shock.

"No way," I manage, shaking my head. Belén is only eight.

"Why not?" she demands.

"Because," I say, "it's dangerous, and lonely, and cold, and you'll be uncomfortable and miserable and get no sleep and be worthless for school tomorrow . . ." I trail off, not able to put into words how terrible of an idea this is.

Her chin juts into the air. "If it's all that bad, you shouldn't have to do it alone."

It's not good to be alone. I clench my hands by my sides in frustration.

"No," I say, keeping it simple.

"We need the money," she says firmly. "You're helping to

get it. My new mami is helping to get it. Even old Doña Elvira breaks rocks and sits with you. You're all doing it for my papi because he's sick. I'm going to help too, and you can't stop me."

"I sure can," I say, getting to my feet. "Come on! We're taking you home right now."

Belén plants her feet, a stubborn crease on her forehead. "You can take me back, but you can't make me stay," she says. "I'll just run out again and come here. And then the mine will be left unguarded, and your abuelita will have to be up all night to keep track of me. What's the point?"

I clench my teeth to prevent myself from shouting at the little girl. She's right: if I drag her home, all those bad things are guaranteed. If Mami were home, we could find a way to make her stay, but Mami might be out all night at the birth. There's no point keeping an old woman and a sick man awake and worried all night, and I do have a job to do. Last night was quiet when Abuelita was here. If Belén stays here, at least I can keep an eye on her until morning, and she won't crawl all over the mountain in the dark with no thought to her own safety.

I chew my lip and consider the fierce little girl, crooked braids and all, standing her ground in front of me. She wants to help her papi. I know how awful it feels to not be able to do anything to change the bad things around you. Given the options we have, this might be the best. Besides, after one night out here with me in the cold, I bet she doesn't try this stunt again.

I reach out and give her crooked braid a tug. "Fine. You win."

Belén grins and throws her skinny arms around my waist.

"Thank you, Ana!" she squeals.

"*Mmm-hmmm.*" I quirk an eyebrow at her. "But when we go home in the morning, you're going to be in soooooo much trouble. Don't expect me to bail you out."

"You bet!" she chirps, all smiles now that she's gotten her way.

I roll my eyes and point her to where I set up my stuff. Belén pulls her schoolbag off her back. In it, she's packed extra blankets and her own bottle of water. I spread all the blankets in one thick layer. Her body is small and will lose heat quickly; we'll need to huddle.

When I glance up, I see that my new sister is examining the little sticks of dynamite that I made with Mami, rolling them around in her hands. There's enough explosive there to kill her if something goes wrong.

"Careful!" I say, and she puts them down gently where I had them before.

"Will we really use those if someone comes?" she asks.

The pile is tiny: the ten mini-sticks of dynamite are grungy and no thicker than my two thumbs together, wrapped in peeling paper. They look like a bunch of nothing, and yet they have the power to move mountains. The power to kill.

"Only if we absolutely have to," I say, and get back to setting up our nest for the night.

———

For the first half of the night, Belén and I chew coca and talk and weave pretty pictures of a fairy-tale life down in the city, but as the dark hours creep by, exhaustion and the cold slowly silence us.

We've been sitting quietly, Belén dozing off and on, when a noise makes me tense. In an instant, Belén is alert beside me.

"Did you hear that?" she whispers, a note of panic in her voice.

I hold up a hand for her to be quiet and listen.

She chews her lip while she waits for my answer, and I briefly wonder whether it's something she's always done, or whether it's something she copied from me.

There's no masking it: those are footsteps. The mountain and the mine echo the sound oddly, but I'm pretty sure they're coming from over the hill, not along the road leading up to the entrance.

There is no good reason for anyone to avoid the road. I make a snap decision.

"You stay here," I whisper, handing her a mini-stick of dynamite and taking three for myself. I light the helmet and leave it with Belén and take the lighter in my other hand. I leave the other six sticks with the rest of our stuff.

"What are you going to do?" Belén is shaking.

"I'm going to climb over the hill and surprise them," I say. "They may not know this mine is guarded again. If I can make some noise, I bet I can scare them off." I point at the dynamite in her hand and the helmet. "Stay near this so they know you can light those in a hurry if you need to, but don't actually. Run away if you have to, but don't use those. Dynamite can kill you as easily as it can kill anyone else."

"Okay," she says, and even though she absolutely should not be here facing any of this, I feel a deep pride welling up in my chest for this brave little sister of mine.

I give her arm a quick squeeze and then climb the incline to the right of the mine entrance, keeping my body low to the ground. I crest the ridge and keep going. I want to be above them when I attack, not below. Gravity will always pull dynamite downhill, and I won't have the luxury of fussing over the timing of my fuses.

Finally, I find a small crevice that is perfect for what I want. It's higher than the hint of a trail that leads over the hill, and it's tucked out of sight. The only thing I don't like about it is that, having turned the corner, I can no longer see Belén or the area in front of the mine. I perch on the rock like a predator and wait for my unsuspecting prey.

After an excruciating few minutes, a shadowy form passes below me.

The tiny wheel of the lighter makes the faintest of rasping sounds as I drag on it with my thumb and light one of my three sticks of dynamite.

I say loudly, "This mine is guarded. Now get out of here." As the man spins on his heel in surprise, I hurl the dynamite at his feet.

And then from around the corner I hear Belén scream.

In an instant I'm scrambling over the mountain. I can't go the quickest route because I just threw dynamite there. If the robber has any sense of what's good for him, he's running too.

"*Help!*" I hear Belén's voice below me.

I'm almost there.

My dynamite goes off behind me. The sound echoes around the small space and the ground shivers under my feet. I hear rocks dislodging and sliding, but I can't check the damage I've caused. I've got to get to Belén.

I imagine a dozen terrible things that could have happened.

I hear the sound of more dynamite exploding. Belén has used her little stick too, even though I told her to run.

I burst around the corner. Belén's dynamite must not have worked well enough because, even in the low light of the stars, I can see her grappling with someone. Belén is kicking and fighting.

It makes me pause. Though I have no problem at all hurling dynamite at would-be robbers, I don't want to hurt Belén. But just then the man I surprised over the hill catches up to them and, using his larger body, shoves Belén against the rock. I hear a sickening crack as her head hits the stone and she crumples at his feet.

Bellowing in fury, I light my last two sticks of dynamite and race toward them.

"Let go of her, you beasts!" I yell.

I'm close enough that the sparkling light from my fuses plays across their shoulders and catches on their faces as the man and the boy turn toward me.

I recognize them.

The man, the one I surprised on the path, is Francisco, who said all those horrible things to me about Daniel being worthless and girls being a curse. The boy is his son, Guillermo.

For a stunned moment I freeze where I am, staring at them. Part of me is hoping against hope that I've seen wrong, that somehow this will turn out to be a misunderstanding. How could they rob their own cooperative?

"Go away!" shouts Guillermo in a rough, ugly voice. "Leave us alone. This isn't your business."

I realize two things.

First, I realize that neither of them has recognized me.

Then, somewhere deep in my brain, I hear the devil laughing. It reminds me of the dream where I challenged him for my life and Daniel's. It makes me glance at my hand and realize the second thing: that I'm still holding two lit sticks of explosives and the fuses are gone.

The dynamite is about to blow up.

Francisco's and Guillermo's eyes shift with mine, and everything happens at once. The two of them dart in opposite directions. I hurl the dynamite high into the air, hoping it will detonate where it can't hurt anyone, and leap toward Belén. I hit the ground hard and curl around her slumped form, shielding her with my body.

I look up just in time to see that, while Francisco sprinted to hide behind the toolshed, Guillermo ran for cover in the mine. The two sticks of dynamite curve in almost graceful arcs through the air and land with a gentle thud on my lookout ledge, where I'd left the other six sticks.

And then, like in my worst dreams, all the dynamite explodes, shearing off the ledge and part of the cliff face, trapping Guillermo inside.

My heart stops.

I can't breathe, can't think.

Francisco crosses the distance between us and grabs me by the arm, dragging me onto my feet. "Idiot!" He shakes me. "What have you done?"

"Let me go!" I shriek, pulling away from him. Then I change my mind. "No. Actually, come with me." I twist in his arms and lurch toward the collapsed mine entrance. "You have to help me! We have to get him out!"

Francisco lets go of me, his glare icy.

I get to the buried entrance and scrabble at the highest chunks of rock I can reach. I pull them off the pile, causing tiny rubble avalanches. Francisco and I have to dance backward out of the way so that our feet don't get buried. The angle of the heap shifts slightly, but I'm no closer to the tunnel behind it.

"You," Francisco says, finally recognizing my face in the moonlight now that he's had a good chance to look at me. "You witch! Causing one disaster wasn't enough? Now you've caused two!"

"There's no time for that now! Didn't you see? Your son is trapped in there! We have to dig him out."

Francisco spits at me and makes a gesture to ward against the evil eye. Then, to my complete astonishment, he starts to jog away.

"Where are you going?" I shriek after him. "He's your *son*. You can't just leave him here!"

Francisco's glance flicks to the pile beside me, and for a moment I think maybe he has a shred of human decency in him, but his eyes are emptier than the mountain.

"He was far back in the tunnel. And that noise is going to bring people—they can help you."

And with no more than that, he turns away and, grabbing a bulky sack off the ground that I hadn't noticed until just now, vanishes into the night.

I know I need to push my bleeding fingers into the jagged gaps between the rocks blocking the mine shaft and dig. I know I need to go over to Belén and make sure she's breathing.

I know these things, but my hands are shaking and a terrible pressure is welling up inside me. Without ever having given myself permission to begin crying, I sink down and bury my face in my hands. The rock fragments on my palms feel like sandpaper against my cheeks. The wetness of my tears leaks through the cracks between my fingers.

"Hey," says a soft voice. A hand on my shoulder shakes me gently.

I jerk away, startled. My hands splay on the rocks behind me and I blink back the tears, trying to see clearly who has found me. Is it another thief, or some drunken miner come to make my troubles even greater? I scrub a hand across my face, blinking furiously against the grit scratching them, and take in the person standing in front of me.

"V-Victor?"

I must sound as confused as I feel, because Victor gives an embarrassed shrug.

"Sorry it took me a minute to come over," he says. "I went to check on the little girl first."

Sniffling, I glance over to the rock face where Francisco slammed Belén. Sure enough, I see that she's been moved and has been propped up slightly, so that her head is higher than her heart.

Victor starts pulling chunks of rock off the pile, two hands at a time, and my hands begin moving automatically, matching his. I feel like maybe it's me who's been hit on the head. Why can't I think?

I turn back to Victor.

"Wait . . . how . . . ?" I swallow and make myself start over. "What are you doing here?"

"I, um, I came back up to get something I'd forgotten at home."

I flick a glance up to the ridge, where I can see the dark outline of Victor's old house. "In the middle of the night?"

Victor ducks his head. "Yeah, well, I'm not really supposed be back here. Papi never paid the last month's rent before he died. The landlord padlocked all our things inside." His voice is so low it's almost a whisper. "I was just leaving when I heard shouting . . . and then blasting. I came over to see if anyone needed help." He takes in my tearstained face. "I guess you do?"

The rock Victor pulls out dislodges a pile of rubble and the two of us have to move away, coughing, until the dust settles again. I know Francisco thinks Guillermo was well clear of the landslide. But what if he wasn't? If Guillermo is trapped underneath this rubble, he could be running out of air . . . or slowly bleeding his life away. I couldn't spare Daniel from being crushed alone, but I can make sure it doesn't happen to someone else.

I climb over the growing skirt of the pile before the dust is completely cleared and keep pulling at the rocks. After a moment, Victor joins me. The work is intense. I don't ask any more questions, and Victor doesn't volunteer anything else.

I know that Francisco is right and that help is no doubt on the way, but no one is here yet. We could wait, but a few minutes might be the difference between life and death. I can't take that chance. My back aches and my hands are in pain. But finally, I pull out a rock and the rubble dislodges in two directions—out and in, creating a narrow entrance shaft.

Leaving Victor to widen the hole, I race across to where Belén is and grab the helmet. It's gone out. I strap the acetylene tank to my hip and fiddle with the dial and the lighter. The flame doesn't catch, and I blow on the spigot, hoping to dislodge whatever dust might have clogged the mechanism. If the metal is bent so that no gas can get through, I'll never be able to fix it here.

I try again and whisper a prayer of thanks when it lights. I carefully put the helmet on my head and climb up the rubble heap to where Victor has opened an entrance about the size of a pothole. I shine the light down it and call for Guillermo.

"I don't hear anything," I say.

"Me neither."

We're both breathing hard from the effort we put in, and neither of us wants to say what needs to be said next. After a moment, taking in how tall Victor is and the width of his shoulders, I take a breath and say it.

"One of us has to go in."

Victor's gaze drifts down to the small, ragged hole in front of us. "I don't think I'll fit," he says. His voice is very soft.

"Victor . . ." My voice quavers. I can't finish. I know it has to be me: we don't have time to widen the tunnel. But the terror of the days I spent lost in the mines is crushing me.

"I won't leave," Victor says, putting a hand on my shoulder. "You're my best friend, remember? If it caves in again, I'll stay here and dig you out. I promise."

I don't trust myself to answer, so I just nod, biting my lower lip. Then I lie down on my belly and squirm into the hole.

22

The tunnels of the main mine had been chiseled smooth, worn by centuries of use. Even the exit vent I crawled out of the last time had been widened by hundreds of years of wind and rain. But these rocks were ripped from their moorings only minutes ago, and their edges are sharp. I feel them press into my body, hard and ice cold, as I push myself, face-first, into the rough tunnel.

The hole is barely wider than my shoulders, and the air inside is so thick with dust, the beam of my light reflects back at me. I can't see through it and my lungs spasm as I try to breathe. When I cough, the edges of my ribs hit the sides of the tunnel. Debris sifts around me. Terror wraps tight like a blanket of needles, digging through my skin.

I pull myself another arm's length in. Then another.

Centimeter by centimeter, I claw my way into the womb of the Pachamama, away from fresh air and freedom. My whole body is encased in rock now—a single false move and I'll be buried.

Victor said he wouldn't leave, I tell myself again and again, but the thought does little to slow my rapid breathing. I know that if the tunnel were to collapse on me, I could easily suffocate before Victor could dig me out. Or, flame-first, I might hit a pocket of gas and the explosion could rip my face off before he has the chance to pull me away. Or . . .

I force myself to stop thinking about these things and pull myself in another arm's length. I feel the scrape of the tunnel ceiling on my heels when I kick to propel myself forward. Directly ahead of me a large boulder blocks part of the space, and I have to flatten myself and tip my head sideways between my outstretched arms to wriggle past it. The rough edge of the ceiling digs into my spine as I push myself over. My acetylene tank catches.

I'm stuck.

With my head tipped to the side, I can't raise my face to see where I'm going. My arms spasm to try to reach around and free my tank, but my elbows bark painfully against the sides of the narrow crawlway.

I can't move forward. I can't see where I am. My face is pinned against my arms, and I can't move them. Rock is digging into the small of my back.

Black dots start to dance in my vision.

I feel like I can't spread my ribs enough to pull in air.

Unable to look around, unable to move, I lose myself to panic.

I don't even know if I'm trying to move forward or backward

anymore, I just need to get out. A scream tears itself from my throat. I kick my feet against the tunnel walls and scrabble with my hands. There's a ripping sound and I feel the rock slice my hips. I don't even know whether the space in front of me is big enough for my body, but terrified and twisted, I shove myself forward.

The first sense I have that I'm coming out of the crawl space is when I can bend my elbows. Pushing against the rock slide, I haul myself forward until I'm half out and can lift my head again in open space.

Sobbing, I raise my face and pull in deep gulps of dust-choked air. I use my hands to lever my hips and legs out of the tiny access tunnel and tumble onto the ground, blind with relief.

For a few moments I lie there on the cold ground, heaving in grainy breaths, waiting for the tide of fear I was drowning in to pull away from me. I am super aware of my body; my face against the smooth floor of an established mine tunnel; every scratch and rip along my aching fingers; the abrasions on my hips; the heaviness of my sneakered feet. I know it must have only been minutes that I was in the crawlway, but it felt like an eternity.

I notice the darkness and reach a trembling hand up to my head. My helmet is still there. I trace the line down from the headlamp and find a dangling tube. In my panic, I must have sheared off my acetylene tank.

This is very bad. I feel around at my feet, but I don't brush against any smooth metal cylinders. I consider striking the lighter in my pocket so I can see. But then I picture my little tank somewhere halfway between myself and freedom. I try to remember whether acetylene is a gas that floats up or seeps down, but I can't. I decide not to chance a flame. I'm still trembling with my last near-death encounter.

"Ana? Ana! Are you okay?" Victor's voice echoes down the access shaft.

I turn my head in slow arcs, trying to orient myself to the sound. There! A moon-shaped grayness in the unending black marks the opening. I put out a hand to steady myself.

"Victor." A coughing spasm racks me when I try to speak. "I'm through!"

"Thank God. I was so worried when you screamed."

I have nothing to say to that.

"Did you find Guillermo?" he asks.

In my mind-crushing panic I had forgotten.

"Guillermo?" I grope around in the dark.

"Here!" says a choked voice beside me.

"Guillermo?" When I reach to my left, my hand brushes a shirt. I sweep my hands over him. "Are you hurt?"

"I . . ."—his voice is clogged with tears and blast dust—"can't feel my legs."

My fingers have to do my seeing for me. My hands trace up his shoulder and find his face. I check his head—no wetness, that's good, at least his skull isn't cracked. He's bowed awkwardly off the floor. I fumble in the darkness until I can pull the loose rocks out from under him and he can rest flat. I trail my hands down his arms and across his chest, pushing away the debris piled on him, then down the side of his leg. I've only made it to his knee when my fingers meet the wall of rubble.

My hands flit over to his other knee; same problem there. I grip the fabric of his jeans and give a small tug, just to see if, by some miracle, his legs will slide free. When I do this, Guillermo gasps in agony.

His legs don't move.

He's trapped.

The pain of me pulling on his legs has fully woken him up, and I can hear his rapid breathing beside me.

"Shh," I say.

"I . . . I . . ." His gulping breaths don't let him finish.

"No, no, don't panic," I say, panicking. "We're going to get you out."

I flutter my hands along the grade of the slope. It doesn't feel good. To test my theory, I pull a few rocks off the top. As soon as I do, a top layer sluices down.

Guillermo hollers in fear and I throw my body over his head and shoulders. Rocks bounce off my back. When the noise of the rockslide stops, I carefully lift myself off his chest and move my hands over the slope again. The angle is gentler, but now he's covered from the waist down.

"Help!" he yells at me.

There's nothing I can do or say to make it better. If I keep pulling at the rocks, the physics of the thing in front of me means I'm likely to bury him completely.

"We need to wait for the miners to help us," I tell him. "They'll know how to get you out."

I hear a commotion above us. The sweep of a flashlight beam lights the access tunnel. The low rumble of male voices and the echo of boots was a sound that frightened me the last time I was in these tunnels, but I am beyond glad to hear them now.

"Victor?" I call. "What's going on?"

"Ana!" He sounds relieved. "Some people are here. Hang on! Was that Guillermo? Are you guys okay?"

"I'm all right." I pause and think about how to say what I need to say next without causing Guillermo to panic. "I found him," I say. "His legs are stuck. I don't know how badly hurt they are, but I can't move the rocks myself. Who's here? Can they help?"

There's a rustle at the opening. Then a hoarse voice calls down.

"Ana?"

"César?" I'm stunned. With how sick he's been, I would never have expected him to come to investigate the blast.

A gale of coughing answers me, and my relief at hearing his voice is instantly washed away by worry and guilt. *This is my fault!* If I hadn't decided it was a good idea to toss dynamite around like it was confetti, he would still be in bed, resting.

I hear César's voice angle away from me. "Okay, men, let's get to work. Enlarge this access tunnel . . ." His voice gets louder again. "Ana, what direction are you?"

"Left . . . my left. To your right."

"Enlarge it away from them," César goes on to his crew.

"Wait!" I call up. "How's Belén?"

There's a long pause.

"Victor is taking her home," he says. "They'll take care of her. I'm sure she'll be fine."

He doesn't sound convinced. My heart twists in my chest. "César?"

"Yes?"

There are so many things I want to say. I want to apologize for being part of what got Belén hurt; apologize for dragging him out in the night wind with his cough. I want to beg him to forgive me for being such a bad daughter so far, and to admit that I think, maybe, I'm happy to be a part of his family.

"I lost my acetylene tank in the tunnel. It might be leaking. Tell the men to be careful as they dig."

"Okay," he says. "We're coming, Ana. Hold tight."

———

I rest my forehead against the rough stone of the rubble wall blocking our exit. Lifting my shirt over my nose and mouth, I try to breathe as deeply as I can through the fabric, listening to the slow, clanking, scraping process of the men enlarging the access tunnel. The dust has sifted somewhat out of the air, but it's still murky and difficult to breathe. I can only imagine how hard it must be for Guillermo, his body seizing up in pain, half a tunnel weighing him down, trapped and having to wait.

The lights from the miners' helmets bob and flash erratically down the access tunnel. Some moments I can see Guillermo, his narrow face pinched and panicked; other moments I can only hear the labored sound of his breathing in the dark.

"Do your legs hurt very badly?" It's probably not the best thing to say, but it's all I can think of.

"Not as badly as when you pulled on them, or when the rocks shifted, but it's not good," he admits through gritted teeth. "How long do you think it will take for them to dig us out?"

I shrug. "I don't know. A while. But they'll get in here as soon as they can. César's out there. He'll make sure they get you out safely."

In the strobe of light, I see the worried look on his face and realize that being dug out by his old supervisor might not be a comforting thought to Guillermo right now.

"What happened?" he asks finally. "All I remember is getting to the mouth of the mine and then I was flying backward. I woke up in the dark, with my legs buried."

I chew the inside of my lip. Guillermo and his papi always thought I never belonged in the mine. I'm not sure he's recognized me yet. If I admit who I am, will he be angry? *Then again,* I think wryly, *what can he do to me with half a mountain holding him down?*

"It was the dynamite that I threw," I admit. "It collapsed the entryway where you were hiding."

"You threw dynamite at me?"

"Not *at* you . . . just, well, away from myself . . . which happened to be toward you, but I never meant it to hurt you . . . or anyone . . . I just . . . It's a long story," I mumble.

Guillermo gives a bitter laugh. "I'm not going anywhere."

And he's right about that, so I scoot closer to him and tell him the whole story of taking the job as *guarda*, Belén joining me, and the mess with the dynamite when he and his father showed up. I hesitate to tell him that Francisco left him here instead of helping to dig him out, but to my surprise, Guillermo doesn't seem shocked by this.

"That was always the plan, if we got separated," he says. "He'll come back for me."

I stare at Guillermo, wondering if he hit his head harder than we thought. "He left," I repeat. "He saw that you'd been buried in the mine and he left you here. He didn't even know if you were okay or dead!"

Guillermo snorts dismissively. "Papi would have trusted me to get out of the way. He knows I know my way around the mine."

I can't believe he's defending this behavior, and it makes me snappish.

"Oh yeah? And how did that work out for you? Do you know your way out from under that pile of rock holding down your lower half?"

There's a long, sullen silence. I regret my nastiness.

"I'm sorry," I whisper. "I didn't look where I was throwing it at all. I just knew I had to get it away from myself and my sister. Even if you were trying to rob the mine, no one deserves what you're suffering."

"We weren't robbing the mine," Guillermo says.

"What?"

For a moment, guilt paralyzes me. What if they were just walking by, minding their own business, and I attacked them? What if this is all my fault and they didn't do anything wrong?

Then I remember how the two of them were sneaking over the hill, not walking on the road, and I remember the bag Francisco took with him when he ran, and I remember

Guillermo saying just a moment ago that splitting up was part of some plan. They were up to something.

"We weren't," he insists. "We were just doing extra, after-hours mining."

"After hours . . ." I trail off, remembering the voices deep in the mountain that shouldn't have been there the night I came down here looking for Daniel. "How long have you been doing this?" I ask suspiciously.

Guillermo shrugs. "Better part of a month," he says. I see him clenching and unclenching his hands by his sides like he can't make up his mind whether to keep talking or not. But talking must be taking his mind off his legs because, finally, he relaxes them and goes on. "We were working off by ourselves one day—César had left us to go deal with some problem or other—and we came across a vein of silver."

"Silver? No way." Everyone knows the silver in this mountain is all gone. There are only tiny filaments of it left in some of the rocks.

"Not a big vein," Guillermo corrects me as if I'm an idiot, "not much thicker than a pencil. But it was good quality, pretty pure."

"And?" I prompt. A pencil-width of silver is not nothing.

"And Papi said maybe we shouldn't tell anyone about it," he goes on, his voice dropping to a mumble. "That it was only a thin thread, and if we gave it to the cooperative, it would have to be shared among all the miners—not even just the ones on our crew, but everyone. He said there might only be a thimbleful of silver, and to divide it out among so many would mean we'd only get centavos."

"So you kept it to yourselves," I say, my voice hard. I feel bile churn in my stomach. Francisco and Guillermo are thieves—worse than thieves, because they decided to rob their coworkers, their neighbors, people they knew were poor, not those who could afford to lose things. "You work in a *cooperative*. Profits are supposed to be shared. Tell me again how that's not stealing?"

"If we had shared it, there wouldn't have been any profit!" he barks at me, and I can hear the echo of his father in his voice. "We had to keep it to ourselves until we knew what we really had. Then we would—Papi said then, if it was a lot, of course we'd share it."

I can hear the desperation in his voice to believe that. It's the same tone he had when he said his father would come back for him. I want to tell him he's an idiot to believe anything Francisco said, but we all want to think the best of our fathers, when we can. It's not like my papi was perfect. I keep my mouth shut.

"We covered it up and told César the air was bad and that we needed to move somewhere else," Guillermo goes on. "Then we came back at night and worked, just the two of us, and collected what we could." He pauses. "But then the thread went deeper than we could reach with our picks, and Papi said we should use some dynamite—just a little, he said. Not so much they'd hear it topside. Just enough to loosen the outer layer . . ." he trails off.

"But you used too much," I say, remembering the zone seven tunnel caving in around me, the puff of air and dust that doused my light.

"I guess." He shrugs. "It became unstable. Part of the lower tunnel collapsed and we had to run. We made it to the top just seconds before César and the others arrived. We pretended we'd come because of the noise too, and joined the cleanup crew. Then they found your brother and the place was swarming. We couldn't go back. Papi said we should take the opportunity to get the metal processed. So we told everyone we had to leave town for a funeral, and we went to Uyuni and paid a man to use the smelter there and extract the silver. We couldn't do it here. It would have raised too many questions. Everyone knows us here."

"But you came back."

"The ore was good quality. Not much, but real pure. Papi wanted to check one last time and see if there was any we had missed, so we came tonight. We didn't know they had hired a new *guarda*."

"Well, they did. But it doesn't matter," I say bitterly. "You got your silver, and you even got out of cleaning up the mess you made getting it. Your stunt nearly killed me—it nearly killed Daniel."

"Whatever," he snaps. "You've made an even bigger mess."

"So—what? We're even?" I snort. "Your explosion buried me, my explosion buried you, and that's that?"

"Hey, if we hadn't set that, they never would have found your brother. You have me to thank that he's a cripple, not a corpse. Besides, you should never have been in the mine anyway. It's probably because you were there that night that our blast went wrong."

I remember why I dislike Guillermo and his father so much.

"Fine," I say, hefting to my feet and turning toward the access tunnel. "I'll leave."

"No!" He reaches out and grabs my ankle, surprisingly strong.

I look over my shoulder at him. "I'm bad luck, right? Won't you be better off if I leave?"

Guillermo's face crumples. His fingers tremble against my ankle. "Please," he whispers. "Please don't leave me here alone."

And I want to hold on to my anger against him. He and his father have been nothing but unpleasant to me and my family. He deserves the consequences of his actions. But then I think of Daniel, how he was hurt and alone in the dark and how much I wish there had been someone to sit with him while he waited for rescue. Even if it were someone who didn't like him.

Guillermo is unpleasant and rude, but we're both just kids trying to survive the Mountain That Eats Men. I sigh. Irony is a sharp, vicious thing. Guillermo constantly harassed me, trying to get me to leave the mine. Now he's terrified I'll do exactly that.

I sink back down beside him. "It's not good to be alone," I say.

"You'll stay with me?" he presses, his fingers still latched on the cuff of my sweatpants. "Promise?"

"I won't leave you." The words taste of ash and rock dust. "I promise."

Guillermo lets go of my ankle and stares at the tunnel ceiling, his eyes losing focus and his breath hitching in pain.

"How are you feeling?" I ask.

"Not good," he says. "Cold. Hurt. Scared."

It's an honest response. "I'm so sorry I hurt you," I say again.

317

"I was here to steal," he says quietly. "You were here to guard. It's as much my fault as yours that I'm buried here."

I nod, accepting that. Glad that what he offered was to take part of the blame rather than offer forgiveness. Guillermo will never be my favorite person in the world, but he's honest and I can respect that. Here, trapped under a mountain together, it feels like maybe we don't have to be enemies. Maybe we can just be two people trying to stay alive who have chosen different roads to get there.

I reach out and take his chilled fingers in mine, offering what quiet comfort I can.

And so we sit there, cold and scared together, and wait for César to save us both.

It's over an hour later when they manage to dig through to us. By the time the first miner climbs out of the expanded access tunnel, Guillermo has started to tremble violently. In the light from the man's electric headlamp I can see that his lips have turned purple.

"I think he's in shock," I whisper to the man.

Three other men climb in behind him. When I see César straighten up, I can't help it, I throw myself at him. He wheezes at the impact, but wraps me in a gentle hug.

"It will be all right, *mi hija*," he says gently. With my cheek pressed against his chest I can hear the rattle of his breathing, but I don't call him on his lie. Instead I step away and point toward Guillermo.

César looks where I point. His eyes widen. "Is that . . . ?"

I nod.

César's expression tightens into a frown. I hear the grumbling behind him from the rest of his team. They all recognize Guillermo.

Despite this, César lays a comforting hand on Guillermo's shoulder.

"Well, boy." He pauses to cough. "Let's make sure the mountain doesn't eat you just yet, hmm?"

Guillermo stares at him, eyes wide and glassy.

"We're going to work on moving the rocks off of your legs," César goes on, between gasps, "and then we're going to get you out of here. It might not be pleasant, but we'll get you out, whatever it takes."

Guillermo seems past speech, but he nods. César heaves himself to his feet, then braces himself against the tunnel wall for support while he gives directions to his men.

"Ebelardo, go get some boards to put around his head so that no rocks fall on his face. Get him a helmet too, if there's an extra in the shed. Oh, and someone go find his father."

"He may be hard to find," I say.

César shoots me a look.

"He was here too. Earlier. He left when this happened."

"We'll deal with that later, then." César looks angry, but the roughness in his voice might just be from the coughing. "Hugo, let's divert the weight of the pile to the right. Once the pressure is off and that angle isn't so steep, we can start pulling these lower rocks off of him."

The miners get to work. César is too weak to help them, but he sits off to the side, giving advice when they need it.

"Can I do anything?" I ask.

César shakes his head. "Climb out if you like."

The looks the other men give me are so cold it's as if they've spoken aloud: *You've done enough.* They may have believed before that women in the mine were unlucky. I've just proved it to them.

I hate being in here with their judgment clouding the already-foul air. I hate seeing César brace his forehead on his crossed arms and spasm with painful coughs. I'm sore and dirty and tired. I want nothing more than to climb up the now-broad exit tunnel and leave this night behind me.

But I remember my promise to Guillermo and settle beside him to wait until the men are done.

No matter the glares, I vow that I will not leave until after he does.

23

Slowly, painstakingly, the men liberate Guillermo from the mountain trying to eat him. When they get to his lower legs and lift the rocks off, he screams, and I can see dark blood staining his jeans. Two of the men leave and come back with a sheet of corrugated tin roofing to serve as a makeshift stretcher. They splint his legs the best they can and lift him onto the metal. Guillermo is moaning in pain, but there's nothing for it but to keep moving him. César fights through his coughing spells to tell them to carry Guillermo down to the health center at the foot of the mountain and stay with him until it opens in an hour's time.

Eventually, the miners are able to wrestle the heavy stretcher through the tunnel. True to my word, I follow the stretcher, not leaving the mine until after Guillermo. I'm sure that at this point he's way past caring where I am, but it matters to me not to break this promise.

When I crawl out, the fact that it's morning surprises me,

though the brightness coming through the shaft would have told me that, had I been paying attention. I look around the entrance to the mine, transformed now by the presence of so many people, and stripped of its shadows by the sun. I check for Victor, but I don't see him.

I feel out of place, floating. The men shuffle off, the stretcher tipping between them. I need to go home and check on Belén and make sure she's okay. And César . . . César is leaning against the cliff, rubbing a tired hand over his lined face. Though he's bent near double with the effort of breathing and talking, he's coordinating with the miners, keeping everyone from bothering me. Wrapping up his conversation, César walks heavily toward me.

"It's been quite a night," he says softly. "Let's go home."

Even though it should only take fifteen minutes, the walk from the mine to César's house takes double that. We creep along, César slumping against the mountain to catch his breath every dozen steps. Finally, not able to bear seeing him struggle on his own, I pull his arm across my shoulders. He's so stooped over it means I can take some of his weight.

"Thank you, Ana."

I turn my head away from him so that he can't see my tears. I let Belén stay with me when I knew it was wrong. I didn't manage to protect her. I didn't prevent a mine robbery. I destroyed the entrance to the mine that will take many man-hours to clean up. I injured Guillermo. I made César leave his sickbed when his body clearly can't handle it. I expected César, in the privacy of the walk home, to finally lay into me for my stupidity, to make clear to me the price tag of all my bad choices, like Papi would have done. I expected anger—or disappointment at least. Somehow, his quiet thanks make me feel even worse. It's hard to be the only one hating yourself when you know you deserve to be hated.

César's wet, racking cough precedes him up the rocky path, and Mami rushes out when we're still meters from the door and helps me get him inside and into bed again. As she works to settle him, my eyes wander over to the little alcove where Belén and I sleep. Belén is lying there, pale and still. Abuelita is sponging her face with a damp cloth. I walk over and lean against the wall, staring down at them. I don't reach for Belén, afraid I'll do even more damage.

"How is she?" I whisper.

"She's alive," says Abuelita. "And so are you. And so is César. What more could we ask from God?"

I could think of a few things. I close my eyes.

A couple of minutes later, I feel Mami standing at my shoulder.

"I'm sorry," I whisper. I feel like I've said that a lot recently. I know it will never be enough.

"What happened, Ana?" Mami's soft voice is my undoing. Tears splash the floor in front of me. I wipe my face with my hands and try to keep my voice steady.

"She snuck out to join me. I let her stay. I didn't think it would be a big deal. But robbers came. They hurt her. I threw dynamite to scare them off, but I collapsed the entrance on Guillermo. He's at the health center now." I choke on the words, and soon the whole story is tumbling out of me, the horror of the night washing over me anew. I find I can't stand any longer. I slide down the wall and curl up on the floor and cry, as if someone had shot me in the belly.

"Hush now, *mi hija*," Mami says, sitting beside me on the floor and stroking my face. "You did what you had to do. We are all still alive. Where there's life, there's hope."

I twist until I can lean my forehead in her lap and let her comfort me for a minute more. Then I get to my feet.

When I go outside to wash, I have to crack through a thin film of ice on the top of the bucket, but I scrub myself anyway, accepting the cold water's punishment. When I'm clean, I head inside to change clothes. Fresh sweatpants, fresh shirt, fresh braids.

Mami makes a broth. I try to bring a bowl to César, but he insists on coming out and sitting with us.

"How is my little girl?" César asks between mouthfuls, pointing toward Belén with his chin.

"She'll be all right," answers Abuelita. "She just had a nasty blow and is sleeping it off. You don't worry; get your rest."

When César has finished his soup, he goes into his room and lies down again. Abuelita and I clean up the meal and try to pretend we can't hear him wheezing as he tries unsuccessfully to fall asleep.

"You rest and sit with Belén," says Mami. "We're going to go break some rocks."

"You're not staying to look after them?" I ask.

Mami gives me a tired smile as she wraps her shawl around her shoulders.

"We're out of money. If Belén doesn't wake up soon, we may need to take her to the hospital. If César's cough gets any worse, we're going to need to take him to the hospital too." She heaves a sigh, one that only poor women know.

"We still haven't paid off the loan for the medical bills from Daniel," Abuelita adds. "They may not treat them if we don't have money. We have to go."

"Do you want me to come and help?"

Mami shakes her head.

"You might as well sleep if you can," she says gently. "You were up all night. But try not to sleep too deeply. If either of them needs something, you'll have to help them with it. If Belén wakes up, try to get her to eat a little bread or drink some tea."

"Okay."

"Hey." Abuelita pats my cheek. "Don't be sad. Who knows? Maybe the miners will have missed a great big chunk of silver, and I'll find it, and we'll all eat steak tonight. Hmm?"

Her words remind me of Francisco and Guillermo's robbery. Sometimes more silver doesn't make things better.

"No sense hanging around when a steak dinner is on the line," I say, hoping my smile looks more real than it feels.

Abuelita gives me a quick peck on the forehead, and she and Mami head out the door. When they've left, I shuffle into the alcove I share with Belén and curl up beside her. I smooth her thick black hair away from her face. Belén has lovely hair. She's going to grow into a real beauty. But now there are traces of blood matted in that lovely hair and her face is pale in the darkness. She still hasn't opened her eyes.

I bite my lip hard and try not to start crying again.

I thought it was bad enough in the mine when the devil guarded every exit. Now it feels like he's loose in the world and I see his bloody handprints everywhere.

———

Hours later, Belén finally wakes up.

"Ana?" I hear, a whisper beside my ear.

"Belén!" I jolt upright and reach out to touch her face. "You're awake! How do you feel?"

"My head hurts."

"Are you hungry? Can I get you some bread?"

"I don't really—" she starts, but I have my orders.

"You need to at least drink something. Stay here, I'll get you some broth."

I hop off the bed and bring a cup to Belén. I sit beside her, prop her against me, and hold the cup to her lips. She sips it slowly. With her leaning on me, my face is right next to her head and I can't help but smell the dried blood and rock dust still caked in her hair. It makes my stomach turn, but I don't move or say anything. It's not her fault that she was injured there. It's Francisco's. And I suppose, in some ways, it's mine. I should never have let her stay.

"How do you feel?" I ask again.

"My head still hurts, but the broth is nice," she says.

She's barely touched it. I smooth her hair away from her face.

"What happened?" she asks. "After I hit my head, I mean. I don't remember anything after that."

I take a deep breath. "Well, it's complicated. A lot happened after that, actually." I'm glad she's sitting in front of me. It's easier to talk to the back of her head than it would be to talk face-to-face. Quickly, I catch her up on the rest of the night after she was knocked out.

"Ay!" Belén exclaims. "You were so brave!" Then, after a pause, "Did they manage to take anything? Is the damage very bad?"

I hesitate. "Maybe?"

In my arms, Belén starts to cry.

"Oh, sweetie!" I give her shoulders a squeeze. "What's wrong?"

"It's our fault," she whispers.

"No, you can't think that way," I tell her.

"No, but it *is*. It's part of being a *guarda*. It was our job to keep the mine safe. If they managed to take anything, then *we* owe the mining cooperative the money to replace it. If the mine got wrecked, *we* have to pay to repair it."

My comfort dies in my throat. She's right. Whoever's working as *guarda*, it's their debt if something gets taken. A feeling in my chest tightens like a winch.

"Maybe I can get a job as a *guarda* too"—Belén sniffs—"at one of the other mines."

"What?" I ask, having been lost in my thoughts. "No way. You're eight!"

"We have to do something." She chews on her lower lip, thinking out loud. "Maybe if I leave school, I can get a job as a *palliri* . . ." She trails off miserably.

I know that no one will ever hire an eight-year-old as a *guarda*. Plus, especially after tonight, César would never let his little girl do such a thing. Hell, after tonight, Mami and César may not even let *me* keep doing the job. I remember, more than a month ago, when I first heard Belén's little-girl dream of becoming a doctor. It had made me laugh. Now I feel like crying. There was never any chance that she would make it. But was it too much to ask that she get just a few more years of hoping for it before this mountain crushed her too? In her sincerity I see a reflection of myself pausing my own dreams because we needed the money. Under my fingers, the dried blood flakes out of Belén's hair and lands on my sweatpants, as brown and dry as the llama bloodstains on the lintels of the mine. From the next room, I hear César coughing.

Sacrifices, I think. *All of us, sacrifices to the devil of these mines.*

I shake my head to clear it from the useless thoughts. Though I wish I had a time machine, I can't go back and change the choices I already made. The only thing I can control is what I do now. I refuse to let Belén give up on her dreams like I had to. I refuse to allow her to become just more grit to be ground between this mountain's molars.

"Belén, listen to me," I whisper to her. My voice is fierce. "You will *never* be a *guarda*."

"But..."

"No. Not now when you're eight. Not when you're older. Never. You are going to stay in school." I close my eyes for a moment, unsure what price I will have to pay to purchase the promise I just made. "Go to sleep now." I gently disentangle myself, laying her flat. "I've got this."

"Where are you going?" she asks.

"First, I'm going to give César some of this broth. Then I'll take care of things. Don't worry."

I tuck her in and drop a quick kiss on her forehead, then I bring the rest of the broth to César. When I enter his bedroom, he's sprawled across the bed. He's in a T-shirt again, sweat standing out on his forehead from the effort it takes to breathe. I feel awkward. I'm used to seeing César fully dressed and in public; in charge of men, working. I hate seeing him sick and weak.

"Ana," he gasps.

I hold out a cup.

"I made some broth for Belén, but she's done with it now. I thought that maybe you'd like some more to help with the cough." César's eyebrows shoot up and I answer his question before he has to ask it. "Belén woke up a little while ago. She doesn't remember much of what happened. Her head hurts, but she was able to take a little broth and she makes sense when she talks. I think she's going to be okay."

César sighs with relief, and when he does, something rattles again.

"I've been praying," he whispers.

I flinch guiltily. It hadn't occurred to me to pray.

"Are you okay for now?" I ask him.

And though he's far from okay, César nods. I close the door to the bedroom behind me softly and start preparing dinner.

I pull a handful of peeled *chuños* from the bucket and salt the water.

I know we won't be having steak.

It's past dark when Abuelita gets home from working as a *palliri*. She must have worked till the absolute last shred of daylight left the sky. Mami still isn't home, but that doesn't surprise me too much. I don't see the flashlight. My guess is that she'll stay out as long as she can, even though she sent Abuelita home.

"*Mmm*, smells good, Ana," Abuelita says. I give her a hug and catch her up on how Belén and César are doing. Then I take a deep breath.

"I'm going back up to the mine," I say. It's abrupt, but with darkness already upon us, there's no time to waste.

"What?" She stills.

I take a deep breath.

"Someone has to be there tonight to guard it. Francisco, or someone else, might come again and take more. It's still officially my job, so it will be our family's debt if more gets taken. We can't afford to be in any more debt." I see Abuelita open her mouth. Whether it's to argue or agree, I don't wait to find out. "It's not a plan for forever. We can talk tomorrow about other ideas, but right now I have to go. It's already late."

I can see emotions chasing themselves across Abuelita's face, but all she says is, "Be careful."

Feeling grim and beaten, I shove some food, a blanket, and

my helmet into my old schoolbag and sling it over my shoulder. On my way out the door I grab four new mini-sticks of dynamite.

This time I do remember to pray that I won't need to use them.

24

When I get to the mouth of El Rosario, I scan the area carefully. I check the shed. The lock is broken from last night, but everything is still inside where it should be, so at least no one has come by yet tonight. The blast pulled my last nest off the cliff face, so I find myself a comfortable-enough spot on the rubble still blocking the entrance to the mine so that I can sit facing the shed. I'm beyond tired, beyond furious at the world that has trapped my family in a corner. I decide that if anyone even *tries* to approach the mine tonight, I'll blast them all before I let them take so much as a pebble from that shed. I stare at the destruction at the mouth of the mine, wondering how long it will take to clean up, wondering what it will cost me.

"Ana, is that you?"

The voice surprises me so much that the flame of my lighter is already halfway toward a stick of dynamite before I notice who it is.

"No no nononono . . ." he says, all in a rush, "don't do that again. It's me!"

"Victor?" Even though he stayed to help me dig Guillermo out and brought Belén home, I still kind of figured he'd make himself scarce. He left, after all. And I'm sure he could still get in trouble if people started asking questions about why he was on the mountain and the landlord figures out he got into his old home.

"What are you doing here?" I ask, glancing around. "Is it just you?"

"Yeah. I scouted around a bit too. I didn't see anyone else."

I relax. I don't want any more surprises.

"Francisco and Guillermo are gone," Victor says.

"Wait! What?"

"The miners dropped Guillermo off at the health center this morning. His legs looked bad, but it turns out the cuts were mostly shallow and only one leg was broken. They were able to set it cleanly. When they went home for lunch, they left him sleeping there, but when they returned, Guillermo was gone. I asked one of my buddies who works at the bus station, and he says he saw a man and a boy on crutches get on a bus headed for Uyuni. I don't think they'll be back."

Some surprises, I realize, I don't mind as much as others. I'm glad that I won't have to face Francisco again. I imagine the vast salt flats of Uyuni and wonder what Guillermo's life will be like there. It's not an easier place to live, trading rock for salt, but it makes sense that's where Francisco took him: Uyuni is where they mine lithium for cell phones and electronics. It should be easy enough for Francisco to get a job there. Plus, it's over two hundred kilometers away—far enough that no one from here is likely to chase him down to make him sorry for what he did.

I'm glad, for Guillermo's sake at least. Miners can be as unkind to thieves as they are to *guardas*.

But even though I'm relieved, a cold dread washes through me. If Francisco's gone, then the small hope I had that the cooperative would make him pay for at least half of the repairs to the mine is gone too. It will be all on me and my family. I sigh. There is no path out of our debt now but to find a way to earn the money the slow way. The hard way. The cooperative will dock César's paycheck, and we'll pull a little out of what we need each week until the debt is paid down, like we did after Papi's burial. It's a hungry road back from disaster. I've traveled it before.

"That's good to know," I decide. "But what are you doing up here? Surely you didn't come all this way, at night, just to tell me the news."

"I was actually visiting your place."

"Oh?"

"I wanted to make sure Belén was better," he says. "And your grandma told me you'd come up here for the night, so I thought, since I was nearby, I'd come say hello."

"Oh. Well, hello, I guess."

"Hi."

I look at him carefully. "And you? How are you doing?"

Victor gives a half laugh. "Oh, you know me, a Sánchez always lands on his feet."

I stare at him until he gives me a real answer.

"I'm okay," he says. "No one figured out I broke into my old house, so I haven't lost my place in mechanic training."

"Wait!" I squeal. "Mechanic training? You got in?"

Victor gives a shy smile. "Yeah. You were right. Joaquín was able to get me in at the garage. I have to work for free, but they're willing to teach me. If I don't ditch, and I prove to them I'm not an idiot or a criminal, they'll let me start as a paid apprentice in six months."

"Victor, that's great!"

His smile stretches. "Yeah," he says again. "It kind of is."

Something occurs to me and I dig in my schoolbag, glad I used it to carry my stuff. Sure enough, there at the bottom is Victor's notebook.

"Here," I say, I pulling it out and handing it to him.

Victor runs his fingers over the pages, pausing when he sees his note.

"I didn't think I'd ever see this again," he says softly.

"Well, I'm officially giving it back. You might need it for taking notes on cars."

Victor grins. "Thanks, Ana."

We sit in comfortable silence for a few minutes. Then something else occurs to me.

"Are you still staying where you were before?"

He nods. "It's the only place I can afford. Even to stay there, I still have to do fights to make rent. But once I get through my apprenticeship, I should be able to move into a better place."

"Good." My cheeks actually hurt, I'm smiling so hard. "That place is a dump."

Victor laughs.

I hate to think that Victor will have to keep letting himself get beaten up for money, but I'm glad to know that he has a way out, a plan for when it will end.

"I'm not sure which is worse," I joke, "being a human punching bag or being a *guarda*. I guess in the fight ring you at least sometimes get to punch back."

"Oh, I don't know." He winks at me, and I see a bit of the sparkle of the old Victor, the one I knew before his papi pulled him out of school to work in the mine. "I hear that sometimes a *guarda* hits back too—except she does it with dynamite. There's this one girl I know who nearly brought the whole mountain down last time someone snuck up on her . . ."

"Ha. Ha. Ha," I say. "Victor Sánchez, you're soooo funny."

"Well," he says, tucking his notebook under his arm and getting to his feet, laughing, "I gotta get going. Catch you later, Ana."

He turns away, and I realize I have one more thing I need to say to him.

"Victor!"

"Yeah?"

"Thank you. For what you did last night. Thank you for staying with me when things were bad, and for taking care of Belén."

Victor smiles his big crooked smile.

"You're welcome," he says simply.

And then he's gone.

I sit there for the rest of the night, alone with the stars.

On the Mountain That Eats Men, hope is a tree from which life slowly snaps off all the branches: it dies a little at a time, year by year, piece by tiny piece. Some days I feel like there aren't enough branches left to keep my tree alive anymore.

I remember the hopes Daniel and I used to pass back and forth like a bag of candy. *We will run away together. Far away from here. Far away from the mountain and the mines. Far away from the rocks and the cold.* For what seems like all of my life, I have wanted nothing more than to leave this mountain. And yet . . . and yet.

As I stare down at the twinkling city of Potosí, I hear the echo of Padre Julio's reedy voice in my head: *Again, the devil took him to an exceedingly high mountain, and showed him all the kingdoms of the world and their glory. He said to him, "I will give you all of these things, if you will fall down and worship me."*

It was the Gospel from church that day I sat between Mami and César, just before he got sick. I had thought, at the time, that it was a judgment on me for wanting a nice life I didn't have. But now I hear it differently. It's not a verse saying the kingdoms of the world and their splendor are bad . . . it's saying that sometimes there is a wrong way to get even the best of things.

The devil knows better than to offer you bad things, I think. *He offers you good things, the wrong way.* Get money by stealing. Feel better by drinking. It's only after you take the bait that you see the trap.

Recently, so much has happened that I haven't really had time to think about anything more than solving the next problem in front of my face. But now, with the icy stars above me and the sleeping city below me, I have plenty of time to think about my life.

I think about mountains filled with devils and darkness, and of sparkling, unreachable cities. I think of Francisco and Guillermo, willing to steal from people poorer than they are, putting my family into even more debt. I always thought I wanted to leave this place no matter what, but now I know that I will not leave those I love to struggle by themselves. I will not steal my future from anyone.

Staring down at the city of Potosí, I trace the stripes of light that outline the roads and count the dark patches of parks and graveyards. Two main roads intersect at Potosí: the 1 and the 5. They loop around a bit in the middle of the city, but the 1 runs in from the south and leaves to the north, stretching all the way to La Paz, one of our capital cities. It's up on the Altiplano and is the seat of the legislative and executive branches of the national government. The 5 comes in from the west from the salt flats of Uyuni, and leaves to the east, looping its way to Sucre, the judicial capital. From there, it meets up with the 7, which takes it to Santa Cruz in the lowlands, the biggest city in the country and our business center, a third capital city in all but name. Yenni's mami is to the north, in La Paz, searching for better work. Guillermo and Francisco are to the west, living off their stolen silver in Uyuni. Daniel is to the east, somewhere along the 5 before Sucre, breathing better air.

The cold wind whipping over the mountain takes my exhale with it, whisking it off to horizons I will never see. I force myself to let go of my sadness. And in the stillness of the hours after midnight, I think. I think about La Paz and Sucre. Of the 1 and the 5. I think of Abuelita handing me an acetylene helmet when I soaked a box of matches.

This is my country and it has more than one capital.

This is my city and it has more than one main road.

This is my home and there is more than one way to light a cook fire.

This is my life. There must be more than one way to live it.

The Inca constructed wonders without the wheel or steel or money or writing or horses, I remind myself. It's time I stopped focusing on all the things I don't have. It's time to start building anyway. And so, instead of resting my head on my crossed arms and letting my thoughts chill me until dawn, I stand, and pace, and find a better way.

———

When I get home, Mami is waiting for me, as she has been every morning I've worked as a *guarda*. I'm exhausted, but when I walk in the door, I'm instantly cheered to see that both César and Belén are up and sitting at the table. With a few days of rest and medicine, César's cough is settling. He's hunched forward, cradling his cup of tea, and Belén is still pale and is wrapped tightly in a blanket, but just seeing the two of them up lifts my spirits.

I sink onto a second bucket that has been placed beside Belén. Mami puts a cup of tea in front of me.

"How was your night?" asks Belén.

"I'm okay, and nothing else was taken," I say, and leave it at that. Abuelita drapes a blanket around my shoulders and gives me a one-armed hug. I feel warmer already.

I sip my tea and consider my new family. Mami, willing to remarry to protect her children. César, willing to leave his sickbed to rescue me. Belén, willing to give up on her dreams to help out. Abuelita, willing to tell me every story she knows until I can stitch together a new truth for myself.

I remember what Victor said at the mouth of the mine: *I won't leave . . . If it caves in again, I'll stay here and dig you out. I promise.*

Maybe it's true that none of us can stop the avalanche of bad things that will try to crush us. But the true tragedy is not the avalanche, it's when each person runs away, trying to get what's best only for themselves, leaving others to die in the rubble. I think of the sacrifices Mami and César and Abuelita and Belén have already been willing to make for me and the sacrifices I've made for them. If we all commit to digging each other out, no matter what, we can make sure that no one gets buried.

I take a deep breath.

"So," I say, "I've been thinking."

———

Three days later, Belén is well enough to return to school. Mami lets her go because it's a Friday: if it exhausts her, she can rest up over the weekend.

Even after spending the night awake as a *guarda*, I walk

with her. Though she no longer has constant headaches, she does sometimes get dizzy, and I won't take the chance of her stumbling off a cliff if I can avoid it.

Belén's friends chirrup with happiness to have her returned to the flock, and we walk in a companionable group over the rocky path from the houses to the school. When we arrive, the little kids knock and are let in by Doña Inés, like always. She has her baby in a sling around her body. We all pause to look in and coo at the beautiful, healthy little girl.

I give Belén a quick hug, and she scampers after her friends. To my left those same boys are still wrestling ore carts in and out of the mine by the school, just as boys have been doing without a break for the past 471 years. *It's not going to change,* I think. *Ever.*

But instead of filling me with sadness, today it fills me with fire. I'm done waiting for the world to change, to give me what I want. It's time to build my future using what I've got now. It's time for *me* to change. I turn to the gate just as Doña Inés is about to close it.

"Wait!" I say. "Please."

Doña Inés is surprised but lets me in with a smile.

I haven't been to school in over a month, but the morning routine hasn't changed. I go and sit in Don Marcelino's office while he sings the national anthem with the kids and gives his daily talk. I can hear him through the open door. Today's topic is Resilience.

Yes, I think with a smile. *Exactly.*

When the talk is done and the kids have surged off for their breakfast, Don Marcelino returns to his office.

"Ana," he says, surprise clearly written all over his face. "How are you?"

"I'm well," I say, gathering my courage for the speech I've rehearsed. "But I was wondering something."

"Yes?" he says, settling himself behind his desk and pushing his square glasses up the bridge of his nose. "What can I do for you?"

They're the same words he used when my request was for him to drive my father's corpse down the mountain. I swallow. All my well-rehearsed words vanish, scattering like rice spilled on a rock floor. When I open my mouth, my old hopes come out instead.

"Someday, I want to leave this place," I confess in a whisper. "Someday, I want to have a nice house in the city and make enough to support my family. I don't want to stay here and marry a miner. I don't want my children to have to live the lives my parents did, and their parents before them." I feel raw, exposed. "But I'm not willing to allow my family to suffer to do that. I won't leave the wrong way. To leave the right way, I need to bring them with me. I need a job better than the ones I can get on this mountain. And to get that better job, I need to finish school."

Don Marcelino smiles. "I'm glad to hear it, Ana. We've missed you."

"Th-thank you," I manage. "But that's only half of it."

He sits quietly, polishing his glasses on a handkerchief, and lets me gather my thoughts.

"Someone once told me that dreams are for little kids," I say finally. "And in some ways, I think he's right. Believing that good things will happen because you want them to is a way only little kids think. Everyone else on this mountain knows better."

Don Marcelino grimaces when I say this but doesn't contradict me. Even though he's from the city, he's worked up here long enough that he knows the rocky outlines of our reality.

"Which is why I need your help," I say. "It's no good to sit and wish for something; you have to work for it too."

Hope kindles in Don Marcelino's eyes. I wonder, for a second, just how hard it must be to choose to run a school and see all your students vanish, one at a time, year after year after year without end.

"Yes?" he prompts.

I take a deep breath.

"I can't come back to school." Don Marcelino's face falls, and I rush on before he can end the conversation. "My family needs the money I make, especially with the robbery and Daniel's medical bills. But . . ." And here I pause, gathering my courage. "But if I'm a *guarda*, I'm alone and it's quiet and I'm not allowed to fall asleep all night long. So . . . maybe . . . I could study then?"

Don Marcelino looks slightly stunned. Stunned, but not angry. I go on.

"You could give me books to read, and exercises to do. I could write them on my overnights and give them to Belén in the mornings. She could bring them in to school . . . if someone was willing to mark them . . . maybe I could eventually learn enough to take the secondary school entrance exams . . . ?"

I trail off.

Don Marcelino starts nodding enthusiastically.

"Yes!" he says, beaming. "Ana, what a great idea! I can certainly arrange that for you. You might need to come in every now and again to have something explained to you or to sit for an exam, but I can arrange this with your teachers." He grins at me. "You're creating your own night school."

My smile is wobbly. I can't believe he said yes. I can't believe that there is a possibility I can still reach for my dreams.

"You really think it might work?" I ask again, just to be sure.

"We'll make it work," he says.

———

Half an hour later I'm standing outside the peeling blue metal door, my arms full of textbooks and supplies. But though the door has clanged behind me, I don't feel shut out. Instead, I'm grinning like a maniac.

I puff a breath out and turn. There is one more thing I have to do.

It hadn't been until the day after the robbery, when César, Belén, and Abuelita were sleeping, that I finally admitted to Mami about the forty-eight bolivianos and fifteen centavos heavy on my conscience. I begged her to let me keep working as a *guarda* until I could earn it back. Mami had thought about it for a few moments, then agreed.

Your debt to your friend is no less important than our family's debt to the cooperative, she had said. With two more nights of *guarda* money, plus what she and Abuelita had been able to earn breaking rocks, we finally had enough to cover food and for me to take what I needed with me when I walked Belén to school this morning.

My pocket swings heavily as I walk down the mountain. The jingle is a cheerful sound. I've hated that I stole from a friend. Now I'm finally going to make it right.

My steps are brisk as I make my way into Potosí. But faced with the imposing slab of the *posada* door, I hesitate for a moment. Taking a deep breath, I force myself to lift my hand and knock.

"Can you get Yenni for me, please?" I ask the gardener who answers. "It'll just be a moment."

He nods and closes the door. I wait on the street, chewing the inside of my lip nervously. Finally, the heavy door creaks open and Yenni is standing on the other side of it.

"Ana?" She looks surprised. "What on earth are you doing here?"

I open my mouth to reassure her that I'm not here to ask for anything else.

"I'm sorry," comes out instead, in a miserable whisper.

"For what?" Yenni scrunches up her forehead, confused.

I reach into my pockets and pull out the handful of coins. I clear my throat.

"The last time I was here, you went shopping. You dropped your coin purse when you left the shop." I find I can't meet her eyes. "I should have given it back to you right away, but instead . . . I borrowed it." I shove the coins into the space between us. "I'm so sorry I took it without asking."

I want to go on, tell her why I took the money, tell her how I felt, but there's a lump clogging my throat and the words are jammed up behind it. Besides, all of that is my problem, not hers. So I just let the apology stand, and hold out the little mountain of silver.

When I feel her warm hands under mine, I open my fingers, and the coins slide away from me. I drop my hands to my sides, feeling like a great weight has been lifted off my chest. I take the coin purse out of my pocket and place it on top of the pile. Then, finally, I look up. Yenni is considering me, the coins cradled in front of her.

"I thought I'd lost the grocery money," she says. Then, after a pause: "They took it out of my wages." She considers me. "I wondered why you never came by for breakfast." After another moment, she nods and tucks the money into the purse, putting it in her pocket. "Well, thank you for bringing it back. It's good to have an honest friend . . . even if it's honest with a delay."

"You still want to be my friend?" I ask, hardly daring to hope.

Yenni smiles.

"Silly," she says, and pulls me in for a hug.

I leave the *posada* happily because that too is a door I know will open again for me in the future.

———

I get to the entry lot of El Rosario right at six.

I stand to one side and watch the miners as they tidy up for the night. I'm starting to know more of them, and as they pack up and head home, they greet me by name, wishing me a quiet Friday night.

"Don't worry," I call after them. "Everything'll still be here in the morning."

They laugh good-naturedly. I've developed a reputation with dynamite.

The last one out, lagging far behind the others, is César. Though I hate how slowly and painfully he moves, after a week of being bedridden, I am so glad to see him on his feet again.

He straightens as he leaves the mine, checking around to make sure everything is where it should be. When he notices me, he comes over.

"Ana," he says.

"Hi, Papi," I say.

The smile that breaks across César's dirty face is like a ray of sunlight through a cloud bank.

"What are you doing here?" he asks. "Now that I'm back, you don't have to work nights anymore."

"I've decided I'm going to keep working as a *guarda*," I say, holding up my books. "It will let me help the family and still continue with school."

César considers me silently for a moment. I play my best card.

"Mami already said yes . . ."

A laugh bursts out of him.

"Daughters!" he says, throwing up his hands. "Who knew they were so much trouble?"

I only notice after he reaches out to playfully tug my braid that it didn't even occur to me to flinch.

I wait until everyone is long gone and it's full night before I strap the acetylene tank to my hip, put the helmet on, and head into the mine. The trip down the main entrance tunnel feels shorter than it did last time, and before I know it, I'm standing in front of the Tío.

I consider him in the flickering glow of my headlamp. Then I take a pencil out of my pocket and hold it in front of his face.

"This is not an offering," I tell him. "It's a promise. A promise that I am going to work hard. I am going to study, and save my money, and find a job that is not guarding your mines or sorting your rubble. I am going to get my family off your mountain. You can't have them. And you can't have me."

I stand there a moment longer, waiting to see if the devil will say anything. But he is nothing more than a statue made of clay, and the only breathing I hear in the tunnel is my own.

I put the pencil at the devil's feet and walk out of the mines.

Later, triple wrapped in blankets on my perch beside the newly cleared entrance to El Rosario, I allow myself a moment before opening my math book. I look down at the city, once the envy of kings, spread below me. Then I tip my head and consider the hill looming above me, and the constellation-spangled sky above it. The Mountain That Eats Men has taken so much: my father's life, my brother's health, my childhood.

But it can only take my hope if I let it.

I choose not to let it.

I will find a path off this mountain that is not bought with the pain of others.

It will be difficult, but I will use the currency of work to buy a new future for myself and those I love.

Girls like me don't get choices handed to us. We have to make them for ourselves.

Just because something is hard doesn't mean you can't do it, I tell myself as I open the book and settle down to my first math problem by the light of my brother's old headlamp. *It just means it might take you a long time.*

Epilogue

—

A long time later.

I set my foot on the mud-spattered running board of the beat-up pickup truck and haul myself into the cab. I wedge the bulging bag of notebooks and colored pens between my feet and wait. For a few moments I sit there alone, wound tight as a spring, drumming my fingers on my knees.

When the driver arrives, he pulls himself into the cab in one smooth motion and turns the key in the ignition. The pickup coughs and hacks like an old miner, but eventually shudders sullenly to life. He shoots a look at me.

"Ready?"

I relax my grip on my knees. I've worked long hours and studied hard to get to where I am. I hope I'm ready.

I remember the expressions on their faces yesterday when I told Mami and Belén that I was going to take a job working as a teacher at the little school up on the Cerro Rico.

You what? Belén had shrieked. She's been shrieking a lot now that her final exams are right around the corner. The quiet, shy girl who hid behind César's legs outside church ten years ago has been replaced by a confident young woman, eager to make her mark on the world. César would be so proud if he could see her. I think he would be proud of me too, and of what we've all managed as a family in the four years since he's been gone. I hope my first papi would also be proud of me: anytime I got something wrong during those long nights of studying as a *guarda*, I copied it over and over until I knew the right answer by heart, just like he used to have me do.

Why? was all that Mami had asked. It was the same question she had put to Daniel when, after the four months it took his cracked ribs to heal, he asked whether he could stay in the lowlands and live with César's cousin for good. With so much more oxygen in the air, he was able to help out around the farm even with his asthma. By the time he visited for Christmas, he was so used to having good air to breathe that he gasped like a tourist when he got off the bus from Sucre. We all teased him that he'd gone soft, but he just grinned and showed off his new farmer's muscles and we had left it at that. César's cousin was thrilled to keep him, and Daniel has built himself a good life in that green valley.

For me, though, the question *Why?* had echoed deeply. Which is why I didn't tell Mami that I was just happy to get a teaching job after all my training. I didn't tell her any of the light, easy answers I handed to my school friends and city acquaintances like so much popcorn at a parade. Instead, I told her the truth.

Because, I said, *somewhere up there is another little boy who's thirsty for the sky, facing a lifetime in the dark. And somewhere up there is another little girl who has no idea how to dig out from under the weight of an unwanted future. They need to know that there are other paths. They need to know that the mountain is only a mountain, and the metal inside it is only metal, but that they are the treasure of the world.*

And Mami had folded me into a hug and hadn't asked me anything more about it.

I smooth my hands over my knees to wipe the sweat off my palms. I look out the windshield and over the city around me to the ugly mountain hulking on the horizon. *This is for you, César,* I think, *for folding me into your family. And this is for you, Abuelita, for showing me the right currency to use to value my life. But most of all, this is for me.*

He's still sitting there, patiently waiting for my answer.

"I'm ready." I cover the butterflies in my stomach with a laugh. "Are you sure this rust bucket will get us there?"

"Well," he says, wrestling the heap into gear and setting off up the streets of San Cristobal, aiming for the peak of the mountain, "if it breaks down, you'll be extra glad your best friend is a mechanic, won't you?"

"Shut up, Victor," I say. But I smile when I say it.

AUTHOR'S NOTE

I am rich Potosí
I am the treasure of the world
I am the king of all mountains
And the envy of all kings
—First coat of arms of the city of Potosí, 1547

My husband died a year ago. It has been very
hard. It has also been a year since anyone
has hit me. I have eleven children. May God
grant that they not suffer as I have.
—Doña Serafina Sandoval Condor, 2016

MY LAST BOOK, *The Bitter Side of Sweet*, looked at the question of child slavery in modern-day chocolate production. There is near-unanimous agreement that forcing children to work, unpaid and unfree, is wrong. However, the fact of the matter is that in most of the world, kids work. After completing *The Bitter Side of Sweet*, I felt challenged to look beyond child slavery to the more nuanced issue of child labor. And few places are more nuanced to consider this question than Bolivia.

The International Labor Organization (ILO) is a branch of the United Nations. It defines child labor as "work that is mentally, physically, socially, or morally dangerous and harmful to children; and interferes with their schooling by: depriving them of the opportunity to attend school; obliging them to leave school prematurely; or requiring them to attempt to combine school attendance with excessively long and heavy work." As of this writing, the ILO estimates that, worldwide, 218 million children age five to seventeen work, with 152 million being victims of child labor. Almost half are between the ages of five and eleven, and 73 million of them work in hazardous conditions. That's a lot of kids!

Bolivia has a very high poverty rate. Many families cannot get by without the money their children bring in. More than three-quarters of a million children under the age of seventeen work in Bolivia. Up until 2014, the minimum age for a child to work was fourteen—the same as the United States, where that is the age restriction for "nonagricultural" jobs. In the U.S., there are also restrictions on how many hours a person under the age of sixteen can work and a prohibition against those under eighteen working in "hazardous occupations." Bolivia, however, made headlines in 2014 by *lowering* the minimum age a child can work. Since then, children in Bolivia can work with their families from the age of ten, and for other people from the age of twelve.

Groups like Human Rights Watch and the United Nations immediately opposed this law. They saw it as opening up more opportunities to exploit impoverished children and keep them out of school. This is certainly a danger: when something becomes legal, more people do it. But what makes the 2014 law interesting is not who was speaking out *against* the law change, but who was asking *for* it.

UNATSBO (Unión de Niños y Niñas Trabajadores de Bolivia) is a union of Bolivian child workers. These were a group of children who were all working to support their families' incomes who realized that, as illegal underage workers, they had no protections under the law. So they banded together and formed a union. They asked that the working age be lowered so they could enter into legal contracts with their employers. However, even the union of child workers agrees there are dangerous jobs that children should not be required to do at any age. Mining is one of those jobs.

Potosí, the southwesternmost *departamento* (similar to a U.S. state) of Bolivia, is home to a mountain that has been mined without a break—or much of a plan—for almost five hundred years. That mountain is the Cerro Rico, and at the foot of it is the city of Potosí. Despite all the agreement that children should not work in mining, estimates are that 3,000–13,000 children between the ages of six and sixteen work in the mines of the Cerro Rico.

Mining is dangerous work: even if one survives the heavy metals, the toxic gases, the unpredictable explosions, and the occasional collapse of the tunnels snaking through the mountain, breathing the rock-dust-laced air without protective equipment inevitably leads to lung disease. Far from being the "Beautiful" or the "Rich" hill that it is sometimes called, to the over eight million people who have perished in it over the centuries, Potosí has another name: the Mountain That Eats Men.

Precious metals have always outweighed the value of human lives on the mountain of Potosí. From the tyrannical *mita* system the Spaniards implemented to exploit indigenous labor, where Incan men were forced to work for months without seeing the light of day, to the thirty thousand enslaved Africans who ground away their lives turning the mighty wheels of the colonial mint, the price of Potosí's silver has always been blood.

There is little silver left in the Cerro Rico anymore, but mining has continued unabated to the present day, with poorer metals such as tin and zinc replacing silver as the mountain's main output. Today, men still flock to the mountain for work whenever there is a bump in mineral and metal prices—just as they travel to the nearby salt flats of Uyuni to harvest the rare metal lithium to be used in our smartphones and the batteries for our electronics.

When you think about it, placing a value on a metal is a strange thing. You can't eat it, nor does it help you in any concrete way. To use money means that everyone in a society agrees that something with no inherent value (a rock, a bit of metal, a piece of paper) is worth something. Usually, that value relates roughly to scarcity: the less of something there is, the more we think it should be worth. Before the discovery of the mines in Potosí, silver was quite rare and was worth three times as much as gold. When the Cerro Rico flooded world markets with silver, silver dropped to being one-sixth the value of gold.

Not every culture in the history of the world has used money. The Inca, the indigenous group that ruled the largest South American empire before the arrival of the Spanish, did not use money. The Spaniards did. In fact, one of the most important reasons the Spaniards sent men to the "New World" was to find more sources of precious metals. The rallying cry of the European explorers is frequently summed up as "God, glory, and gold." Wave after wave of explorers came in search of El Dorado, a mythical Native American city said to be made entirely of gold.

Though they never found El Dorado, the Spanish did discover so much silver in the one hill of the Cerro Rico that it bankrolled (and then, due to the Spanish crown's international debt, bankrupted) Spain as a global superpower, and inflated currencies as far afield as the Ottoman Empire and the Ming Dynasty.

Potosí was hugely famous in the sixteenth and seventeenth centuries. In the 1600s, it was the fourth largest city in the Christian world. It was a hub of wealth and power: it was larger than London, Paris, and Madrid. Rumors circulated that the city streets were paved with silver. The first epigraph on this author's note, from the city's first coat of arms in 1547, captures this sense of grandeur. It was "the king of all mountains and the envy of all kings." Today, it is the poorest city in one of the poorest countries in the western hemisphere. Most have never heard of it.

The second epigraph is from a mother I met working as a *palliri* on a slag heap of the Cerro Rico when I took my research trip for this book in 2016. Doña Serafina Sandoval Condor was sending her youngest child, a seven-year-old, to school in the back of a pickup truck along with her daughter's child, also seven. That daughter worked the slag heap beside Doña Sandoval. Her greatest wish in life was that her kids not suffer as she had.

That research trip was the first time I had been back to Bolivia in over twenty years. I lived in Bolivia from the age of five, when my family moved there from Ecuador, until the age of ten, when we left to move to the Dominican Republic. We likely would have stayed longer, but my eyes were damaged as a result of ultraviolet radiation leaking through a hole in the ozone layer of the atmosphere, and the doctor finally gave my family the ultimatum: move before the next dry season or she'll go blind.

Though my eyes healed in the decades since I left my child-hood home, I was unsure if it was safe to return to those altitudes for my research trip. The doctors couldn't guarantee anything, but I wanted desperately to go. So, with the tenuous approval of an ophthalmologist and a large bag of various eye drops, I headed back to Bolivia in 2016. It was worth the risk: it was an amazing trip. I even got to visit my old elementary school!

Completely by chance, I arrived in Potosí on the first of April—the 471st anniversary of the Spaniards finding silver in the mountain. I watched the parade and listened to the speeches much like Ana does in this book.

Then I went up the mountain.

Through the generosity of the organization Voces Libres, I was able to tag along for the day to Escuela Robertitio, a tiny school for miners' children high on the Cerro Rico. I interviewed the teachers and the school psychologist about their work, and I talked to the children about their hopes and dreams.

What stunned me most was the difference that emerged between groups of kids. When I chatted with the six- to eight-year-olds and asked them what they wanted to do with their lives, they all had enthusiastic answers. One wanted to be a teacher, another a beautician. But when I asked the same question to the older kids, the eleven- to thirteen-year-olds, they had no answers. They merely shrugged. By that age, most of the boys were working in the mine after school and the girls were working as *palliris*, breaking refuse rock with their families to try to make ends meet. Many of them had already given up hope of doing anything different with their lives. Instead, they mapped that hope onto their younger siblings. "Maybe my little brother can get away," one of the older girls told me, not meeting my eyes.

The clash between the two realities shown in this note's epigraphs—the blinding wealth produced by the mountain and the crushing poverty experienced by those who have extracted that wealth over the centuries—is the core injustice that drove me to tell this story. I wanted to explore how a girl could dig out from under the weight of generational poverty where the generations began in the 1500s. I wanted to showcase Bolivia, in all its stunning Andean glory and societal complexity, for readers unfamiliar with the country. But most of all, I wanted to write a possible future for the girls—Jadahi, Emily, Noelia, Joela, Jimena, Cintia, and Emiliane—I had met on the Mountain That Eats Men. May they not suffer as their forebearers have.

A NOTE *on the* USE OF ITALICS, LANGUAGES, *and the* BIBLE

THERE HAS RECENTLY been some discussion over whether non-English words should or should not be italicized in a predominantly English text. The argument is that such italicization serves to highlight the foreignness of those words and is not the way bilingual people think or speak. However, the story I wanted to tell in *Treasure of the World* was not one of bilingual identity. In this book, my characters are not codeswitching between English and other languages: they are not using English at all. For clarity, I have chosen to italicize non-English words—not to highlight that they are a change from the way my characters have been speaking, but to remind my readers that the characters are speaking a language that is not English throughout.

So how, in an English-language text, could I best represent Spanish? Whenever possible, I have tried to reflect the fact that my characters are speaking Spanish at the level of word choice and grammar. For example, I have used Spanish colloquialisms ("if you give him a hand, he'll take your arm") rather than their English equivalents ("give him an inch, he'll take a mile") and kept the subjunctive mood, which is optional in English but mandatory in Spanish. Similarly, the response Ana gives to the readings in church is not the response one would give in English, but a translation of the Mass response from the Spanish. My hope was that, though these choices might make the phrasing feel jarring to Anglophone readers, moments like this would help sink them into the cadence of the language my characters would really be speaking. In addition, some of the Spanish used in this book may not be familiar even to native speakers, as many of the terms are regionally specific to Bolivia.

And what of the Quechua? Variations in the spelling of Quechua come from the fact that the Inca had no written language. More than one modern spelling has evolved to capture the sound of the oral language. Moreover, Quechua is spoken from southern Colombia to northern Argentina and has many regional variations. I took the phrases and spellings used in this book from my graduate school studies with Francisco Tandioy Jansasoy at Indiana University. Though the words I have used are quite basic and likely do not vary regionally, it is possible—as Francisco taught me the type of Quechua (Inga) that was his native language growing up in the Sibundoy Valley in highland Putumayo, Colombia—that there may be discrepancies between the words I have used on the page and the Quechua spoken by the families of the Cerro Rico. I was not able to check it on my research trip as, sadly, my "classroom Quechua" did not stretch far enough for me to do much more than greet my sources politely. To conduct more detailed interviews, I was assisted by a Spanish-Quechua interpreter familiar with the local dialect.

Lastly, the Bible translation used in the text is from the World English Bible, a public domain Modern English translation of the Holy Bible found on biblegateway.com. The Catholic Church rotates biblical readings based on church season. The Gospel reading that Ana hears in the cathedral (Matthew 4:1–11, the temptation of Christ in the desert) is traditionally the reading used for the first Sunday in Lent. In 2016, the first of April was the Friday after Easter. This would most definitely *not* be the reading you would hear in a Catholic Mass on this day. However, as the passage had interesting resonances with the fictional story I wanted to tell, I used it anyway.

All other errors and omissions in the text are entirely my own.

GLOSSARY

AGRADISEYKI (Quechua): thank you (borrowed from the Spanish *agradecer*)

ALLYISIAMI (Quechua): response to *puangi/puangichi*: "Fine"

ALTIPLANO (Spanish): literally "high plain," a plateau of land at 12,000 ft where the Andes are the widest, covering a large expanse of southeastern Peru and western Bolivia

API (Quechua): a drink made from ground purple corn, water, citrus fruit, and spices

¡AY, DIOS! (Spanish): Oh, God!

AYMARA: indigenous language spoken in Bolivia. Estimates are that around 1.6 million people across South America speak Aymara today. Also used to refer to the ethnic group whose primary language is Aymara.

Casa de la Moneda (Spanish): literally, "house of coin." Name of the mint in Potosí where the silver of the mountain was turned into ingots and money.

Cerro Rico (Spanish): Rich Hill

cholita (regionalism): historically a derogatory term for indigenous women in Bolivia. Today, women have taken over the term and claimed it as a source of cultural pride. The "look" of a cholita is standard: many layered, colorful skirts, a long shawl, flat shoes, a bowler hat, and braids. Pride in this term has come about in parallel with grass-roots indigenous movements; discrimination against women who choose to wear cultural dress is lower today than in the past.

chuño (regionalism): a Bolivian staple: small potatoes that have been freeze-dried and thawed multiple times to extend their shelf life. Cooked into stews and soups.

cielo (Spanish): sky; heaven

coca: leaf of the coca plant. (No relationship to cocoa/cacao, an entirely different plant, which is used to make chocolate.) Coca leaves are chewed by indigenous people throughout the Andes. Though the plant is the raw material that is used to produce the addictive drug cocaine, in its natural form it is only a mild stimulant and appetite suppressant. In Bolivia, it is cheaper than food, and many poor families use it to make it through the day on only one meal. Coca is also a deeply important part of indigenous culture and is used both in religious rituals and traditional healing.

———

DINAMITA (Spanish): dynamite

DON (Spanish): term of respect for a man, similar to "Mr."

DOÑA (Spanish): term of respect for a woman, similar to "Mrs."

———

GUARDA (Spanish): someone who guards the mines overnight to prevent robbery; usually women or girls

———

HUYANA CAPAC (1464/1468–1524): eleventh emperor of the Incan empire

INCA: indigenous people of the Andes

———

MANTA (Spanish): large square of woven wool cloth that can be used as a shawl or poncho or folded to make a sling for carrying babies or a pouch for carrying goods.

MI HIJA (Spanish): my daughter

MI HIJO (Spanish): my son

MINERAL (Spanish): literally, mineral. Used colloquially by the people on the Cerro Rico to refer to the various metals and ores that have a market value, such as tin, zinc, and aluminum.

———

PACHAMAMA (Quechua): Mother Earth

PADRE (Spanish): literally, father. Term of address for a Catholic priest.

PALLIRI (regionalism): Used on the Cerro Rico to refer to a woman whose job it is to break open refuse rocks from the mines by hand, looking for trace amounts of leftover metal.

POSADA (Spanish): inn

POTOC'XI: "a thunderous noise." Though this is part of a myth about the origin of the name "Potosí," it does not fit the phonology of Quechua, the language spoken by the Inca. Possibly Aymara in origin.

PUANGI (Quechua): hello (to one person); literally: an abbreviation for "How was the dawn for you?"

PUANGICHI (Quechua): hello (to more than one person)

———

QUECHUA: indigenous language spoken by the Inca and by their descendants. Estimates are that eight to ten million people across South America speak Quechua today. Also occasionally used to refer to the ethnic group whose primary language is Quechua.

—

EL ROSARIO (Spanish): literally, "the rosary," Catholic prayer beads and the sequence of prayers that are said on them. Many mines are named for religious figures.

—

SALTEÑA (Spanish): a baked, meat-filled pastry; empanada

SAQSAYHUAMÁN: Incan fortress near Cusco, Peru, capital of the Incan empire

SILICOSIS: a lung disease caused by breathing in dust that contains the mineral silica. Over time, it builds up in the lungs, scarring them and making it more and more difficult to breathe. Left untreated, it leads to death.

SORROCHE (regionalism): sickness caused by the lack of oxygen at high altitudes. Symptoms can include nausea, exhaustion, weakness, dizziness, insomnia, pins and needles, shortness of breath, headache.

SUMAJ ORCKO (Quechua): Beautiful Hill

—

Tío (Spanish): literally, uncle. Used by the miners of the Cerro Rico to refer to the statues of the devil guarding the mine shafts.

—

LA VERDE (Spanish): slang term for the Bolivian national football team, one of the ten members of FIFA's South American Football Confederation.

—

YACHAC (Quechua): term for a shamanistic healer in Ecuador and Bolivia

ACKNOWLEDGMENTS

GETTING ANY BOOK from idea to publication is a tremendous undertaking, and this book required more assistance than many to make it there. A huge thank-you to everyone who has supported me personally over the past five years or has helped this book in a creative or technical capacity.

To my dad, to whom this book is dedicated, and who left his heart on the *altiplano* years ago. For traveling with me, opening doors where I didn't even know to look for handles, and for being willing to wait over five years for "his" book to be ready.

To my family, for supporting me as I dug deep to find the treasure in this book. Most especially, to Nick, for ceaselessly supporting me, including solo parenting a feverish four-year-old and two boisterous boys for the two weeks I was in another hemisphere. You have never once doubted me in this crazy thing that I do, though I often doubt myself. Thank you for loving me and being my solid rock every step of the way.

To my amazing writer friends and those who supported

this book on its bumpy road to publication. First and foremost, my amazing critique group: Annie Gaughen, Annie Cardi, Katie Slivensky, and Allison Pottern. You guys are the absolute best. Thanks also to Trish Ryan for encouraging me to give this book the time it needed, to Annamary Sullivan for the many phone calls reminding me that "benching" a book is an investment in the future, and to Daniela DeSousa and Samantha Negrete, for the last-minute consult, even though it was midnight in Madrid.

To Caryn Wiseman, my agent, and to all those at Penguin Random House who helped turn this book from an idea into a reality. Special thanks to assistant editor Caitlin Tutterow, art director Cecilia Yung, and assistant art director Eileen Savage for the beautiful cover. Deepest thanks to Stacey Barney, editor extraordinaire, for helping me bring out the heart in this book that mattered so much to me.

I am indebted to the producers and directors of two documentaries that I used in my research: Kief Davidson and Richard Ladkani's *The Devil's Miner* (2005) and Raul de la Fuente's *Minerita* (2013). *The Devil's Miner* was my first introduction to the Cerro's child miners. I have named my fictional mine El Rosario in tribute to the real El Rosario mine in which Basilio and Bernardino Vargas worked. And though I only discovered it recently, I would also like to acknowledge Ander Izagirre's book *The Mountain That Eats Men*. Thank you all for working to make known the plight of the children of the Cerro Rico.

To Francisco Tandioy Jansassoy, native speaker of Inga (Quechua) and co-founder of Musu Runakuna, a political action group that works closely with Inga elders to promote Inga language, cultural expression, and land rights, and my teacher at Indiana University. Thank you for introducing me to your culture and teaching me the fascinating basics of your native language.

Lastly, to all those who helped me while on my research trip in Bolivia, my thanks:

Este libro ha sido una empresa dura de realizar que ha llevado varios años. Quiero dar las gracias enormemente a las siguientes personas, quienes me ayudaron durante mi viaje de investigación a Bolivia en 2016:

A la Dra. Rosario (Nilda) Caballero Aracena, doctora, trabajadora de desarrollo y ayudante extraordinaria: Mil gracias por presentarme a personas que fueron claves durante el proceso, por actuar como intérprete del quechua al español y por dirigir la excursión por la montaña.

A Zenon Paucara, trabajador de campo en la Fundación Voces Libres: Gracias por dejarme acompañarle mientras conducía a los niños del Cerro Rico a la Escuela Robertito y por compartir sus experiencias conmigo.

A Fabiola Sandivel Miranda Vela, abogada de CEPROMIN: Gracias por ayudarme a ver la realidad de las mujeres de la montaña, y por su trabajo protegiendo a todas esas mujeres maltratadas y guiando a los niños que quieren abandonar la montaña mediante los programas de capacitación.

A José Manuel (Manolo) Diez Canseco y Jorge Marcelo Velásquez Bonilla: Gracias por auxiliarme con contactos y alojamiento en la ciudad de Potosí.

A Vanessa Giselle Nera Zeherina, psicóloga escolar en la Escuela Robertito: Gracias por su generosidad al compartir su trabajo y por presentarme a los estudiantes que tiene bajo su cuidado.

Por último, a las mujeres y los niños del Cerro Rico: Gracias por compartir sus historias, vidas y penas conmigo con tanta generosidad. Debo una mención especial a Doña Serafina Sandoval Condor, madre de once y viuda del Cerro Rico, y a Emiliane (trece años), Rober (trece), Jadahi (doce), Edwin (doce), Cintia (once), Emily (diez), Joel (diez), Noelia (ocho), y Jimena (seis), estudiantes de la Escuela Robertito.